HEIR OF THE PROMISE: BOOK ONE

CHAD MUESSIG

CM

CHAD MUESSIG
BOOKS

THE SWORD OF THE SPIRIT

While Noah, Shem, Ham, Japheth, and the Flood are figures and events rooted in the biblical narrative, this novel is a work of fiction. All other characters, organizations, and events portrayed in the story that are not drawn directly from Scripture are either the product of the author's imagination or are used fictitiously. This work is not intended to be a literal or theological interpretation of biblical texts, but a creative exploration inspired by them.

Book Cover by Miblart

Maps by Chad Muessig

Aram's sketchbook art by Chad Muessig and Robert Muessig

ISBN 979-8-9989994-0-6 (paperback)
ISBN 979-8-9989994-1-3 (hardcover)
ISBN 979-8-9989994-2-0 (ebook)

Library of Congress Control Number: 2025910627

First Edition July 2025

Published by Chad Muessig Books
Vineland, NJ
@ChadMuessigBooks

For my wife,

Your love, faith, and steady presence made this possible.
Every word carries a piece of you.

Contents

ADAMAH
Havilah
Pishon Valley
Pishon
Cush
Eden
Tigris
Nod
Gihon
Euphrates
Assyria

Shem's Journey
Pishon
Northbridge
Eden
Enoch
North Road
Pishon Marsh
Tigris
Ararat
East Road
Garden
Centergrove
West Road
Gihon
Euphrates
Assyria
Asshur

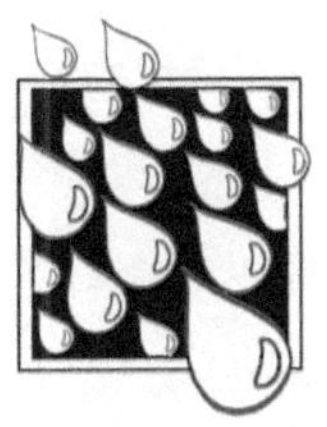

Prologue

THE GREAT FLOOD, 17 CHESHVAN 1656...

"In the six hundredth year of Noah's life, in the second month, the seventeenth day of the month, on that day all the fountains of the great deep were broken up, and the windows of heaven were opened. And the rain was on the earth forty days and forty nights."

-*The First Book of Moses*:
***Genesis*: *Chapter* 7, *Verses* 11-12**

PART ONE
Consequences

"'My Spirit shall not strive with man forever, for he is indeed flesh; yet his days shall be 120 years.'

'I will destroy man whom I have created from the face of Adamah, both man and beast, creeping thing and birds of the air, for I am sorry that I have made them.'

But Noah found grace in the eyes of the Lord."

-T***he First Book of Moses:***
Genesis: Chapter 6, Verses 3, 7

Chapter 1

Rocks and Dreams

85 YEARS EARLIER...

Shem's hands ached from another day of backbreaking labor in the fields. He could feel the prickly thorns still embedded in his skin, a reminder of the never-ending battle against nature that consumed his life. As he cursed his fate and longed for something more, his father would recite the same old saying: "Tending crops was easy until Adam defied Yahweh."

But Shem couldn't shake the feeling of resentment towards this punishment for someone else's mistake. Why were they still paying for Adam's disobedience? His mind wandered to dreams of a life beyond these cursed lands, where adventure and purpose awaited him. He yearned for wide open horizons, free from the oppressive traditions that held him captive. But each day, he was forced to continue breaking boulders, pulling weeds, and battling against the unforgiving land. The conflict between duty and desire waged on within him, leaving him feeling trapped and restless in this endless cycle.

Shem tightened his grip on the ancient leather straps attached to his trusty dinosaur, Rocky. Despite being centuries old, Rocky remained a reliable farming ankylosaurus. However, after hours of smashing boulders with his clubbed tail, he could become temperamental. Shem had learned to be cautious and avoid falling from Rocky's back onto one of the many sharp spikes adorning his shell. The lumbering beast was taller than any man, and accidents had injured many farmhands.

A group of colorful compsognathus darted past them from behind, skillfully dodging between Rocky's legs. Shem marveled at their agility as they chirped at Rocky in what seemed like defiance before narrowly avoiding being crushed by his powerful tail. As Rocky shattered a boulder into fragments, one 'compy' even seemed to take offense, scurrying away in protest.

Shem lowered his head behind his arm to shield his eyes from the flying debris, relying on his thick, hide-covered sleeve for protection. As he cleared the dust off his sleeve, he noticed a solitary horse rider approaching from the direction of the compy stampede that had seemingly triggered it. Sweeping sweat and grime from his forehead and shading his eyes against the glaring sun, he recognized the figure as Ningangar, his father's ranch foreman, dressed entirely in black with his customary wide-brimmed hat concealing his face.

He was tall and slender, yet his presence was commanding. His demeanor was always relaxed, yet he had an air of a coiled serpent ready to strike. His shirt hung partially unbuttoned, untucked, as if such formalities were beneath him. Atop his large black stallion, he exuded a natural ease. His skin was pale and unblemished except for a prominent scar trailing down the left side of his face, narrowly missing his almond-shaped eye. Shem never inquired about its origin; it seemed impolite to do so. Besides, the scar, along with his dark, intense eyes, gave him an aura that discouraged such intimate questions. The black beard and the sword at his hip completed his intimidating silhouette. Approaching Rocky, he drew level with Shem, their gazes nearly meeting.

Nin, as he was known, possessed a pleasant baritone voice that belied his appearance. As he tilted his hat back, he remarked, “It appears you’ve made some headway on this, what was it you termed it? A bootless errand?” With a gesture of his black-gloved hand, he indicated the field.

“Well, no thanks to this relic of a work dino. I’m surprised I got anything done at all,” Shem replied with a smirk, to hide his embarrassment of being reminded of his earlier ‘complaint.’

Rocky snorted.

Nin looked down at the old ankylosaur, and said, “Looks like you offended old Rocky, here.” They both laughed. Shem relaxed a bit, since Nin used his pet name for the dinosaur.

He continued, “I know you hate mundane farm work, but you’ll inherit all this someday. Your father started at the bottom, and so must you.”

Realizing that Nin wasn’t going to yell at him, he said, “Come on, Nin, it’s more likely that I’ll need to start my own. He’s already over 500 years old, with no sign of slowing down. Oh, and let’s not forget my older brother.” Shem said, dejectedly, as he flicked another stone from his dark brown hair.

“Well then, the lesson is well learned!” Nin smiled, “Way to be positive about the situation!” He exclaimed, with a telling smirk on his scared face.

Shem looked confused, "Wait, what?" Realization dawned on him, "Oh, you're mocking me. Whatever."

Nin, getting serious, "It's my job to mold you into a proper ranch foreman, like me, someday. If that knowledge makes you my replacement, or another business owner, then I have done my job. Either way, your father has accomplished his goal of training you. You will never forget these lessons. And, who knows, maybe you'll fit some adventures in there, too."

"Maybe," Shem sighed, "I hope I get some adventures in there...some day."

Nin shook his head, "That's what you got out of all that?" He appeared to gaze off towards a far off land, "It's not all it's cracked up to be."

Shem noticed that he was looking south, and glanced in that direction, "What have you seen? The Floating Mines of Uruk? The great city of Asshur? The ruins of Eridu? The grass plains of Nod? The jungles of Cush?"

Nin put his hands out, like he was halting a wagon, "Woah, slow down, son. Adamah is a large world, nobody sees it all. Be happy where you are now, right here in Eden. You have plenty of time."

Shem, crossed his arms in feigned thought, "Well, you are as old as my father-I figured you must've seen most places. Guess not." A small smirk escaped his lips.

"Oh, no you don't," laughed Nin. "I'm not falling for that. I am here to check on your progress and get you for the midday meal. Not make travel arrangements. Besides, I may be older. I lost track."

The midday meal was a grand affair. Shem's father, every day without fail, had a lavish feast laid out for all the ranch hands, shipwrights, farmers, and workers in his employ. It was a tradition as old as Shem's memories, always at noon, when the sun crowned the sky above their lands. As the High Priest, his father would also offer a sacrifice to Yahweh for them at this hour. To Shem, however, the ritual was nothing but a disruption. He preferred solitude at meal times, or spending time with his friends.

"Ok," Shem shielded his eyes, looking up to the sky with a sigh, "about an hour, then?"

"About that, yeah," answered Nin. "Set Rocky to grazing, then make your way there. You'll have just enough time. If you don't slack. Take the direct way." He focused directly on Shem's eyes.

Shem raised his hands in surrender, "I would never dream of taking the long way." Nin grunted, history being what it was.

He scratched at his beard, appearing rapt in thought. Instead, he simply adjusted his hat down on his head, spun his stallion, and rode off in the direction he had arrived. Probably asserting himself to others on his way back. This field was the furthest from the great hall, where the meal was always held, and most didn't own a watch.

Shem gave the command for Rocky to kneel down, at the same time loosening the bridal and locking the mechanism in place. Looking around to see if any one was watching, Shem launched himself off of Rocky's shell backwards, tucking into a backflip and sticking the landing.

"And the crowd cheers," bowing to an imaginary audience. A little blue compy, that had been foraging in the brush nearby, chirped at him and ran off. "Oh well, Rocky, no one can appreciate talent anymore, " he said, as he strutted over to Rocky, took the bit out his mouth, and unhooked the headpiece and cheek straps. Rocky snorted, seemingly in thanks. Or maybe in agreement. Or laughing. Who can tell with ankylosaur.

Shem paused briefly, weighing his options for the journey home. There was the quicker path that led straight to the hall, pleasing his father. Or there was the scenic route that would take him along the river through Ararat, their quaint town, offering a chance encounter with friends, especially Adi.

Adi. With her blonde, wild hair and blue eyes. Together, they would ride off into the sunset someday. Unless their fathers had something to say about it, that is. If it were up to them, they would take over the family businesses and continue what they built. Adi was as strong-willed as Shem was curious, which meant their days together were filled with discovery-and more than a few heated arguments. Still, they always ended up laughing. And there was something magical about that. She knew him so well; she'd probably be waiting at the town's edge, pretending to be surprised. Shem could almost hear her voice in his head: "Got lost again, did you?"

A sense of resignation settled in as he contemplated the choice between enjoyment and duty. Except realistically, there was no real choice to mull over. Being late again wasn't on the table, and just being on time wouldn't cut it either. As the adage goes, to be early is to be on time, and to be on time is to be late. Nin had already scolded him for lateness. The direct path was the only viable choice, for defying Noah was out of the question.

After carefully securing his bridle and hide jacket to one of Rocky's bony shell protrusions, Shem set off towards his destination. The sun was shining brightly through the tall trees as he followed Nin's path. Small compys scattered and chirped in their wake, being chased by an irate chicken like children fleeing from a scolding mother. Shem couldn't help but laugh at the comical scene, imagining what the chicken would do if she actually caught one of the nimble creatures.

The path through the dense grove of trees was narrow and uneven, made up of trampled underbrush from Rocky's frequent trips to the western field. As he reached the top of a small rise, Shem emerged into the open expanse of a forenoon sky.

The field where Shem had spent all morning was located at the western edge of a vast valley that housed Noah's farms and estates. Looking towards the East, he could see rows upon rows of farmland and expansive vineyards stretching out before him. To the south, hidden behind more trees, plumes of smoke rose into the air marking the location of various cooking fires in town. Trees lined the edges of the fields, creating a patchwork of different tiers cut into the hilly terrain like layers on a cake. Dirt roads and paths connected them all, bustling with activity as farm hands and workers moved back and forth.

In the distance to the north, beyond the farmlands, Shem could see herds of sheep grazing peacefully alongside sturdy pachycephalosaurus, prominent domed heads, standing out among the rugged foothills. The landscape was both grand and serene, a testament to Noah's thriving community and industry.

As he made his way down to the main road, Shem heard a sharp screech pierce through the air above him. Shielding his eyes from the bright sun, he scanned the sky and caught sight of a lone pterosaur soaring high overhead. Its massive wingspan filled the sky as it glided on a current of wind, carrying a figure on its back. Shem's heart raced as he realized it was one of the legendary Flying Knights of Eden.

The pterosaur seemed to dance in the sky, effortlessly riding the wind with grace and power. Shem couldn't help but feel a sense of awe and wonder at the sight.

Excitement bubbled up inside him as he thought about the possibility of being recruited by these brave warriors. He quickened his pace, eager to reach the ranch and discover why they'd come here.

He had heard countless stories about the Flying Knights from his friends around campfires. They were renowned for their bravery and skill in defending their land against the Assyrian Empire's attempts at conquest hundreds of years ago. Led by their fearless captain, Anatu, they rode into battle on the backs of giant pterosaurs like Tanniym. Elam would be so jealous.

Elam was so much more than Shem's best friend; he was like a brother. Their bond had been forged in the crucible of shared childhood memories and dreams. Their fathers were both influential figures in the politics of their small town, which meant that Shem and Elam spent countless hours together from a young age.

The two boys had grown up pretending to be the legendary knights of Eden, gallant protectors of their beloved homeland. They'd spend sun-drenched afternoons charging down the dusty farm roads, wooden swords clutched tightly in their hands as they battled invisible Assyrian invaders. Shem could still hear the echoes of their laughter ringing out over the fields as they celebrated another hard-fought victory against their unseen foes.

Elam was always there by his side - steadfast and reliable. He was his confidante, his sparring partner, his partner in crime. Elam's intelligence and strong sense of justice often made him the butt of jokes among other kids, but to Shem he was a rock.

In many ways, Elam embodied everything that Shem admired: courage, wisdom and an unyielding spirit. And even though they were now older, and life had become more complex than pretend battles on farm roads, Shem knew that their friendship was one thing that would never change.

Shem couldn't help but imagine the thrilling adventures that awaited him if he were to join their ranks. But first, he had to make it to the ranch and see if this encounter was truly a call to action from the Flying Knights of Eden.

While daydreaming of old wars and new adventures, Shem almost walked right into someone coming off a side road, behind an outcropping of rock. After catching his balance and trying not to fall into a ravine, he looked up at who it was.

"Raphael!" Shem, righting himself, said, "I didn't see you!."

Raphael just smiled and dipped his head, seemingly to say, "It's ok". He adjusted the small lamb that was draped over his shoulders.

Raphael never spoke. Shem wasn't even sure how he knew what his name was. Someone told him at some point, he imagined. He came to work for his family some time ago, and was one of Noah's shepherds for his personal flock of sheep. He seemed to be nice enough. As much as one can judge that from someone who never said a word.

He waited for Shem to compose himself, then proceeded to walk alongside him. He was of average build, with pale blonde hair and blue, almost clear, eyes. His skin was tan from being out in the sun, yet Shem couldn't tell what his age was. He was the same height as Shem, so he could be under 20, like himself, or a few hundred. Nothing stood out to differentiate that about him. No wrinkles, blemishes, scars, hair color and certainly not his voice. Raphael was a mystery, to be sure. Yet, Shem felt at ease around him, so he didn't mind the company.

"I'm guessing, you're bringing the lamb for sacrifice today?" asked Shem.

No answer, of course. Just a smile.

"Probably not a grain offering then?" Shem chuckled to himself.

Silence.

"What's your thoughts? Well-being offering? Sin? Guilt?" Shem asked Raphael.

At this, Raphael just stared at him.

"Oh, ok. All of it then." Shem looked down at the ground, embarrassed. "I guess that makes sense. Father has been doing mostly burnt offerings lately." No longer finding it funny. They walked the rest of the way in silence.

Getting closer to the ranch, the farms and trees gave way to fenced enclosures, the cows sunbathing, enjoying the beautiful day. Farm hands and workers merged with them on the road to the meeting. Shem received all the "Hellos" and other niceties that befitted the son of their employer. They all but ignored Raphael.

"How are you on this fine day, Shem?"

"How's your father been?"

"Tell him I said, 'hi'"

And one lady asked, "So, what do ya think he'll talk about today?"

That last question struck Shem as ludicrous. "What will he talk about?" Shem asked, incredulously. "The same thing he always talks about, I imagine. That the world, Adamah-our country, Eden-everything is coming to an end?" He could feel his ears heat up in frustration.

The woman that asked the rhetorical question, Sheila, was taken back. She didn't expect an answer or Shem's change in attitude, for that matter. She wiped her hands on her already dirty pants, and humphed in indignation. He didn't intend to cause offense, but he was frustrated. Frustrated at everyone trying to curry favor with his father. Frustrated that they all acted like they believed what Noah said. Frustrated that he was stuck in this life. Shem stared dismally at the ground and kept walking. He thought he caught a look of disapproval from Raphael, but wasn't sure.

Coming to the end of the road, there was a row of giant boulders that made a natural wall for the east end of the enclosure, on Shem's left. On his right, the woods opened up into a large clearing where his father's estates lay. Directly ahead of Shem, in the center of a clearing, was a small well.

The well made up the center of the ranch area. It was the first thing that Noah built when he acquired the land. It was small, made of wood, and still produced water, even though it was over a hundred years old. Even the wood never rotted, still a bright golden-yellow, like it was built yesterday. Off to the right, all of the staff houses were located. The largest of those was Shem's family's house. It was a two story house built of logs. It was the largest, yet the oldest in the area. Between the houses, down the hill, was the road that led to town.

On the left side of the clearing were all the storage buildings and stables, the heart of Gopher Ranch, which continued further to the north and west, on the other side of the fenced enclosures. Directly, on the other side of the well, was the great hall.

The great hall was where Noah gathered all his employees for parties, meetings, and the random get-togethers. It was an old building , constructed by Noah with loving care.

It had a high gable, a fascia clad with carved animals, and a large tree carved into the middle of the gable end, above the door. Due to its beauty and elegance, many townsfolk would rent it for weddings and banquets. This was also the hall where Noah sacrificed to Yahweh.

As he approached the area, Shem could see a large crowd gathering in the open area past the well, in front of the great hall. In the center of the crowd, was the knight on the back of a light blue and white striped pterosaur.

Chapter 2

Midday Surprise

The pterosaur's presence was truly awe-inspiring, with a regal blue crest atop its disproportionately large head. Every detail seemed to be meticulously crafted - the long, yellow-tipped bill, the keen brown eyes that took in everything around them, and even the pale reddish orange throat pouch. Its body, covered in fine fur-like fibers, radiated power and strength as it stood on striped blue and white muscles, ready to defend itself at any moment.

Its magnificent wings - like a bat's but much larger - were folded neatly behind the creature's back, supported by thorn-shaped fingers that could easily tear through flesh. Even its small clawed feet held a sense of grace and purpose as they firmly planted on the ground below. This was no mere beast, but a majestic being beyond imagination.

"He's beautiful." Shem breathed, wishing he could fly away on it right now.

"He is a she, and her name is Alouette," said a woman's voice from above.

Shem gazed in astonishment at the rider adorned in white. He was entranced by the majestic pterosaur, but he couldn't believe his eyes when he comprehended who was speaking. *A woman? She's a knight?*

The knight's armor was crafted from pristine white leather, adorned with intricate engravings and held together by straps and buckles. The spaulders on her shoulders were etched with symbols of power and strength. Her boots, reaching up to her knees, were no less ornate with their elaborate designs. Adorning her head was a gleaming helmet with a bird-like visor, crowned with a long blue plume that trailed behind her.

As she spoke to Shem, she removed her helmet and placed it atop Alouette's saddle horn, revealing a blue cloth around her neck and two swords secured upon her back. With effortless grace, she dismounted from the pterosaur and stood before Shem, surprising him with her shorter stature. Yet, she exuded an aura of grandeur and authority that had been amplified while riding the powerful creature.

The emblem emblazoned on her breastplate marked her as a member of Eden's Knights - their symbol, the Tree of Life from the Garden of Eden, known to all but seen by none. She retrieved her helmet from the saddle and let out a chirping sound, prompting Alouette to take flight once again.

Turning to face Shem with piercing blue eyes, plush pink lips, and smooth olive skin, she swept her long golden-blonde hair - intricately braided with feathers - over her shoulder and strode towards the great hall with determination and confidence radiating from every step. Chin held high, she commanded attention without uttering another word.

In that moment, Shem was struck speechless in awe of this formidable woman who seemed to possess an otherworldly presence. Like a tempest about to unleash its fury, she marched towards the great hall with purpose, her regal demeanor demanding respect and admiration. Shem couldn't help but feel a mixture of fear, fascination, and reverence for this enigmatic knight before him.

Maybe she's of royal blood. His gaze was fixated on her as she marched away, leaving behind a trail of lilac that perfumed the air.

Each step she took seemed to be filled with purpose and determination, captivating him entirely. Even her armor seemed to hug her curves in all the right places, adding to her allure. The heat rose to his cheeks, causing him to turn away, lest anyone notice.

As she disappeared from view and the commotion died down, the crowd erupted in a flurry of chatter.

"Why's she here?"

"Did you see the mighty dragon?"

"That wasn't a dragon at all!"

"She's a vision of beauty."

"A woman knight? Preposterous!"

The cacophony of voices blended together, but Shem could feel their excitement in the air. It seemed that he was not alone in his quest for adventure.

Shem watched Nin ride up on his majestic black stallion. Nin swung down, tethering his horse to a post outside the hall and gave Shem a knowing wink before strolling inside. The rest of the townspeople took notice and began making their way into the hall as well.

Shem followed suit, albeit a little slower. *Here we go.*

Inside the grand hall, the air was thick with the enticing aroma of roasted meat and cedar, a sacred scent that filled the space in honor of Yahweh. At the far end of the expansive hall, Arit stood diligently preparing the altar for today's ceremony. He was one of Noah's most trusted celebrants, having served on his council since before Shem was even born.

The altar itself sat atop a raised, half-circle platform made of smooth slate tiles, its three steps spanning the width of the room. Carved into the same gray tiles were intricate designs, carefully arranged in a circular pattern around the massive boulder that served as the centerpiece of the altar. The boulder had been smoothed over time from countless flames and offerings, and now stood sturdy and strong as it held piles of wood ready to be set ablaze. And behind it all, towering over the hall, was a magnificent window that stretched from wall to wall, its rounded top divided into three sections. Sunlight streamed through this beautiful masterpiece, casting a warm glow over every inch of the holy space.

Peering through the window, Shem was struck by the serene blue sky. It seemed like the perfect backdrop for a sacrifice to Yahweh. But as he gazed out, the same doubts always crept in. *Does our offering truly matter to you, Yahweh? Or is all this just senseless tradition?*

Beneath the window, a grand barn door stood open, revealing the breathtaking view of Lake Ararat from the terrace. In the doorway stood Shem's father, his silhouette commanding attention in the center. He was always alone during this time, and everyone knew not to disturb him. His powerful presence could be felt even from across the hall.

Shem's gaze shifted towards a group of workers, who seemed to be gossiping and gesturing towards the front of the room. Curiosity piqued, he followed their line of sight and saw the Eden Knight standing alone by one of the grand columns, her arms crossed in frustration and foot tapping impatiently. It seemed she had tried to speak with Noah, but was met with resistance.

Scanning the length of the hall, past the elaborately adorned table in the center, Shem noticed Nin on the opposite end from where the visitor stood. His eyes were fixed on her, as if he feared she would snatch all the delicacies that adorned the banquet table.

Shem turned to walk around the left side of the long table when he heard his name being called from behind. It was his older brother, Japheth, who was walking over with a girl Shem didn't recognize.

"Hold on for a sec, Shem," Japheth said as they approached.

"What's up, Japh?" Shem replied, turning to face them. *What'd I do now?*

Japheth was only two years older than Shem but acted like he was decades ahead in maturity. To Shem, his brother seemed to think he knew everything and was in charge. Standing a few inches taller than Shem, he had a much bigger build - no matter how hard Shem tried, he could never beat him in a wrestling match.

Even their appearances couldn't be more different; Japheth had blue eyes, flaxen hair, and light skin while Shem had brown eyes, dark brown hair, and an olive complexion. They were like night and day.

His brother motioned for him to follow as they walked under the balcony towards the tables set up from back to front. They stopped in front of a wall sconce that held a crystal light, providing some visibility in the dimly lit room. Shem braced himself for whatever transgression he had committed this time.

Fidgeting with the tableware, Shem anticipated Japheth's inevitable confrontation. "Just so you know, I'll grab the tools off of Rocky once we're finished here. Got it?"

Japheth raised an eyebrow in confusion before letting out a hearty chuckle. "Huh, that's rich. But sure, good job." He shook his head patronizingly but continued, "First of all, why did you just throw yourself under the wagon? And secondly, that wasn't even the reason I called you over here." He gestured towards the young woman beside him. "This is Adataneses, my soon-to-be wife. She's agreed to marry me."

Poor girl, she has no idea what she's getting into.

Adataneses stepped forward with a shy smile and introduced herself, "Hi, my friends call me Ada. And since we'll be family now, you can too." She twisted her blouse nervously as if trying to hide her discomfort.

Shem couldn't help but notice how young she seemed, but then again, Japheth always acted more mature than his years.

Japheth playfully wrapped his arm around her waist and said, "You remember her, right Shem? Her parents own the Ararat Bakery in town. We deliver grains to them all the time."

Shem scratched his head, remembering where he had seen her before. "Oh yeah, I remember now. Welcome to the 'family', I guess," he mumbled awkwardly. Not knowing what else to say. Usually, Japheth was not this cordial to him, and he was struggling to come up with a snarky retort to ease his discomfort.

Shem's eyes darted around the wooden balcony, searching for an escape route as he tried to maintain a polite facade. He couldn't help but feel happy for Japheth and his betrothed, Ada. She was undeniably cute and well-mannered, even if she did have a few too many freckles. Shem considered making a snarky comment, but her infectious grin stopped him in his tracks. Instead, he just burst out laughing.

Jepheth raised an eyebrow suspiciously, "What's so funny? She's going to be part of the family, you know."

"Oh, I'm well aware of that," Shem replied through his laughter. "It was just a silly thought."

Before Japheth could press further, Arit's voice echoed through the hall, signaling everyone to gather.

Saved by Arit.

As they made their way to the front, Shem leaned into Jepheth's ear and whispered, "I'm actually surprised you asked her to marry you."

Japheth looked offended and mouthed silently, "What?!"

To which Shem responded with a sly smile, "I thought you were already married to the ranch." He walked away not looking back at Japheth's bewildered expression.

As he walked away, Ada's questioning voice still echoed in his ears. He could almost envision the look on his brother's face as he desperately tried to defend himself.

Shem strode over and positioned himself next to Nin, who was leaning nonchalantly against a column with his arms folded. Glancing over to where the visitor had been standing earlier, Shem noticed that she was now standing upright with her arms also folded and a clear displeased expression on her face.

Before Shem could inquire about her, Nin spoke up, "Looks like you're getting along well with your brother."

Nin didn't miss a beat.

Shem replied, "Well, I suppose he was on his best behavior. Didn't want to embarrass himself in front of his new wife-to-be."

Nin gave him a knowing look and said, "Ah, so you've met Ada. And YOU were going to be the one embarrassing HIM?"

Without making eye contact, Shem responded slyly, "I have quite the talent for verbally sparring with him. And yes, she did seem lovely."

Nin chuckled, "Funny how it's always you who gets offended more than he does."

"That's what I mean, Nin. I know you must be older than you claim because your memory is failing." Shem couldn't contain his laughter.

Nin simply grunted and turned towards the front of the room as Arit called for their attention.

The room fell silent as Arit made his way up onto the elevated platform, standing before the altar. He wore plain gray robes that were cinched at the waist with a rope, and his feet were bare. His hair, as white as the clouds, was pulled back with a leather thong. The deep black of his skin contrasted with a few wrinkles that hinted at his advanced age.

He lifted his arms, palms open in a gesture of supplication to the audience gathered before him. With rich, powerful vocals that rang out like bells, he began to sing, filling the space with his melodious baritone voice. Each note flowed effortlessly from his lips, weaving together to create a breathtaking symphony that captivated all who listened. His voice was like liquid gold, dripping with emotion and passion, leaving the crowd spellbound and yearning for more.

"Oh Lord, my rock and protector,
Why do you whisper to my soul
To flee like a bird from its nest?
For the evil ones roam free,
Shooting their arrows from dark corners
At those with pure hearts.
Law and order crumble before us,
And what can the righteous do?
But The Lord remains in his sacred garden,
Watching everything closely,
Searching the souls of all on Adamah.
He sees both the good and the bad,
And abhors those who revel in violence.
His wrath will rain upon the wicked,
Drowning them in floods of destruction.
For the just Lord loves righteousness,
And the righteous will behold his face.
The Lord reigns in his holy garden,
Ever vigilant and in control,
Looking deep into every heart
Of those on this world below.
For the just Lord loves righteousness,
And the virtuous will see his face.
The virtuous will see his face,
The virtuous will see his face."

Arit's voice soared through the air, holding a final note that seemed to stretch on for eternity. The audience was captivated, hanging onto every word and melody as tears glistened in their eyes. The only other sounds were a few sniffles here and there, a testament to the emotion that Arit's performance had evoked in them

Shem turned his head to the left, rubbing his tingling nose. In the corner of the hall, Raphael kneeled with a sheep in his lap. The light from the window illuminated tears streaming down his cheeks as he looked directly at Shem. It made him uneasy, so he avoided his gaze and quickly looked away.

Arit began to speak again, "I am grateful, Yahweh, for the privilege of relaying this beautiful message from Noah. He composed this hymn after many conversations with you and he wishes for all to understand your heart. Our prayer is that everyone in this room will acknowledge you as the Creator and Lord of All."

Arit turned around and noticed that Noah had joined him at the altar. He motioned towards him and said, "Please welcome Noah." Then Arit stepped to the right side of the platform.

A gentle breeze wafted through the open doors, causing Noah's gray robes to flutter in its wake. The gathered crowd stood in anticipation of what was to come next. Shem breathed in the sweet scent of honeysuckle, feeling refreshed and reminded of Yahweh's creation.

For Shem, the afternoon sacrifice had become routine. He closed his eyes and reflected on his faith. Did others feel the same way, or did they struggle with their belief like he did? Were they as devout as his father, truly believing in a loving creator who watched over his people? Could this gentle breeze be a sign of Yahweh's presence among them?

The bleating of a lamb broke Shem from his thoughts as Raphael handed the small animal to Noah at the altar. Noah cradled it gently before placing it on top of the pile of logs on the altar, as if caring for a small child.

"Listen," Noah's voice echoed through the room, "Yahweh created us in His image. We were given one rule: not to eat from the tree of The Knowledge of Good and Evil. But we betrayed Him. Since that moment, our actions have been a betrayal. 35 years ago, the Lord spoke to me. He saw how wicked humanity had become on Adamah, with every thought and inclination being evil all the time. He regretted creating us and was deeply troubled." Noah's voice cracked with emotion. His face was etched with sorrow, tears streaming down his cheeks as he spoke.

He held up his left hand, now grasping a knife, gesturing to encompass the entire room. "So the Lord told me, 'I will wipe out all of humanity and animals from Adamah - for I regret making them.'"

Noah lowered his head, his long dark hair covering his face as he placed his right hand firmly on the lamb's head. With a swift motion, he slit its throat with the knife.

As blood dripped onto the altar, Noah said, "Repent."

Arit approached him with a crystal torch lighter and handed it to him.

Igniting the wood on the altar, Noah repeated, "Repent," this time even louder.

The cool breeze that had surrounded Shem now blew towards the altar, carrying Noah and Arit's robes in its wake. The fire blazed up, engulfing the lamb in flames and smoke which swirled in a vortex and rose up through the chimney in the ceiling.

One last time, Noah shouted, "REPENT!"

Chapter 3

Royal Struggle

Shem sat at the long wooden table with his brother Japheth and his friends, half-listening to their conversation as he took a sip of wine. He could see that his brother was talking about ranch business, but Shem's attention was more focused on the knight arguing with their father Noah at the foot of the steps that led to the altar.

One of Japheth's friends, Halvin, chimed in, "But shouldn't we be more concerned about foreign invaders? They could pose a bigger threat than just vagabonds."

Shem looked over at his brother to gauge his response but instead noticed Ada's face. She had a look of intense fear and her hand trembled as she brought her cup to her lips.

Suddenly, Shem's attention was fully captured by Halvin's last remark. "Wait, did you say there are invaders coming?" he blurted out.

Halvin nodded, "It must be why the knight from Stone Crest is here. Why else would the High Council have found it important enough to send her?"

Some of Japheth's friends tapped their cups on the table in agreement, while Shem couldn't help but feel a sense of dread creeping over him.

But before he could say anything else, Japheth cut in dismissively. "Don't worry about it, Shem. You're always lost in your daydreams anyways. Just leave the ranch business to us."

Feeling frustrated and belittled by his brother's words, Shem stood up abruptly and pushed his chair back. Japheth also stood up, but Ada grabbed his arm in an attempt to stop him.

Japheth ignored her and continued to taunt Shem. "Go back to your chores or whatever it is you do. Don't worry about things you don't understand."

Feeling hurt and angry, Shem knew deep down that there was something more to the knight's visit. He could feel it in his gut. But he also knew that Japheth had already made up his mind, and he didn't want to get into a fight with him. So instead of engaging further, he stormed off towards the back of the room while Japheth and his friends laughed at him.

His mind was a whirlwind of conflicting thoughts. He replayed the conversation over and over, wishing he had said something different. Japheth's words echoed in his head, causing fear to bubble up inside him. Ada's expression of fear only added to his turmoil. Halvin's logical arguments clashed with his gut feeling that something bigger was at play. But despite this, he couldn't shake off the feeling of being dismissed and laughed at because of his age. He couldn't explain how he knew it, but he just did.

The crowd began to thin out, having satisfied their appetites. Some lingered, chatting and laughing, while others made their way towards the exit to resume their tasks.

Shem's anger and frustration grew as he struggled through the crowd, desperately trying to find a way out. Meanwhile, his younger brother Ham stood calmly by the wall near the door, sporting his usual smile. In contrast to Shem's fair skin and straight hair, Ham had dark brown skin and braided ponytails cascading down his back. His deep black eyes shone like stars in the night sky.

"Hey there, Shemy," Ham greeted with a mouthful of bread. Shem cringed at the nickname he despised.

He reluctantly replied, "Hi Ham. Where have you been?"

Ham took another bite and smugly replied, "Right here, being the wall's best friend. In case I need to make a quick getaway."

"Well, you might want to use that escape plan soon," joked Shem. "Because there are rumors of wandering vagabonds threatening Eden."

"Seriously? Did the knight tell you that?" Ham asked skeptically.

Shem raised an eyebrow suspiciously and answered, "No, but Japh and his crew were talking about it so it must be true."

"That's strange," Ham remarked with a mischievous grin, "usually Japh is too busy bossing people around to worry about anything like that."

Shem couldn't help but laugh; Ham had a way of diffusing his tension during fights with Japheth. Even though he was younger, he always knew how to get to the heart of the matter. "Well actually," Shem continued, "Halvin brought up concerns and Japh was debating him. And then I made the mistake of interrupting them."

"You really stepped in it this time," Ham chuckled.

"Yeah, I never know when to keep my mouth shut," Shem admitted. Then he turned the tables on Ham, pointing out, "But if you were trying to make a quick escape, why are you still here?"

Ham shrugged nonchalantly and explained, "'Cause Mother said not to skip out on today's midday meal. As if I ever would." He rolled his eyes playfully. "And Father wanted us all to meet afterward."

"Did she say why?" Shem inquired.

"I don't know," Ham shrugged again, "but probably something about the messenger Father sent to the house after the knight arrived."

"Well, nobody told me about any meeting," Shem said.

"Probably because you're always such a devoted son and never miss a meal," Ham teased sarcastically.

Shem playfully nudged his brother and leaned against the wall next to him. It was comforting to have Ham by his side, always able to lighten the mood. He started surveying the room and noticed Noah, Nin, and the knight in conversation below at the head of the long table. Japheth and Ada were making their way over to join them, as if summoned. Ham nudged Shem again and they both headed towards the front, ready to finally find out what was going on.

"Look, Shem, I'm sorry..." Japheth began as he approached.

Shem interrupted him, "Forget about it," not really wanting to get into it again. "Ada probably put you up to it anyway," He thought.

Never missing a moment, Ham said, “Hi Japh, always keeping things pleasant, I see.”

“Shut up Ham. Nothing to do with you...” started Japheth.

“Enough, boys!” barked Noah. “I didn’t call you all here to listen to you bickering like a bunch of compies.”

Before any of the brothers could retort, Noah continued, “We need to discuss a few troubling events. Our visitor, Lady Aryana of the Knights of Eden, has brought some news. We will listen to her and give her all due respect.”

“Thank you, Sir Noah.” The knight said, “I was sent by the High Council, to bring warning to Ararat, and your ranch. Most of the areas and regions are no stranger to bandits and vagabonds. Which is why most of you carry arms of some sort. Well, I am here to tell you that things have gotten dire.”

Ham winked at Japheth, as to say Shem was right. Shem elbowed him to stop. This was what he wanted to hear. Maybe she had come to recruit for Eden’s armies. This could be the adventure he was craving.

Lady Aryana raised her eyebrow at the little exchange, but continued, “As citizens of Eden, we stay armed in defense of our land. Our people make up the militia that is the first defense against any and all invaders. That is how it has always been, except in times of war.”

“Did you say war?” Shem couldn’t contain himself any longer. “Is Eden building her armies up? Are you here to recruit? Is Assyria invading again?”

The knight looked at Noah, who just shook his head, and said, “No. We have no reason to believe that they would invade again, at this point. But, we are concerned with rumors of armies gathering in the east. " Putting her hand up to stop Shem, “Before you ask, we are aware that Eden extends all the way to the Eastern Sea. The only thing we know of the armies is that they are there, and it seems that they hold no loyalty to any land. They appear to be mercenaries and malcontents that have banded together with the sole purpose of stealing and destruction. To what end we have no knowledge."

Japheth jumped in at that point, "Pardon me my lady. I don't understand. There are many towns between here and the east coast. Surely, we aren't in any danger here?" Ada was holding tightly to his arm.

She responded, "The consensus is that the armies are concealing themselves in the Great Forest that surrounds The Garden. Most people won't travel there, and it is impenetrable from the sky. With mages in their midst, they could conceal their movements as they attack random towns and cities. Even this one."

Noah spoke, "Mages! Surely, you don't believe that they have that kind of power at their disposal? Most witchcraft is nothing more than conjured illusions and ugly words."

She responded, "Sir, I meant no disrespect." Her cheeks were starting to flush. "But, you know the tools that The Serpent and his minions have at their disposal. I know you believe in the power of Yahweh, but they believe just as strongly in his power. And...they may have Nephilim with them. Giants."

Lady Aryana was clenching her fists at her sides, but her face displayed worry. Noah turned his back on the small group and started pacing. He looked deep in thought. Ada was watching all this with tears in her eyes.

Seeing Ada's distress, Japheth started to speak, "If we're in that much danger, then we'll start building a wall around the town. We can protect the people that way, and ramp up our militia training. I'll tell the local sheriff right away." He started pacing as well.

"Wait. Wait." Lady Aryan said, "A fence? To build one that could withstand a giant? It would take years. Training would help, but who would lead them, you?"

"You bet I could. Father tell her..." started Japheth.

"Japheth, please.," responded Noah, "Lady Aryana,all we've heard is fear mongering. What is it you've come for? It can't be just to raise an alarm that has already been sounded. You know who I am, and what I have warned of. My sons, and all of our workers are well trained in warfare. Ningangar has that well in hand. So what is it then?" He placed his hand on Nin's shoulder, which made him look uncomfortable.

"Sir, w..." She started to reply.

Noah, interrupted her, "and please Lady Aryana, stop calling me sir. I gave up that moniker years ago."

Lady Aryana, fidgeting with one of her many clasps, responded, "This is awkward, sir...I mean Noah. We need your help. For the reasons you, yourself just stated. Your men are all well trained. We need someone to come and train our soldiers. It's been hundreds of years since they've seen war, and they have become.....lazy." She seemed embarrassed to have said that last part out loud.

"Many, like yourself, have walked away from the army. From the order of knights, even. They believe that we are in a time of universal peace, and that wars are a thing of the past. They won't listen to reason. It's almost as if they are part of some mass influence. The world has gone crazy." She paused, and seemed to lose her composure.

Noah placed his hand on her shoulder, gesturing for her to continue.

"We, my brother and I, thought that if we could convince you to come back, that it would make a difference. Your family were the founders of The Knights of Eden, after all."

Noah, with a smile, spoke in a soft voice, “Ah, Anatu. How is your brother?”

“He is busy trying to hold it all together. It was his idea to come and seek you out. The High Counsel was reluctant but acquiesced in the end.”

Shem’s head was spinning. His family started the Knights of Eden? Anatu, the hero of his childhood stories, was her brother? Giants? He couldn’t believe his ears.

He spoke before he could stop himself, “Father is royalty? Captain Anatu, the hero of the Assyian war, is your brother? Did he really kill over a hundred invaders?”

Lady Aryana, trying to hide her smile, looked at Noah and said, “Of course your family is royalty. You can trace your lineage directly to Adam, himself. There is no higher nobility, I would say. " Looking back to Shem, she continued, “As far as Anatu goes, it was more like a thousand.” Her smile, diminishing, “Alas, he is too old to fight in any wars now. That is why we need the wise Noah.”

“While I appreciate the.....” Noah started to respond. Then, before he could finish his statement, Nin stepped forward and made a gesture for everyone to be silent.

In the distance, coming from Ararat, a bell started to chime.

Noah's voice crackled with urgency as he quickly untied the rope belt from his waist. “It appears the attack is sooner than expected.”

Lady Aryana's eyes narrowed in determination as she let out a piercing whistle and charged towards the doors leading to the terrace.

With everyone in tow, Noah raced towards the back door of the hall, barking orders. "Nin, Japheth, gather the men and weapons. Shem and Ham, take Ada to the house and defend her and your mother with your lives. Use the sword over the mantle if necessary."

Shem turned to his father, his pulse quickening to a frantic beat. "What about you?"

"I'm heading to town to fight off whoever or whatever is attacking us. Now go, protect your mother." Without hesitation, Noah ripped off his cumbersome robe and pulled out a large dagger from his pants belt.

Shem watched in trepidation as his father disappeared down the hill towards danger. Running towards the house, he saw Japheth and Halvin among the armed men of their ranch, rushing to join Noah in defense of their home. Nin galloped past on his mighty stallion, determined to join the battle.

As they closed the door behind them, Shem caught a glimpse of Lady Aryana riding her pterosaur, Alouette, towards the fray overhead. With a heavy heart, Shem hoped that this wasn't just the beginning of a brutal and bloody fight for survival.

Shem's mother, Emzara, welcomed them all into the cozy kitchen of their home. Her warm smile calmed their nerves as she tended to each of them, offering comforting drinks and a place to sit at the table.

With her kind nature and gentle touch, Emzara embodied all the best qualities of her children. Shem inherited her peaceful demeanor, while her bright blue eyes reminded them of Japheth and her dark hair mirrored Ham's. As always, she was concerned for their well-being and had just finished wiping her hands on her apron after pouring the drinks.

Looking at each of them with concern in her eyes, Emzara asked, "Is everyone alright? I heard the bell ringing, it's been so long since we've been attacked out here."

Ham was quick to respond, "Whatever it is, it seems to be happening down in town. Meanwhile, we're stuck here babysitting you and Ada."

Shem shot his brother a disapproving look before turning to check on Ada, who looked pale and shaken. "Mom, I think Ada may need something. She doesn't look well."

"My family..." Ada whimpered.

Emzara gently placed her hands on Ada's cheeks and said, "Oh my poor dear, come here and sit down." She led her over to the table and handed her a cup.

Ada took a shaky sip of the strong drink in the cup and sputtered in response.

"Just take small sips, dear," Emzara instructed. "It's quite strong."

Feeling overwhelmed, Ada put her head in her hands on the table and began to sob. Emzara rubbed her back soothingly and whispered comforting words until Ada's tears stopped flowing.

Shem trailed after Ham, the familiar creaking of the wooden floorboards beneath his feet. They passed by the table where Ada sat, her fingers delicately tracing patterns on the surface. The sweet scent of wood and flowers enveloped Shem's senses as they entered the front room of their home. His mother had a knack for arranging vases of freshly cut blooms all around the house, lending a sense of comfort and tranquility to their modest abode. Ham paused in front of the wide window that looked out onto the winding road leading down to Ararat.

Standing beside Ham, Shem could see the tops of the roofs of Ararat, the bustling town nestled in the forested hill below them. His eyes scanned over the familiar streets and buildings, his heart aching to be down there with all the action. He just couldn't ignore the nagging worry for his friends, especially Adi.

His thoughts raced as he wondered if she was safe. He clenched his fists at his sides, feeling the dryness in his mouth and the pounding of his heart. *Is she ok?*

Glancing over at the fireplace mantle, Shem resisted the urge to grab his father's sword and rush to her aide. But his father had given him an order to stay put.

Ham's low voice broke through Shem's inner turmoil. "Go. Go help your friends. Take the sword and go. I'll handle things here."

Shem looked at him in surprise. *How does he always know what I'm feeling?* "I can't..." Shem protested.

Ham shrugged. "I'll find a way to defend them without it. Besides, the trouble is down there."

Shem's gaze drifted longingly out the window towards the town. *I'd rather face a whole army than disobey my father's command...but...*

A deafening bang against the back door jolted Shem's heart into a frantic rhythm. His eyes locked with Ham's in the shared realization that danger has arrived at their doorstep. The women screamed in terror from the dining room, sending chills down Shem's spine.

With each successive bang on the door, Shem's chest tightened, and his breathing became shallow as he heard muffled voices outside. *They're trying to break in.*

"Ham, watch the front door. I'll handle this," Shem commanded, adrenaline coursing through his veins.

He quickly snatched up his father's sword from the fireplace, only to realize it's far lighter than any weapon he's ever wielded. But there's no time to ponder its mystery as the back door gave way with a resounding crash against the wall.

With a fierce determination, Shem positioned himself in front of his mother and Ada, shielding them from the attacker with his body. The sound of metal clashing filled the room as he blocked a powerful strike from a massive black battle axe with his own sword.

Their eyes locked in a deadly stare, Shem could smell the stench of sweat emanating from the man before him. His greasy black hair hung in stringy strands around his pale, tattooed skin. Black eye makeup and facial tattoos only added to his menacing appearance, as his yellowed teeth were clenched in a snarl while pushing against Shem's defenses with brute force.

Just as Shem felt like he's about to give way under the pressure, a sharp blow to his gut took the wind out of him and sent him crashing into a nearby cabinet. Dazed and disoriented, he struggled to get back on his feet as the man advanced on him, intent on finishing the job.

But then Ham's voice cut through the chaos, hurling curses at their assailant and buying Shem enough time to gather his wits. With all of his strength, he swung his sword at the man's legs, slicing through both in one swift motion. The man fell backwards onto a table, screaming in agony as blood pooled beneath him.

Shem stood over the fallen man, unsure of what to do next. He had never killed someone before and still was unsure of his inclination to do so. The man's hateful gaze bored into him even as death approached.

Behind him, Ham yelled out a warning just in time for Shem to dodge a swing from the dying man's battle axe. Without further hesitation, Shem leaped onto the man's chest and drove his sword deep into his heart. A final gasp escaped the man before falling silent.

In shock and disbelief at what he had just done, Shem staggered to the front door, leaving the sword embedded in the man's chest. His head was spinning as he stepped out into the sunlight and took a deep breath, grateful it was over.

But the scene before him told another tale.

CHAPTER 4

Controlled Fear

The chaos of battle overwhelmed Shem's senses as he stepped out of the house. The man who had forced his way inside was not alone; it seemed like a small army had invaded Gopher Ranch. While most of Noah's militia had rushed to town upon hearing the loud bell, another group attacked from beyond the foothills.

Shem watched in horror as these invaders mercilessly killed people he had grown up with and cared for. Women were shrieking and fleeing from the black-clad killers. Some of the farm workers tried to fight back with their tools, but they were no match. These attackers had no identifying mark or banner; their only goal was violence and terror. Shem couldn't determine how many there were, but they definitely outnumbered the farm hands and workers.

All the training he had received from Nin did not prepare him for this moment. He regretted not paying closer attention during their lessons. He had never taken it seriously, just like the deserters from Eden's army. In that moment, he realized he was no better than them. He knew he needed to find a way to turn the tide of this senseless slaughter; he needed help and quickly

Stepping off the porch, he reached out and grabbed onto a worker's arm as they ran past him.

"Hey you. Elben. Quick, run to town and get help," Shem urgently instructed the panicked boy. Despite his attempts to break free, Shem held onto his arm tightly.

"Listen, this is important. Go to town and find Noah. Can you do that for me?" Shem tightened his grip on the boy's other arm, making sure he was paying attention.

This time, Elben responded with determination between heavy breaths, "Get. Noah. Got it."

Satisfied that he had gotten through to him, Shem released his arms and watched as Elben ran off in the direction of town. He could only hope that the message had been received. The boy was barely older than him and seemed to be on the verge of breaking down under the pressure.

Without warning, Shem was violently knocked off his feet by a man lunging at him from the left. The attacker landed on top of Shem, his crazed eyes fixated on stabbing him with a gleaming dagger. Panic set in as Shem realized he left his own weapon in the house.

Desperately, he struggled against the man's wrist holding the dagger, but it became clear that his assailant was much stronger. Just when it seemed like all hope was lost, the man suddenly went limp, dropping the knife, narrowly missing Shem's head. He lay on top of Shem until Ham came and shoved him off with a swift kick.

Peering over at the motionless man, Shem saw an axe lodged between his shoulder blades. With a sense of relief, he got up and handed Ham the fallen man's dagger. "Thanks for the assist," he said with a grateful smile.

"Any time, Shemy," said Ham, scanning their surroundings. "We need to level the playing field. It's just us against them."

Shem nodded in agreement, feeling a surge of determination. "Hopefully we can make a difference. We're all they've got."

As they prepared to defend their home once again, Ham reached behind the door jam and pulled out Noah's sword, handing it to Shem. "You may need this," he says grimly.

Grasping the weapon tightly, Shem steeled himself for the coming battle. "Let's go," he declared, raising the sword towards the nearest group of invaders with fierce determination in his eyes.

Shem's muscles strained as he fought his way through a swarm of ruthless invaders, determined to reach a group of defenseless women at the well. Despite their initial appearance, Shem soon realized that these attackers were no match for his and Ham's years of combat training.

With each ferocious swipe and thrust, Shem and Ham quickly overpowered the clumsy invaders and made their way to the women's side. They trembled with fear and gratitude, huddled together as Shem and Nin stood guard.

But just as they began to catch their breath, one of the women let out a blood-curdling scream and pointed behind Shem. He spun around just in time to see a towering figure charging towards them, brandishing a massive sword dripping with fresh blood. With a surge of adrenaline, Shem readied himself for another intense battle.

A raspy, arrogant voice broke the tense silence. "Well, well, well. What do we have here?"

Shem's heart raced as he faced the new threat, glancing at Ham for support.

The man towered over them, exuding confidence and strength. Dressed in all black like the rest of the invaders, he stood out with his long golden hair and beard adorned with braids. His dark eye makeup traced intricate patterns down his face, making him seem even more menacing.

With a smug smile, he spoke again. "Looks like we have a couple of fighters here, huh boys?"

Panic tightened Shem's chest as he noticed a group of men surrounding them and the women. They laughed at the man's comment, their weapons at the ready.

"This must be their leader," Shem whispered to Ham.

Thinking quickly, Shem decided to keep them talking while they came up with a plan. "Who are you and why have you invaded our town?" he demanded.

The man - now revealed as Arnulf - threw his head back in laughter. "Oh ho, it's your town, is it? And who might you be, m'lord?"

Shem knew he was being sarcastic but answered anyway. "I am Shem, son of Noah. This land belongs to my family."

Ham groaned and shook his head in disapproval.

Arnulf chuckled and turned to face Ham. "And what about you?"

"None of your business," Ham spat back defiantly. "I'm not afraid of some random invaders."

Arnulf nodded to one of his burly men who promptly punched Ham in the stomach without warning.

As Ham doubled over in pain, the giant growled, "You think we're here by accident?"

Shem raised his sword in anger. "What does that mean? Why are you doing this?"

But Arnulf simply waved his hand dismissively. "You are outnumbered and we have other villages to pillage. But because you two have shown some fight, I wanted to give you a chance to talk."

His hand rested on the hilt of his long sword as he continued, "But thanks to your friend here, you know too much. And since you have nothing we want, our conversation is over."

Ham held up his dagger in defiance while Shem gripped his sword tightly with both hands.

"Fine with us," Ham retorted. "We're not afraid of death."

Shem muttered under his breath, "Defiant even in the face of death."

Arnulf smirked and drew his black sword from its scabbard. "I admire your courage. But thanks to my loyal companion here, you've sealed your fate."

The women they had sworn to protect were now huddled in terror, whimpering and crying as their attackers closed in. His heart constricted at the thought of his parents' safety, praying they were unharmed in this chaos. He desperately hoped his friends had escaped the worst of the onslaught. As he steadied himself and braced for what was coming, he could only pray that Japheth and Ada's fairytale ending wouldn't be cut short by these violent invaders.

With a deep breath, he planted his feet firmly and prepared to defend those he cared for with his life. The enemy drew closer, their weapons glinting with malice.

A screech echoed above the clearing, causing everyone to freeze in fear. Shem's heart raced with hope as he watched Lady Aryana riding Alouette, swooping down towards the invading force. The pterosaur dove into the crowd, her powerful talons snatching two men and hurling them across the clearing. As she ascended back into the sky, Lady

Aryana drew her twin swords from over her shoulders and let out a fierce cry.

With Alouette's guidance, she charged towards the black-clad men for another attack. The pterosaur grabbed another assailant while Lady Aryana launched herself head-first into the fray like a cannonball. With agile flips and leaps, she dispatched several more attackers before they could even register what was happening.

Shem struggled to keep up with her lightning-fast movements as she sliced through their ranks like a reaper mowing down wheat. A whirlwind of steel and fury, Lady Aryana single-handedly took on their enemies with lethal precision.

Taking advantage of the distraction, Shem lunged at Arnulf, his sword aimed straight for the man's heart. But Arnulf was prepared, easily parrying the blow and dodging Ham's attack at the same time.

"Oho, it seems the little men have some fight in them," taunted Arnulf as he deflected another strike from Shem's sword.

He grabbed Ham's wrist as the boy lunged at him, twisting his body and delivering a brutal blow to Ham's face with the pommel of his sword. Ham fell to the ground with a cry of pain.

Enraged, Shem swung wildly at Arnulf, his anger clouding his judgment.

"Tsk tsk, such a temper," laughed Arnulf as he effortlessly blocked and parried Shem's attacks. "You'll never defeat me if you let your emotions take control."

Finally growing tired of the game, Arnulf disarmed Shem with an expert twist of his wrist. Shem stood there helplessly as Arnulf held his own sword to his throat, daring him to make a move. He couldn't understand why he wasn't dead yet - surely this man was more skilled than him. *Why doesn't he just end it?*

Meanwhile, chaos raged around them as Lady Aryana cut down men left and right like an avenging angel. The sound of screams and battle cries filled the clearing as others attempted to counter her deadly onslaught.

Shem felt utterly helpless - his brother lay unconscious at his feet, the women cowering behind him, and his enemy's sword pressed against his throat. He raised his hands in surrender, unsure of what else he could do. But instead of striking him down, Arnulf simply tilted his head and smiled wickedly.

In a sudden move, Arnulf sheathed his sword and took off running towards the town. Shem was confused by the change in events. *Why did he just let me live?*

He knelt down beside his brother and listened for signs of life. He was relieved to hear him breathing. "Can someone please take care of my brother?" Shem asked the women, standing up and retrieving his sword.

An older woman with white hair came over to help him tend to his brother. The tension in the clearing dissipated as the fighting died down. Lady Aryana stood among the fallen bodies of the invaders, her white leather armor stained with blood. She watched as a few remaining men followed their leader's orders and ran away down the road.

The sound of swords clashing echoed back towards them from further down the road. Shem felt sick but knew he had to join the fight once again. He dragged his tired body towards the new commotion.

"Young lord, you can barely stand let alone fight," Lady Aryana said as she approached him, her scent of lilacs mixing with the smell of battle. She placed her hand on his sword arm to steady him as he struggled to catch his breath.

"The rest of your family is right behind me," she continued. "We realized it was probably a trap when we only found a few invaders in town."

Shem was confused. "A trap? For who?"

"That's what we're about to find out," Lady Aryana replied, gesturing towards a group of men approaching them.

Among Japheth, Halvin, and Nin, was their leader, Arnulf. He had been disarmed and bound with iron cuffs in front of his body, blood dripping from his blonde beard and a scowl on his face. The rest of them were unscathed.

Shem made his way over to where Ham lay sprawled out on the ground, a noticeable lump already forming on the side of his head. He crouched down next to him, brushing away some loose strands of hair that had fallen across Ham's face. His heart pounded in his chest as he awaited any sign of consciousness from his younger brother.

Finally, Ham's eyes fluttered open, squinting against the harsh daylight that filtered through the treetops above them. He groaned and lifted a hand to gingerly touch the tender spot on his head. Shem waited as Ham winced and then slowly propped himself up onto one elbow.

"So," Ham began, his voice raspy and weak but still infused with its usual humor. "Did I sleep through anything exciting?" His words were slurred slightly but they brought an immediate sense of relief to Shem.

He replied with a sly grin, "Oh, just my heroic victory over the entire army of invaders."

Rubbing his chin thoughtfully, Ham grumbled, “Of course, that's why I decided to take a little snooze.”

Shem playfully nudged him in mock annoyance.

He turned as Lady Aryana strode up to the prisoner, her gaze piercing him. "Why did you attack?" She demanded, not giving him a chance to respond before continuing with an angered tone. "Tell me."

The prisoner, Arnulf, responded by spitting blood on the ground in front of her, a twisted smile on his face.

Without hesitation, Lady Aryana punched him in the jaw.

Noah approached from behind and voiced his disapproval. "Lady Aryana, now is not the time for this. And certainly not this method."

With a nod from Noah, the group surrounding the prisoner grabbed his arms and began leading him towards the great hall.

Defiantly raising her chin, Lady Aryana turned on her heel and followed behind.

Noah embraced his sons Shem and Ham tightly. "Oh boys, I am so sorry," he said with genuine remorse. "It took us some time to realize there was trouble here at the ranch."

"It's okay, Father," said Shem.

"Yeah," said Ham. "We had it under control."

Chuckling, Noah stepped back and looked them over. "Well, we were already regrouping when young Elben arrived. He was quite hysterical."

"I sent him to find you," Shem said. "I tried to calm him down and make him listen, but I guess it didn't work."

"We got the message loud and clear," replied Noah with a smile. "By the way, where is your mother? Is she alright? Ada?"

A cool early evening breeze swept through the town of Ararat. The townsfolk chattered animatedly over dinner, their voices carrying through the air as they gathered around tables with their loved ones. Nestled by a babbling river that flowed into Lake Ararat, the residents had long felt shielded from the turmoil that gripped the rest of Adamah. Their focus had always been on cherishing moments of tranquility with family. Today, that sense of security was brutally shattered.

Shem, accompanied by his closest friends - Adi, Elam, and the brothers Lud and Aram, sought sanctuary in the loft of the ancient Burchard barn. The barn had a history; its original owner, Burchard, once ran a bustling livery from here but had since succumbed to the sweet allure of retirement. The boarding stables now stood vacant and the loft, once brimming with haystacks, served as their regular hideaway when they yearned for an escape from the world's prying eyes.

Lud and Aram were sons of an ingenious inventor and watch maker who mysteriously vanished years ago when they were still young boys. Their father's sudden disappearance left them spending a lot of time with Shem and Elam as their fathers tried to unravel the mystery that surrounded the inventor's sudden disappearance. As a result of this shared experience, they became a tight-knit group where each member found solace in one another.

In the wake of their father's departure, Lud and Aram stepped up to take care of their mother while also lending their technical expertise around town whenever required.

Or at least Aram did most of the repairs, whereas Lud was more of the comedy relief of the two.

"These apples are great as usual. Thanks Adi," said Lud with a mouthful, "Did you do something different to 'em?"

"Oh yeah, Lud, Dad grew that tree facing north." Adi said with a roll of her eyes. It was her family that owned the property, turning it into an apple orchard.

The familiar rhythm of their playful banter brought solace to him as he leaned against the wooden frame of the hay loft, gazing out at the tranquil waters of Lake Ararat.

Adi was nestled beside him, her small frame snug against his. Shem observed how her mousy blonde hair was tied back in a modest bun, highlighting her gentle features. He gazed at her fondly, entranced by the way she looked back at him. Her striking blue eyes mirrored the sunlight filtering through the foliage.

Elam, cutting to the heart of the matter, said, "I don't know how you can be so calm. You literally fought in a battle. Like...people died."

"I know. I was there. I even killed a few," said Shem, despondently.

"Elam. Come on." Adi said, squeezing Shem's leg.

Shem really didn't mind. He understood that Elam had good intentions and genuinely wanted to understand what had transpired. However, Elam looked mortified by Adi's reprimand, lowering his head in embarrassment as his face turned a deep shade of red, contrasting with his rich, dark brown skin. He nervously ran his hand through his long dark curls.

"Oh stop, Adi, we want the details. Did you fight off a hundred men, like Anatu did in the Assyrian war against

General Ouza and his forces?" said Lud, dancing around with a pretend sword, vanquishing his brother.

Aram acted as though he took a mighty blow through the heart, holding his chest and slowly falling to the floor.

Having spent most of his childhood with these two brothers, he was used to their playfulness. Though Lud was a year older, they could've been twins. Both of them had blond hair, blue eyes, were tall and built like "brick houses." Except Lud liked to joke all the time and Aram barely said a word.

"Actually," said Shem, "I was told by his sister, The Lady Aryana, that he killed over a thousand."

"What?! His sister? She actually spoke to you?" Exclaimed Lud. The three boys all looked at each other in shock. "We heard she was beautiful."

Adi's tone was serious as she scolded them, "That's not something to joke about, boys. Shem could have been seriously hurt, or even killed, just like those poor farmers."

Shem lightly wiped away a tear from her eye. He felt regret as he took her hand, not wanting to see her upset. "I'm sorry, Adelaide. I didn't mean to hurt you," he said quietly, using her full name.

In response, Adi folded her arms in defiance.

Shem looked up at the boys, who all nonchalantly shrugged and pretended to admire the ceiling. Aram returned to his sketch, which was his usual tactic for appearing occupied.

Lud mumbled something about, "...wishing he could meet a beautiful princess."

Elam, sitting against the opposite door jam from Shem, came to the rescue, and said, "Wanna know what I heard?"

They all perked up at that. Elam's father was Ararat's town sheriff, which gave him access to all sorts of juicy information.

The two boys leaned a little closer in anticipation.

"We were eating dinner. Mom, Dad, and all of us kids. And he started telling Mom about his day," said Elam, pausing to make sure he had their attention. Lud and Eram gestured to hurry up in anticipation.

Elam rolled his eyes. "Soooo, he started talking about that bandit they captured, today. They put him in Dad's jail until they can decide what to do with him."

"Let me guess," said Lud, "he couldn't remember anything?"

Eram laughed at his brother's offhand remark.

"Not exactly," Elam continued. "He did say something that dad found concerning. My dad said, when they asked him if there were more of them, he just laughed."

Shem jumped in, at this point, "Well, he seemed to laugh a lot, even when threatening to kill me." Feeling Adi flinch, he added, "Sorry."

He felt bad that he was so cavalier about what happened, but he couldn't help himself. The image of that first dead man and all the blood, on top of almost dying multiple times that morning, took its toll on him. He didn't feel upset about it. In fact, he just felt numb, like he was seeing everything from outside his own body. Shem was glad to have this time with his friends, but on the other hand, they could never understand what he was going through. That thought made him feel very alone.

Elam looked at Shem sideways and said, "Right, he's a strange one, that one. But dad said, not only did he laugh, he said, 'you have no idea what's coming. Wait until you meet Anu the Destroyer.' That's a direct quote." He stood up, obviously troubled over what he heard. "What if there are more of them hiding in our town? What if there's a whole army over the hill? Worse...what if there are Nephilim waiting to strike? I mean, with a name like Anu, it must be a giant." His voice rising in pitch, continued, "Oh, and right before I left to come here, I even heard dad mention the word 'spy, ' while talking to Mom in the other room."

Now he was pacing back and forth with his fingers in his mouth with worry. This was not uncommon for Elam. Shem and his friends always joked about how hungry he was every time he started chewing his nails. This was different, though, hearing what happened to Shem today, plus the information from his Dad, was just too much for him.

"Ok. Elam. Please take a breath. Sit down," said Shem.

Elam continued to wear a path into the loft floor, so Shem continued, "Look, they all wore black and stunk really bad. So they would kinda stand out, right? Plus, hiding a whole army nearby would be hard, with Lady Aryana patrolling the area. As far as Nephilim go, they kinda stand out. We'd see them. They are giants, after all. And...a spy? Come on. Really? Why here?"

Elam scratched his hair in thought and stared Shem directly in the eyes, trying to ascertain whether or not he was just pacifying him. "Ok, you're right. We would know if there was something going on, right?" He looked at the other boys, who just shrugged.

Then Lud added, "I mean Nephilim come in different sizes though. One could hide right behind old Betsy and we would never see it. We don't even notice her half the time." He winked at Aram with a smile. He laughed in return.

"Thanks guys," said Shem. He couldn't help but look out of the hay door towards the lake where old Betsy the Brontosaurus was eating from a tall tree on the far side with her long slender neck. Even with her body half submerged in water, she was taller than any man. The thought of a giant hiding behind her gave him a shiver. *Thanks a lot.*

Looking at his watch, Aram spoke, "It's six thirty."

He was the only one of the friends that owned one. Being the oldest of the two brothers, their father, being a clockmaker, passed it on to him from one of their grandparents before he disappeared.

Lud added to his brother's announcement, "We better get going if we want to make the town meeting. Maybe WE'LL get some excitement today."

Aram continued, "Excitement like Shem getting beat by his father for speaking out at a town meeting. " Both brothers looked at each other.

At the same time, they both said, "Again." They laughed at their own joke.

Adi punched Shem in the leg.

"What did I do?" said Shem.

Lud answered for her, "You're a boy, that's what you did." All of them laughed, that time. Adi didn't find it funny, and punched him again.

"Ouch. Stoppit you!" exclaimed Shem.

This time Adi looked up at him with a smile and giggled.

CHAPTER 5

Trivial Matters

The evening was still as Shem and his friends made their way through the orchard toward the center of town. Not a single bird or cricket chirped, nor a frog croaked, adding to the fear in their minds of coming trouble. The only sound that could be heard was the sound of their boots crunching the cursed earth beneath their feet.

They all screamed as one when a little compy ran between them from out of the darkness of the surrounding trees and up the cart path they were traipsing. Adi grabbed onto Shem's arm, turning her paler than she already was. Elam held his stomach like he could lose his dinner. The brothers started laughing.

"You should see the looks on your faces," said Lud, all too amused with himself.

Elam straightened his shirt. "You screamed too."

Lud, looking incredulous, said, "Yeah, like I'm scared of a little lizard."

Walking backwards, while he was chiding Elam, Lud tripped over a root and stumbled for a ways before righting himself. Elam, Adi and Aram all laughed at the unintended consequences of Lud's mockery.

Lud punched Aram in the arm, kicking at the root that personally assaulted him.

Elam, noticing that Shem and Adi were still walking arm in arm, said, "Come on guys we got to hurry if we don't wanna miss anything." He picked up his pace, walking between Lud and Aram. They turned and followed on his heel, Lud singing a wedding tune.

Shem was used to the wedding jokes, as Adi and he had been in each other's lives since they were infants. Their father's had betrothed them to each other at birth, since their parents were so close. They were practically family already.

He appreciated that his friends were willing to give him space, but he wasn't sure if he wanted it today. He knew Adi would want to talk about what happened, but he really didn't want to discuss it.

Almost on cue, "What's wrong? You've been distant."

"I'm fine. Really. I was even joking around earlier," said Shem. *Here we go.*

"See?" Adi said, pointing her little finger at his nose. "That's what I mean. What's wrong?"

"I'm ok. I don't know what else to tell you. Stop asking," he said, feeling the frustration bubble up.

"Don't get testy with me. I know you...and I know when something is wrong."

Shem's cheeks flushed with warmth. He wasn't angry at her, just feeling a bit exasperated that she couldn't let go of the issue. He simply wanted to move on from the past, as talking about it wouldn't change anything.

"What?" The tone of her voice got higher.

Uh oh.

"Is it me?"

"You?" said Shem, his own voice getting louder. "Why would it be you? You haven't done anything wrong!" Realizing he sounded angry, added, "I love you."

She stopped walking.

He took an extra step, then realized she wasn't walking. *I blew it.* He stopped and turned to face her.

"There is something, though. Or you wouldn't have said, 'Why would IT be you?' You said, 'IT'. There is an IT!" she said, eyes starting to get shiny.

Shem struggled with what to say. He knew if he kept putting her off, the tears would flow. He also knew that if he made something up, she would call him on it. So he told her what he thought. "OK. If you want the truth...here it is. I just killed a man today. Probably more than one. For like my whole life, I've been taught that Yahweh is our creator, that he would protect us if we served him. We sacrifice to Him everyday, yet He still allowed this to happen to me."

His anger was getting the better of him. "Then, instead of just letting me sit in silence, I need to answer a million dumb questions about, if I'm ok or not?! Really?!" he said, with his hands up in protest. *There, that should do it!*

He knew he handled it wrong when the tears started down her face. By the way she looked at him, he also knew that they were tears of anger.

Shem braced himself, already formulating a follow up as she replied, "So...let me get this straight. Instead of letting me in, you decided that I can't help? And on top of that...don't interrupt me...it's Yahweh's fault? Have you lost your mind? Maybe, just maybe....I'm going out on a limb here... Yahweh did help you. That's why you're alive, you DOPE!" Adi was breathing hard, and was gearing up for more.

Shem jumped in, sputtering with exasperation. "Oh that's just right. I'm the one that almost got killed, and you somehow make this about you. If He is soooo powerful, couldn't He have stopped the attack all together." *There. Take that!* He folded his arms in self satisfaction.

Adi smiled, and shook her head in mock understanding. "Oh He could've. But...if you remember what your father's been telling you, Yahweh is done with the hearts of man and plans on destroying all of Adamah. Besides, we all know how you feel about attending Noah's midday meal everyday. So I'd say He's sick of another ungrateful human that expects special treatment." At that, she stormed past him, sniffling as she walked by.

Shem was in shock; he couldn't move. She just couldn't understand what he was going through. She was being selfish. He was the one this happened to, and he had a right to keep his thoughts private. He could feel tears of frustration run down his face, and that made him more angry, more alone.

"Ok." Shem said out loud. "Get it together." Leaning on his knees, he took a few deep breaths. Then, standing up straight, he shook off the anguish, wiped his face, and started down the path to join his friends.

Better to feel nothing at all.

As Shem made his way to Town Hall, the grand building loomed before him, its double doors beckoning visitors inside. The intricate stonework and ornate carvings adorned the exterior, a testament to the skilled Ararat craftsmen who had constructed it. A steady buzz of chatter and excitement emanated from within, drawing in curious townspeople who wanted to witness the night's events. As Shem approached the entrance to join his friends who were already there waiting, he could see his father and the council members gathered inside, at the front of the large hall, their voices carrying through the rows of polished wooden benches where eager onlookers had already taken their seats. The warm glow of crystal lanterns cast a soft light over the scene, creating an atmosphere of anticipation and reverence.

"Where's Adi?" said Elam, as Shem approached them.

Shem responded, "I thought she was with you? Damn. We had a fight. I'll go look for her."

"Just give her space, Shem. She'll be ok. You know she always comes around."

Shem said, "Yeah, but I was a huge brontosaurus dung pile to her this time."

"Ugh," said Elam, "I shouldn't have left you two alone, given your mood." He shook his head with a grimace.

"You too?" Shem asked.

Elam answered, "It was obvious to everyone but you, apparently." He chuckled. "But, hey, you had a tough morning. I'd be all in pieces by now, if it were me."

Shem just shook his head, "What a bone head." He thought.

"Are we going to do this, or not?" Said Lud, pointing to the inside, where everyone was taking their seats.

Elam answered, "Yeah, what are you waiting for? Come on," as he held his hands out in mock submission to royalty.

Lud took the hint, and with a bow, walked into the hall like he was the star of the show.

As the rest of them caught up to Lud, he pointed to the back row in the room, which happened to be empty. "I figured this spot was best in case we wanna make an escape." He winked at Aram as his brother took a seat.

"You're probably right, " said Elam as he joined Aram. "They can't hear you talk back here."

"Real funny," said Lud, acting wounded. "Or, so Shem is tempted to yell out again."

"Stop it you two. They're about to start," said Shem, not feeling their jokes at the moment.

To his friends' credit, they didn't offer any further jokes. They did cover their mouths to suppress their laughter, though.

They started the meeting like they usually did, with a roll call of Ararat council members, and finished with a word of prayer by Noah. Upon finishing his prayer, Noah began pronouncing the end of Adamah once again, to the moans and shuffling of feet of many in the room.

Shem wished he could slide under the bench, with embarrassment.

"Noah. Noah, we've heard all the warnings," said the Mayor, interrupting Noah's forceful pronouncement that they have all heard many times. "But that warning doesn't help us now. We have an immediate problem. Let's hear from the Sheriff." He pointed to Elam's father, who sat at the head table with the council due to his elected position.

"Thank you, Mister Mayor. The man we have in our cell is indicative of a larger problem," the Sheriff said, addressing the room. "Like, why is he here? Is this the beginning of an invasion? Are the Assyrians rattling their swords again? Is Tubal-Cain and his evil sister, Naamah, reviving their plans for expansion? Will..."

Someone whose voice Shem didn't recognize interrupted, "Come on Abban, more fear mongering from you?

Every time the wind blows, you people think it's Assyria. Sometimes I think you want to go to war."

The Sheriff responded, apoplectic, "I'm trying to speak facts, here, Declan, and you're talking politics." The Sheriff was addressing a man that was close to the front of the room. "It's not an election year, and I have nothing to gain from hyperbole."

Declan, a short man with unkempt wispy blonde hair, turned to face the room. "If that's true, then why do you keep us in the dark? It took forever just to get plumbing and sewage around here. If we were to foster an alliance with Assyi....."

The Mayor interrupted, "Declan, this is not getting us anywhere. You know that the Sheriff has nothing to do with those things."

"Now wait a minute," said Declan, trying to get control back. "We could use the education that their schools provide..."

Talking over Declan, as if he never stopped his thought, the Mayor continued. "His job is law and order. Now then. Let us continue. Audrey, I see your hand, and I'm so sorry for your loss."

Audrey, a pretty red-headed woman, stood up and spoke. Her voice sounded raspy like she had been crying. "Thank you, Cy. Everyone has been very supportive of me and my daughter, after losing...my husband this morning. Given that we don't have any of the Assyrian schools or the engineering guilds in Eden...as Mister Declan so eloquently pointed out, are any steps being taken to find my husband's replacement as black smith?" The Mayor answered, "That's a great question, Audrey, thank you, and again we're sorry. In fact, we were already discussing that very thing, just before the meeting. We will let you know what we decide."

“This is boring, Shem,” whispered Lud. “Me and Aram are getting out of here. We’ll go find Adi for you.”

“After he looks for that tall red head he saw earlier, outside the hall,” said Aram, a little too loud for his brother's comfort.

Shem responded with a thumbs up.

Lud rolled his eyes and scooted past Shem and Elam with Aram in tow.

Elam scooted closer to Shem, and said, “I hate to say I agree with Lud, but not much is being discussed about today, is it?”

“Not so far,” whispered Shem. “You can go too, if you want. I’ll let you know if you miss anything. Or if your Dad gets into a fist fight with Declan.”

Elam looked down in thought, shook his head as if he really considered the ramifications of that, then slid past Shem and headed towards the door to join the brothers.

Listening to numerous complaints from the various townspeople made Shem’s eyes start to get heavy, the craziness of the day finally taking its toll. Just as he thought he heard enough, he saw Nin as he walked to the front of the room, where he found a seat in the front row. *That’s odd. He’s never late to anything.*

The conversation continued about whether or not Japheth’s idea to place a fence around all of Ararat was expedient or not. Shem perked up when there was some talk of sending a party to neighboring towns to warn them, but it was shot down by others, and it went nowhere. The meeting droned on and on.

The back and forth between different people was usually quite entertaining, but tonight, though, it was annoying. There were so many horrible things that could happen, and all they wanted to do was argue over trivial matters. This went on for sometime, and once again Shem had his fill and was about to join his friends.

As Shem began to push himself to his feet, he heard boots stomp into the hall behind him. Gasps of horror escaped the mouths of many in the room, and it then went completely silent. Shem watched in horror as a bloodied Sheriff's Deputy hurried to the front. It instantly brought images of the morning back to his head. He gasped in spite of himself, placing a hand over his mouth, so as not to draw attention to himself. He couldn't believe what he saw.

He made his way to the front of the room, and stood in front of the council. The Deputy was an average sized man with dark curly hair, dressed in one of the tan uniforms that were standard issue for them, and looked as though he had just fought for his life. All that Shem could focus on was the look of panic in his eyes when he walked by him, like whatever he had seen had stolen his soul. His blood stained hands were shaking, and he held a bloody towel with which he was wiping them.

The mayor stood up, and addressed the distraught officer. "What happened, Deputy? Are you harmed?"

The deputy just stood there, shaking.

"Sheldon." The Sheriff himself approached him. "Son, what happened?" He put his hand on his shoulder and spoke softly to him.

The deputy had trouble articulating. "I came to the jail to start my shift, and..."

"It's ok, now, go ahead, please continue," said the Sheriff, with sympathy.

Taking a deep breath, the deputy continued, "I went to start my shift at the office. I got there and didn't see Tig anywhere, and I knew he was supposed to be watching the prisoner. He had told me earlier that day. So I went looking for him." Wringing his bloody hands in the bloody towel, he managed to keep talking, "I got to the back, where the jail is, and....and...Tig was laying there face down in his own blood. His throat was slit." After a long hesitation, and gasps from the crowd, he continued. "I...I....tried to stop the bleeding...with this towel. I was too late. He was dead." Deputy Sheldon, just hung his head, having run out of energy at last.

The Sheriff just stood there, looking at the ceiling in dismay, his hand still on Sheldon's shoulder offering as much comfort as he could. There wasn't a sound in the room, and Shem had to use all his strength not to scream in anguish. He was so glad Elam wasn't here to see this, as most of the deputies have been around his family forever.

"*What about the prisoner*?" The mayor verbally voiced Shem's thoughts to the deputy.

Deputy Sheldon, now seated in a chair that someone brought up for him, said, "His throat was slit, too. He's dead." Looking at the Sheriff, he said, "I'm sorry, Sir. I failed. I couldn't save him. I couldn't find who did it. All I could do was come here. I just...." He trailed off, head in his hands.

"It's ok Sheldon, there's nothing to be done. Seems as if you'd be dead as well if you were there." The Sheriff just patted his shoulder, looking at the mayor with sorrow in his eyes.

Shem watched as the people started to fumble out of the hall. A few started moving at first, then eventually the rest started moving for the door. It was anything but orderly, and all attempts to reclaim order were ignored. There was crying and people yelling in fear about killers coming to hurt their family and loved ones. Panic was rising quickly among the townspeople. He realized he needed to get out of there fast before he was stuck in the stampede.

"What is going on, Yahweh?" He growled to himself in anger as he made his way outside to the town square.

"Going somewhere?" said Nin's voice from behind him as he exited the building.

"Well, I wasn't trying to run into anyone I knew." Said Shem.

Nin responded, "I guess that cloud passed, huh?" He came and stood next to Shem, putting his hand on his shoulder, he added, "You ok? It was a lot to deal with today."

"You were late." Not feeling like discussing it again.

Nin just made a grunt in the back of his throat.

Kicking at an invisible stone on the ground, Shem fumbled for something else to say. He really wanted to get back to his friends.

Almost like he read Shem's mind, Nin said, "Your friends went down the main street towards Adi's family store. I'm sure you'll find them there safe and sound snacking on apples."

"Uh thanks...I'll be going then," said Shem, making to walk past Nin, but he grabbed his arm.

"Listen. Not everyone has been through what you experienced today. If you need to talk, I'm here. No religious mumbo-jumbo either." Nin looked like that thought made him very uncomfortable.

"Oh, thanks Nin, but I'm good," said Shem, knowing that he was anything but. Plus, Nin wasn't exactly the kind of person to confide in.

Nin said, "Ok, have it your way." He let go of Shem's arm, but added, "Noah wanted me to see you home safely."

"Tell him," Shem said, "that you couldn't find me." He headed across the square towards Main Street. *My father is probably going to kill me.*

He thought he could hear Nin chuckle as he walked away.

Shem's friends were gathered exactly where Nin had predicted, gathered around the front porch of Rania's Fresh Apples, proudly owned and operated by Adi's parents. As Shem approached the quaint storefront, he heard the laughter of Lud and Aram echoing through the cobblestone street. The scent of freshly baked apples wafted towards him, mixed with the aroma of warm cinnamon and sugar. Shem couldn't help but smile as he watched Aram and Lud toss apple cores at each other. It was moments like these that made their small town feel like a close-knit family.

"Look who finally arrived. It's sourpuss Shem!" hollered Lud to Elam and Adi, perched on the porch with a half-eaten bucket of apples. Shem could tell the general store must have stayed open later than usual as he saw townsfolk strolling back from their meeting. He checked if the other shop across the street was still open but nearly got run over by an unusually speedy horse and carriage. A voice bellowed obscenities at the reckless driver as they zoomed past. *Idiot.*

Shem, beside himself, since his life just flashed before his eyes, stumbled onto the creaky wooden porch. “Hey guys,” he said, still trying to catch his breath. “How are you?”

Elam took a long sip of the drink he was holding, before answering. "Oh we're fine. Just discussing how much of a bone head you are.” He laughed, nudging Adi, who was sitting next to him. She just simply smiled.

"Nah, don't lie, El. We were taking bets on how long you'd be grounded for. We were sure you'd get into trouble. Like usual." He laughed at his own joke while throwing another apple at his brother.

Shem tried to find the humor in what was said, but was distracted by his earlier argument with Adi, and what he saw at the Town Hall. *She's smiling, at least.*

He walked up to the bench, hoping she had forgotten the whole ordeal. "I was a bone head," he said. "I am sorry."

Elam said, "Oh I already forgave you." He acted indignant when Adi pushed him. "Ok. Ok. I know when 'three's' a crowd. Behave you two," he said, getting up from the bench. He took a bow, and grabbed an apple from the bin as he stepped off of the porch.

Shem laughed as Elam hurled the fresh apple at Lud, but overthrew him and narrowly missed a passerby walking home from the meeting. Lud and Aram pointed at Elam and started laughing, as he was apologizing profusely to the random towns person.

"So," said Shem, so only Adi could hear, "I guess I owe you an apology." It wasn't a question.

She responded, still looking down at her lap, "I guess so. Probably Yahweh, too."

Shem reached over and tilted her head towards him, with the tip of his finger under her chin. Kissing her gently on the forehead, he said, "I'm sorry. You know I love you." *Yahweh can wait.*

She cuddled up to him, wrapping her arm around his in comfort. He contemplated telling her about tonight's events at the meeting but decided to let a sleeping dog lie for now.

He was content, just enjoying the sound of her breathing with her head on his shoulder, watching his friends chase each other around, under the street lights. A gentle breeze blew through the porch, carrying the smell of honeysuckle, his favorite smell. Placing his head against the large window behind him, he could hear Adi's mom, Rania, and her little sister, Reem, inside discussing school work. Shem, closing his eyes, wanted the peace of this moment to last forever.

The peace was short-lived. The street lamps started to rattle when a distant thumping, like a large tyrannosaurus stomping down the street, shook the porch and bench where they were sitting. Then there was screaming.

CHAPTER 6

Thunderous Terror

A distant rhythmic thumping, like a large tyrannosaurus lumbering down the street, shook the porch, rattling buckets and window panes alike.

Then there was more screaming.

Shem and Adi, both sat up in alarm. The world seemed as though it stopped and not a sound could be heard except the steady cadence.

Boom boom.

The three boys in the street froze in place, just looking at each other, expressionless, feeling the rumbling under their feet.

Boom boom.

The surrounding shops and houses came alive as people were awakened by the steady drum of terror approaching.

Boom boom.

Even the crickets and tree frogs were singing no songs. All life seemed to be hanging on the edge of a knife with the sound getting closer.

Boom boom.

The door to Shem's right slammed open, almost giving him a heart attack. Adi's mom, with her sister holding onto an apron string, came flying out of the shop in a panic, looking as though she saw a ghost.

Boom boom.

"Wha...what is that horrendous noise?" she said.

Adi answered, "Not sure, mom. Sounds like a dinosaur!"

"Here?" Shem yelled, trying to keep the panic from overcoming him. "The ones that would be that big never come into town."

BOOM BOOM.

The townspeople scrambled out onto their porches, frantically searching for the source of the thundering sound that filled the air. Families huddled together in terror, fear etched into their faces as they tried to find safety. Shem strained his eyes but couldn't see anything through the thick barrier of trees and buildings that blocked his view. The town itself seems to be shaking with each earth-shattering thud, causing even the streetlamps to sway dangerously on their posts. Whatever was approaching was not just powerful, but was a force to be reckoned with.

BOOM BOOM.

The steady sound of the monstrous terror drew closer, accompanied by the deafening crash of bricks and wood as buildings were reduced to rubble. The air was filled with the desperate screams of people running for their lives. Shem and Adi bolted towards the street with their friends.

Shem's heart was racing with adrenaline as he ran, hoping for a better vantage point to witness the carnage unfolding before them.

Shem's footsteps echoed on the cobblestone as he approached Elam. "You know what this is, right?" Elam asked with awe in his voice.

"You think it's a...? In Ararat?" Shem said, in disbelief.

The sound of chaos filled the air as people poured into the street, drawn by the commotion. Adi's mother and sister joined them, their faces etched with fear and surprise. Shem scanned the growing crowd, realizing that the entire town was now on high alert.

Calls for help echoed through the streets, mingling with panicked screams and urgent orders. Adi's father Bartel appeared, his usually neat blonde hair now wild and pulled back into a long braid. Sweat dripped down his bushy beard as he charged toward them, his usually calm demeanor replaced by wild-eyed urgency. His sword gleamed in his hand, poised for battle. With a commanding presence, he pushed his family back and took up a defensive position, barking out orders to those around him.

"Rania, get Adi and Reem back into the house now! Shem, take your friends with you. They are not prepared to handle this." His voice was hard and commanding, leaving no room for argument.

Lud's eyebrows shot up in disbelief. "We're not equipped? And you are?"

The man's face hardened with determination. "Boy, you never know when to just follow orders, do you?" He gave Lud a cold stare, daring him to challenge his authority.

Shem stepped forward, defending Lud before he could regret his next words. "Sir, what can we do then? Is help on the way?"

The deafening sounds of smashing and destruction echoed through the cobblestone streets, shaking the ground beneath their feet. People scrambled for safety, but instead, more and more gathered in the streets or on their porches, drawn to the chaos like moths to a flame. Shem could hear screams and shouts from down the street, mingled with the terrified plea of a woman begging for mercy. But her cries were abruptly cut off, replaced by a chilling silence that sent shivers down Shem's spine.

Shem's body trembled with the urge to flee, but he forced himself to stand firm as Adi grabbed onto his arm in desperation. Biting back his own fear, he tried to put up a brave front for her sake. Glancing at his friends for support, he saw them all frozen in shock and fear. In the chaos, Shem saw Reem's mother clutching her daughter tightly, trying to calm her as she sobbed uncontrollably.

"Listen," Bartel barked urgently, grasping Shem's shoulder with a vice-like grip. His eyes darted around frantically, scanning for any sign of danger. "Your father is on his way with the militia, but we don't have much time. You need to get out of here."

His voice echoed across the street as he started yelling, "LISTEN! Everyone run! It's not safe here. Get to safety NOW!"

The sound of destruction rumbled down the street, causing some to try and pull their loved ones away from the danger, but most were rooted to the spot, refusing to leave until they knew what was happening.

A brave soul shouted back at Bartel's warning, "What safety? We need to know what we're up against."

Despite their trembling limbs and racing hearts, curiosity and determination overrode self-preservation.

The memory of the afternoon's events consumed Shem's thoughts, stirring up a deep desire to fight. Yet, he also struggled with his innate urge to flee from danger. Even though he was prepared to confront The Serpent himself, conflicting emotions tore at him, leaving him uncertain and unbalanced. Is *this worth risking my life*?

Shem ripped his arm out of Adi's grasp, his heart racing with adrenaline as he prepared to face the unseen threat before him. But as he stepped forward, a piercing screech echoed through the air, causing him to freeze in fear and uncertainty. His gaze shot upwards to see Lady Aryana on her trusted pterosaur Alouette, soaring towards the chaos that was unfolding down the street. Despite the danger, a spark of hope ignited within Shem.

Adi's panicked voice broke through his thoughts. "What are you doing? You can't just charge into battle without a weapon!" She grabbed onto his arm again, trying to hold him back.

Elam joined in, desperation lacing his words. "Please, we have to think this through. This isn't some random enemy we're facing." He gripped onto Shem's other arm, pleading for reason.

But Shem could not listen any longer. The screams of innocent people being hurt and killed resonated through his mind, pushing him over the edge of rage and despair.

"We have to do something!" he roared, shaking with anger and emotion. "I can't just stand here and watch as more lives are lost! Get off of me!" With a ferocious yank, he tore himself away from their grasp, determined to take action despite the overwhelming odds against them.

The terrifying sounds of destruction echoed through the town, as if the very earth itself was being torn apart. The people cowered in fear, their mouths agape as they witnessed buildings being ripped from their foundations. But amidst the chaos, a screeching Alouette joined the fray, defending the townspeople with fierce determination.

Shem's heart pounded in his chest as he prepared to run towards the source of the destruction. But before he could move, an enormous presence appeared in the night sky. The people gasped in horror, believing that their world was coming to an end on this very night. Kneeling to the ground, Shem watched in terror as a massive piece of building materialized into view and hurtled towards Yohan's Tailor Shop. With a deafening crash, the brick and mortar wall smashed into the store across the street from Rania's.

Bricks and splintered wood rained down on them like deadly projectiles, sending shards flying in all directions. In a split second, Yohan's family, who had come outside to investigate the commotion, were caught in the blast. Shem instinctively ducked his head and shielded his eyes from the sharp debris hurtling towards him. His heart sank as he couldn't see if Yohan or his family had survived the impact. More cries of pain echoed through the chaos as others were struck by pieces of flying shrapnel.

Lud's voice pierced through the chaos, yelling at Shem over the deafening screams and panicked shouts of those around them. "We're easy targets out here!" Without hesitation, Aram grabbed Lud's arm and they sprinted to their left, towards the alley next to Adi's family shop. Elam shot Shem an urgent look before turning and running with the two brothers. The building that was just hit exploded into flames, consuming the neighboring trees and structures in a matter of seconds. The townspeople scattered in all directions, some frantically seeking help from the nearby fire brigade while others froze in terror, their screams competing with the raging inferno. With adrenaline pumping, those who were able followed the boys' lead and fled down the back alleys, desperate to escape the terror unfolding before them.

Bartel desperately pulled his family back down the street, trying to protect them from the chaos unfolding around them. "Please, we have to go," he urged his wife and children.

But Adi refused to leave Shem's side. "I'm staying with him. You go ahead," she insisted.

Shem, knowing the danger they were all in, pleaded with her. "Adi, please, you should go with your father."

Determined to stay by Shem's side, Adi stood her ground. "I am not leaving you! Do you want to run or argue?!"

Feeling helpless, Shem took her hand and led her away from the chaotic streets. He could feel Bartel's disappointed gaze on them as they passed by. "I'm sorry," he silently mouthed to her father before disappearing into an alleyway. The sounds of destruction behind them only fueled their fear as they made their way through the narrow alleys, hoping to find safety amidst the rubble and chaos.

At the next intersection, Shem's friends were waiting for them with anxious expressions. Elam was busily pulling out splinters from his arm, wincing in pain whenever he jarred it against someone rushing by. Lud and Aram stood on tiptoes, peering around the corner, their voices rising in a heated conversation. The bustling chaos of people darting in every direction only added to the tension and urgency in the air. It felt like being caught in a whirlwind of energy and noise. Shem's heart rate quickened as he joined his friends and tried to make sense of the situation.

Elam's voice was urgent as he laid out the options to Shem, sweat beading on his forehead as his eyes darted between the two choices. "Lud wants to head back towards town center, but Aram thinks the farm is safer since there are no people. What do you think?"

Shem's response cut through the air like a knife. "Neither." His words were met with shocked gasps from Elam and Adi.

Before they could even defend their choices, Shem spoke again with a grim tone. "There is no safe place," he said, his mind replaying the events of the day. "We thought we were safe at home, but we were attacked there. The deputy thought he was keeping a prisoner safe, but they were murdered."

Elam's reaction was one of disbelief. "What did you just say?" he asked, unable to comprehend.

Realizing his mistake that he hadn't told Elam what had happened yet, Shem tried to backtrack. "I meant to tell you earlier, but I never had the chance." But seeing Elam's distraught expression, he knew there was no going back now. "I'm sorry, Elam...we'll talk about it later. But right now, all I know is that something big is happening and I can't escape this feeling that it's a trap."

Lud chimed in nervously. "So you somehow think this is about you? Obviously, you've had a rough day. I understand that you're upset and not thinking clearly, but if not town center or Buchard's, where should we go?"

"I am thinking clearly," Shem replied firmly. "These events are just not sitting right with me. Those men who attacked us earlier and this current danger are somehow connected. I can't explain how I know...but I just do."

Suddenly, a nearby building shook violently, bricks crumbling and falling as the walls swayed dangerously. Smoke and dust filled the alleyway, choking their lungs and burning their eyes.

Without hesitation, Shem took off running towards certain danger-motioning everyone to follow. He could hear them protesting behind him, but they stayed close, Adi's hand still tightly gripping his own.

They raced down the road where Shem led them into an alley leading back to the main street they had originally fled from.

As they paused at the end of the narrow alleyway, Shem's heart skipped a beat as he took in the nightmarish scene down Main Street where, from this vantage, he had a clear unobstructed view. The rooftops were engulfed in flames, casting a fiery glow over the destruction that lay ahead. Buildings were reduced to rubble, with bodies scattered among the debris. A thick cloud of smoke and dust hung in the air, coating everything in a hazy red and yellow light. And at the center of it all stood a figure straight out of his childhood nightmares: a Nephilim.

Shem had heard stories of these giants before, but nothing could have prepared him for the sheer awe and terror he felt at seeing one in person. Towering over the already impressive buildings of Main Street, the nephilim's massive form was an imposing sight to behold. Broad-shouldered and muscular, with a braided black beard and exposed snarling teeth, he exuded an aura of power and danger. His head was completely shaven, adorned instead with intricate tattoos matching those of the invaders Shem had faced earlier. And around his waist hung a loincloth made of animal hides, while a necklace of human skulls dangled from his neck like a grisly trophy.

Elam's hands gripped Shem's shoulders, his fingers digging into the fabric of his tunic. Despite the chaos and noise surrounding them, the intensity in Elam's eyes was impossible to ignore. "I told you it was a giant," he said, voice urgent with warning. "The prisoner's words were true."

Shem's heart raced as he looked at the massive figure before him. The tattoos covering his face and arms marked him as one of the invaders they had encountered earlier. Panic and dread filled Shem as he recognized the man standing before them - Anu: The Destroyer.

"How could something so colossal hide?" Elam's voice trembled with fear, mirroring Shem's own emotions.

Adi, barely audible above the commotion, offered a possible explanation. "Perhaps some kind of dark magic or divination?"

A chill ran down Shem's spine as he recalled Aryana's warning about the invaders' use of dark arts. "That's even more proof that they are united," he said grimly, realizing the dire situation they were facing.

Aram, pointing at the giant, got their attention. “Looks like we have help.”

Through the thick, acrid smoke, Shem strained to make out the chaotic scene unfolding before him. The giant swung his massive arms in a frenzy, trying to swat at the small figure darting around his head. Lady Aryana, bravely perched atop Alouette, darted back and forth, desperately trying to divert Anu’s attention away from the innocent townspeople.

Shem watched as a wall was ripped off a nearby building and hurled towards her, narrowly missing its target.

The heavy debris soared through the air with a deafening whoosh before crashing into another building in a shower of splintered wood and shattered glass, causing panicked screams to fill the air.

An endless stream of bodies came into view, their footsteps stampeding the ground as they rushed past Adi's family shop. The militia had finally arrived, their faces hardened with determination and fear as they prepared to face this monstrous threat. Shem could feel the sheer force of all the able-bodied men of Ararat gathering near his position, their weapons glinting in the streetlights, ready to take on Anu. Battle cries shook the air, drowning out the sounds of crumbling buildings and screams of terror. The chaotic symphony of dust and smoke filled his nostrils, thickening the air with a sense of impending doom.

The deep, rumbling sound of Anu's voice echoed through the cave, sending shivers down their spines. "Humans. I eat you," he declared.

Lud's eyes widened in amazement. "Wow," he said, his voice tinged with sarcasm, "He's a bright one."

Elam rolled his eyes at Lud's comment and turned to Aram. "Anakim," he stated.

Lud furrowed his brows in confusion. "A what?"

Aram sighed and explained, "It's the skulls around the neck that give it away."

Lud's gaze shifted back and forth between Elam and Aram. "What are you two going on about?"

"The Anakim," replied Elam, "are the dumbest of all the Nephilim. They are known by the skulls they collect from the humans they kill."

Aram chimed in, "They are also the largest and most destructive."

Shem felt his head spinning with this new information. "That's just great," he muttered, trying to wrap his mind around the situation, "Most destructive." As if things couldn't get any worse.

The battle raged on, chaos and destruction reigning over Main Street as the giant Anu relentlessly advanced towards their hiding spot. The militia fought desperately against him, hurling spears and firing arrows, but their efforts were futile against his massive frame. Some managed to strike his legs with spears, but most only bounced off his bulging muscles.

Noah, armed only with a large dagger, had his arm around an injured Japheth as he barked orders at the men trying to gain control of Anu by lassoing his ankle with a rope. But their attempts were short-lived as the giant lifted his leg and brought it down with earth-shattering force, crushing both bricks and men in one fell swoop. The screams of the soldiers pierced through the air, sending chills down the friends' spines.

Ducking for cover as debris from the destroyed buildings rained down around them, the friends retreated further into the alleyway. Adi trembled visibly, her voice shaking as she asked, "What are we doing here?"

Shem was overcome with determination as he reached down to grab a fallen sword. Aram's hand shot out to stop him, concern etched on his face. "It's not smart," he warned.

But Shem was fueled by anger and frustration at their inability to make a difference in this hopeless situation. "They need all the help they can get!" he roared, the rage causing tears to stream down his cheeks. The sounds of destruction and death surrounded them as they huddled in helplessness.

Shem's heart raced as he watched the chaos unfolding in front of him. Rania, her face twisted with fear and determination, was hunched over someone on the ground while Reem sobbed uncontrollably by her side. He was sickened as he recognized the injured figure as Bartel, Adi's father. He knew her family was not safe from the mindless violence surrounding them - at any moment they could be trampled by the deadly melee.

Through the throngs of raging townspeople, the towering giant bulldozed through, seemingly unaffected by their weapons. Shem watched in terror as the giant swung wildly at Alouette, her small form staying just out of reach of his brute strength. Lady Aryana held on, swiping at the giant with her dual swords, delivering many gashes and cuts from her relentless attacks.

Shem's heart raced with a sense of impending doom as he watched Anu wade through the sea of soldiers and townspeople, their invisible presence no match for the unstoppable force. With every passing second, Shem felt the weight of their failure to stop this chaotic nightmare bearing down on them, suffocating and paralyzing their ability to save themselves and their loved ones. Suddenly, Aryana's ferocious attack shifted the tide of battle towards their refuge, and Shem's friends scrambled to avoid falling debris as the giant ripped away half of the building. In desperation, they all dove out of the way, narrowly avoiding being crushed by the debris that rained down upon them with destructive fury.

The giant's massive arms swung wildly as he brandished his new weapon, trying to swat away the pesky nuisances flying around his head. Shem struggled to free himself from the pile of rubble that had trapped him, only to catch a glimpse of his father staring straight at him with an unreadable expression. Despite disobeying Nin earlier, Shem couldn't decide if he was relieved or worried that his father had found him in this chaos. But they had bigger problems to worry about. The giant was barreling down Main Street, heading straight for Adi's family and the townspeople gathered there. The militia behind him was desperately trying to secure a rope around a nearby tree, but their efforts were futile against the strength of Anu's leg. The giant continued his rampage, leaving destruction in his wake.

Shem dragged himself to the edge of the alley and peered out, heart racing as he saw Adi's parents still huddled in the same spot where he last saw them. But then he noticed something even more unsettling - Reem, their youngest sibling, was inexplicably moving toward their shop, putting herself in grave danger.

Shem's adrenaline pounded in his chest as Adi struggled to stand next to him, her eyes widening in shock and terror as she finally saw the danger her family was in. "Dad! Mom!" Her voice cracked with fear and desperation.

The scream of Alouette overhead made Shem look up just in time to witness Lady Aryana's next attack on Anu's face. In a desperate attempt to defend himself, Anu hurled a piece of debris towards Lady Aryana. The projectile narrowly missed her but hurtled towards Adi's family's shop with deadly force.

Time seemed to slow down as Reem, Adi's sister, ran towards the building, unaware of the impending danger.

Before Shem could even react, Adi had already taken off towards her sister, risking her own life to save her. The impact of the makeshift weapon against the front of the two-story building was deafening, sending a shockwave through the air and blasting it into pieces. Shem could only stare in disbelief as Reem disappeared under the rubble and debris.

Rainia, who had left her husband's side to stop Reem from entering the crumbling building, arrived at the same time as Adi. But it was too late. The remainder of the facade collapsed just at that moment, burying both Adi and her mother under a mountain of stone, brick, and wood beams.

The sound of shattering wood and crumbling bricks filled Shem's ears as he was grabbed by his friends and pulled away. He struggled against their grip, his heart wrenching at what he just witnessed. He needed to save them. He needed to get to Adi before it was too late. *Why won't they let me go? What is that screaming?*

A sharp blow landed on Shem's face, causing his vision to blur. The sound of screaming abruptly ceased as he was knocked onto his side.

"That was a little too hard, don't you think?" Someone's voice reached his ears.

Another voice responded, "He wouldn't stop. And he was heading out there."

Through the haze of pain and confusion, Shem managed to pull himself up against the wall behind him. He tasted the metallic tang of blood in his mouth and struggled to clear his thoughts. All he knew was that he needed to reach Adi.

Elam, tears streaming down his face, grabbed Shem by both sides of his face, searching for any signs of injury. "Are you okay?"

Lud answered for him, "That's a dumb question."

As Shem's senses slowly returned, he could finally make out who was talking to whom. "What was all the screaming about?"

"I told you it was too hard," Aram muttered.

Lud leaned over Elam to get a better look at Shem's condition. "Forget it. You're alright now." Although the concern in his voice said otherwise.

The giant let out a deafening roar of rage, his eyes bulging with fury as the rope tightened around Anu's ankle. With a massive tree as its anchor and an army of militia tugging on it for dear life, the rope held strong against the giant's brute strength. But still they hacked at his leg, determined to bring him down and end this devastating rampage once and for all.

With a primal roar of his own fueled by anguish and grief, Shem lunged at Elam with all his might, slamming him into the unsuspecting Lud and Aram behind. The force of their impact reverberated through the narrow alleyway as bodies collided and were sent flying in all directions. Ignoring the chaos around him, Shem charged towards Adi and her family in the middle of the war zone, plowing through soldiers who were caught unawares, helpless against his berserker strength.

Bartel, now fully aware of the horrific scene before him, was kneeling in a puddle of his own blood. He desperately scoured through the debris of his former home and shop. Shem rushed to his side but could only stare in shock and disbelief.

The tears ran freely down Shem's face as he gazed upon the ruins of Rainia's Fresh Fruit Shop, with Adi, her mother and sister buried under the rubble. In that moment, Shem felt like his heart had been ripped out and shattered into a million pieces, leaving him frozen and helpless in despair.

With every breath, Shem felt like he was suffocating. The smoke and rubble surrounding him were choking him, but it was the pain in his heart that truly took his breath away. He wanted to give up, to let himself be consumed by the devastation around him. But a small part of him still held onto hope for vengeance against the one responsible for all this destruction, Anu. As he turned to face the giant, Raphael appeared by his side, wielding a sword with a fierce determination in his eyes. *Why is he here?*

Picking up a discarded sword, Shem began walking towards the battle to confront this evil. But before he travelled too far, Nin materialized from out of the smoke. *Him too?*

"Don't try to stop me," Shem said.

Nin unsheathed his sword and joined Shem in walking towards the menacing sight ahead. Anu was still struggling to reach Lady Aryana while being attacked by the militia. The wind carried the scents of fire, soot, and ash towards them as they drew near. The scene was engulfed in flames and black smoke, making it seem like Yahweh had accelerated His plan to destroy Adamah. Despite the danger, Shem, Raphael, and now Nin were determined to face it head-on.

The colossal creature continued to thrash and stomp, desperately trying to free his foot from the grip of the tree, while swinging wildly at the swooping pterosaur. The militia, vastly outnumbered and outmatched, fought with unrelenting determination against their opponent. As the wind picked up, rain began to mix in, creating a swirling tempest of smoke and ash that whipped back towards the giant's face. Despite the chaos and danger, the soldiers stood strong, unflinching in their fight for survival.

Anu's movements halted suddenly, as if his body had been drawn to a far-off sound. He stood amidst the chaos and commotion, his eyes scanning the area with intensity. Turning on his heel, he gave the rope a strong tug, causing the soldiers gripping it to strain against its resistance. The others surrounding them also paused in their actions, captivated by Anu's sudden stillness. No longer raining destruction upon them, he simply stood in silent contemplation, an enigma amongst the chaos.

Noah's eyes widened in terror as he snapped to the source of the giant's hesitation. "Shem, go back!" he bellowed desperately, his voice echoing through the chaos.

Shem paid no heed as he continued towards the danger that lay ahead. “Anu! Today you will die!”

Staring down at him with a cold, twisted smile, he chuckled. Anu leaned in closer, as if to crush Shem, but then paused. Suddenly, his head tilted to the side like a dog trying to interpret a master's command. With a sharp intake of breath, he recoiled and jerked back his hand as if burned.

"The giant slayer!" He shrieked in terror, his eyes widening with madness before he frantically turned and began tugging in earnest at his leg restraint.

Noah barked orders to the soldiers, his voice ringing out like steel against stone. They quickly scattered, making way for Anu as he charged towards them. His massive form barreled down the street, causing chaos and panic among the fleeing civilians. Desperate to escape, Anu thrashed and pulled at the rope binding him, muscles straining and veins popping in his neck. But with a sharp nod from Noah, one of the soldiers swiftly brought his axe down, severing the rope and sending the giant tumbling into a nearby building. With a roar of fury, Anu fought his way free from the debris and continued on his destructive rampage, leaving behind a trail of devastation and shattered families in his wake.

With a heavy heart, Shem let the sword fall from his trembling hand. He turned to face the destruction that lay before him - the ruins of the store where he had found solace and friendship. His life in Ararat was shattered, along with any dreams of a normal future. Tears streamed down his face as he stood alone in the rain.

I failed you, Adi. I broke my promise.

CHAPTER 7

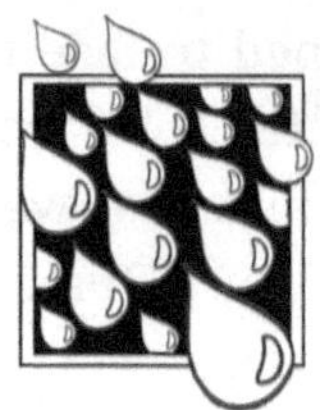

Restless Intentions

The following days became a somber cascade of rain, enveloping the world in a shroud of depression and gloom. Although the rain helped extinguish the fires, it only intensified the bleakness that seeped into Shem's very marrow as he assisted the townsfolk in sifting through the remnants of their upturned lives.

Everything he touched evoked memories of the past before the calamity, and his desire to move forward grew stronger. Sleep, too, became a bothersome interruption for which he had no patience.

The funeral did not bring any solace. It only served to slow the pace of things when time could be better spent pursuing the monster responsible for these heinous acts.

Shem did not wish to spend his time standing idly by, listening to his father's eulogy, and being reminded once more of Yahweh's punishment of death upon His people. There was no benefit to it. Grieving could wait until after justice or vengeance had been served.

His friends had good intentions, but they couldn't truly comprehend his feelings. Although Adi was a friend to all, his bond with her was profoundly deeper. As her betrothed, his sole duty was her protection—a duty at which he had failed. How could he safeguard his family and friends while passively sitting on a farm, mourning and healing? He vowed not to fail again.

The funeral's gloomy remnants departed like a fog drifting off as Shem stood with his closest friends in the hushed seclusion of the now empty yet somber cemetery. His voice, barely above a whisper, revealed his intent to depart Ararat and pursue those behind the onslaught. The mere utterance of Anu, the towering giant haunting their nightmares, cast an icy chill over the gathering.

"Shem," Elam gasped out, his shock on full display. "You can't be serious." His dark eyes were wide pools of disbelief and fear. "That's...that's suicide!"

"Elam's right for once," Lud interjected with a scoff, rolling his eyes dramatically. "Now you're a hero of legend? You've lost your mind."

Yet despite their frantic pleas and protests, Shem remained unyielding. He didn't quiver or waver under their concerned gazes or heated retorts. Instead, he paced back and forth, planning for his journey in silence. His path might have been unclear and his plan to topple a giant single-handedly crazy at best, but there was a firm resolve etched onto his face that echoed louder than any words could.

Aram watched him silently for a moment before finally speaking up. "Maybe...maybe he's onto something," he murmured thoughtfully.

But it was like trying to reroute a river with bare hands-futile. Shem was determined-a solid wall against their pleas for reason and safety. Their attempts to change his mind transformed into an emotionally charged debate–each friend voicing their fears and doubts while Shem paced in stoic silence.

Lost in endless thoughts of self-doubt, Shem frantically rummaged through his room for essentials to bring on his journey. His hands trembled as he tried to pack, the tragic events playing on an endless loop in his mind. He second-guessed every decision, agonizing over what he could have done differently.

Did I cause this? Could I have acted faster? The gnawing doubts and self-blame clouded his mind, making it hard to focus on his impending departure.

"This isn't going to bring her back, Shem," his mother's voice echoed from the doorway.

Shem inhaled deeply, steadying himself. "And will sitting around?"

"Do you believe that's all we do? Just sit idly by?" she countered.

"That wasn't my intention," he replied, feeling the tension rise.

"Yet that's what came across," she pointed out gently.

Shem turned to face her. "How am I supposed to guard our family while tending crops?"

"That's not the issue here, Shem. You're restless, always have been. But fleeing isn't the solution. You know what your father prophesied."

He averted his gaze, unable to bear her concerned look. "So we're supposed to till the fields, make endless offerings and just await Adamah's end? That's 85 years away! What purpose does that serve?"

"The purpose is faith, Shem. Yahweh has a plan." She stepped forward and wrapped him in a comforting embrace.

Feeling his throat tighten and eyes well up with unshed tears, he straightened up and took another deep breath. He wouldn't crumble now; he had a mission to accomplish and couldn't let anything deter him.

But he couldn't face her again for fear of succumbing to his emotions.

She held him tighter as if sensing his internal struggle. "Shem, I understand you're hurting right now but remember we love you dearly."

His mother's tears soaked through the fabric of his shirt onto his skin–an additional assault on his wavering determination. He gently disengaged from her embrace and resumed packing his bag with a newfound urgency–a silent signal that he was done with the conversation. He felt her presence recede towards the door.

Just as she was about to exit, he called out, "Mom." She paused in the doorway and waited for him to speak. After a moment of silence, Shem said, "Pray for me."

"Always," she replied softly before leaving him alone in his room.

Shem found Ham lounging in the parlor as he descended the staircase. "Well, look at you, all grown up," Ham teased.

"Pot calling the kettle black?" Shem retorted, a defensive edge lining his words.

Ham chuckled lightly. "Don't get me wrong. I'm not here to stop you. But do you really think father will just let you walk away?"

Shem shrugged, trying to appear nonchalant, but his voice betrayed him. "I don't know...and I'm not going to ask."

"And if he orders you to stay?" Ham asked with a knowing smirk.

"I won't." Shem's words were firm but lacked conviction.

Ham crossed his arms and leaned back in his chair. "Keep that spirit when it happens."

"When it happens?" Shem echoed, catching onto Ham's self-satisfied tone.

"Well, considering mother just stormed out of here crying, I'd say father will find out soon enough," Ham said smugly. "I just wanted to make sure you're ready for that."

"Really." Shem spat out the word like an accusation.

Ham feigned hurt at his brother's skepticism. "Hey! I've always had your back!"

Shem raised his hands in a half-hearted apology before changing the subject. "Guess this is goodbye then."

"Do you even know where you're going?" Ham asked with an amused grin.

Shem glanced past Ham's shoulder into the distance. "Not really sure yet... Maybe East towards Center Grove or possibly the coast where Lady Aryana mentioned the invaders are gathering."

"The coast? That's weeks away from here! And what do you plan on doing once you find them?" Ham pressed on.

"Why all these questions?" Shem snapped back irritably.

"Just curious," came Ham's nonchalant reply.

Feeling guilty for snapping at him, Shem forced a smile. “Sorry. I don’t know, maybe Eden is assembling an army. I could join them... Why are you acting like the older brother all of a sudden?”

Ham softened his voice, "So... Is it true what I heard?"

"About what?" Shem's defensive guard was back up.

Ham hesitated, as if choosing his words carefully. “I heard that you walked right up to the giant...like you...”

"Like I wanted to die," Shem finished for him, trying to deflect with a joke, “The real question is why did he run?”

"I suppose a straight answer is too much to ask for," Ham sighed.

Shem just raised his eyebrows in response. *How can I give you an answer I don’t have?*

Ham laughed and gave Shem’s shoulders a friendly pat. “Alright...one last question.”

“You sure?” Shem chuckled weakly.

"How are you planning on getting wherever it is you're going?” Ham asked.

Shem rolled his eyes at the absurdity of the question. "By horse? How else does one travel?"

At this, Ham burst into laughter as if Shem had shared a hilarious joke. "Gallimimus."

“So that’s what all the questions were about. Father’s messenger dino’s.” Shem looked out in amazement over an indoor enclosure of fully saddled Gallimimus. “You already had them ready to go.”

The space was cavernous, with massive wooden beams arched overhead, supporting a vaulted ceiling that seemed to touch the sky. Sunlight streamed through strategically placed skylights, casting a warm glow over the sandy floor below.

The air was thick with the earthy scent of hay and the musky odor of the creatures within. The graceful Gallimimus milled about, their long necks swaying gracefully as they moved.

Ham smiled as he leaned against the fence and stroked the soft black fibers of one of the males. "Aren't they beautiful?"

The bird-like dinosaur shook its white feather-like arms, which looked more like fluffy shirt sleeves with three sharp talons for hands.

Each creature stood taller than a man, perched on elongated legs that ended in three-toed feet. Their long necks and counterbalancing tails stretched longer than a horse-drawn carriage. Adorned with soft black or brownish-gray fibers, brief white wing-arms, and a striking tail plume, they presented a majestic sight.

Stretching to look up at the closest male's eyes and beak, Shem asked, "Why these instead of a horse?" It jerked its head down to look at him, then to the ground to peck at something in the hay.

"Terrain and speed. They can run as fast as a horse, but are not hindered by Eden's rugged countryside. They'll be less likely to come up lame," said Ham, as if it were the most obvious thing ever.

Shem counted the dinosaurs in the pen. "Wait. Why did you saddle ten of them?"

"I gave the order," said Nin, entering the room.

Shem wasn't sure what to make of this new development. *Did he go running to Nin?*

He was about to snap at Ham in protest, but more people shuffled into the barn behind him. Still in disbelief, he realized that Elam, Lud and Aram had joined his conspiracy to leave home.

All Shem could say was, "I'm confused."

Ham put his hands up in surrender.

"Don't be angry with your brother, I orchestrated all of this," said Nin.

Shem looked at Ham. "That's what you were doing in the house? Stalling for time?"

"Come on Shem, you weren't exactly quiet about your intentions," said Elam, chiming in the conversation.

Lud jumped in. "Yeah so if there's anyone to blame, it's your own mouth." He laughed way too loud.

Elam, slightly annoyed, placed a hand on Lud's shoulder. "We were all concerned that you were gonna run off on your own and chase down that monstrosity. We were coming up with a plan to talk you out of it or tie you up...or something like that. Nin overheard us and suggested that we all go with you instead."

"Naturally, I'll be part of this group. Your father would have my head if anything should happen to you," Nin said with a wink at Shem.

Shem gesturing towards the dino's, said, "That still leaves five galli's unspoken for."

"We have a few more joining us," said Nin, looking towards the door. "Let's prepare; they'll arrive soon."

In the next few minutes, they got their packs and equipment ready for the journey. Elam equipped Lud and Aram with swords from his father's armory and gave Shem a long dagger. Their packs included clothing, various pocket knives, flint, and spices for food they planned to gather along the way. Aram, ever the tinkerer, also packed a clockmaker's toolkit and, naturally, his sketchbook.

Shem, growing impatient with the delay, turned to Elam and said, "If we don't leave soon, my father will find out."

"You assume he hasn't already?" Elam replied.

Shem glanced at the door and agreed, "Good point. We need to go. Right now."

Nin approached them both. "Relax, boys. I've got everything under control. Trust me. Look."

More people started gathering in the barn. Halvin, Japheth's friend, arrived carrying a short sword and a pack slung over his shoulder. His dark hair was tied into a top knot, and he looked ready for a fight. Among the newcomers was Adi's father, Bartel, who had cut his long hair and had dark circles under his tired eyes. He was equipped with a sword and wore leather armor.

Raphael stood out as the most unusual member of the group. His presence was puzzling; with a sword strapped to his back, he had no pack and wore his usual light-colored clothes, as if he was just going for a casual walk to tend to Noah's sheep.

The final arrivals were two women. One, taller than most men, had auburn hair and was armed with a pair of short swords at her hips. She carried a pack on her back and seemed about the same age as Shem and his friends. She was unfamiliar to him. The second woman, who was familiar, looked related, sharing similar hair and features but was slightly older. She carried no visible weapons, but her pack rattled with the sound of pots and pans.

The older of the two walked up to Nin and Shem. "I'm Audrey, and this is my daughter, Eloise. I lost my husband, her father, during the attack. She's been trained as a militia member her entire life, and I handle the cooking." She stated it plainly, as if listing ingredients.

He offered her a smile and glanced at her daughter, who appeared lost in her thoughts with an irritated expression. "Thanks for joining us... I guess."

Elam leaned closer to Shem. "She's the one who spoke up at the town meeting."

Hearing laughter from behind, Shem turned to see what amused the others. Lud gestured for him to come over.

"That's her," Lud said. "She's the redhead I saw that night at the meeting."

Shem, not wanting to revisit that evening, simply stared at Lud.

"What?" Lud asked, raising his hands in confusion.

Aram gently pulled his brother back. "Too soon," he whispered.

As Lud processed the situation, realization dawned on his face. "Oh no... Shem, I'm sorry, I didn't mean to..."

"Forget it," Shem replied, noticing Nin glancing his way.

Nin spoke loudly enough for everyone to hear. "We have everyone now. Let's get going."

“Not so fast,” said a terse voice from the barn entrance.

Without turning around, Shem recognized his father’s tone. A surge of fear tightened his chest, and suddenly, his carefully laid plans seemed doomed. *What if he orders me to stay?*

Torn between his resolve to leave and his doubts about his own strength, he finally faced his father.

Before Shem could utter a word, Nin and Raphael stepped in with Noah, joined by his brother Japheth, whose arm was in a sling. Helplessly, Shem watched them speak in whispers, their hushed tones too soft to decipher from afar. Noah's expression revealed neither pleasure nor anger.

What is he holding?

Soon the brief conversation ended. Raphael rejoined the others, while Nin motioned for Shem to come forward to Noah. With every step toward his father, a mix of nervousness and panic threatened to overwhelm him. Shame at even having thought of disobedience mingled with anger at the prospect of being forced to stay. His stomach churned with unease, a physical testament to the anxiety that would have overwhelmed him if he had eaten.

"Father," Shem said, too weary to meet his gaze.

Noah rested his arms on each of Shem's shoulders. "Look at me son. Have you nothing to say, but 'Father'?"

Shem's mind was racing. *Should I ask for permission, or tell him I'm leaving?*

He wasn't sure if there was a right decision at all—he only knew he had to go. "I plan to track down the giant that attacked Ararat—and the men who sent him."

"Really? You're about to do what an entire militia couldn't manage?" Noah said.

Caught off guard, Shem didn't yet know how to answer. Shem hadn't figured that part out yet. He just knew he had to go.

"No need to answer," Noah sighed. "I suspect you don't have a true answer anyway. I believe your motives run far deeper than just revenge—although I can see that element in it."

Wounded by the implication, Shem's tone turned sharper than he intended. "I would never lie to you, Father!"

Laughing it off, Noah said, "I wish that were so. I really do. But, nevertheless, I'm not going to make you choose. And before you can incriminate yourself further, I am going to give you three things for your journey."

"My journey? I don't understand. What about your proclamation? The end of Adamah. Mother said...."

Noah cut off his barrage of questions. "Your mother has her own reasons for keeping you here—as only a mother could have. My proclamation is no different. Yahweh's will is unchanging; whether you stay or leave, the end will come. It was foreseen by your great-great-grandfather Enoch before he went to join our Lord, and Yahweh Himself confirmed it to me. I let you go because I believe the Lord has a purpose for you, a plan that must be forged in fire."

"What plan? Father, I don't see how Yahweh...."

"Then be quiet. There's more. First, I give you Ningangar. He has been my ranch foreman and trusted companion for years. He has business with Bartel in Center Grove, and I have charged him with keeping you safe on this errand. Second, I entrust you to Raphael, my personal shepherd. I promise you, he's a blessing—even if you can't see it right now." Noah nodded toward Raphael. "Finally, I give you this." Noah held up the object he held at his side.

Shem gasped as he realized it was the sword from the fireplace mantle, now unwrapped by Noah from its cloth covering, sheathed in a scabbard of unknown material. As the sword was drawn, its sinuous blade gleamed brilliantly in the barn's dim light.

Noah turned the sword in his grasp, tenderly caressing the plant-like tendrils emanating from its guard and quillon. The ricasso resembled vines climbing the blade, while the pommel bore the image of the Tree of Life, its branches outstretched in homage to the Creator.

Everyone in the room paused to admire this magnificent weapon.

He gazed into the distance, lost in thought, as though the memory brought him pain. "Its name is Davar-an angelic name meaning The Word of Yahweh or in essence, The Sword of the Spirit. This sword was sung into existence from a gopher tree—a tree that originated in The Garden and was nurtured by Adam. When Adam and Eve were exiled for their sin, they carried its seeds with them, which were then passed on to Seth. Only one forest of this magnificent tree remains, known only to our lineage. Our ranch is named after that forest, and both the forest and the sword stand as a testament that Yahweh, our Creator, reigns supreme."

Presenting the sword to Shem, Noah declared, "This is a weapon of The Knights of Eden, forged for righteousness. It carries a noble, distinguished history and will be your steadfast ally. Cherish this relic of Eden as your inheritance."

Shem grasped the sword with a sense of awe. Gazing into its rich, wooden hue, the pale sword appeared to dim as he wielded it—or perhaps the room itself grew brighter? Swinging it that fateful morning felt like slicing through air, yet it lacked any feeling of significance. Unbeknownst to him, the sword was imbued with profound meaning, and suddenly, he felt utterly undeserving of its weight.

Snapping him back to the moment, Lud spoke. "So, you plan to fend off a giant with a tree branch? *That's* the stuff of legends," he chuckled at his own jest.

"This is no ordinary tree branch, my son." He explained, ignoring Lud. "The essence of this wood has been transformed by Yahweh himself. It once stood in a forest, indistinguishable from the others, but now it is as sturdy and sharp as any blade tempered in flame, and nearly indestructible." He helped his son fasten the leather baldric across his shoulder.

As the rest of the companions began making their way to the enclosure to mount their galli's, Japheth, with Ham at his side, approached Shem.

"So, I guess this is it," said Japheth.

Shem replied, "I guess that depends on Yahweh's will, doesn't it?"

Ham, shaking his head, said, "Yeah, okay. Just give us a hug, Shemy."

Japheth, gripping Shem's shoulder with his one good arm, said, "Shem, I know you like to jest about 'Yahweh's will,' but it's dangerous out there. If it were up to me I wouldn't let you go. " After squeezing his shoulder, he turned and walked over to his father.

"Has all the answers, doesn't he?" said Ham.

Shem looked at the ground. "He gets me so angry. He's always so..."

"Smug," they both said simultaneously. With a smile, they embraced each other, possibly for the last time.

As Ham walked back towards his father and brother, he called over his shoulder, "Oh, by the way, watch out for the Nephilim that can turn you to stone with just a glance."

PART TWO
Awakenings

"I will put enmity between you and the woman, and between your seed and her Seed; He shall bruise your head, and you shall bruise His heel."

The First Book of Moses:
Genesis: Chapter 3, Verse 15

CHAPTER 8

The Jolly Giant

The advantages of using the gallimimus became apparent shortly after leaving Ararat. The terrain was a patchwork of crags, hills, and valleys so treacherous that even the most agile horses would have faltered long before. Riding these swift, muscular dinosaurs offered an exhilarating yet jarring experience, a stark contrast to the preferred mode of travel on foot, unaccustomed to the constant jostling and bouncing as they sped across Eden's rugged landscape.

The conversation was subdued, with most of the companions lost in their thoughts, pondering if following Shem into the unknown had been wise. Ararat, the only home they had known, was a peaceful haven now shattered by a brutal attack.

Shem, steeped in melancholy, reflected on a past now forever altered. He recalled the days spent in the fields with Rocky, bemoaning his mundane existence, never imagining his desire for change would be fulfilled so harshly. *Are you happy, Yahweh?*

Farming would not be missed, yet he sighed at the drastic change in his life. Adi, too, would never experience the world beyond her small town, never feel his touch, his caress through her blonde hair, or a gentle kiss. All opportunities lost, thanks to the invaders and Anu: The Destroyer. *You're all gonna pay.*

Center Grove was their destination, a bustling city renowned for its trade, nestled at the heart of Eden's crossroads. Tales of its vibrant commerce had reached him from travelers passing through Ararat and Nin's own journeys. The city thrived on the north-south road, connecting Havilah in the north with Assyria in the south, facilitating seamless trade. To the east, a road stretched all the way to the coast, while the westward path led to Eden's capital, StoneCrest. Center Grove was a tapestry of diverse cultures and beliefs, a place where beauty and immorality danced in a delicate balance, each culture converging before venturing to their final destinations.

As the companions travelled most of the day, the number of homesteads and farms increased. They bypassed most to maintain their pace, but as the day waned, Nin suggested they seek an inn or welcoming abode for the night. He was aware of one nearby, just beyond the next rise.

However, without warning, Nin came to an abrupt halt, on high alert.

Riding up alongside Nin, who was now standing in his saddle, Shem asked, "What is it?

"Look," Nin said, pointing to a plume of smoke over the hill.

"Cooking fire maybe?" said Shem.

Nin climbed down from his galli. "It's too dark and too much of it. Come on." He walked cautiously towards the crest of the hill at a crouch.

Reaching the crest alongside Nin, hidden in the tall grass and rocks, Shem caught sight of the smoke's source.

A quaint settlement, a cluster of structures, nestled along a winding road that snaked through a narrow valley. From their vantage point, it seemed as though flames engulfed one or several buildings, yet the distance obscured finer details.

"I can't see what happened. Can you? Some of the buildings are on fire. If only we had Lady Aryanna to do a fly over," said Shem.

Nin pulled a spyglass from his jacket's inner pocket. "Unfortunately, she's not here. She had to report what happened in Ararat to her superiors." He extended the tube, making it longer, placing it up to his eye. "But we do have this. It's not good." He handed it to Shem. "Look."

Focusing the spyglass, he said, "I can see two buildings burning, and what looks like a bonfire further back. No people though."

"What's burning?" Asked Elam, as he crept up beside Shem and looked out over the ridge. "Oh, boy."

Shem, still looking through the spyglass, said, "Yeah, looks like trouble."

"We're going to go around, right?" He said, as he watched Nin extract himself from the ridge.

Shem answered, "Go around? What if someone needs help? Anu could be here. That's why we came." He got up and went to join Nin and the others.

Elam put his head in his hands, and said to know one in particular, "Sure. Why not?"

The companions gathered around their gallis, awaiting Nin's guidance. As Shem approached, he noticed Raphael's gaze fixed on him once again. *Why does he do that?*

"We're going down there, right?" he said to Nin.

"Sure we are," said Lud, laughing as usual, "let's just walk into an unknown area that's on fire. Sounds like a great idea."

Aram elbowed him.

"What?" Lud said.

Bartel, ignoring the exchange between them, addressed Nin, "I agree with Shem. We should check it out. But we should be smart about it. I'll go first and make sure it's clear."

"Great," said Shem, "I'll go with him."

Nin shook his head, adjusting his hat. "I am definitely not sending you two together. You'd take on a whole army if I'd let you. Bartel, take Aram with you and scout the area. Report back here either way. Do not get into trouble."

"Was that an order, Nin?" Bartel said, with a tilt of his head.

Seeing that Nin wasn't responding to his taunt, Bartel threw his pack down and adjusted his sword belt before moving along the ridge, with Aram giving Shem a reassuring pat on the shoulder as he followed.

Shem stood there, seething with frustration, watching them tread carefully on a path that ran parallel to the settlement. It was supposed to be his mission, yet Nin had chosen Aram. He was the one who should be confronting any dangers that lay ahead, not them. With fists clenched, he simmered in silence.

Nin turned to the rest of the group. "Let's gather their packs and beasts. We'll move along the ridge to a closer position. Just be ready for anything." Looking at Lud, he added, "And be quiet."

Lud held his hands up in protest.

Shem found himself walking between Eloise, the tall auburn haired girl, and Lud. He gave her a smile, but was in no mood for conversation so he just walked his galli in silence.

"You don't remember me, do you?" she said, quietly.

Glancing in her direction, Shem said, "Um, no. Sorry."

"My father is...was the blacksmith for Ararat. You picked up orders for your ranch before," she said.

"Oh yeah, I remember now," Shem said, not really wanting to make small talk.

"Since Father was killed... Anyway, we thought maybe to return to our homeland in Havilah," she said, with a sniff.

That peaked his interest. "Homeland? I just assumed you were from Ararat, like all of us. Eloise, right?"

"Yeah," she said. "My father was hired by the Ararat Council to be the town blacksmith after the last one had died. That was about 70 years ago. I was only about 20 at the time." Then lowering her voice slightly, she added, "and to be honest, I just needed to get her away from Ararat. With everything that happened, I fear for her well-being. I couldn't imagine if something happened to her. She's just so heartbroken."

I know how she feels. Realizing he hadn't expressed his sympathy yet, he quickly said, "I'd think you'd both be pretty upset."

She hesitated and sniffed before answering. "Yeah...I am, too."

Not wishing to get into an emotional discussion with someone he had just met, he asked, "How did your father get hired all the way out here?

She smiled, and said, "Do you know anything about the schools?"

Shem shook his head, "Not really. They were founded by Tubal-Cain, I was told."

"That's true, although they are managed by The Conclave-the religion of the Serpent's leaders," she said, "My father graduated from the school of the forge-The University of Havilah. It's where most of the blacksmiths, swordsmiths and armorers get their training in our region. Eden doesn't have any Conclave-run schools, so places like Ararat need to hire out those kinds of services, or train their own."

Shem thought that was strange. "Why wouldn't Eden have a school? Havilah does?"

Eloise furrowed her brow. "I believe it goes back to the first thing you said. Tubal-Cain. Eden was founded by the Sethites, yet he was from the line of Cain. So, Eden refused to allow any of his schools to be established here. And yes, in the Pishon Valley, we have the University."

"That makes no sense. It could benefit the people," said Shem.

Looking at the ground, she said, "Religion. Different beliefs. Wars. Bad blood? Life is long, and grudges longer, I guess."

"Different religions?" said Shem.

She took in a deep breath, with pride, and smiled at Shem. "My family worships Azazel: god of the hammer. It was he that taught Tubal-Cain how to forge iron. We have held to the old traditions for generations."

Shem was taken aback by her confession, and couldn't help feeling embarrassed by his own lack of respect for his own family's traditions.

There was no time for further questions as Nin signaled the group to stop, and gestured for him to come to the front of the group while securing his dinosaur to a tree branch.

As Shem joined the others, Lud finally found the courage to introduce himself to 'the redhead' that caught his attention that fateful night outside Town Hall.

"Shem, head over to the crest of the ridge. See if you can see them," said Nin, as Shem arrived with the others.

Shem, glad for something to do, hurried towards his goal, staying low to avoid detection.

The landscape here was still a tapestry of crags, tall grass, and sporadic trees, yet the ridge was flattening out. To his left, the road snaked through the rolling terrain, disappearing behind the foliage and undulating hills.

Flat on his belly, he inched to the crest and noted they had considerably narrowed the gap to the settlement. The view from here was dominated by a large two-story structure, its front porch exuding the charm of an inn, complete with a sign proclaiming it "The Jolly Giant," masking the view of the smoldering buildings behind.

Amidst the smaller structures surrounding the Inn, Shem noticed that the distant fire was, in fact, a large bonfire rather than the campfire he had initially presumed. As he peered through the dimming twilight, an oddly moving figure caught his eye, resembling a stringless marionette flitting among the buildings. Could it be a person? Perhaps Bartel or Aram, distorted by the deceptive twilight.

Recalling the spyglass on his belt, he raised it to his eye and fine-tuned the focus. He surveyed the area around the buildings where he suspected movement, but found nothing. Aiming at the upper floor of the Inn, the darkness within was too profound to discern anything, though he was certain he had seen something. Peering closer at the front door, he noticed it slightly open with a sign on a tripod beside it reading "Vacancies," confirming the building was indeed an inn. Yet there were still no signs of anyone.

Shem lowered the spyglass, lost in thought, and froze when he heard the snap of a twig right beside him.

"Gotchu!" exclaimed a voice as a large man leaped onto him, knocking the wind out of him.

He rolled onto his back, the giant atop him, dropping the spyglass as he struggled for his life. His sword was unreachable pinned beneath him, and his hands were now trapped on the ground.

"Shem. Shem. Stop. It's me!" Shem recognized Aram's voice as he regained his senses.

With his heart pounding, Shem snapped in anger, "What the bloody hell are you doing?"

"Sorry," Aram said, gesturing to the companions who were all smiling or outright laughing. "They pointed at your spot, so I figured I'd surprise you." He released Shem and stood up. "Nice hiding place, though."

"Yeah, well, I could've killed you," Shem retorted, embarrassed. He dusted himself off, retrieved the spyglass, and staggered to his feet, his knees still trembling from the shock.

"I doubt it," Lud chimed in, "you looked like a turtle on its back, flailing, 'Help me, I'm stuck in the mud.'" He mimicked a helpless turtle, waving his arms in the air.

"Whatever," Shem dismissed.

Still chuckling, Elam remarked, “I can’t fathom how a man so large can move so silently.”

“Yeah, that’s impressive,” agreed Halvan, “I was sure you’d hear him.”

Audrey interjected, cutting through the mirth, “You boys can continue this later. It’s getting dark. Is it safe to head to the settlement now?”

Receiving his pack from Halvin, Bartel confirmed, “We’ve scouted the area; it seems safe. Clearly, something happened here. That large fire in the back is burning dead bodies, so the question remains, who placed them there and what happened?”

“We saw blood and evidence of a struggle in different places— broken furniture and such—but the area is deserted. Oh, and there’s an Inn that appears untouched,” Aram added.

Nin interjected, “Alright, let’s head there and settle in for the night. We’ll discuss this later.”

Shem, recalling his observation from the ridge, got Nin’s attention. “Hold on. I thought I saw someone,—or something—down there.”

Bartel, advancing towards the settlement, halted and replied, “We’ve checked everything, son. There’s nothing. We would’ve noticed it.”

“Right,” Aram chimed in, “We were quite thorough. Sorry. And sorry for scaring you.”

Shem grinned and responded, “It’s alright. But, you didn’t scare me, though,” his unease about the incident lingering. He was uncertain whether he was more disturbed by the strange entity he spotted or by Aram’s sudden appearance.

“Of course not,” Aram said.

Nin, leading the way, declared, "Okay, let's move. But let's stay alert. Something killed those people and threw them on a pyre."

"Oh, it's absolutely lovely," Audrey exclaimed as they neared the large inn's front porch.

"The Jolly Giant" was meticulously maintained, with a spacious front porch that showed evidence of daily sweeping and mopping, and bright blue curtains were visible through the windows. There were two seating areas on the porch, furnished with large couches and chairs adorned with plump black and white checkered cushions, and small end tables and center tables held vases of freshly cut flowers.

Halven lifted a cup from the center table and inhaled its scent. "It smells like tea and feels cold. Could it be from this morning?"

"Indeed, whatever transpired here must've been recent," Bartel replied. "We've come across other beverages and food throughout this settlement, and all of it is still fresh."

"It seems like something unexpected happened while they were just going about their normal activities. I didn't feel like they were aware of any danger," said Aram, looking at Bartel to see if he agreed.

Eager to enter, Audrey began moving toward the inn's entrance. "Let's go in and eat," she suggested. "I'm sure we're all hungry. I'll make my way to the kitchen."

"Hold on," Nin said, "One of us should go in first, just in case." He slipped past her and gently pushed the door open.

"I'm telling you, there's nothing here," Aram said to Shem, shrugging as they made their way into the inn.

The common room was eerily spacious compared to the dim, cramped inns and taverns scattered throughout Ararat. Eloise, moving slowly, followed her mother inside and pressed a pad on the dark-paneled wall next to the door. The air felt heavy with unsettling energy as the soft crystal glow from the multiple chandeliers flickered to life, casting a ghostly light across the room. The two-story high ceiling seemed to loom above them, shadowy and oppressive.

Tables sat ominously around the room, some sparsely adorned with half-eaten plates of food, remnants of hasty meals abandoned.

Eloise's eyes darted nervously around the space, on high alert. "It definitely happened during the day. All the lights were out," she murmured, her voice barely above a whisper.

"Or someone shut them off," Halvin replied, a slight edge of suspicion lacing his tone.

"A little nervous energy, huh Halvin?" Lud chuckled, but the sound echoed hollowly in the tense silence that followed.

Halvin's eyes narrowed at Lud's comment, but he didn't rise to the bait. Instead, he moved purposefully into the room, his gaze sweeping every corner and shadow. "This isn't about nerves," he said quietly. "Something terrible happened here, and we need to understand what. For all we know, it could be connected to Ararat."

The mention of their ravaged home silenced any further attempts at levity. Halvin's words hung in the air, a stark reminder of why they were here.

Shem felt it too— that something had transpired that was far from ordinary. The shadows flickered closer, and the weight of unseen eyes seemed to press upon them, urging them to uncover the secrets lurking in the depths of the common room.

At the back of the room, shrouded in shadows, stood a dual staircase that spiraled upward, leading to a balcony that stretched the entire length of the room. Above, the faint creaks of the wooden floorboards echoed the unsettling silence.

Flickering firelight cast long, dancing shapes across the walls, and the air felt thick with unspoken secrets. Between the stairs, on the ground floor, a dark hallway seemed to beckon, leading away from the common room and into uncertainty.

The source of the firelight, a rustic fireplace loomed ominously to their right, its natural river stones climbing to the ceiling like skeletal fingers reaching for escape. The large mantelpiece, heavy with an array of chotskies that appeared to be carved from stone, ceramic, and wood, seemed to watch those who dared to approach. Vases of freshly cut flowers provided an eerie contrast, their vibrant colors almost mocking the growing tension in the room.

On the left, the bar stretched out like a dark boat in the night, made of polished wood that glimmered ominously in the low light. Its surface was littered with cups and plates of food, but the emptiness of the room gave them a feeling of abandonment.

Behind the bar, shadows swirled around stacks of bottles, glasses, and cups as if they held more than just drinks. Above it all, a sign loomed, "The Jolly Giant - Est 1510," but the jovial name felt like a cruel joke amidst the eerie atmosphere.

"Looks like there were about 8-10 people in here. So many dead," Elam muttered, his voice barely breaking the heavy silence that hung in the air.

Shem, not surprised at his friend's attention to detail, took in the table settings littered with half-eaten food, and replied, "Where did they..."

His words were cut off as a sudden violent slam echoed through the room, causing everyone to jump. The front door had been thrown shut behind him, they all turned instinctively, hands twitching toward their swords.

The door bounced off its frame, creaking ominously as it slowly swung ajar, thickening the air with unease. Raphael cautiously approached the door, his hand on the hilt of the sword on his back.

He slowly pulled the door open, peering into the darkness beyond, straining to hear any hint of what lurked outside. The shadows danced along the walls, and Shem's skin prickled with a chill, feeling increasingly uneasy.

With a shrug Raphael stepped back, closing the door with a soft click before latching it securely.

"This place gives me the creeps," Lud said dramatically, glancing around as if he expected something to jump out at him. "I'm starting to wonder if it was a mistake leaving home."

Eloise rolled her eyes and muttered something about "skittish compies" while strutting over to the bar with her mother, a confident sway in her step.

Lud, reacting to the sting of her comment, shot back, "Hey, I'm no coward. I just don't like surprises, okay?"

With a playful glint in her eye, Eloise tossed a smile over her shoulder that said she found him utterly amusing. "Sure, Mr. Tough Guy," she teased.

Rubbing her hand along the bar, Eloise's eyes widened as she admired the accents and fixtures. "Look, Mom, it's got Havilah gold plating. They spared no expense here. The craftsmanship is exquisite. It reminds me of Dad."

"Yes, it does, dear," Audrey replied, her voice cracking. She moved behind the bar and grabbed a cup from the back counter, her fingers trembling slightly as she turned on the faucet. It sputtered ominously before falling silent. Her brow furrowed as she bent under the sink, kicking the pipes in frustration and trying again. Still nothing. "That's odd. Everything appears to be operational, yet—why is the sink dry? You can't run an inn without water."

"Maybe they lived on wine," Halvin suggested from his seat at the bar, a smirk barely disguising his concern.

Audrey shook her head, sliding a bottle of dark liquid and a glass toward him. She laughed sharply, the sound echoing too loudly in the unsettling silence as he struggled with the cork.

"Bartel, did you see anything that would explain this?" she asked, her voice tight.

Bartel shook his head. "There's a water tank out back, but I didn't examine it closely enough to see if the pipes are compromised. We can go take a look."

"Please do," she said, a hint of urgency in her tone. "I'll need water if I'm gonna cook anything."

Audrey strode towards the door at the end of the bar, determination in her step. "In the meantime, I'll check the kitchen to see what we have."

Eloise followed, her hand on a sword.

"Alright, while they figure that out, I'll check on the water situation," Bartel said, his voice steady and confident, like usual.

Aram dropping his pack next to Bartel's, said, "I have my tools with me. I'll join you."

"Me too," Shem chimed in, feeling anxious as he placed his pack with the others.

"Good," Nin said. "The women have food under control. Halvin, you and Raphael stay here in case they run into any problems. Elam. Lud. Come with me. We need to get the galli's stabled for the night."

The air was thick with apprehension as they moved to follow Nin's instructions.

Chapter 9

Blood and Sacrifice

The water tower loomed in the murky darkness, an intimidating silhouette just beyond the inn's back door. At its base stood a rickety shed, its weathered planks barely holding together. Moonlight glinted off rusty hinges as gusts of wind creaked the door open and closed. Inside, in the darkness and a musty odor was Aram, doing his best to figure out what was wrong. Shem and Bartel stood by the door, keeping him company.

Shem stared off into the darkness, deep in thought. *Who rekindled that fire in the inn? And what happened in the hours before?*

The weight of uncertainty gnawed mercilessly at him. Shem's heart raced as he considered the huge bonfire across the clearing. *Were the same people that stoked those flames responsible for the dead ones? Did they just clean up the aftermath, or was something far more evil going on?*

Hints of movement in the shadows sent shivers down his spine. Who—or what—was lurking just out of sight? His instincts screamed that they were not alone. A quiet whisper of danger rustled through the air, and without knowing why,

Shem felt the urge to run. Every nerve in his body was on high alert, straining to catch the faintest sound or flicker of movement that might betray an unseen menace ready to pounce.

"Any luck yet, Aram?" Shem said, his voice trembling slightly as he anxiously scanned the flickering shadows cast by the fires. The buildings on his right had crumbled to embers, their charred remains a haunting reminder of the chaos. At the same time, the bonfire in the central clearing roared defiantly, illuminating the darkness around them.

From the dim confines of the shed, Aram's voice came out, thick with urgency. "It looks like the pipe was being replaced, but it's still half-done. Just give me a few minutes—I think I can get it working."

"Do you need anything?" Shem asked, his voice barely a whisper as a gnawing dread curled in his stomach. The eerie silence enveloped him, pressing down like a heavy fog. "I'm going to go check something out." He scanned the area, his heart pounding wildly. A flicker of movement caught his eye above—a quick, darting shadow. Adrenaline surged as he squinted, only to realize it was just a few birds perched on the water tower. Yet their presence felt disturbingly ominous against the smoldering wreckage behind them.

Aram shouted from within, "I'm good."

Bartel eyed Shem closely, the flicker of unease in his own gaze evident. "Is everything ok? You look a little jumpy." The wind picked up, whispering through the charred remains of the buildings, filling the air with a sense of foreboding. "I told you...we searched the place and didn't find anything. The stables are over there." He gestured toward the far side of the clearing, where shadows seemed to loom menacingly, hiding secrets in the swaying darkness. "And those burning houses?

Looked to be homes—maybe a small smithy. And that large fire...well, I told you what that was."

Shem couldn't shake the feeling that something was still out there, watching them. The stillness was almost mocking, as if it were waiting for the right moment to unleash its terrible truth. He took a step forward, feeling the weight of unseen eyes, each rustle in the underbrush sending chills down his spine.

"That's actually why I want to look around. Something feels off." Just then, a loud crash echoed from the stables, jolting him to attention. The voices inside grew clearer, and he recognized Nin and the others securing the dinosaurs for the night. Bartel's laughter cut through the tension, and he said, "Just one thing is making you uneasy?"

Ignoring Bartel's attempt at humor, Shem walked towards the bonfire, its flickering flames casting an eerie glow that danced ominously across the clearing. Shadows twisted and turned around him, creating the illusion of movement just outside his line of sight. He glanced towards the stable on his left, where he could see his companions bustling about, their voices muffled and anxious. A chill ran down his spine; he felt as if something was watching them.

Pressing on, he approached a fenced enclosure, where a few white and black spotted cows lay motionless in the hay, their eyes glinting like dark gemstones in the fire-light. He leaned against the fence, heart racing, and caught sight of a secondary pen containing sheep, their soft bleating almost deafening in the still night. Something felt off; the animals seemed restless, their movements erratic.

Suddenly, a rustle from the shadows beyond the enclosures sent a jolt of fear through him. Turning his gaze, he spotted a shadow moving just outside the glow of the fire, unnoticed by his companions. He swallowed hard, every instinct screaming at him to stay alert. On the far side, he could see a coop where a couple of chickens roamed, clucking softly as if oblivious to the tension in the air. But then one of the chickens froze, staring into the gloom, its feathers ruffled, as if sensing the danger that lurked just beyond the light.

Panic flickered in Shem's mind; he sensed they weren't alone. Who—or what—was out there in the darkness?

He pressed onward toward the flickering fire that cast eerie shadows in the night. The crackling flames danced in the air, illuminating the clearing just enough to reveal a few buildings on the other side—structures untouched by the blaze. Maybe there was something worth salvaging. He started to head in that direction, but a movement beyond the fire stopped him in his tracks.

Heart pounding, he froze, squinting into the dim light, desperate to discern the source of the disturbance. The heat from the fire enveloped him, but a chill slithered down his spine. What he saw sent adrenaline surging through his veins: a large, dark shape moving slowly, almost stealthily. It was too massive to be a person, and as he focused harder, recognition washed over him—an ankylosaurus.

A wave of dread fell over him. That must be their farm out there. But the question gnawed at him: Why wasn't it stabled? Was it a stray? Or was it evidence of something far worse lurking in the shadows? He felt exposed and vulnerable, the fire casting long, sinister shadows that flickered ominously around him. He knew he had to make a decision: retreat into the safety of the darkness or venture closer to uncover whatever lay beyond the flames. The night held its breath, and so did he.

He pressed on, each step echoing in the stillness of the compound. As he moved deeper into the shadows, the ground beneath him shifted unexpectedly, a damp chill creeping up from the earth. He glanced down, and his heart raced.

There it was—a star meticulously drawn in the dirt, its five points stark against the darkened soil, glistening with a viscous, wet substance that seemed to pulsate with a life of its own. A shiver prickled at the nape of his neck, the hairs standing up as if warning him of an unseen presence. Was he truly alone?

The wind fell silent, the world around him fading into an eerie hush. The oppressive weight of something unseen settled in, pressing against him, urging him to flee. Yet his feet were rooted in place, drawn to the strange symbol, as if it called to him with whispered promises of knowledge—or peril. The flickering shadows danced eerily upon the sigil of a forgotten ritual. In the center lay the remnants of once-lit candles, now reduced to mere stubs, their wax pooling in ominous shapes that suggested long hours spent in silence. Surrounding them were the bones of an unknown creature, haphazardly piled as if discarded after a grim event. They glistened in the dim light, damp and eerily glimmering, absorbed in the moisture of the earth beneath them.

What happened here? The very air seemed thick with unspoken secrets, a heavy weight pressing down on Shem like a thick fog.

A whisper of wind rustled the leaves around this desolate altar, chilling his spine and drawing a chilling connection between the scene and the dark echoes of the past.

What kind of ceremony was this? And who, or what, did those bones belong too?

Shem tensed as he heard footsteps approaching. Quickly. Each stride charged with urgency. His heart raced as he strained to identify the source of the approaching danger.

Suddenly, a man burst into view, launching himself at Shem with a primal force that took him by surprise. The impact sent him crashing backward, pain exploding in his chest as they tumbled out of the ritual site, the world spinning around him.

As he hit the ground hard, instinct kicked in. Shem curled his chin to his chest, using the momentum to roll and spring back to his feet, adrenaline coursing through him. He pivoted just in time, his senses heightened, to meet the next assault. The man charged again, fists flying in a blur, and Shem instinctively raised his arm to block the punch, the force reverberating through his body. Breathing heavily, he narrowed his eyes, preparing for the next strike, knowing that every second counted.

With a crazed look in his eyes, the man lunged at Shem for another attack, panting heavily. Shem quickly drew his dagger and braced himself as they collided, falling to the ground once again. The assailant let out a moan of pain and stopped moving. Shem pushed the man off of him and stood up, ready for the next move. The man lay on the ground, clutching his side and grimacing in agony.

He didn't know how long he stood there, frozen in shock and fear. His attacker lay on the ground, moaning and writhing in agony. Shem's head was spinning, trying to make sense of what had just happened. *Why am I always fighting for my life?*

Yesterday, he was just a simple farmer, living in the middle of nowhere. But now, his hands were trembling and numb as the realization dawned on him - he had again drawn blood from another human being. The metallic scent of blood mingled with the dirt and sweat in the air, making Shem feel sick to his stomach. He couldn't believe this was happening again, and his mind raced with questions and uncertainty.

"Shem! Are you ok?" Bartel inquired as he reached Shem's side first, his arm already around him and searching for any injuries. Finding none, he asked, "Is he one of them?"

Shem just stared at him; mind blank.

Aram came up behind Bartel, sword drawn and scanning the surroundings for any other potential assailants.

The middle-aged man's lips twitched, low murmurs spilling out incoherently as tears streamed down his dirt-stained face. His wide eyes were filled with terror and pain, his hands tightly clasped over a deep gash on his left side. Despite his fine clothing - black pants and a white shirt that would have been considered elegant if not for the blood and grime - he looked like a broken man, driven to madness by some unknown force.

His gaze fixed on Aram's sword, he begged, "Please...kill me."

Bartel made a move to do just that, but Shem stopped him with a hand on his arm. “He seems… helpless,” he said, torn between feelings of anger and pity for the man. “Maybe he can tell us what happened?”

“Please...please,” the man continued to plead under his breath.

Bartel’s anger was evident as he spoke. “This man has been lurking in the shadows and just tried to kill you. You want mercy? What if he’s part of that group that attacked Ararat?”

Shem hesitated, unsure whether to trust or condemn the man before them. “I...I don’t know. What if he’s not? He doesn’t even have a weapon,” he said slowly, studying the man’s disheveled appearance. “And he doesn’t look like the others.”

The sound of approaching footsteps from behind suggested that their companions from the stables had heard the commotion and were arriving to help.

Shem leaned closer to the man; determined to find answers. “Let’s find out who this is.”

“Careful,” warned Nin from behind them.

Undeterred, Shem reached out a hand towards the shaking figure. “My name is Shem. What’s yours?”

But the man recoiled at the sound of Shem’s voice and flinched away from his outstretched hand.

“It’s ok,” reassured Shem, “I won’t hurt you anymore.”

“Anymore?” questioned Elam with surprise. “We’re hurting people now?”

Bartel interjected with a smirk, “Easy, sheriff, our boy here put up quite a defense. That’s how he got that gut wound. Shem’s reflexes saved his life.”

Ignoring them, Shem moved closer to the man. “Just tell me your name. We can help you.”

"No one can help me," whimpered the man, shrinking back into himself. "My soul is damned. It's too late...too late."

Nin stepped up beside Shem and suggested, "Let's get him inside and into the light."

Aram jumped in, "I'll get his wound tended to. Come on, Lud, give me a hand."

"This night just keeps getting better," mumbled Lud.

Together, they helped the injured man to his feet. He offered no resistance and simply slumped between them as they made their way to the Inn, out of the damp, night air.

Shem watched in bewilderment as the man who had viciously attacked him just moments ago now seemed like a helpless creature. He couldn't shake off the feeling of guilt for contributing to this man's suffering. In silence, he followed his companions into the Inn.

As they reached the back door and climbed the small steps, Nin asked Aram, "Did you fix the water problem?"

"Yeah," replied Aram, "it was an easy fix. Just a disconnected pipe."

Nin furrowed his brow in thought. "Disconnected? That's strange."

Aram explained, "It looked like someone was trying to replace it, but it was only half finished. Like they were interrupted."

Despite being inside the safety of the Inn, Shem's senses were still on high alert and his heart continued to race. He couldn't shake off the feeling that they were still in danger. Maybe this man could provide answers about the mysterious star drawn in the clearing. Or maybe he was just a lone survivor, unable to cope with the tragic events that had unfolded in this place. The unknown sent shivers down Shem's spine as they made their way deeper into the Inn.

Entering the common room, the flickering light from the hearth cast eerie shadows across the room. The injured man's labored breathing echoed in the tense silence. Shem's kept expecting someone to jump out at him, as he followed behind his friends.

Halvin and Raphael immediately rushed to his side with concern. "What happened," said Halvin, "Who is this?"

"We don't know much at this point. Just that he had a run in with Shem's dagger, " said Bartel, sliding chairs out of their way.

Aram and Lud gently lowered the man onto a bench near the fire. Nin quickly gathered some clean cloths and a bowl of water to tend to his wound. As he worked, the man's eyes remained unfocused, his lips moving in silent prayer or madness.

"What's your name?" Shem asked again, crouching beside him. "Please, we want to help you."

The man's gaze suddenly snapped to Shem's face, a flicker of recognition in his wild eyes. "Armaros," he whispered. "My name is Armaros."

"Armaros," said Shem, "Good. Why did you attack me? What happened to you?"

"I...I...I thought you were more of them," said Armaros, looking from face to face.

Bartel jumped in, and aggressively said, "More of who? Are we in danger here?"

"Slow down," said Nin, still kneeled down in front of the man, tending to his wound, "He's overwhelmed."

"Overwhelmed? Overwhelmed? This could be the beginning of another attack. He needs to..." started Bartel.

Nin stood to face him. "Yes. Overwhelmed. Look at him." Leading Bartel away from the frightened man, he said, "Let's give him some space. Why don't you go get something to eat? Look...Audrey is coming out of the kitchen now."

"Don't placate me, Nin..."

"Come on, Mr Bartel," said Lud, "Let's see what she's got. I could eat too." He walked over towards the bar area, where Audrey placed a large platter of food. Bartel hesitated, staring at Armaros in suspicion, then joined Lud. The look he gave Nin was even worse.

Refusing to acknowledge Bartel's unspoken challenge, Nin gestured for everyone else to join them, as well, "Go eat. I'll try to figure out what happened here." Shem and Elam remained behind.

Shem wasn't about to let someone else handle this. "I think I'll stay and hear what he has to say." After all, he was the one the man had attacked, and an uneasy feeling lingered in the pit of his stomach that he couldn't quite identify.

"So be it," Nin said.

Kneeling down to eye level with Armaros, Shem continued, "Yeah, you're going to talk to me, because your safe now, right, Armaros?" He needed to understand what had happened. Was he a victim of an assault like they had experienced in Ararat, or was it something else?

Looking at the man, Shem noted that he didn't seem that big, yet he had hit him with a force that still throbbed in Shem's arm.

Instead of responding, Armaros buried his head in his hands and whimpered. Shem felt uncertain about how to get the man to communicate. There had to be an answer, and he sensed that time was running out.

“It’s pointless” said Nin, “Let’s find a room to put him in for the night.”

"And then what?" Elam asked, his voice tinged with frustration. "Are we supposed to tie him up and force the information out of him? I don't know about you, but I'm getting really tired of violence always being the solution!"

Nin, taken aback by Elam's sudden reaction, replied, "Alright... I understand we're all exhausted. Perhaps consider involving Lauren? A woman's perspective might help?"

Shem looked over to the bar in thought. “That might be a good idea.”

Nin approached the bar and signaled to get Audrey's attention.

Sensing her approach, Shem stood and stepped aside. Wiping her hands on her pants, she knelt down to see Armaros more clearly. She placed her hand under his chin, and though he flinched away from her touch at first, she persisted until he allowed her to guide his face up to meet hers.

The expression on her face shifted from sympathy to surprise. “Armaros! Oh, my poor dear, what happened?” She looked up at Nin and said, “This is Armaros, the innkeeper. This is his family’s establishment.” She wrapped her arms around him in a warm embrace. His arms remained slumped in his lap as he cried in the crook of her neck, sobbing uncontrollably.

After a few minutes he was able to compose himself, as she dabbed the tears from his eyes, and just waited for him to talk. He said, “Audrey...I haven’t seen you in years. How’s your husband?” He was still speaking in between sobs as he fought to control himself further.

“Oh, it was horrible.” Audrey took a deep breath. “Our town was attacked by invaders and a giant. My Cormac was taken from me too soon. He died in the attack." Tears escaped her eyes, as she continued, "It's just me and Eloise now. We're heading home, back to The Pishon Valley in Havilah. What about you? Where's your family? What happened?"

Audrey's words struck home with Armaros, and he said, "He was killed by invaders? How long ago?"

She responded, "Recently. Things happened so fast. Why?

Shem interjected, "Is that really what happened? Invaders? I don't see any signs of a fight?"

Armaros maintained his gaze on Audrey as he spoke, "The invaders were here. They wore black and were covered in tattoos. They've been here since last night, I think. There was no fight." Tears began to stream down his cheeks once more. "They were like pests, consuming all we had without paying. They were abusive, and...and..."

"It's ok. Take your time," said Audrey.

Summoning his energy, he spoke, "They rounded up all the women and brought them to our house." He gestured behind him toward the fireplace.

Shem glanced in the direction he indicated and asked, "Is that one of the houses on fire? What happened? Why did they do that?"

Nin clenched his jaw and made a gesture with his hand, cutting off Shem's questions.

Armaros shook his head. "Yes, the closest house was ours. But I started the fire...earlier today." Looking at Shem, his brows furled in anger, and he said, "These animals came here and destroyed our lives, taking our women, killing our staff. I had to do something." His face was red, his hands visibly shaking. "They took my wife, Darina to our house, and.... I could hear the screams. I was helpless. So weak."

Shem could only stare in horror, his heart pounding with a renewed desire for revenge that made him tremble.

Audrey seized his hands and pulled him closer to meet his eyes. "What have you done, Armaros?"

In despair, Armaros said, "I prayed to Nergal, the god of vengeance and death."

She put her hands to her face in horror and shock, and drew a symbol in the air with her hand. Then collecting her thoughts, she looked up at Shem and Nin. “Nergal is one of the Cainite gods of The Serpent. One of the cults from our homeland. Praying to him is bold, but not a problem, unless he evoked the rites. It would involve blood and sacrifice.”

Shem felt the hairs on his head stand on end, again. That feeling of impending doom returned in a rush, as he recalled the disturbing star drawn in the sand. “He may have done that,” he said, in barely a wisper.

“What do you mean? What do you know of our rites?” she said, in almost a panic.

Shem, looking from her face to Nin’s, he said, “Out back, I stepped in a star drawn on the ground in some dark liquid. There were candles and bones I believe.” He could feel his blood pound in his ears.

Trying to calm his friend, Elam put his hand on Shem’s shoulder.

She grabbed Armaros by the collar, shaking him vigorously. "Was it you? Did you draw the pentagram and recite the incantation? Did you invite him?" Her face flushed with a deep red as she edged closer to panic.

“I’m sorry! I didn’t know what to do. They destroyed my world. I...I wanted vengeance, " he said, crying once again tears streaming down his face once more.

Gripping his shirt tightly, she demanded, "What happened after that? Did he appear?"

"Wait...what? Are you saying you think this god or demon or whatever just showed up because he was called?" Shem replied, baffled.

"That's impossible...right?" Elam whispered, his voice almost inaudible.

Nin crossed his arms thoughtfully.

Lauren, still clutching the shaken man, looked at the boys and shouted, "Be quiet! You have no idea of the power at play here. These are forces beyond your understanding." Turning back to Armaros, she inquired, "So? Did he respond?"

"I...I'm not certain. It feels like he responded," Armaros murmured, his voice barely above a whisper. "I'd trudged out to the old water tower, starting to mend the pipe. But then...then it all goes blank. When I came to, I was sprawled out in the open clearing, my body smeared with earth and grime." He paused for a moment, swallowing hard before continuing. "My clothes were ripped apart as if by wild beasts. Every inch of me throbbed with pain. And there they were - the invaders - scattered around me like discarded toys." His voice dropped even lower as he added, "Their bodies twisted into unnatural shapes... lifeless... each and every one of them." With that final confession, Armaros collapsed forward onto his hands, every bit of energy drained from him.

Audrey released Armaros, letting her hands fall to her sides as she bowed her head in surrender. "You might have doomed us as well," she said.

"What?" Elam exclaimed in surprise.

Confused, Shem asked, "What do you mean by that?"

Nin, moving past Lauren, assisted Armaros to his feet. "That's enough for tonight. Let's get him to a room to rest," he suggested.

"Hold on," Shem protested, "That's it? They claim their god just killed all these people, and now she's saying we're doomed too, and you just say, 'that's enough?'"

Guiding Armaros toward the stairs, Nin paused and replied, "Yes, Shem, that's exactly what I said! You're about to find out there's a lot more to this world than you ever imagined."

Shem stood there, stunned, as Nin led Armaros upstairs, grappling with the gravity of what he'd just heard. *Could it really be true?*

The notion that this god wielded such immense power sent a shiver through him. His entire upbringing had instilled in him the belief that vengeance belonged solely to Yahweh—an idea he had embraced without question. Yet, here he was, on a journey his father had permitted, one that seemed to contradict the very teachings he'd held dear.

In that moment of contemplation, doubt crept in. *Was there another path to the justice he sought, one that diverged from his father's wisdom?*

Perhaps this notion of divine retribution was more complicated than he had been led to believe. It struck him that his father's insistence on self-control might have been rooted in a deeper understanding of the natural order, which he was just beginning to grasp. *Is this why Yahweh plans to destroy Adamah?*

Questions whirled in his mind, leaving a lingering sense of confusion. He needed answers—craved them—yet felt utterly lost on how to find them. As he sank into these thoughts, the world around him faded, and he became ensnared in a web of contemplation. It was then that he caught Raphael's gaze once more, a silent reminder that he was not alone in this bewildering moment.

CHAPTER 10

Conjured Menace

The dim light of the fire cast dancing shadows on Shem and his companions as they sat together, deep into the evening. Their voices were low and hushed, discussing the events that had transpired in the past few days. Most of the group had retired to their beds, scattered throughout the inn's various rooms upstairs.

The tables that had once been filled with food and drinks were now pushed aside, making room for the boys to spread out and get comfortable.

Shem found himself in a plush chair, his booted feet propped up near the warmth of the freshly stoked fire. His stomach was full from their meal and he couldn't help but feel a sense of contentment wash over him, despite the weight of recent events weighing on his mind.

Elam sat next to him, mirroring his relaxed posture, while Aram and Lud occupied chairs and a bench on the opposite side of the fire. Lud lounged lazily on the bench, one arm draped over his eyes, while Aram sketched in his book in a nearby chair.

It was a rare moment of rest for them all, but for Shem it was bittersweet as memories of what could have haunted his thoughts once again. *I miss you so much, Adi.*

Conversations around the room died down as Armaros' tale of solo victory against a horde of outlaws, thanks to some mystical aid, took root in their minds.

Aram was the one who broke the silence, setting his sketchbook aside. "Are we actually buying this story?" he asked, skepticism lining his voice. "One guy versus an entire gang...and we're supposed to believe it just like that?"

"He said some 'god' helped him. That's a twisted way of saying demons, right Shem?" Elam chimed in, turning towards his friend.

The first to react was Lud with a nervous question, "Okay, but *how* did he manage that?"

Shem found himself lost in thought, staring at the flickering fire in front of him without an answer. *How do I explain something I can't even wrap my head around?* He wondered aloud if these so-called demons were truly as powerful and whether Yahweh would ever grant him such strength.

Elam gave a dismissive snort and straightened up. "Don't be naive Shem. You know how The Serpent's minions operate. These cults and their followers might seem harmless initially but they hide enormous power - remember what happened with that Nephilim." His voice turned sour as he remembered their recent run-in with the giant.

Aram raised an eyebrow doubtfully and shot back, "The giant was tangible though. Real."

"And huge," Lud added shakily. "Let's not forget huge."

"Also," Aram continued addressing Elam directly, "How can you claim to know what they're capable of? Maybe there's a logical explanation for all this."

Elam looked shocked at this suggestion. “Is that what you really think? These cults are evil forces, Aram! We've all been taught the same lessons!”

Aram simply shrugged and returned to his sketch.

“But Eloise and her mother...” Shem started, only to be cut off by Lud.

“What about them?” Lud asked curiously, leaning in closer.

“They are followers of Azazel,” Shem said quietly.

Lud's eyes widened in shock. “No way! They seem so nice, not at all ‘evilish’.”

Elam rolled his eyes and shook his head incredulously. “Evilish? Being good doesn't mean they're serving Yahweh. In fact, it makes them more dangerous because you let your guard down around them.”

Lud nudged Aram with an elbow and grinned, “She is pretty though.” Aram just smirked back, eyes still on his sketch.

“That's exactly my point,” Shem jumped in, "just because they believe differently doesn't make them evil."

Elam sighed heavily at this statement. “Armaros might be a decent guy but if he did get help from an evil force to seek revenge as he claims, there will be consequences.”

“Assuming it's true,” Aram added doubtfully.

“I still think we need to look into this further,” Shem insisted firmly. “We've always been taught that vengeance belongs to Yahweh yet it was Nergal or some other deity who helped him.” He paused before adding, “Maybe I'll ask Audrey for her take on this.” He didn't mention the look of horror she had when she found out what Armaros had done which only added to his internal struggle even more.

“Firstly,” Elam rebutted sharply, “they're demons, not gods. And secondly, I want no part in this investigation. You can't imagine the possible repercussions." He crossed his arms and closed his eyes signaling the end of discussion from his side.

Shem's mind was a whirlwind of conflicting thoughts. *I'll never forget that giant.* He was torn, unsure whether to believe Aram's insistence that it was a matter of science or to accept the terrifying reality of a demon capable of slaughtering so many.

But amidst all these doubts, one thing echoed in his mind - the impending destruction of Adamah by Yahweh's hand. It was a constant warning ingrained into him since childhood - *Repent before it's too late.* The power of Yahweh was undeniable, but would He help Shem now in his time of need? Was it even right to seek vengeance for the agony the giant had wrought upon him? Or would turning to demons offer a more viable path? Shem's head throbbed with these conflicting questions. *Would you even answer my prayers*?

Suddenly, a loud crash reverberated throughout the inn, making the chandelier sway wildly and startling everyone. The boys leapt to their feet, adrenaline coursing through their bodies as they prepared for whatever might happen next.

Doors flew open on the mezzanine level, revealing the rest of the group who had been roused from their slumber by the commotion. In hushed voices, they cautiously made their way towards a closed door at the center of the balcony, with Bartel and Halvin taking position on one side and Nin on the other. Audrey stayed close behind her daughter, who stood ready with her swords drawn.

Meanwhile, the boys retrieved their weapons from beside their chairs and crept towards the bottom of the stairs. Raphael appeared from the back hallway, his sword unsheathed and ready for battle as he joined them.

With a swift motion, Shem unsheathed Davar and joined his companions. His grip on the sword tightened as he considered its lack of glowing power in his grasp, unlike what it did for his father.

But any thoughts were quickly silenced as a blood-curdling scream pierced through the closed door. It was unlike anything Shem had ever heard, a cacophony of torment and anguish that sounded like a thousand men wailing in unison. The chilling sound was then followed by a sinister laughter that sent shivers down his spine, filling him with dread and a sense of impending doom.

Swords unsheathed, glints of resolve shining in their eyes, Bartel and Halvin burst through the door with a thunderous crash, ready to face whatever lay ahead. The air erupted with the clash of metal and fierce battle cries as Nin charged in right behind them. The sound of battle froze the boys in terror at the foot of the stairs.

Shem's heart was pounding like a drum in his chest.

Suddenly, Nin was violently thrown from the room, his body slamming against the sturdy balcony railing before collapsing to the ground motionless- the door banging shut.

Before anyone could even react, the door exploded outward in a spray of splinters, sending Bartel and Halvin hurtling through the air like rag dolls. They crashed down to the main room below, landing with bone-crushing force onto a large table that shattered beneath them.

Shem and Raphael rushed to their friends' side, horrified by what they saw. Halvin lay moaning in pain, blood streaming from deep gashes on his face. Bartel, though alive, was unresponsive and incapacitated just like Nin.

Eloise stood over Nin, her body tense and ready to defend against whatever horror was approaching, while her mother was frantically drawing unknown sigils in the air in a desperate attempt to save her companions' lives.

Aram and Lud leapt into action, scrambling up the staircase to come to their rescue. But before they could reach them, a blur of movement from within the dark room grabbed Eloise and tossed her towards the boys with incredible speed. The impact sent them all tumbling down the stairs in a chaotic heap.

Elam just managed to dodge the pile of his friends as they came at him. "Do you have a scientific answer now?" he yelled at Aram, who was tangled up with Lud and Eloise.

Shem and Raphael stood firm, ready to face whatever emerged from the darkness.

Shem could hear his friends' grunts and cries as they struggled to get back on their feet. "Are you guys okay?"

The only answer he got from them was cursing as they tried to get back to their feet with assistance from Elam.

Whatever they were facing was causing as much chaos as the giant had, amplifying his own fear and helplessness. He stood rooted to the spot, unsure of what he could do but determined to stand by his friends.

Meanwhile, Audrey remained bowed down in front of the door, seemingly frozen in supplication to whatever she saw or heard from her position on the mezzanine above. She was sobbing, adding another layer of unease to the already tense situation.

A figure stepped into the dim light cast by the flickering fire, causing the hairs on the back of Shem's arms to rise. It was a man, or at least it resembled one, but there was something off about him. His movements were stiff and jerky, like a marionette being controlled by unseen hands. His arms hung limply at his sides as though they were being pulled by strings.

It took Shem a moment to recognize him—this was Armaros, the same creature he had seen through his spyglass earlier that day. But now he looked even worse than before; covered in multiple sword wounds and with a twisted smile stretched across his face.

Ignoring Nin unmoving at his feet, Armaros turned his attention to Audrey who remained prostrated before him. A deep, guttural laugh bubbled up from within him as he towered over her.

"Leave her alone!" Eloise's voice rang out, her determination to protect her mother evident despite being tangled up with the boys on the stairs.

With a cruel smirk, Armaros disregarded Eloise's desperate pleas and yanked Audrey up by her hair. The helpless woman cried out in pain as he forced her to stand, while his possessed eyes turned towards Eloise with his twisted grin.

"Ah, the little lioness," he purred, his voice a sickening blend of honey and gravel. "So eager to protect, so willing to sacrifice. But tell me, child, are you truly ready to die for your mommy?"

Eloise's hand shook as she raised her sword towards him, her voice trembling but determined. "If you lay one finger on her, you will pay for it," she declared, her words laced with steel.

Shem stood frozen in terror as Armaros descended the stairs, dragging Audrey along behind him by her hair like a rag doll. The sound of her cries echoed through the air, fueling Eloise's determination to end this madness and save her mother from the clutches of evil.

Armaros' laughter echoed through the room, a chilling sound that sent shivers down Shem's spine. He reached the bottom of the stairs, still clutching Audrey by her hair. Eloise lunged down the other staircase, her sword aimed at Armaros' chest, but he effortlessly sidestepped her attack, his movements fluid and unnatural.

Lud, Aram and Elam were close behind her, poised to strike at this shell of a man, swords flashing in the firelight.

They all came up short when he yanked Audrey around and used her as a human shield. "I wouldn't come any closer if I were you," he said with a snarling smile.

"Such spirit," he hissed, his black eyes gleaming with malevolent amusement, now refocused on Eloise. "But spirit alone won't save you or your precious mother."

Raphael, leaping into action, charged at Armaros from behind, hoping to catch him off guard. But the creature sensed his approach, whirling around and backhanding Raphael with such force that he was sent flying across the room, crashing into the wall with a sickening thud.

Amidst peals of laughter, Armaros taunted Raphael who lay slumped on the floor. "Not yet, servant," he sneered. His voice was thick with malice and amusement.

Shem felt helpless as he stood by with his friends.

But as Eloise swung at him again, he suddenly spoke in a human voice, almost gentle. "Eloise," he said, grabbing her wrist with his free hand, "it is pointless to fight."

Eloise stumbled to her knees, her strength drained in an instant at the sound of her own name. "Dad," she choked out, her voice small and hopeless. A mix of emotions were etched on her face - anger, fear, sadness - all directed at the man before her who was speaking in the voice of her once beloved protector and mentor—her father.

Shem's heart sank as he watched Eloise's resolve crumble.

"Don't listen to him!" yelled Lud, trying to come to her rescue, but was being held back by his brother.

Elam put his hand on Lud's chest. "Just wait, or he'll kill Audrey."

The realization that Armaros was somehow channeling or possessing her father added a new layer of horror to the already nightmarish situation. Shem knew he had to act, to do something to break the spell that seemed to have fallen over Eloise.

"Eloise, he's trying to trick you!" Shem shouted, his voice cracking with desperation. "That's not your father!"

Armaros's eyes burned with otherworldly malice as he turned them towards Shem. His voice was a grotesque blend of Eloise's father and something far more sinister, dripping with pure distain. "Ah, the little son of Noah," he sneered, his lips curling into a menacing smile. "Perhaps you'd like to speak to someone else?"

Shem's grip on his sword tightened, his hands trembling as he defiantly met Armaros's gaze. "Who are you? I'm not afraid," he said, refusing to show any fear in front of this monstrous being.

But deep down, he knew that hearing that one person's voice in this form was the last thing he wanted. No, *no, no...please no.*

Despite his friends being close by, Shem couldn't shake the feeling of dread that filled him after witnessing the creature effortlessly toss them around like toy soldiers. *He's going to kill us all!*

"I am Azazel, god of the forge, leader of the watchers, chief among the host of heaven, sent to Adamah to guide mankind against the tyrannical rule of the vindictive God of heaven, Yahweh," his voice boomed with authority and malice. "Join me and you can have your revenge against those abominable invaders and that wretched giant," he sneered as he towered above Audrey with a menacing glare.

Audrey's eyes widened in fear as she realized the true nature of this twisted deity. With tears in her eyes and trembling hands, she reached out to Shem for help.

But Azazel's grip tightened around her neck, cutting off her cries for mercy. "This poor soul and her daughter know that I am the only way," he taunted. "They serve me, and so shall you."

Shem's heart filled with rage and sorrow as he was about to witness the merciless death of an innocent woman at the hands of this self-proclaimed god.

He raised his sword in defiance, knowing now that he could never ask an evil demon such as this for any kind of help with his petty request for vengeance.

But before he could strike, Azazel's hand twisted with a sudden motion, snapping Audrey's neck with a sickening crack. Shem let out a guttural cry of anguish as he charged towards the vile creature, determined to put a stop to this evil being.

"Why would you attack me, Shem? You promised to protect me." The words pierced through Shem's heart, bringing him up short— paralyzing him. His sword clattered to the ground, useless against the voice of Azazel that twisted and distorted the very memory of Adi he held dear.

He knew deep down that this was not his beloved, but his mind couldn't help but yearn for her. In that moment, everything faded away except for Adi standing before him, as beautiful and radiant as he remembered.

Tears streamed down his face as he begged her for forgiveness. "I tried, Adi. I swear I did. I would never hurt you. I couldn't save you."

"You failed," came the angry retort, an accusatory finger pointed in his direction. "You were never strong enough for me. Perhaps Elam would have been a better choice." Her words stung like venom, fueling the anguish in his heart. He would do anything to save her, even if it meant sacrificing himself. His friends' voices were distant background noise compared to the overwhelming desire to please Adi.

It wasn't until she mentioned her father's presence that reality snapped back into focus. But it was too late. Before Shem could even react, Adi's head was severed from her body by her father's sword. A scream ripped from Shem's throat as he fell to his knees, reaching for his own weapon with a desperate need for revenge.

Elam and his friends had to physically restrain him from attacking Bartel and the others who had betrayed them. Shem's thoughts were a jumbled mess as he struggled against their hold. He could see both Adi's headless body and Armaros' lifeless form beside him, unable to comprehend what had just happened. Bartel had killed Armaros...but then why did it feel like he had just lost Adi all over again? The conflicting emotions and images overwhelmed him, until he finally surrendered to the numbness that enveloped him.

As Shem's body went limp in his friends' arms, the world around him seemed to blur and fade. The sounds of his friends' voices grew distant, replaced by a hollow ringing in his ears. He felt himself slipping away from the gruesome scene, but he couldn't muster the strength or will to resist.

Time passed in a haze. Shem drifted in and out of consciousness, catching fragments of hushed conversations and worried glances from his companions. Shem remained detached from it all, lost in a fog of grief and confusion.

It wasn't until a few days later that he finally stirred, his parched throat forcing him to seek water. As he sat up in a small bed wincing at the ache in his muscles, he found Elam sitting beside him, a look of relief washing over his friend's face.

"You're awake," Elam said softly, offering Shem a cup of water."We were starting to worry."

Shem took a long drink, the cool liquid soothing his raw throat. As the fog in his mind began to clear, the memories came rushing back - Armaros, Adi's voice, the brutal beheading.

He squeezed his eyes shut, willing the images away.

"What happened?" he croaked, his voice barely above a whisper.

Elam sighed, running a hand through his disheveled hair.

"Bartel... he saw an opening and took it. Armaros, or Azazel— whatever his name, was distracted by you, and he struck. It was over in seconds."

Shem closed his eyes. *This had to be a nightmare.*

"It wasn't her," Elam said, placing a hand on Shem's shoulder. "You know that, right? Azazal possessed him and was playing tricks with your mind."

Shem nodded weakly, but the pain in his chest told a different story. Logically, he understood it had been an illusion—a cruel manipulation. But his heart ached as if he'd lost Adi all over again.

The heavy door to Shem's small room creaked open, and in slipped Bartel, his broad frame towering over Nin who stood uncomfortably by his side. The two men exchanged a silent glance before cautiously venturing further into the room.

Shem, still feeling like he got mauled by Rocky, lay propped up on pillows in bed, unsure if he was ready for visitors.

"He's awake," announced Elam, sounding relieved. "Finally."

Shem's mind was foggy as he tried to remember how long he had been unconscious. "How long was I out for?"

"Three days," answered Nin, standing rigid by the door.

"What's his problem?" Shem muttered to Elam, not wanting to show any weakness in front of Bartel.

Elam chuckled and glanced at Nin before answering. "I don't think he likes it when someone gets the better of him in battle."

Bartel let out a hearty laugh and strode across the room towards Shem. "Well, for one, I am grateful that Yahweh saw fit to spare us all and deliver us from Azazel himself." He enveloped Shem in a tight embrace. "And I'm even more thankful that I regained my senses in time to stop whatever he was doing to you."

Feeling awkward at Bartel's display of affection, Shem managed a weak smile and said, "I'm glad you killed him. That's for sure. I could feel myself getting sucked in."

"Oh, he didn't kill him," interjected Nin with arms folded across his chest. "Armaros is dead, but not Azazel. You can be sure he's still alive." He leaned against the doorframe, looking smug.

Feeling like he had missed something between Bartel and Nin, Shem asked, "I'm not sure what happened or who it was, but why didn't he affect you, Bartel? Why did I fall under his spell and not you? All he did was say my name and everything faded away." He tried to hide his embarrassment.

"He got lucky," said Nin with a sneer.

Bartel's face turned red with anger. "Luck had nothing to do with it, foreman. I am under the protection of Yahweh. His divine shield would not allow for a 'demon' to take hold of my soul. Luck indeed." His emphasis on the word 'demon' did not go unnoticed by Shem.

"That means I don't have that protection," Shem muttered dejectedly.

"Son," Bartel said, noticing Shem's downcast demeanor. "It is a personal choice we all must make between ourselves and our Lord. You can choose to serve Yahweh - Creator of the universe and Lord of all - or you can choose to serve The Serpent and join his rebellion. But you cannot serve both."

Shem felt embarrassed and ashamed at the truth in Bartel's words. He had heard similar sermons from his father his whole life, but in his pride, he had always pushed them away, thinking he could do it all on his own.

All he could think about was getting away from the farm, his father, and the mundane cursed life he lived. Never once did he consider the cost of making the wrong decision - or no decision at all.

At that moment, he thought of Eve in The Garden faced with the same choice: "Do I eat the forbidden fruit or not?" And now, that same pivotal moment was before him, and he had to make the same choice.

"Bah," scoffed Nin, "men cannot hope to survive in this war between gods."

"So according to you," retorted Bartel, "we should just give up hope of redemption?"

"Hope is just a childish dream," Nin replied coldly. "We are adults. The gods don't care about us, and I make my own choices."

Seated on the edge of Shem's bed, Bartel placed a comforting hand on his shoulder. "Yahweh is Lord and He has a plan. Trust in Him. It's the only way, especially if you want to be with Adi again someday in the bosom of our ancestors." A pang of sorrow crossed Bartel's face as he mentioned his lost family. "I miss my daughters and wife terribly, but I have hope that I will join them again someday. And I want that for you too."

Standing abruptly, Bartel strode back across the room towards the door, pausing in front of Nin before exiting. "I'll pray for your soul."

Nin stood silently, avoiding eye contact with Bartel.

The weight of Bartel's words hung heavy in the room as silence enveloped them all once more. Shem thought about his father and the teachings he had forsaken in his desire for independence and adventure. He realized that he had never truly considered the cost of not making a choice until now.

As Bartel's footsteps faded down the hallway, Shem was left to contemplate his future and the decision he must make between serving Yahweh or succumbing to the temptations of The Serpent and his demons. *What'd I do?*

Chapter 11

Shifted Balance

As the first light of dawn crept over the horizon, the group climbed onto their gallimimus and headed toward Center Grove. They took the road leading east, which passed the inn where they had spent the previous night. This was the connecting route to the main road that led into the city from the west, and they knew they were just a few hours away.

The morning mist from the underground springs still lingered on the ground, wrapping the hillside in an ethereal mist that cast a dreamlike aura over everything. It felt almost otherworldly, especially after the experiences of the last few days.

After his terrifying encounter with Azazel, Shem woke to find Eloise in a similar state. She too had been incapacitated for some time, but unlike him, she had awoken to a harrowing realization - her mother had been killed by the demonic creature. Lud rode by her side, trying to coax her back to health with jokes and conversation, but she remained silent and distant.

Shem could only imagine that she was numb from the shock and grief, much like he was after Adi's death, except Eloise was still dealing with the loss of her father as well, which made her ordeal far worse. She didn't even shed a tear at her mother's funeral last night, when they honored her with a traditional pyre ceremony, as was custom for her people.

The group rode in silence, the rhythmic thudding of their mounts' feet the only sound breaking through the morning stillness.

As they crested a small hill, the mist began to thin, revealing the sprawling expanse of Center Grove in the distance. The city's towering spires pierced the sky penetrating a canopy of huge trees, their gleaming surfaces catching the early morning light. In spite of the circumstances, the sight was still breathtaking.

Nin cleared his throat, breaking the silence. "We should reach the city gates by midday," he said, his voice stoic as usual. "Once we're inside, we can seek out the Council of Elders. They'll want to hear about what happened."

Shem nodded absently, his thoughts still consumed by the events of the past few days and the looming threat of Azazel hanging over them. But as they descended the hill and rode closer to Center Grove, he found himself increasingly captivated by the magnificent city sprawling before them.

The ancient trees just beyond the city were absolutely colossal, their trunks wider than houses and their branches reaching hundreds of feet into the sky, forming a backdrop that seemed to stretch on forever.

As they descended the hill, the road widened and merged with the western road. More travelers began to appear: merchants with heavily laden carts, pilgrims on foot, and the occasional patrol of city guards on horseback.

As the group approached the city gates, the bustling sounds of Center Grove started to fill the air. Market vendors called out their wares, children laughed and played in the streets, and the smell of freshly baked bread wafted from nearby bakeries.

"We should stick together once we're in the city," proposed Bartel, glancing around at the lively crowd. "It's easy to get separated in these busy streets."

Shem nodded in agreement, his eyes scanning the surroundings warily. "And keep an eye out for any suspicious characters. We can't afford to let our guard down, especially with Azazel still out there."

Eloise finally spoke up, her voice barely above a whisper. "What if he finds us here? What if we're not safe even within the city walls?"

Lud tried his best to comfort her, with a sideways look at Shem. "We'll keep a lookout, Eloise. It's a large city, and maybe there's someone inside that understands what happened and can come up with a plan to face him together."

Elam leaned in close to Shem, his voice a whisper. “What's our plan once we're inside? We can't exactly announce that a demon is on the loose.”

Bartel, riding in front of the boys, leaned back to join the conversation. “We'll save it for the council. They're familiar with demons. Trust me—they won't take this lightly.”

Approaching the towering city gates, Nin signaled for their group to halt. With a graceful dismount from his mount, he strode confidently towards the guards standing watch. As he engaged in conversation with them, the rest of the companions eagerly took the opportunity to stretch their stiff muscles.

In awe, Elam's jaw dropped as he gazed upon the majestic sight of Center Grove. “Would you look at that.”

Shem couldn't help but share in his wonder at the sprawling city before them. From this vantage point, they could see a magnificent bridge spanning a wide river that wound its way north and south. On either side of the river, buildings and houses stretched as far as the eye could see.

But it was the heart of the city on the far side of the river, built into a lush forest of towering trees, that truly caught their attention. The massive trees dwarfed even the tallest structures in the city, their branches stretching upwards to touch the sky. The houses and buildings were cleverly incorporated into and around the trees, their sloped roofs peeking out like spikes from the forest canopy. They could see intricate archways, stairs, windows, and artistic wood siding blending seamlessly with and carefully cut around the natural curves of each tree. It was a breathtaking blend of nature and architecture that left them all speechless.

Nin returned from his conversation with the guards, a satisfied smile on his face. "We've been granted entry," he announced. "But we must leave our mounts here. The city's interior is not designed for large animals."

As they began to unload their belongings, Shem couldn't tear his eyes away from the magnificent sight before them. "How did they build all of this?" he asked, gesturing towards the tree-integrated structures.

"The people of Center Grove have lived in harmony with these trees for generations," Bartel explained, his voice filled with reverence. "They say their ancestors made a pact with the forest itself, allowing them to shape their homes within its embrace without harming the trees."

Once inside, they were immediately enveloped by the bustling energy of the city. The main thoroughfare, which continued across the bridge, was lined with colorful market stalls, their vendors loudly hawking wares from across Adamah. The air was thick with the mingled scents of exotic spices, freshly baked bread, and the earthy aroma of the surrounding forest

As they passed through the market over the bridge the group was immediately enveloped by the cool shade of the towering trees. The air was thick with the scent of moss and rich earth, a stark contrast to the craggy lands they had traveled through for days. The sounds of the city seemed to fade away, replaced by the gentle rustling of leaves and the occasional call of a bird high in the canopy.

Nin led them along a winding path that spiraled upwards around the trunk of an enormous tree. Wooden platforms jutted out at various levels, connected by an intricate network of bridges and staircases. As they climbed higher, Shem marveled at the ingenuity of the construction. Each step and handrail was carefully crafted to follow the natural contours of the tree, as if they had grown there alongside the branches.

"We're heading to the Elders' Grove," Bartel explained as they ascended. "It's where the city's leaders convene and where we'll be able to warn them about the impending danger."

As they climbed higher, the group began to notice intricate carvings etched into the tree bark. Symbols and patterns swirled around the trunk, telling stories of the city's history and the forest's ancient wisdom.

Shem ran his fingers along one of the carvings, feeling the grooves worn smooth by countless hands before his.

"Hands off," Lud piped up with a mischievous grin. "The trees have the memory of an elephant! They'll remember every tickle and whisper. Who knows, they might start gossiping about your secrets!" His laughter echoed through the woods, and soon the others were laughing in spite of themselves, unable to resist his silliness.

Finally, they reached a large circular platform nestled high in the canopy. It was like stepping into another world, surrounded by ancient trees whose trunks were so wide that it would take ten men linking arms to encircle them. The gnarled branches stretched out and intertwined above, creating a natural dome that shielded the platform from the sun's rays.

In the center of the platform stood a group of elderly men, their faces weathered and wise from years spent among the trees. They seemed to emanate a sense of calm and wisdom, as if they held the secrets of the forest within their minds and hearts.

The leaves rustled overhead as Lud whispered to Aram, "I'm not sure who's older, those guys or the trees." They both tried to stifle their laughter as Bartel gave them a stern look.

Elam opened his mouth to say something to Shem but was silenced by another disapproving glare from Bartel. Their attention was then drawn to an ancient-looking man making his way towards the group.

The man's long, white hair and waist-length beard gave him a wise and weathered appearance. His slow, shuffling gait and deeply wrinkled face added to the impression that he held all the secrets of the universe. As he approached, Shem couldn't escape a feeling of familiarity.

Despite his age, the man's voice was strong and sure as he addressed the group. "Welcome to Center Grove, we've been expecting you." The companions exchanged shocked glances, except for Nin who seemed unfazed by anything.

"Magic," muttered Halvin under his breath.

The old man laughed at this. "Oh, nothing like that," he replied with surprisingly sharp hearing. "We have a visitor from the capital. I believe you know her."

"Aryana," exclaimed Shem a little too loudly. It would be good to see her again.

The man smiled at Shem's response. "Yes, Lady Aryana. She arrived late yesterday."

"So, you are aware of why we have come?" Nin asked, stepping towards the man.

His demeanor shifted slightly at this question. "Yes, Ningangar," he replied without meeting Nin's gaze. "I was relieved to hear that my grandson was unharmed and had accompanied you."

"My apologies for not introducing..." Nin was interrupted by a raised finger from the man, who now turned his gaze on Shem with a warm smile.

Shem was puzzled by this exchange. Grandson? He wondered who that could be. As he grew older, Shem was realizing just how interconnected the family lines in Eden were.

The man stepped around Nin and stood before Shem. "And it brings me great joy to see my great-grandson standing before me, now."

"You're my great-grandfather?" Shem asked with wonder.

Elam couldn't contain his shock and blurted out, "That would make you..."

"Over 800 years old? 884, to be exact," the man chuckled. "My name is Methuselah, son of Enoch, father of Lamech, and grandfather to Noah." He placed a hand on Shem's shoulder. "And great-grandfather to you."

Shem was at a loss for words. His father had spoken of Methuselah, of course, but always in the context of the great patriarchs and their responsibility to pass on the history of The Garden and the coming Redeemer. It had never occurred to him that this man, his great grandfather, was still alive.

Methuselah, seeing Shem's hesitation, wrapped him up in a bear hug that could rival any farmhand's grip. "Your friend was correct," he said, with a grin. "I've got more rings than half these old redwoods."

At this, Lud's face flushed a deep shade of red, looking as though he'd been caught stealing eggs from the henhouse.

Aram and Elam couldn't help but dissolve into laughter at Lud's comical mortification.

Shem returned the embrace, feeling a strange mix of wonder and familiarity. As they parted, Methuselah's eyes twinkled with mischief. "Now, let's not stand here all day. I'm sure you're all hungry after your journey."

He turned and began shuffling towards a building that was part of one of the trees that surrounded the platform, gesturing for the group to follow. As they walked, Shem found himself falling into step beside his great grandfather.

"Grandfather," he began hesitantly, "I...I have so many questions. About our family, about the past, about..."

Methuselah chuckled softly. "About everything, I imagine. Don't worry, my boy. We'll have plenty of time for questions and answers. But first, let's fill those empty stomachs of yours," Methuselah finished with a wink. "Questions are best pondered over a hearty meal."

As they approached the tree-building, Shem marveled at its construction. The trunk had been hollowed out and expanded, with windows and balconies seamlessly integrated into its living wood. Branches curved to form archways and natural staircases, while leaves provided a canopy overhead.

Inside, the air was cool and fragrant with the scent of wood. Methuselah led them to a large circular room where a table was already set with an array of fruits, breads, and steaming dishes. Aryana stood at the sight of Shem and his companions.

"You finally showed up," she declared, arms crossed like a stern school teacher, seemingly annoyed with the whole gang. "I was about to send out a search party." A tiny, sly grin peeked out from behind her mock disapproval.

As they settled around the table, Shem couldn't help but notice the way Nin's eyes lingered on Aryana, like back at the midday meal, not so long ago. There was a tension there, unspoken but palpable. He filed the observation away for later consideration.

Methuselah took his place at the head of the table, his weathered hands resting on the polished wood. "Before we begin, let us give thanks for this meal and for the safe arrival of our guests," he intoned, bowing his head.

"Now then," he said, his voice carrying a hint of mischief, "who wants to tell me about this adventure of yours?"

Lud, taking his opportunity to tell a story, launched into an animated recounting of their journey, complete with dramatic gestures and sound effects. The others chimed in occasionally to correct details or add their own perspectives, while Methuselah listened intently, nodding at the appropriate moments.

As he prattled on, Shem found himself stealing glances at his great-grandfather, still marveling at the fact that he was sitting with a living legend.

"But tell me," Methuselah continued, his gaze sharpening, "what do you make of these attacks? Of the invaders in Ararat?"

The mood around the table sobered quickly. Nin cleared his throat, all traces of his usual nonchalance gone. "It's worse than we initially thought. The attack on Ararat seems to be just the beginning."

Lady Aryana nodded grimly. "The capital is in turmoil. There are whispers of a growing attack against Eden, of those who seek to challenge the old ways. We believe there is a force gathering in the great forest, to the east." She leaned forward; her brow furrowed. "We've received reports of similar incursions all across Eden. Small raiding parties at first but growing bolder and more organized. Usually, they include Nephilim as well, like the one in Ararat."

Methuselah nodded gravely. "As I feared. The time of reckoning approaches."

"What do you mean, grandfather?" Shem asked, a chill running down his spine.

The ancient patriarch sighed; his eyes distant. "There is much you don't know, Shem." He paused, considering his words carefully. "Adamah is changing. The balance we've maintained for centuries has shifted."

Nin spoke up, his voice uncharacteristically sarcastic, "So...more of the end of the world talk. Noah has been talking about this for almost forty years. Fanciful tales won't solve this problem."

Methuselah's eyebrows raised at the tone of Nin's voice. "Ah, I remember...My grandson's foreman isn't a believer," his voice now carrying an edge. "It doesn't matter whether you believe it or not. It was prophesied by my own father, Enoch, before he was caught up in the sky to join our Lord, Yahweh."

"Prophesied?" Elam interjected; confusion evident in his voice. "I thought Noah was the first to predict the end of Adamah."

Methuselah's eyes swept across the table, taking in the curious and concerned faces before him. He leaned back in his chair, his fingers interlacing as he gathered his thoughts.

"My father, Enoch, walked with Yahweh in a way few have ever known," he began, his voice low and reverent. "But, before he was taken, he foretold of a great judgement that would befall Adamah. He said that the Lord is coming with countless thousands of his holy ones to execute judgement on the people of the world, and he said that it's because of the ungodliness and the insults that man has spoken against Him. Even my name, as given by Yahweh to my father, means 'when he dies, it will be sent.'"

Shem felt shivers run down his spine. His father had been preaching something similar his whole life but hearing it from Methuselah made it feel more real, more imminent. "What will be sent? When you die?"

"We are not sure what form the judgement will take, but it will be world ending...that is what was prophesied," said Methuselah, grimly. "As far as my death goes...I will live until the end comes."

"So based on what Noah has been saying, you only have 85 years left." said Nin, shaking his head. "And you're ok with that?" It wasn't a question.

Methuselah fixed Nin with a steady gaze. "I am at peace with whatever Yahweh has planned, Ningangar. My years have been long and full. But this is not about me." He turned to address the whole table. "The corruption Enoch spoke of, the evil that has taken root in Adamah - it grows stronger every day. The Nephilim are but one symptom of a deeper sickness."

Shem leaned forward, feeling a knot form in his stomach. "But what can we do? How do we fight this... corruption?"

Methuselah's gaze softened as he looked at his great-grandson. "That, my boy, is why your father has been telling everyone about the impending doom. The only way to fight the corruption and survive the coming cataclysm is to repent and place your faith in The Lord, Yahweh."

Shem nodded slowly, processing his great-grandfather's words. The gravity of the situation settled over the table like a heavy fog.

Halvin broke the silence, his voice steady but tinged with concern. "These attacks, the growing unrest - they're all connected, aren't they? To this... corruption...this ungodliness you speak of?"

Methuselah nodded solemnly. "Indeed, son. The evil that has taken root manifests in many ways. The Nephilim, the violence, the demon possessions, the turning away from

Yahweh's ways - they are all branches of the same poisoned tree."

"Demon possessions? Like what happened with Azazel?" asked Eloise, her fists clenched tightly on the table. "I was taught that he was a god." She was breathing heavily.

Methuselah, with a look of loving concern, said, "My dear child, you've been through so much, and I'm so sorry for your loss. Alas, no, Azazel is no god. He, just like the Serpent, Satan, was one of Yahweh's heavenly host of angels." He paused to look around the table, with his eyes stopping at Raphael.

"Long ago, at creation, Yahweh sent a host of angels to watch over Adamah. Chief among those was Lucifer, or Satan, with Azazel and Semyaza his top two chieftains. After Yahweh created Adam and Eve, Satan possessed a beautiful dragon and, in his jealousy and pride, tempted Eve to rebel against Yahweh and eat of the forbidden fruit from the Tree of The Knowledge of Good and Evil.

"Due to their rebellion, Yahweh placed a curse on Satan, on Adam for also eating from the tree, and on the land itself. He even cursed the dragon that Satan had inhabited, as it willingly participated, declaring that it and its descendants would forever crawl in the dust without limbs or wings as a serpent.

"Yet, in His mercy, Yahweh promised to send a Redeemer to ultimately vanquish Satan. Semyaza and Azazel, intent on thwarting Yahweh's plans, persuaded hundreds of their fellow beings to corrupt or pollute the bloodline."

"Pollute the bloodline?" Eloise was visibly shaking, as if she was cold from a fever. Lud wrapped a blanket from his pack around her.

"Yes," continued Methuselah, directing his attention back to her. "That is why we have the Nephilim. Those sons of

Yahweh, or fallen angels, took the human women as brides. Their union created those abominations. They have been wreaking havoc ever since. They felt that if they could pollute the bloodline of Adam or destroy it, then Yahweh's plan for a future son of Adam, a Redeemer, could never happen."

Shem, hearing most of this from his father's teachings, wasn't sure how this affected them directly. "If Azazel is one of the leaders, why would he concern himself with us?"

Methuselah's eyes saddened as he looked at Shem. "Their ultimate goal has remained the same - to stop Yahweh's plan. And now that Noah has prophesied the destruction of Adamah 35 years ago - 85 years in our future - they are trying to speed up their plan."

"But why us? Why me?"

"Because, my boy, you are a descendant of the patriarchs and could potentially be a threat to them. You could hold the lineage of the chosen one or even be the Redeemer yourself. The destruction of Adamah means that Yahweh's plan for a coming Redeemer may be happening soon. They must believe that their time is running out." Methuselah's words hung heavily in the air, filling the room with a sense of urgency and danger.

Bartel, who had been quietly observing, finally spoke up. "But surely there must be something we can do beyond just... waiting for this judgement? We can't just sit idly by while Eden falls to these invaders and wipes us all out."

"Yes. It seems to me," said Nin, "that the invaders don't care what you believe.

The old patriarch's eyes gleamed with approval. "You're right, Bartel. We cannot simply wait. While faith in Yahweh is our ultimate salvation, we are called to be His hands and feet in this world." Methuselah leaned forward, his voice gaining strength. “That is why you are here. Each of you has a role to play in the days to come.”

He turned to Shem. “Your father’s work is crucial, for Yahweh is using him specifically. Eden must be defended, its people protected, for as long as possible.”

Aryana nodded, her expression resolute. “The capital is mobilizing its forces, but we need more than just soldiers. We need information, strategy, and unity among the remaining faithful.”

Methuselah’s eyes scanned the group before him. “And now, this is where you come in,” he said. “Yahweh has brought you to me for a specific purpose. I will pray on it and we’ll meet again tomorrow morning. Until then, feel free to make yourselves at home. We have arranged for a villa nearer to the ground so that you may easily access the market and see our city.”

CHAPTER 12

A Tapestry of Chaos

Shem and his companions relaxed in the comfort of the villa at the base of the tree city in the woods district of Center Grove. The sun was beginning to set, painting the sky in vibrant oranges and pinks, but Shem's curiosity about this new city urged him to explore. As they made their way towards the entrance, Shem couldn't help but notice the plethora of colors and scents that filled his senses.

However, Lud seemed uncharacteristically disinterested in adventure. "I think I'll stay here with Eloise," he said, glancing towards the room where she lay napping. "It's been a rough one for her. She may need someone to talk to."

Shem was surprised by Lud's empathy but didn't question it. "Okay, we'll let you know what we find," he replied, seeking confirmation from Elam before turning to Aram. "You staying or going?"

"Three's a crowd," Aram responded with a grin. "I'll tag along with you guys. All this talk about spirits and stuff has me antsy."

Shem looked around at the others in the room. "Anyone else staying back?"

Aryana stood up from the plush couch she had been lounging on. "I'll come with you. It's not often I get to see a place from ground level. Plus, someone should keep an eye on you guys."

"I'll take Raphael and Halvin with me to the local school office on some ranch business." said Bartel.

Shem, confused, said, "I thought Eden didn't allow the schools in their land?"

"Wow, you must've been paying attention. They don't, but they still recognize that skilled workers are hard to find, so they allow field offices and representatives to be here. It's a compromise but needed. Ararat needs a new blacksmith, so we need to fill out the proper forms," said Bartel.

Nin shook his head when asked if he would join them, stating he had other errands to attend to elsewhere before making a quick exit from the villa.

Shem looked at Bartel in confusion. "Did I miss something?"

"No, he keeps his own counsel. Besides, I don't trust.... " Catching that everyone was looking at him, he decided against continuing that line of thought, "But that is a story for another day. You kids stay out of trouble. Follow Lady Aryana's lead."

Bartel, waving for Raphael and Halvin to follow, left in the same manner as Nin, leaving the rest of them to themselves.

"Let's go see the market," said Shem, excited to get going and do something other than think about prophecies, wars, and demons.

The market was a vibrant tapestry of colors and sounds stretching across the bridge that spanned the Piston River. Shem's eyes widened as he took in the sights: stalls overflowing with exotic fruits, artisans crafting intricate wooden carvings, and merchants calling out their wares in a cacophony of voices.

Aryana led the way, her graceful steps guiding them through the bustling crowd. Shem noticed how people seemed to part for her, a mix of reverence and curiosity in their eyes. He wondered what it would be like to join the ranks of the Eden Knights and command that kind of respect.

"Look at those fruits," Elam exclaimed, pointing to a nearby stall. "I've never seen anything like them."

The vendor, a wizened woman with kind eyes, smiled at them. "Ah, visitors from afar! These are sunburst melons, a specialty of our city. Would you like to try one?"

Shem nodded eagerly, and the woman cut a slice of the vibrant orange fruit. As he bit into it, a burst of sweet, tangy flavor exploded on his tongue. "It's incredible," he said, juice dripping down his chin.

Aram chuckled at Shem's enthusiasm, reaching for a slice himself. "Not bad," he admitted after tasting it. "Though I still prefer the apples from back home."

"Yeah," said Shem, feeling that tinge of pain, when recalling thoughts of Adi's apple store.

As they continued through the market, Shem found himself captivated by the variety of goods on display. Colorful textiles hung from awnings, their intricate patterns telling stories of far-off lands. Aromatic spices filled the air, tickling his nose with unfamiliar scents.

Aryana paused at a stall selling jewelry, her fingers tracing the delicate metalwork of a gold pendant. "This craftsmanship is exquisite," she murmured, almost to herself.

Shem watched her, struck by how different she seemed here, away from the formalities of the council chambers. Her guard was down, revealing a curiosity that matched his own.

"Thank you, I crafted them myself. The gold is from our mines in the mountains of Havilah." said a small, petite girl with kinky dark hair with a huge proud smile.

"You're from Havilah? We have a friend from there." said Shem.

Looking annoyed at the interruption, she said, "Really?" then renewed her attention on Aryana. "My uncle and I travel from the Pishon Valley to Assyria selling our jewelry. It's a family business." Reaching under the table, she pulled out a few more pieces. "I've also made these. You'll notice that they are inlaid with jade."

A look of sadness showed on Aryana's face for a flash, then her mood changed. "They are very beautiful, but I have to decline. Warriors don't have time for trinkets. Pretty or otherwise." She walked away towards the next stall.

"We also have perfume from the north, made from Bdellium," She yelled at Aryana's back as she walked away. Looking dejected, she put the jewelry back in its draw and slammed it shut.

As the boys followed behind Aryna, Shem lingered. "Sorry about that. They look very pretty. Your jewelry is beautiful."

With a small smile she said, "Would you like to buy one for your girl?" gesturing towards Aryana.

“Her?” Shem was shocked that she would think they were together. “Oh, no, not us. I have a....I mean I had....um... .I’m single.” He didn’t want to go into details, having just met her. “I’m Shem.”

She huffed in defeat. “Sorry Shem. Breakups are tough. Maybe next time.”

“What? No...we didn’t break up.” Shem was at a loss for words. “Never mind.”

“Okaay,” she said, looking confused. “My name is Sedee. This is our last day here, and I’m short of our goal. I wasn’t tryin’ to be pushy.” A passerby caught her eye, and she held up the original pendant again, yelling in their direction. “Gold from Havilah!”

Shem watched as Sedee tried to catch the attention of the passerby with her beautiful jewelry. He couldn't help but feel a sense of empathy for her situation.

"Is business slow today?" Shem asked, trying to start a conversation and show his support.

Sedee sighed, looking a bit defeated. "Yeah, it's been a tough week. People seem more interested in the exotic spices and fabrics than handmade jewelry these days."

Shem nodded sympathetically. "Your jewelry is truly stunning, though. I'm sure someone will appreciate its beauty."

A small glimmer of hope appeared in Sedee's eyes. "Thank you, Shem. I put my heart and soul into each piece, hoping that they find their way to someone who appreciates them."

Shem, seeing his friends losing him in the crowd, quickly said, "I wish you luck with your sales, Sedee. Your craftsmanship deserves recognition."

Sedee smiled gratefully at Shem's words. "Thank you, Shem. Perhaps you'll come across someone who would love one of my pieces."

Shem jogged to catch up with his friends, his mind still lingering on the awkward interaction with Sedee. As he reached them, Elam raised an eyebrow. "Making new friends already?"

"Just trying to be polite," Shem mumbled, his cheeks flushing slightly.

Aryana turned to them, her eyes bright with curiosity. "What do you all think of the market so far? It's quite different from what you're used to, isn't it?"

Shem, still thinking about the cute jeweler, barely heard her.

Although Elam nodded enthusiastically, "It's amazing! I've never seen so many different things in one place before. Those fruits, the spices, the crafts... it's overwhelming."

As they crossed over the bridge market, the group came upon a large open area where a crowd had gathered. In the center, a group of performers were putting on a show, their bodies twisting and bending in impossible ways as they danced to the beat of drums and flutes.

"Now, this I wanna see!" Aram exclaimed, exuding an enthusiasm that was hard to ignore.

"Another one of your artsy things?" Elam asked, a hint of amusement in his voice.

"Absolutely! You know I can't resist. The swirls of color, the depth of emotion... it's all so tangible," Aram defended with a wave of his hand as if painting the air itself. "None of that spiritual mumbo jumbo," he added with a grin. "Just pure, unadulterated expression."

Shem couldn't help but smile for his friend, who seems to get very chatty when art is involved.

They made their way closer to the performance, finding a spot where they could see clearly. The dancers moved with fluid grace, their colorful costumes shimmering in the late afternoon sun. One performer balanced precariously on a tall pole, swaying in time with the music as the crowd gasped and cheered.

Shem found himself captivated by the spectacle. He glanced at Aryana, noticing how her eyes followed the dancers' movements with intense focus. She actually seemed to be enjoying herself. "Have you seen anything like this before?" he asked.

"I have, back in the capital where I grew up. Every once in a while a troupe of skilled gymnasts would journey to Stone Crest to mesmerize the High Council and the King with their daring performances." Her eyes lit up with longing as she spoke. "There was a time when I yearned to be one of them. So elegant, so liberated." Her face fell as she pondered the long forgotten memory. "But who has the luxury of such dreams? Dancing, jewels, love - those are mere fantasies for children. Now, our nation is on the brink of war and it's time for us adults to prepare."

Shem felt a pang of sadness at Aryana's words. He wanted to say something comforting, but before he could, a commotion erupted near the edge of the crowd.

"Stop! Thief!" a girl's voice yelled.

Heads turned to see a young boy darting through the throng, clutching something to his chest. Hot on his heels was the cute girl from the jewelry cart, Sedee, red-faced and puffing as she gave chase.

Without hesitation, Aryana sprang into action. She moved with lightning speed, weaving through the startled onlookers. In a flash, she had caught up to the boy, grabbing him by the collar of his tattered shirt.

"Let me go!" the child cried, struggling against her grip.

Shem and the others pushed their way through the crowd to join Aryana. Sedee arrived moments later, breathless and flushed.

"Thank you," she panted, reaching for the small pouch the boy still clutched tightly. "He snatched this right off my table when I wasn't looking."

The boy, no more than ten years old, glared defiantly at them all with fiery determination burning in his eyes. His small frame shook with anger as he spat out his words. "I didn't do nothin' wrong!" he growled. "You rich folk got plenty. I'm just tryin' to protect my family!"

Aryana's grip on the boy's collar loosened slightly, her expression softening as she looked into his desperate eyes. "What does that mean? Protect your family?"

The boy nodded vigorously, tears welling in his eyes as he recounted his family's struggles. "My da left home, and my ma and sister are helpless. I didn't know what else to do."

"Helpless? What's that mean? From who?" interjected Elam, peering down at the young boy.

But the boy, wiping away his tears, looked at Elam like he was crazy. "From the coming invaders and Nepitim," he answered firmly.

Aryana knelt down to his level and gently pried the small pouch from his hand. "You mean the Nephilim," she corrected him. "And how did you come about this information?"

In that moment, the little boy's demeanor changed from hopeless to confident as a mischievous grin spread across his face. "Ask the son of Noah, he knows," he said smugly, with a deep guttural voice, before bursting into laughter. "We are coming for you Shem. You're ours!" With a quick bite to Aryana's hand, the boy wriggled free from her grasp and disappeared into the bustling crowd.

Handing the pouch to Sedee, Aryana expressed her concern. “That was troubling. How did that boy know you, Shem?”

"That was no boy," Shem said, his voice heavy with concern. "It was Azazel. Somehow, he discovered my location and must've used the boy as a vessel." He paused, feeling his stomach twist into knots as the realization hit him like a punch to the gut.

"But how?" Elam said, trying to make sense of it all. "How could he have found you here?"

Shem's mind raced with possibilities, each more unsettling than the last. “Maybe he followed me? Or maybe he's got spies... No, no that's absurd." His words tumbled out in a jumble of confusion and fear.

"Or perhaps..." His voice trailed off as another thought struck him. "Maybe it's not about 'how' but 'why'. Maybe my grandfather is right? Am I that important to their plans?" The questions hung in the air like an ominous cloud, threatening to unleash a storm of uncertainty and dread.

Shem watched as Sedee's eyes widened, a flicker of fear crossing her features. "I thought I was just chasing a petty thief," she admitted, her voice tinged with concern. She ran a hand through her hair and sighed heavily.

Aryana raised an eyebrow at that, looking between Shem and Sedee. "And now?" she prompted.

"Now," Sedee replied, glancing at Shem before turning her gaze back to Aryana, "I'm not sure what that was, or if I even want to know."

"That's probably the best," Shem said, trying to deflect what happened with a small smile.

Sedee nodded, catching the hint. "That's right," she said earnestly. She looked at them both for a moment before adding, "if I could just get my jewel, I'll be more than happy to get back to my cart. It's worth a year's worth of wages for my family."

"Thankfully we were able to get it back, then," Shem said with a chuckle, earning him an amused smirk from Aryana and even managing to draw out a reluctant grin from Sedee as he handed her the valuable item.

Nodding a thank you at Aryana, she paused in front of Shem and smiled sweetly. "Told you we'd meet again." She ran off, disappearing into the crowd.

As Shem gazed at her retreating form amidst the bustling crowd, time seemed to stand still. In that fleeting moment, all else faded away, leaving only the captivating memory of her mesmerizing blue eyes etched in his mind. *What a beautiful smile.*

Breaking Shem' from his trance, Aryana was urging them to make haste and inform the others of Azazel's threats.

"I don't like the sound of this," she stated firmly as she began leading them back towards the safety of their villa. "We need to warn the elders before it's too late."

As they walked, they could hear a sudden hush fall over the crowded festival grounds. Even the acrobats ceased their routines as a deep rumbling filled the air - the unmistakable thudding footsteps of an approaching giant, evoking frightening memories of the attack on Ararat.

"Too late," said Aram, drawing his sword from its scabbard.

The ground shook beneath their feet as the thunderous footsteps drew closer. Panic spread through the crowd like wildfire, people screaming and scattering in all directions. Shem's heart raced as he scanned the area, trying to locate the source of the commotion.

Suddenly, a massive figure emerged from behind a cluster of tall buildings. It was Anu: The Destroyer, easily three stories tall, with bulging muscles and a face contorted in rage—skull necklace hanging from his neck. In one meaty hand, he clutched a crude club fashioned from a tree trunk.

"Anu," Aryana hissed, her hand flying to the hilts of her dual swords. "We need to evacuate the civilians. Shem, Elam - help get people to safety. Aram and I will try to distract him." Looking to the sky, she gave a loud whistle, calling Alouette to battle.

Shem's instincts kicked in as he sprang into action, grabbing Elam's arm. "Come on!" he shouted, pulling his friend towards the panicking crowd. They began ushering people away from the approaching giant, directing them towards safer ground.

"This way!" Shem called out, gesturing frantically. "Get to higher ground, away from the market!"

Elam's voice rang out beside him, steady and authoritative despite the chaos. "Stay calm and move quickly! Head to the forest!"

As they worked, Shem caught glimpses of Aryana and Aram engaging the massive Nephilim. Aryana's swords flashed in the fading sunlight as she darted around Anu's legs, slashing at his ankles. Aram, looking small but determined, jabbed at the giant's knees with his own blade.

Shem's heart pounded as he guided terrified civilians to safety, all while keeping one eye on the battle unfolding behind him. Aryana and Aram looked like insects darting around the towering Nephilim's feet, their blades glinting as they struck at his massive legs.

Suddenly, a piercing screech filled the air. Shem looked up to see Alouette diving from the sky, talons extended. The great pterosaur raked her claws across Anu's face, causing the giant to roar in pain and anger.

"Look out!" Elam shouted, pulling Shem back just as Anu's club smashed into the ground where they had been standing moments before. The impact sent tremors through the earth, toppling nearby market stalls.

A cold wave of fear surged through Shem as he watched his friends being attacked by the monstrous creature before him. His heart raced with anger and determination as he drew his sword, Davar, from its scabbard on his back.

For the first time, the weapon glimmered with a faint light, pulsing with power as he pointed it at the towering foe. Shem's hand shook slightly, but he steadied his grip and prepared to face off against this terrifying giant.

Shem knew he had to act fast to help his friends. "Elam, keep evacuating people!" Shem shouted. "I'm going to help Aryana and Aram!"

Before Elam could protest, Shem was sprinting towards the battle. Alouette swooped down for another attack, distracting Anu momentarily. Shem seized the opportunity, darting between the giant's legs and slashing at the back of his knee.

Anu bellowed in pain and rage, whirling around to face this new threat. His massive club came crashing down, but Shem rolled out of the way just in time. The ground shook from the impact, nearly throwing Shem off balance.

"Shem, what are you doing?" Aryana yelled, her face a mix of anger and concern. "Get out of there!"

But Shem stood his ground, Davar held high. "No! I'm tired of being scared. We face this together!"

As Shem stood his ground, Davar began to pulse with an intense light. The sword's energy seemed to flow through him, filling him with a surge of courage and strength he'd never felt before.

Anu's eyes locked onto Shem, narrowing with recognition and hatred. "Son of Noah," the giant growled, his voice like rolling thunder. "That ancient relic will not save you!"

The Nephilim swung his massive club again, but this time Shem was ready. He dodged with newfound agility, then thrust Davar upward. The glowing blade sliced into Anu's forearm, severing his hand from his arm and drawing a roar of pain from the giant.

Aryana seized the moment, leaping onto Anu's back and driving her swords deep into his shoulder. Aram, following her lead, hacked at the giant's ankles with renewed vigor.

Anu howled in agony, his severed hand and club crashing to the ground with a thunderous impact. The giant staggered backward, nearly crushing several buildings as he flailed wildly.

"Now!" Aryana shouted, still clinging to Anu's back. "Hit him while he's off balance!"

Shem didn't hesitate. With Davar pulsing brightly in his hands, he charged forward. The sword seemed to guide his movements as he slashed at Anu's legs, opening deep gashes that oozed dark blood.

Alouette screeched overhead, diving once more to rake her talons across the Nephilim's face. Blinded and in pain, Anu stumbled, crashing to one knee.

With a fierce battle cry, Aram charged forward, determined to inflict more damage on his enemy. But Anu was not done yet. In one swift motion, he lashed out and grabbed Alouette as she frantically clawed at his face. With a powerful thrust, he flung her into the nearest building, leaving her limp body sprawled across the rubble.

The sight of her being tossed aside like a ragdoll caused Aryana to falter momentarily, loosening her grip on the giant's shoulders. Seizing the opportunity, Anu spun around and hurled her off his back, ripping her swords from his skin with ease.

Aram, caught off guard by the sudden turn of events, stumbled backwards in shock. Without hesitation, Anu bolted between the buildings and disappeared from sight.

"We can't let him get away!" shouted Shem, still in pursuit. "He must pay for what he's done."

But Shem came up short, as they were met with a heart-wrenching sight. Aryana knelt over Alouette's motionless body, her hand covered in blood as she desperately tried to heal her fallen pterosaur.

"Is she...?" Shem couldn't bring himself to finish the thought.

Aryana's quiet voice cut through the chaos. "She lives," she said, her tone tinged with sadness and determination. "But it will be some time before she can fight again."

Shem's chest heaved as he caught his breath, adrenaline still coursing through his veins. He looked around at the destruction Anu had left in his wake - toppled buildings, crushed market stalls, and terrified citizens peeking out from their hiding spots.

"We need to go after him," Shem said, gripping Davar tightly. The sword's glow had dimmed, but he could still feel its power thrumming through him.

Elam jogged up to join them, his face pale but determined. "The town guard is securing the perimeter. But Anu could return at any moment."

Aryana stood slowly, her hands and clothes stained with Alouette's blood. "We can't leave her," she said softly, gesturing to the injured pterosaur.

Aram nodded, sheathing his blade

"We'll need to split up," Shem said, his voice firm. "Aryana, you stay with Alouette. Get her to safety and tend to her wounds. Elam, coordinate with the town guard to fortify our defenses. Aram and I will track Anu." Shem's heart raced at the prospect of pursuing the giant, of finally ending his rampage. "We can't let him escape. Who knows how many more towns he could destroy?"

Aryana looked torn, her eyes darting between her injured companion and the direction Anu had fled. Finally, she sighed. "Be careful," she warned, locking eyes with Shem. "That sword may have given you strength, but Anu is still incredibly dangerous."

"We will," Shem promised, tightening his grip on Davar, hoping that it was enough.

Shem and Aram set off at a brisk pace, following the trail of destruction left by Anu. Overturned carts, crushed fences, and blood splattered on the cobblestone roads from his grievous injury.

"He's heading north through this side of town but working his way towards the river," Aram observed, his voice tight with tension. "If he crosses and gets to the forest, we'll lose him."

Shem nodded grimly, picking up speed. The weight of Davar on his back was comforting, a reminder of the power he'd wielded against Anu. *But why did Davar come to life now?*

As they raced through the winding streets, following the trail of destruction, Shem's mind whirled with questions. The sword's power had surprised him, but deep down, he suspected it was more than just the weapon. Something had awakened within him during the battle, a strength he never knew he possessed.

"Aram," Shem panted as they ran, "did you see what happened back there? With Davar, I mean."

Aram glanced at him, his expression a mix of awe and concern. "I saw you wield it like a warrior of old. But now is not the time for questions. Look!"

They rounded a corner and skidded to a halt. Before them lay a scene of utter devastation. Entire buildings had been flattened, creating a clear path through the densely packed houses. At the end of this makeshift road, the river gurgled, its waters-tinged orange in the fading light. And there, hunched by the bank, was the massive form of Anu. The giant was cradling his severed hand, dark blood seeping between his fingers.

Shem's heart pounded. This was their chance. He reached for Davar, but Aram's hand on his arm stopped him.

"Wait," Aram whispered, his eyes fixed on the wounded giant. "We need a plan. He's cornered and desperate - that makes him even more dangerous."

Shem nodded, forcing himself to take a deep breath. The urge to charge in was almost overwhelming, but Aram was right. They needed to be smart about this.

"Okay," Shem said quietly, scanning the area. "We need to keep him from crossing the river. If we can trap him here..."

Suddenly, Anu's massive head swiveled towards them. Even from this distance, Shem could see the rage burning in the giant's eyes. With a roar that shook the very ground, Anu lurched to his feet.

"Son of Noah!" the giant bellowed, his voice dripping with hatred. "Come to finish what you started?"

Shem's heart caught in his throat, but he steeled himself, drawing Davar from its sheath. The sword hummed to life, its faint glow intensifying as if sensing the impending battle.

"It's over, Anu!" Shem shouted back, his voice steadier than he felt. "You can't escape!" *Please, Lord Yahweh, be with me.*

The giant's laughter boomed across the devastated street.

Aram tensed beside Shem, his own weapon at the ready. "We need to flank him," he said, under his breath. "It's the only way it'll work."

Shem nodded, his mind racing. "I'll draw his attention. You circle around and—"

But before he could finish, Anu charged forward with shocking speed for his size. The ground trembled beneath his thunderous footsteps as he barreled towards them, his one good hand balled into a massive fist.

"Move!" Shem yelled, diving to the side. Aram rolled in the opposite direction just as Anu's fist smashed into the spot where they had been standing, leaving a crater in the cobblestones.

Shem scrambled to his feet, Davar glowing brightly in his hand. He slashed at Anu's leg as the giant passed, opening a fresh gash. Anu roared in pain and fury, whirling to face him.

"Aram, now!" Shem shouted, backing away to keep Anu's attention.

Seizing the opportunity, Aram darted behind the giant, slashing at the back of the giant's knees with his blade. Anu howled in pain, staggering forward. Shem seized the moment, charging in with Davar raised high.

The sword seemed to sing as it cut through the air, its glow intensifying as Shem brought it down on Anu's injured arm. The giant's scream of agony shook the very foundations of the nearby buildings.

"You cannot defeat me, boy!" Anu roared, his voice a mixture of pain and rage. "I am eternal! I am—"

His words were cut short as Aram's blade found its mark, embedding itself deep in the giant's calf. Anu's leg buckled, sending him crashing to one knee.

Shem felt a surge of power coursing through him, Davar pulsing with an otherworldly light. He charged forward, the sword raised high. "This ends now, Anu!" he shouted, his voice ringing with a confidence he didn't know he possessed.

Anu's eyes widened with a mix of fury and fear. The giant lashed out with his remaining hand, but Shem was faster. He ducked under the massive swing and thrust Davar upward with all his might.

The glowing blade sank deep into Anu's chest, piercing through his heart. The giant's roar of pain shook the earth, his massive body convulsing as he toppled backward.

Shem held on tight to Davar, pulling the sword from Anu's massive chest as he fell.

There was a tremendous splash as Anu's massive form crashed into the shallow river, sending a tidal wave of water surging over the banks. His enormous body, now lifeless, lay just under the surface of the clear water.

CHAPTER 13

Fleeting Haven

The streets surrounding the fallen giant were quickly filling up with a rising tide of town people, eager to catch a glimpse of the men who had brought it down. At first, their expressions were filled with genuine curiosity and relief at the monster's demise, but quickly they began to swarm like bees around a hive of honey.

Their voices rose to a deafening buzz as they pressed in closer and closer, causing Shem to feel suffocated and trapped within the crowd.

As his adrenaline began to wear off, he could feel his legs growing weak with fatigue. "We have to find a way out of here," he whispered urgently to Aram over the noise of the crowd. "Something doesn't feel right." Shem's senses were on high alert, his instincts telling him that danger lurked within the chaotic sea of bodies surrounding them.

"Yeah, they sound more angry than relieved," Aram said, as he slowly sheathed his sword.

Following his lead, Shem secured Davar as well and started pushing through the dense crowd. The clamor of voices and bodies pressing against each other made it difficult to move.

Amid the chaos, Shem's gaze caught the eyes of a woman in the crowd. She had tattoos etched on her face and a wicked grin on her lips. And she was staring directly at him.

"Over here!" The woman's voice cut through the noise, drawing attention to them. She pointed eagerly in Shem's direction. "It's the son of Noah. He murdered the poor creature in cold blood."

Another voice joined in from somewhere deeper in the throng, a man this time. "I saw it all! That giant only tried to warn us of invaders from the east, but he slew it with his magic sword!"

A chorus of accusations rose up from different parts of the crowd, all directed at Shem. "He's just like his father, trying to destroy Adamah!" Their words echoed and mixed together, creating an overwhelming din.

Shem's heart pounded in his chest as he pushed his way through the chaotic crowd. People were screaming and running in all directions, and he could feel a sense of panic rising within him. He quickly scanned the area for any signs of their pursuers, hoping to find a safe path for them to follow.

Shem followed closely behind Aram, his breaths coming out in short gasps as they weaved through the throngs of people.

As they approached a break in the crowd, Shem spotted a safe place and shouted, "Look, over there! Let's duck into that alley."

Aram nodded and they both sprinted towards the narrow passage between two buildings. They ran blindly through multiple alleys, twisting and turning until they finally came to a stop. Shem leaned against the nearest building, trying to catch his breath while Aram kept watch for their enemies.

"What just happened?" asked Aram, still on guard.

"I think it's the invaders." Shem was struggling to catch his breath. "I caught the eye of one of them...tattoos and all."

"Surely lots of people have tattoos."

"Not like those," said Shem with a wry smile. "All over her face."

Aram's eyes widened in understanding. "Oh. I see your point then. It looks like their strategy has changed."

"Yeah, now I'm their direct target...you know, as Son of Noah," said Shem, shaking his head in disbelief. *What changed?*

As they caught their breath, Aram scanned the alleyway nervously. "Okay, it seems like we've managed to escape for now." He motioned for Shem to follow him. "We need to find the others and come up with a plan."

"Maybe we should make our way back to the villa."

Aram led them to the next junction in the alley. "Not a bad idea. But we'll have to cross that market bridge, which means we'll be exposed."

"No," said Shem, coming to a stop. "I would be exposed. But you could slip out and find a cloak or something to disguise me. Bring it back and we can blend in with the crowd and make our way back to the villa." He put a reassuring hand on his friend's shoulder. "At the next intersection, we'll split up. You go towards the market, and I'll head towards the town's outer wall...towards the entrance. We'll meet there."

Aram looked hesitant but ultimately agreed, "I'm not sure I like it, but I don't see any other options." He paused for a moment, and then with a sigh, said, "Ok, let's go then." He turned and rushed to the next intersection.

Shem lingered for a moment, then moving in the opposite direction, he set off toward the town's outer wall. He traveled southward, torn between wanting to escape the chaos and seeking safety at the main entrance, praying that Elam was there waiting with the guards.

Exhaustion washed over Shem like a tidal wave as he came to a hiding spot between a building and the wall; he couldn't fight it anymore. His legs gave out beneath him, and he slumped against the cool stone wall.

But what troubled him most was the enemy's sudden change in tactics. Instead of Azazel trying to deceive or possess him, a crowd was directly threatening him. And these attacks felt more personal than those back in Ararat. *Was this part of their plan all along?*

The mere thought of Adi dying because of some sick plan by the enemy made Shem sick to his stomach. *Yahweh, couldn't there have been another way?*

This thought surprised him; he had never considered Yahweh's role in his life before, especially in times of danger. *Am I that desperate?*

After his conversation with Bartel at the inn, Shem had come to the realization that he never wanted to experience that evil in his head ever again. That fear of that, and the hope of seeing Adi again, had pushed him towards seeking protection from Yahweh. *Was this what changed?*

Shem knew he needed to talk to his great grandfather again—to seek some answers and guidance. He felt conflicted and confused, torn between his pain and his newfound faith in Yahweh. But two things were certain—he never wanted to feel that close to Azazel's grasp ever again, and he needed help.

A hand unexpectedly clasped his shoulder, jolting him from his thoughts. Shem sprang up, prepared to defend himself, but eased up when he recognized Aram's familiar face.

"Easy there," Aram said, slightly out of breath. He held out a dark cloak. "Here, put this on quickly."

Shem quickly donned the dark cloak, grateful for the added layer of disguise it provided. As he adjusted the fabric around him, he asked Aram, "What's it look like out there? Did anyone follow you?"

Aram peered cautiously around the corner before responding, "I don't think so, but we should move fast. The crowd's getting restless."

Nodding in understanding, Shem whispered, "Now for the real trick...to make our way through the market bridge unnoticed."

As they made their way through the crowded streets, Shem couldn't shake off the nagging feeling of being watched. He whispered to Aram, "Do you feel it too? Like eyes are following our every move?"

Aram nodded solemnly, his expression mirroring Shem's unease. "It's probably just the large crowd. Stay alert and keep moving," he replied in a low voice.

They weaved through the maze of alleys and groups of people, trying to avoid drawing attention to themselves, finally reaching the market bridge.

Shem felt a surge of relief wash over him, when just as they were about to cross, a familiar voice called out from behind them.

"Shem! Aram! What are you doing here?" Elam's voice cut through the din of the market, causing heads to turn in their direction.

Shem turned around to see Elam striding towards them with a group of guards in tow. With a sense of gratitude and relief, he replied, "Elam, we need your help. The crowd has turned on me, and we're trying to make our way back to the villa safely."

Elam looked confused but gestured for them to follow him. As they crossed the market bridge under his watchful eye, Shem couldn't help but feel a glimmer of hope amidst the chaos that surrounded them.

As they merged into the stream of people heading over the bridge, Shem kept his head down, trying to blend in with the crowd as they made their way across. The noise of the mob still echoed in the distance, but it seemed to be moving away from them.

"Almost there," Aram whispered, guiding Shem with a gentle hand on his back.

As they neared the end of the bridge, a group of guards stood at the far end, carefully inspecting everyone who passed.

"Just keep walking," Elam said, back over his shoulder. "The guards are friendly."

Shem's heart pounded as they approached the guards. He could feel sweat beading on his forehead beneath the hood. Just a few more steps...

"There he is!" a woman's shrill voice pierced the air. "The Son of Noah!"

Shem froze in place— muscles tense and ready to spring into action. A quick glance at Aram confirmed what they both already knew - they couldn't run from this. The crowd on the bridge roared like a raging river, pushing Shem and Aram into Elam and the unyielding guards. In the chaos and confusion, Shem felt Aram's hand grip his arm tightly, grounding him in the chaos.

Shem's heart pounded with a surging rush of hope as he spotted Bartel coming towards them with another group of guards. Acting in unison, they surged past the boys, their brute force pushing back the seething mass of people.

Shem, Aram and Elam stumbled forward as the guards created a barrier between them and the angry mob. Bartel rushed over; his face etched with concern.

"Are you alright?" he asked, gripping Shem's shoulder.

Shem nodded, still catching his breath. "We're fine. But what's happening? Why did they turn on me?"

Bartel's expression darkened. "It seems our enemies have been busy spreading lies. They've convinced many that you're a threat to the town."

Halvin joined them, his sword drawn. "We need to get you both out of here. The villa isn't safe anymore."

As they spoke, the crowd's shouts grew louder, more insistent. The guards were struggling to hold them back.

"This way," Bartel urged, gesturing towards a narrow path through the large trees. "We have a safe house prepared."

Shem hesitated, glancing back at the roaring crowd. "But what about the people? These tattooed troublemakers are going to destroy the city."

Halvin stepped forward, his usually calm demeanor tinged with urgency. "We don't have a choice right now, Shem. We need to regroup and figure out what's really going on."

Reluctantly, Shem nodded and followed the others down the hidden path. The dense foliage quickly swallowed them up, muffling the angry shouts behind them. As they hurried along, Shem's mind raced with questions.

"How did this happen so quickly?" he asked, ducking under a low-hanging branch. "One minute we were heroes, the next they wanted our heads."

The grave tone of Bartel's voice matched his expression. "It seems that the invaders have infiltrated every corner. They've been sowing seeds of doubt for weeks. The guards have been keeping an eye on them, especially the ones with tattoos." Lowering his voice, he added, "But the real question is...where is Nin during all this?"

Shem shook his head. "I assumed he was with you. He's not at the safe house?"

Bartel's tense demeanor gave away his answer. "We haven't seen him since he went on his...errand." He made air quotes with his fingers.

As they walked side by side up a wooden ramp that seemed to have grown organically from the massive tree it was connected to, Shem was concerned about Bartel's implication. "You think he's involved?"

Shem's question hung in the air as they continued along the winding path, the dense foliage still concealing them from prying eyes. Bartel's gaze was troubled, his brow furrowed in thought.

"I can't say for certain," Bartel finally replied, his voice heavy with uncertainty. "Nin is a man of many secrets, even to us. It's possible that he's playing a deeper game than any of us realize."

Aram, who had been walking silently alongside Shem, spoke up for the first time since their escape from the angry mob. "But why would Nin betray us? We've always been loyal to him, and he's been part of Shem's family forever."

Bartel gave them a sidelong glance. "All I know is I've never trusted him. Not from the moment your father brought him on board. I used to work on the ranch too, you know."

Shem was surprised by this revelation; he had always known Bartel as a friend of his father's, especially since he was promised to Adi. "I didn't know that. I thought you two were just childhood friends or something, not that you were employed by my family."

"We are friends," Bartel paused momentarily, his face softening as he continued. "But some time before you were born, I met my...wife...Rania. We wanted to start a family and create our own life away from the ranch. So when old man Burchard was selling his livery, we jumped at the opportunity to purchase it and take over the ranch's orchard."

"Our farm grew apples too?" Shem's curiosity was piqued.

Bartel let out a hearty laugh. "Yeah, your father gave it to us as a wedding gift. And with the acquisition of Burchard's neighboring property, we were able to open a storefront in town and even trade with other nearby farms."

Shem found this glimpse into Adi's family history fascinating and surprisingly less painful than expected. "That sounds perfect. But what about Nin?"

"Cutting right to the chase, huh?" Bartel's expression turned serious. "Because he came out of nowhere. I know it sounds petty, but he came without any references. No one had ever heard of him." He clenched his fist in frustration. "And we don't even know what he believes."

Shem was confused. "Does that even matter?" he asked, pausing before adding, "in fact, I'm not sure I knew what I believed until recently."

Bartel didn't miss Shem's comment. "So you finally understand that knowing about Yahweh isn't the same as truly believing," he said with a hint of pride, draping an arm around Shem's shoulders as they continued up the seemingly never-ending ramp of the tree.

"I didn't realize it was a problem," Shem admitted.

"It's not just his beliefs," Bartel clarified, pointing to a junction that led them onto a bridge connecting to another tree ramp. "It's the timing of it all. He showed up just at the right moment, was given the highest position of trust on the ranch and has been primarily responsible for your training...if you really think about it. It all seemed too convenient to me. But...Noah trusts him, and since I trust Noah, I had to accept him...do you understand?"

Shem murmured that he did, unsure of what to do with this new information. He was glad to have learned more about Adi's family history but hated the thought of there being tension between two men he respected and relied on for his safety. Was Bartel right to be suspicious or was there simply a misunderstanding? *Where was he, though?*

The group reached a wide platform perched high in the canopy of trees. It stretched out like a giant wooden road, connecting various structures and buildings that were integrated into the trunks and branches of the trees. People could be seen traversing the platform, moving gracefully between the structures with ease. The buildings themselves seemed to blend seamlessly with the forest, as if they had grown from the trees themselves. It was a stunning sight; unlike anything they had ever seen before. The air was filled with the sounds of chatter and laughter, as well as the occasional trill of various birds. It was like stepping into a whole new world suspended above the ground below.

Bartel strode confidently onto the platform, his steps purposeful and determined. "Welcome to the old city of Center Grove," he announced as they reached their destination.

Shem's eyes widened in disbelief. "But what about the bustling shops and market bridge we saw on the ground?" he asked, still trying to take in the sight before him.

"Up here, in the forest canopy, reside generations of families who founded and built this tree city," Bartel explained with a furrowed brow. "As word of its beauty spread, the city expanded outwards, into the surrounding countryside. Unfortunately, with outside influences came a focus on commerce and now there are two cities within one - with riots happening down there that would never happen here. This part of the city remains loyal to the old ways."

Shem was beginning to realize just how sheltered his life had been. "How do you know all of this history? I've only heard stories about this place."

Bartel's expression softened. "I used to travel here often when I was your father's Ranch Foreman."

Shem nodded, understanding now what Nin may be up to - perhaps ranch business. He couldn't fathom why anyone would think Nin couldn't be trusted after spending his entire life learning from him and being under his tutelage. Bartel must be mistaken.

As if on cue, they approached a long walkway that led to a large structure at its end. Leaning against the rail was none other than Nin himself.

Shem's worries melted away as he saw Nin safe and sound. "Nin! We were worried something had happened to you." He glanced at Bartel, for any sign of concern or suspicion.

Ignoring Nin completely, Bartel walked past him and entered the building without a word.

The rest of the party followed suit, giving Nin a brief nod as they passed. Shem waited for them to pass before addressing Nin. "You worried us, Nin. That crowd in town was out of control."

Nin simply smiled and said, "You worry too much." He tilted his wide-brimmed hat back on his head and continued, "Besides, who could ever hurt me?"

Shem thought of the demons and giants they had encountered on their journey and shuddered. "I don't know, Nin, I think there are quite a few things that could pose a threat to you." He couldn't take danger lightly anymore after everything he had seen.

Nin's smile faded slightly at Shem's serious tone. "I told you I had errands to run." He paused before adding, "But if you must know, I transferred all of our mounts to the East Gate. Remember, they cannot travel through the city - so any travelers heading East must take their larger transportation across the Southern causeway and stable their animals at the East Gate." Then he flashed a mischievous grin. "If I knew you were going to start trouble, though, I would have taken you with me."

Shem couldn't help but laugh at Nin's words. "Trouble? No trouble."

Nin folded his arms in mock smugness. "It sounds like you actually started a war."

Shem joined in Nin's laughter before Nin gestured for him to follow. "Come on, let's go inside with the others."

In the generous expanse of the room, the companions found a fleeting haven from the perils lurking beyond. The walls, adorned with elaborate etchings and vibrant murals, wove a tapestry of opulence that contrasted starkly against the untamed world outside.

As Shem took in this sight, a tension he hadn't realized he'd been carrying uncoiled within him. Lud and Eloise were already present, nestled comfortably around an enormous table sculpted by skilled hands in the dining area. The air was heavy with the soothing scent of freshly brewed tea that they cradled in their palms.

With Aram, Elam and Halvin joining them, they huddled together at the table like a flock seeking warmth on a cool night. Their voices reverberated through the cavernous living space, punctuating its silence with snippets of conversation.

On one side of this sanctuary, Bartel and Raphael sprawled languidly in plush individual chairs while across from them, Shem, breathing a sigh of relief, sank into an invitingly long couch before a grand window that framed an awe-inspiring panorama of their treetop city.

Tiny lamps perched on side tables scattered about the room spilled their warm light onto every surface; painting everything in hues of comfort and calmness. Nin stood nonchalantly by the entrance door - his posture casual yet radiating an ever-vigilant readiness for any unforeseen danger.

As they shared stories and experiences of their day, Shem felt his heart brimming with gratitude for this long-needed interlude of tranquility amidst their otherwise turbulent day.

Lud, his voice carrying across the room, addressed Shem with a concerned tone. "What happened to Lady Aryana? And Alouette?"

Aram, his brow furrowed with worry, answered first. “They should be fine,” he reassured. “They were with the town guard when we last saw them.

Elam just shook his head, the sorrow written all over his face.

Shem’s mood soured at the thought of her ordeal. “Yeah, poor Alouette was injured in the battle against Anu.” The weight of the situation settled heavily on his shoulders as he spoke the words aloud. “She had to stay behind with her when we went after the giant.” The gravity of her predicament hung heavily in the air.

“Ever since we left home, it’s been one devastating thing after another. I didn’t sign up for this,” said Lud, uncharacteristically melancholy.

Elam, who had been silent until now, shared a quiet observation. "Our journey has been filled with unexpected twists and turns, but we accomplished what we set out to do...we got justice for Ararat."

Bartel leaned forward, his face etched with concern. “We were told that you wielded your father’s magic sword of power.”

Raphael sat up in his chair, as if that held great interest to him.

“Indeed,” Halvin agreed, his hand resting on the hilt of his sword. “It seems that Shem, here, fought like a hero of old. Like a true Eden Knight.”

Lud cleared his throat with a short laugh, drawing everyone’s attention. “So...we’re still talking about Shem?”

They all turned to look at Shem.

Shem felt his cheeks flush as all eyes turned to him. He shifted uncomfortably on the couch, suddenly feeling very small under their scrutiny.

"It wasn't just me," he said quickly, gesturing to Aram. "We all fought. And like I said, without Alouette's help..."

"But you were the one who struck the final blow," Aram interjected, his voice filled with admiration. "With that glowing sword. I've never heard of anything like it."

Shem pulled the sword from its sheath, laying it across his lap. In the dim light of the room, it looked ordinary - just an artist's rendition of a wooden sword. Nothing special.

"I don't understand it myself," Shem admitted, running his fingers along the beautiful Gopher blade, tracing his fingers along the vines that crept along the fuller. "One minute it was just a regular sword, the next it was glowing and...I felt this surge of power. Like I knew exactly what to do."

Nin stepped closer; his eyes fixed on the sword. "May I?" he asked, holding out his hand.

Shem hesitated for just a moment before handing it over. Nin examined the blade carefully, turning it over in his hands.

"Extraordinary," he murmured. "so...this is one of the fabled weapons."

Bartel leaned forward, his suspicion evident. "And where exactly did you hear of this weapon, Nin?"

Nin ignored the question, his focus still on the sword. "This was your father's blade," he said, handing it back to Shem. "Only he could possibly understand what kind of power it holds."

Then, fixing a cold, unflinching glare on Bartel, he hissed through gritted teeth, "Don't mince words. Spit it out if you have something to say." The words dripped with a venomous threat, daring Bartel to speak any further insinuations.

A tense silence fell over the room as Nin and Bartel glared at each other. Shem's eyes darted nervously between the two men, unsure of how to diffuse the situation.

Halvin cleared his throat loudly. "Perhaps we should focus on more pressing matters," he suggested, his tone carefully neutral. "Like what our next move should be."

Elam nodded in agreement. "Halvin's right. We need a plan. The town is in chaos, the guard overwhelmed, and our enemies are clearly growing bolder."

Shem gratefully seized the change of subject. "Is there a way we can help them?"

"It's too dangerous to go back down there right now," Halvin said, shaking his head. "We'd be walking right into a trap."

"But we can't just sit here and wait," Shem urged, his voice trembling with anticipation.

Suddenly, a loud thud shook the door, causing everyone to jump in terror. They knew it was only a matter of time before their pursuers found them.

CHAPTER 14

The Long Shadow

The group froze, eyes locked on the door. Nin moved silently, pressing himself against the wall beside it. He motioned for everyone else to stay quiet.

Another thud rattled the door, followed by muffled voices outside. Shem's hand tightened around the hilt of his sword, his heart pounding.

Suddenly, a familiar voice called out. "Shem? Aram? Are you in there?"

Relief washed over Shem as he recognized Aryana's voice. He started to move towards the door, but Halvin held up a hand, signaling him to wait.

"Aryana?" Halvin called back. "Is that you? How did you find us?"

"Yes!" came the reply, the frustration apparent in her voice. "Now, Halvin, let me in or.... will you just let me in?"

Halvin smiled awkwardly at Shem. "Yeah...it's her."

Nin nodded to Halvin, who cautiously opened the door. Aryana stumbled in, looking disheveled and out of breath.

Halvin attempted to quickly shut the door behind her, but was stopped by someone's foot. Before he could react, another man stepped into the room, with a pleasant look on his face.

"Grandpa," said Shem, rushing to the middle aged, bearded man, and catching him in an embrace. He couldn't believe he was looking into the face of his beloved grandfather, Lamech. "I can't believe you're here! It's been years!"

"Thank Yahweh," Aryana panted, leaning against the wall. "We barely made it out of there." Gesturing towards the newcomer, she said, "He found me with the guards and told me where to find you." She sank into a nearby chair, her usually immaculate appearance marred by dirt, sweat and blood. "The situation in town is worse than we thought," she said grimly. "The lies have spread like wildfire. People are calling for Shem's arrest - or worse."

Shem felt his stomach drop. "But why? What are they saying about me?" He released his grip on Lamech.

Aryana's face darkened. "They're claiming you're in league with the demons. That you orchestrated the attack on the town to seize power for yourself."

"That's ridiculous!" Elam exclaimed.

"Of course it's ridiculous," Lamech said, his deep voice carrying a calming authority. "But fear makes people believe the unbelievable." He turned to Shem, placing a strong hand on his grandson's shoulder. "We'll set things right, son. But first, we need to understand what we're up against."

Shem nodded, grateful for his grandfather's steadying presence. "But how did you know where to find us, Grandpa?" he asked.

Lamech's eyes reflected his smile. "I may be old, but I still have a few tricks up my sleeve. Your great-grand father and I have been tracking these invaders for some time. When we heard about the trouble brewing, we knew it was time." He laughed to himself, and added, "As far as finding you...that was easy. You're standing in my house."

Shem's eyes widened in surprise. "Your house? But I thought this was just a safe house...Oh...is Grandma Betenos here, too?"

Lamech chuckled, his eyes crinkling at the corners. "It's actually a vacation home, but it's also been in our family since I built it. Your father and his siblings used to play here as children. And your grandmother is safely home, back at the farm, up the northern road towards Northbridge."

The revelation sent a wave of warmth through Shem. Somehow, even in this unfamiliar place, he felt a connection to his roots, to his family's history. "What brought you all the way here, then?"

"Methuselah sent word of strange people showing up in Center Grove, and asked if I could lend a hand. So I brought a group of my own guard to help with the investigation."

Nin stepped forward, his expression serious. "Now that you investigated, what can you tell us about these invaders?"

Lamech's face grew grave. "They're more organized than we initially thought. They've been infiltrating towns and cities across the land, sowing discord and turning people against each other. Their ultimate goal seems to be to weaken our defenses and pave the way for a full-scale invasion."

Shem felt a chill run down his spine. "But why? What do they want?"

"Who knows," Lamech said simply. "Maybe power? Maybe they just want what's not theirs, or maybe they desire to ultimately snuff out any last followers of Yahweh. We've dealt with this kind of thing forever."

Bartel paced back and forth, his brow furrowed in deep thought. "Yeah, we've faced these invaders in Ararat as well," he said, his brow furrowed. "But this time it feels different—like they were expecting us. And, this feels coordinated."

"I agree, it was definitely organized, that's why we think this is a prelude to something larger," added Lamech, running a hand through his hair in frustration. "We're just not sure who or what we're up against, and who is orchestrating it all. The only dominant marking that stands out among all the other tattoos is an eye." He paused, lost in thought before adding, "It seems like they belong to a specific cult. But which one? Who do they serve?"

Shem felt a heavy sense of dread wash over him as he realized that he was at the center of it all. *Azazel.* "It's the only thing that makes sense," he muttered under his breath.

"What was that?" asked Nin, his eyes narrowing in suspicion.

"Oh...nothing," Shem replied sheepishly, knowing that he needed to reveal the truth to them. "When I...the four of us," gesturing to the others who were with him earlier, "we were in the market and stopped a little boy from stealing from a merchant. Only...it wasn't a boy...well...it was a boy, but he was possessed by...Azazel."

Bartel gripped Shem's shoulders in shock. "Again? Why didn't you tell us that sooner?"

"A lot has happened since then," Shem admitted with embarrassment. "I mean, we fought a giant. Besides...Azazel didn't try to...recruit? Is that the right word?"

"Possess," said Bartel, releasing his hold on Shem and resumed pacing..

"Right...he didn't try to possess me this time. He just threatened me. Said that he found me and that I would be theirs...whatever that means," Shem explained, still confused by Azazel's new tactics. "Then Anu attacked." He raised his hands in a helpless shrug, unsure of the connection.

Bartel abruptly stopped pacing and locked eyes with Shem. "That's because you surrendered to Yahweh after the incident at the inn," he said with a proud smile at his own revelation. "Remember what I told you? A demon cannot possess someone who belongs to Yahweh."

"That means," added Nin, his voice low and grave, "the only course of action they have is to capture or kill you."

A troubled expression flickered across Lamech's face. "Okay...that may be their plan, but it still doesn't explain how they knew you were here. Or even at the inn. Someone must have contact with Azazel."

"Well, he's a demon," Elam chimed in. "Doesn't he just... know?"

Lamech let out a laugh before shaking his head. "No, son, it doesn't work like that. Despite what some believe, demons are not gods. They can't be everywhere at once. Only Yahweh can do that." His expression turned serious as he continued, "Which means someone has been tracking you, young Shem."

Shem felt his heart skip a beat at his grandfather's words. The idea that someone had been watching him, reporting his movements to Azazel, was deeply unsettling. He glanced around the room, suddenly suspicious of everyone present.

"But who?" Lud asked, voicing the question on everyone's mind. "Who would betray us like that?"

"We're all dead," whispered Eloise, grabbing onto Lud's arm.

"It could be anyone," Halvin said grimly. "Someone could've followed us from Ararat."

Shem's mind raced, trying to connect the dots from the chaos of the past few weeks. *Who would've betrayed us?*

Bartel, his eyes blazing with accusation, stopped in front of Nin and declared, "We all know who has betrayed us."

"We do?" Lud's confusion was evident on his face.

Nin remained unreadable, but met Bartel's gaze head on. "What's on your mind, storyteller?"

Bartel's voice rose as he shouted at Nin, his fist clenched and ready to strike. "What did you call me?"

Raphael, who had been sitting calmly until now, leapt from his seat and positioned himself between the two men. Shem braced himself for a potentially violent confrontation, uncertain of which side he would even be on - both of these men were like fathers to him.

"Enough!" Lamech's voice boomed through the room as he forcefully pulled Raphael out of harm's way. Stepping in between Bartel and Nin, he looked at each man sternly. "This petty bickering is playing right into our enemy's hands. We must rise above base desires."

The tension in the room was palpable as Lamech stood between Bartel and Nin, his stern gaze silencing their argument. Shem felt torn, his loyalties divided between the two men who had been such important figures in his life.

Bartel took a deep breath, visibly trying to calm himself. "You're right," he admitted grudgingly. "I apologize for losing my temper."

Nin nodded stiffly, his face unreadable. "As do I," he said, though his tone held little warmth.

Lamech looked between them, his expression grave. "We cannot afford to be divided. Our enemies are counting on that."

"So what do we do now?" Aram's question hung in the air as everyone looked to Lamech expectantly.

The older man stroked his beard thoughtfully before speaking.

"We need to gather more information," Lamech said decisively. "We can't act until we know more about what we're up against and who's behind it all."

"I agree," Elam nodded. "But how do we do that without putting ourselves at risk? The town is in chaos, and they're looking for Shem."

Shem's heart sank as he spoke the words, knowing that it would bring pain to those he loved. "I think I need to leave Center Grove," he said, feeling a lump in his throat. His great-grandfather Methuselah had been praying for a solution to their problems, but Shem couldn't shake off the feeling of guilt for what he was about to do. Turning to Bartel, his trusted friend and advisor, he asked in desperation, "Is this really what seeking Yahweh's will means? Causing harm and pain to others?"

Bartel's expression softened as he looked at Shem. "Sometimes, yes," he said gently. "Following His will isn't always easy or painless. But it's always right."

Lamech placed a comforting hand on Shem's shoulder. "Your heart is in the right place, my boy. But leaving alone would be too dangerous. We need to think this through."

Shem's hands shook as he voiced his concerns. "But staying puts everyone in danger," he said, sick with worry.

Bartel stepped closer to Shem, placing a reassuring hand on his shoulder. "Listen...we'll figure it out. But, no matter what happens, you won't be in this alone."

Nin chimed in in agreement, causing Bartel to roll his eyes. "Besides...your father would kill us if we let anything happen to you," he said with a wink of his eye.

Lud couldn't help but laugh at Nin's statement. "Um, I guess you came close to royally screwing that up," he said, with his familiar grin, earning sharp glances from both Nin and Bartel. "What?"

Halvin spoke up with a suggestion. "What if we divided up? Someone could take Shem back to Ararat, and the rest could stay and help the guard hunt down these invaders. Maybe even uncover who is behind it all. I volunteer to do the hunting. Ararat, or Eden for that matter, won't be safe until they're all taken out for good."

The group fell silent, considering Halvin's idea. Lamech turned to face him, looking thoughtful. "The idea has some merit, but it begs the question of who will go with Shem? And is it wise to divide your party?" He glanced around at the group assembled before him before nodding to himself. "Let's discuss this further in the morning. For now, let's rest and replenish ourselves." He gestured towards the stocked pantries and comfortable rooms around them. "We'll come up with a plan first thing in the morning."

As he moved towards the door, Lamech pulled Shem aside for a private conversation. He gently placed his hand on the back of Shem's neck, drawing him closer. "Listen...if you have truly surrendered to Yahweh as your friends say, then start praying," he said in a soft tone.

Shem's brow furrowed in uncertainty. "But how will I know if he answers?" he asked, unsure of the deeper life of a believer.

Lamech offered him a kind smile. "That's the thing. We don't always know His plans for sure," he said, pointing up towards the heavens. "But...if you pray to Him, Yahweh will guide your path...even as you make your own plans." With a nod goodbye, Lamech left the cozy house and stepped out into the cool night air, leaving Shem to contemplate his words.

As the evening wore on, Shem and his friends huddled together in the snug kitchen, their laughter echoing off the stone walls. The aroma of a rich stew filled the air, warming them from within as they savored every bite. Afterwards, they retreated to the comfort of the dining room, where a roaring fire bathed everything in a soft amber glow.

Lud was idly tracing patterns on the worn wooden table with his finger when he finally broke their comfortable silence. "I don't know," he said slowly, looking up to meet each of their gazes in turn. His voice was quiet but firm, carrying an unspoken weight that demanded attention.

"I think it's time for me to head back home." He sighed heavily, his shoulders sagging as if he bore the weight of the world. "I've seen enough to know... this isn't fun anymore."

"Lud, are you sure?" Aram asked gently, leaning forward to place a comforting hand on his brother's arm. "What about our plan to search for dad?"

Lud shook his head, a look of frustration overtaking his sad smile. "No...that was always *your* plan. He ran out on us. You were just too young to remember what that did to mom."

Shem, feeling Lud's tension rise, interjected. "Where do you think he went, Aram?"

Aram leaned back in his chair, a faraway look in his eyes as he considered Shem's question. "I'm not sure exactly," he admitted, his voice tinged with a mix of excitement and uncertainty. "But I have this feeling that he's out there somewhere, waiting to be found."

He stood up and began to pace, his hands gesturing animatedly as he spoke. "Think about it - there are so many places he could be. Maybe he's in one of the great cities, like Enoch or Asshur, working as an engineer on some great invention. Or perhaps he went into hiding off into the wilderness and needs help."

Aram's eyes shone with a fierce determination as he continued. "Imagine if we found him, Lud. We could bring him home, reunite our family. And think of all the knowledge and wisdom he could share with us! The things he must have seen and experienced..."

Lud shook his head, a hint of exasperation creeping into his voice. "I understand your desire to find him. But we have to be realistic." He fixed his brother with a stern gaze, his voice firm but not unkind. "It's been years, Aram. If he wanted to be found, don't you think he would have sent word by now? Some sign that he was still out there, thinking of us?"

He leaned forward, his elbows resting on the table as he continued. "I know it's hard to accept, but we have to face the possibility that he left because he wanted to. That maybe he found a new life somewhere else, and didn't want to be a part of ours anymore."

Shem's heart ached as he watched the painful exchange between Aram and Lud. He could see the yearning in Aram's eyes, the desperate hope that clung to the idea of finding their long-lost father. But he could also understand Lud's hardheadedness, the weariness that came from years of unanswered questions and dashed expectations.

Elam, who had been quietly listening, spoke up. "I know how you feel, Lud," he said softly, his voice carrying a note of empathy. "I feel it too." His eyes grew distant as he spoke, his voice tinged with a mix of longing and resolve. "I understand the desire to go back, to be with family and protect what's yours. There's a part of me that feels the same pull."

He leaned forward, pulling his long curly hair out of his face as he continued. "My father had been hinting that it's time for me to start learning more about the family business - law enforcement, keeping the peace. He says it's the best way for me to defend Ararat in the future, to keep our people safe. He wasn't happy that I left to help my friends...as you could imagine."

Halvin's eyes flashed with intensity as he joined the conversation, his voice low and urgent. "I understand the desire to protect your home, Elam. But the only way to truly defend Ararat, to keep our people safe, is to hunt down these invaders at their source. We have to uncover the evil behind them, root it out before it spreads further."

He stood up, his tall frame casting a long shadow in the flickering firelight. "And think about it, Lud, the best way to care for your mom is to make sure these evil men never return!" Then, looking at Aram, he added, "Once we end this threat, then maybe we can investigate your father."

Shem sat quietly, absorbing the impassioned words of his friends as they debated their next steps. The flickering firelight cast dancing shadows on the walls, mirroring the turmoil he felt within.

On one hand, he understood Lud's weariness and longing for home. The events of the past weeks had taken a heavy toll on all of them, physically and emotionally. The idea of returning to the comfort and familiarity of their families, of stepping back from this dangerous quest—held an undeniable appeal.

And yet, as he listened to Halvin and Elam speak of their duty, their responsibility to protect their people and uncover the truth behind the invaders, Shem felt a stirring in his heart. He glanced down at the sword resting at his side - Davar, the Sword of the Spirit. Its weight was a constant reminder of the power he had been entrusted with, the calling that had been placed upon him.

As the fire crackled and popped, casting a warm glow over the room, Shem's mind drifted back to the moment he had first grasped Davar's hilt, that fateful day in his living room. *Lord, what should I do?*

As the night wore on, they slowly made their way to their respective rooms, each one uniquely built into the large tree that the house was nestled within. Surrounding the house was a vast deck, with stairs leading to other rooms as if it had been continuously expanded upon over time by Lamech and his growing family.

Bartel, Halvin, and Raphael found comfortable rooms on the upper level, while Elam, Aram, and Lud settled into a spacious room below the main house. Eloise and Aryana shared a charming room on the main floor near the kitchen.

Shem noticed that, earlier, Nin had separated himself from the group and was sitting out on the deck, lost in thought. Once everyone else had retired for the night, Shem joined him, drawn to Nin's quiet contemplation amidst the peaceful surroundings

As he stepped onto the large deck under the trees in Center Grove, an enchanting scene unfolded. The crystal lighting, carefully scattered amongst the trees, gave the illusion of stars twinkling above and casting a soft glow under the dense canopy.

Shem leaned against the wooden railing; his eyes wide with wonder as he took in the sight. Countless fireflies danced around him, their tiny lights creating a magical ambiance that was almost as bright as the crystals themselves. A symphony of sounds filled the air - the chirping of crickets and croaking of tree frogs blended together in a soothing melody.

Nin sat nearby, reclining in a plush chair with his feet propped up on the railing. His hat was pulled low over his eyes.

Alone now with Nin, Shem felt the weight of unanswered questions pressing on his mind. He could no longer ignore the tension that seemed to exist between Nin and Bartel. "Nin...why doesn't Bartel like you?"

Nin's posture remained unchanged as he responded, "He doesn't? I never knew that..."

Frustration seeped into Shem's voice as he probed further, determined to get some answers. "I need to know."

Amused by Shem's persistence, Nin lifted the brim of his hat so he could meet Shem's gaze. "You *need* to?"

Shem was starting to feel like a pawn in some unknown game. "Stop dodging me, Nin."

Nin couldn't help but smile at Shem's frustration. "I'm sure he already told you. He likes to tell stories."

"Bartel's no liar," Shem retorted, his frustration now bubbling to the surface. "Does he have a reason not to trust you?"

A hint of sadness crept into Nin's expression before it was quickly masked again. "He's a Sethite. They don't need a reason to distrust people of other faiths." He paused, deep in thought for a moment before continuing, "Funny thing is, he never even asked what I believe. And I wouldn't have told him even if he did. A man's religion should be personal and private."

Shem couldn't help but feel the sting of Nin's words as the surrounding wildlife seemed to echo them back at him. "Do you feel the same about me now that I'm one?"

Nin shook his head, pulling his hat back down over his eyes. “If you’ve known me your whole life, then you shouldn’t need someone else’s words to form your opinion of me.”

Shem felt a twinge of guilt for doubting Nin’s trust and loyalty. “I’ve known you my whole life, and yet I know nothing about your past. In fact...nobody does, as far as I can tell.”

Nin’s eyes narrowed slightly at Shem’s words. “And what makes Bartel so trustworthy? You don’t know his history either.”

“Well...he told me something at least,” Shem countered, feeling defensive. “All you’ve done is hurl insults at me. That hurts.”

But Nin remained unfazed, his voice taking on a stern tone. “Life is full of pain, boy. I didn’t train you to be weak.”

As tears threatened to spill from his eyes, Shem turned and walked away, no longer able to bear the weight of their conversation. *Is he right? Am I really this disloyal and untrusting? Maybe I should’ve just kept it to myself?* All he knew was that tomorrow was a big day, and he needed some rest before facing it.

Shem stood in front of the empty bed, feeling utterly defeated and consumed by guilt. He didn’t like how the conversation with Nin went, and the decision tomorrow hung heavy on his heart, leaving him troubled and restless. Doubts plagued his mind - *did I truly surrender to Yahweh? Would He forgive my doubt? Would my prayers even be heard?*

His heart felt heavy as he knelt in front of the bed, mimicking the prayers he had seen his father do countless times before. *Oh great Creator, all-knowing Lord*, he began, tears streaming down his face, *I come before you...*

PART THREE
Forgotten

"Then the Lord saw that the wickedness of man was great in Adamah, and that every intent of the thoughts of his heart was only evil continually..."

-***The First Book of Moses:***

Genesis: Chapter 6, Verse 5

Chapter 15

Some Wild Adventure

Shem awoke from a restless night and found himself with his companions atop the tallest spire in Center Grove. From their vantage point, they could see Eden spread out before them in all its breathtaking beauty.

Earlier, just before dawn, an aide from the council arrived to lead them up to the palatial structure where they had dined the day before, bringing them a delicious breakfast of hearty oats, fresh fruit, crusty breads, and sweet cakes on the balcony overlooking the council platform. They were joined by Methuselah and Lamech, who refused to discuss any serious matters until after they had their morning tea and a respectable breakfast.

After a satisfying meal, the companions were led across winding walkways and ramps that, like all the others, seemed to be woven into the trees themselves, reaching what Shem believed to be the highest point in the entire world. The air felt cooler up here, and he couldn't help but notice the abundance of birds making their homes in this elevated sanctuary - cooing doves nestled among the wooden rafters.

The circular room they entered was sizable enough to accommodate a large group of people, constructed entirely of wood that appeared to have grown seamlessly from the surrounding trees. Four large windows framed each direction of the compass, providing breathtaking views of the skies above and the newer section of town below, with its bustling market bridge over the river. He strained his eyes in hopes of catching a glimpse of his home in the distance, feeling a twinge of sadness for all that had been lost but also holding onto hope that he will see his family once again, upon his return. Across the rugged terrain in front of him, he spotted a herd of majestic triceratops grazing peacefully, their three horns and four sturdy legs standing out against their bulky bodies and spiked tails.

As he gazed out at a flock of birds soaring beneath him, it struck Shem as odd that there didn't seem to be any large crowds or mass movement of people down on the ground. In fact, everything appeared to be business as usual. Other than people sifting through the rubble of the demolished buildings, and a few additional guards patrolling the streets in their green uniforms, there was nothing out of the ordinary to be seen.

Turning to his companions, all equally mesmerized by the views from the other windows, Shem couldn't help but voice his observation. "Does anyone else find it strange that it's so peaceful down there?"

Methuselah nodded, his weathered face creasing with concern. "Aye, lad. It's unsettling, to say the least. It appears that the tattooed invaders slipped away in the night. Our spies couldn't track them all, but some were spotted heading east."

"So that means the threat is over? They returned to their base?" Elam asked, turning to his friends in excitement.

Lamech frowned, his brow furrowing. “I wish it were so. I fear it’s a trap.” He placed his hand on Shem’s shoulder. “All intended to lure you out.”

“I agree,” said Bartel, “They wouldn’t have gone through this much trouble to just walk away.” Tugging on his beard in frustration, he added, “I just wish we knew what they were up to.”

Shem felt a chill run down his spine at Lamech’s words. He turned back to the window, scanning the horizon with renewed intensity. “All this for me? I don’t get it...I’m no redeemer. I’m just a farmer.”

Elam stepped closer, his voice low and serious. “Well...not *just* a farmer. You are the son of the man who yells about the end of Adamah.”

Methuselah nodded solemnly. “Aye, young Shem, you are just a farmer...for the time being. But the odds are in favor that the Redeemer will come through your line. And, as Elam has so eloquently stated, your father’s words have spread far and wide. There are those who fear them...and those, like Azazel, who seek to prevent them from coming true.”

A sudden gust of wind whistled through the wooden chamber, causing the structure to creak and sway slightly. Nin stepped forward, his voice tense. “So...then, what is it you suggest?”

Bartel, nodding solemnly, turned to Methuselah. “Sir,” he spoke with reverence, “you mentioned praying for guidance. So with all that has happened, what do you believe is the next step?”

Methuselah’s gaze was full of wisdom and faith as he replied, “I have been interceding before Yahweh day and night with prayer and sacrifice. As you know, we can only do our best with what has been given to us, and trust in Him to provide the rest." He then turned to Shem with a knowing look and added, "And what I believe we should do next..."

"Wait." In that moment, Shem realized that their collective fate rested on this very decision. He felt a sense of urgency rise within him as he interrupted his great grandfather and boldly spoke up. "If you'll allow me." He stepped forward to address his friends as a whole. "I was the one who initiated this journey. It was my desire for revenge that set us on this path. But through recent events," he glanced at Eloise with deep sadness, "I have come to realize that I placed too much faith in my own abilities and was carried away by dark desires and emotions. And it ultimately cost Audrey her life."

"It wasn't your fault, Shem," Eloise began to protest his confession.

"But..." Shem continued, hanging his head in shame. "But it was. My pride led us away from my father's protection and wisdom, and nearly into the hands of Azazel." Shem felt Bartel move closer to him, offering support. "I've learned the hard way that I can't fight this battle alone. I recognized that my way was wrong."

"What are you trying to say, Shem?" Elam asked.

"I'm saying...that I finally understand the message my father has been preaching all of my life." A smile spread across Shem's face as he shared his newfound realization with everyone. "I have placed my faith in Him," he pointed to the heavens, "and His promised Redeemer." He took a deep breath and prepared for the difficult part.

"There's more?" Lud interjected, earning an elbow from Eloise and a disapproving glance from Aram.

Shem chuckled at his friend's attempt at humor. "Yes, there is. The hard part is what I believe Yahweh now expects of me."

"We're with you," Aryana spoke up, taking Shem's hand in hers. He felt a warmth radiating through her touch and noticed that she was no longer wearing her armor, dressed all in black instead.

Feeling emboldened by her support, and a little surprised by her tenderness, Shem continued. "After spending time in prayer, I believe that I am supposed to continue my journey east."

But before he could explain further, the room erupted into chaos as all of his friends began talking over each other at once. Shem couldn't discern whether they were in favor or against his plan, although he suspected the latter.

To his surprise, Nin was the first to voice his thoughts. "We need to listen to Shem." Despite his calm tone, there was a firmness in Nin's words that silenced all the chatter immediately. Everyone turned to look at him in shock.

"We followed him at the beginning," Nin continued, pushing his hat back on his head. "So why do we doubt him now when he speaks with maturity?"

Shem felt a strange mixture of flattery and offense at Nin's words.

"I will go with him, wherever that leads, and continue to be his protector," Nin declared. Then, with a hint of teasing in his voice, he added, "Although after what happened with Anu, he probably won't need it." Shem thought he saw a small smirk on Nin's face.

Shem felt a surge of gratitude towards Nin, but before he could respond, Elam stepped forward, his face etched with concern.

"Hold on," Elam said, raising his hands. "I understand your newfound faith, Shem, but how do you know that heading east isn't exactly what Azazel wants? You could be walking right into his trap."

Lud nodded in agreement. “Elam’s right. It’s too dangerous. We should return to Ararat and plan a defense.”

Shem took a deep breath, feeling the weight of their concern. “I appreciate your worries, truly, and I listened carefully to your concerns and perspectives last night around the table, and I can’t shake this feeling that Halvin was right. I think we’re meant to go east. It’s not about revenge anymore. It’s about fulfilling a greater purpose. And I see that purpose as stopping the threat to Eden, and more specifically, defending the remaining good in this world that Azazel would snuff out.”

Before anyone could respond, Bartel stepped forward, his eyes blazing with determination. “I’m coming too,” he declared firmly. “I have no reason to go home, and someone needs to keep you both out of trouble.”

Aram chuckled, shaking his head. “Count me in. I’m not sure about all this ‘higher purpose’ stuff, but you know where my heart is, and why I can’t return home yet.”

“You have me with you, too, Shem,” said Eloise, with resolution in her voice. “I have lost both of my parents to this evil, and if I can stop even one family from sharing their fates, then I’m in.”

Lud looked down, apparently torn. “Shem, are you sure about this? We barely escaped with our lives last time. My mom…” He paused in thought, looking at Eloise and his brother in turn.

Shem met his gaze, his heart breaking for his now emotional friend. “I understand your concern. I wouldn’t blame you if you don’t choose to go. But I have to believe that this time is different. ”

“I’m with you, Shem,” said Lud, offering Shem a smile.

Shem looked at Elam, feeling horrible putting his friend in this position.

Raphael stepped forward with a smile and an affirmative nod, nudging Elam along with him.

Realizing that he was the only one not to respond, Elam placed his hands on his hips. “What? Did you think I would leave all you guys, and go home without you ?” He said, with a look of incredulity on his face. “You’re crazier than I thought. Of course I’m with you.”

Methuselah nodded approvingly, his wrinkled face creasing into a smile. “Ah…I miss the days of my youth. So…it appears that we came to the same conclusion. Yahweh is indeed good.” He winked at Shem. Then, his expression became more serious, and he said, “Yet…you are not indestructible. Stay in prayer.”

As Shem looked around at his companions, a mix of determination and uncertainty on their faces, he felt a surge of both excitement and trepidation. The weight of his decision hung heavy in the air.

“I know it’s a lot to hear,” Shem said softly, his eyes meeting each of theirs in turn. “But I truly believe this is what I need to do. I can’t begin to tell you how grateful I am that you are doing this with me.”

Aryana squeezed his hand gently. “I may not fully understand your faith, Shem, but I’d like to join you guys, too. Alouette needs time to heal, and I’d like to find this enemy as well and report back to the council.”

Shem felt a lump form in his throat as he looked at his friends, their loyalty and bravery overwhelming him. He swallowed hard, trying to find the right words to express his gratitude.

Methuselah stepped forward, his weathered hand resting on Shem’s shoulder. “Remember, lad, Yahweh doesn’t call the equipped. He equips the called. You have His strength behind you.”

Lamech nodded in agreement. "And you have our strength as well. We may be old, but we're not useless yet."

Bartel stroked his beard thoughtfully. "If we're to embark on this journey, we need to be prepared. Supplies, weapons, maybe a few soldiers."

Shem nodded gratefully at Bartel's practical suggestion. "You're right. We can't rush into this unprepared."

"I can help with that," Aryana offered. "My family has connections with some of the best outfitters in Eden. We can get you all properly equipped for the journey."

Methuselah's eyes twinkled. "And I believe I can convince the council to provide a small escort. Nothing too conspicuous, mind you, but enough to offer some protection."

As the group began discussing logistics, Shem felt a tap on his shoulder. He turned to find Elam looking at him with a mix of concern and curiosity.

"Shem," Elam said quietly, pulling him aside. "I know you said this isn't about revenge anymore, but... what exactly are we hoping to accomplish by going east? What's our end goal here?"

Shem took a deep breath, considering Elam's question carefully. He gazed out the window at the vast expanse of Eden stretching before them, feeling the weight of their impending journey.

"Honestly, Elam? I'm not entirely sure," Shem admitted, his voice low. "But I feel it in my bones - we need to go east. Maybe we'll find answers about Azazel and his plans. Maybe we'll discover something about...whatever Yahweh's plan is. Or maybe..." he paused, a slight smile playing on his lips, "Maybe we'll just end up on some wild adventure that changes us all and forges us like steel for whatever is to come."

Elam raised an eyebrow, a hint of amusement in his eyes. "A wild adventure, huh? Well, I suppose that's as good a reason as any."

Their conversation was interrupted by Lud's booming voice. "Hey, you two!" Lud called out, his voice carrying across the room. "Stop your secret plotting and come help us figure out how many pairs of socks we need for this grand adventure!"

Shem and Elam exchanged amused glances before rejoining the group. The circular room was now abuzz with activity as everyone pitched in to plan their journey.

The eastern gate stood in stark contrast to the western gate. Hidden deep within the dense woods of Center Grove, its entrance was a masterpiece of intricate design with wooden beams woven together to form a sturdy arch over the road into town. The road leading up to it from the western gate crossed the bustling market bridge, meandering through towering trees and underbrush before arriving at the artisan gates that marked the eastern boundary of Center Grove. Surrounding the gate complex were quaint buildings and stables bustling with activity from the contingent of town guards and visitor's trusty steeds.

These were the first sights and sounds to greet Shem and his companions as they approached, signaling their arrival at this crucial point on their journey eastward. It was here, in the shadow of the impressive gate structure, that they would gather and prepare for the next leg of their adventure.

They walked together, newly equipped with leather armor, thanks to Lady Aryana. Along the way, Elam reflected on the openness to the sky of the town's beautiful amphitheater, where they spent the morning in sacrifice. Shem couldn't help but feel a sense of gratitude at the thought. "After all those years of mindlessly attending the midday meal and sacrifice with my father, I never truly appreciated its significance," he admitted with a smile. "It's something how a change of heart can completely change one's perspective."

Elam shook his head sadly. "It's a shame that so few were in attendance."

Shem couldn't deny that it was odd. "I suppose as we travel further from home, fewer people will see the importance of such rituals."

Nin interjected, "It's not the location. People are the same wherever you go. Those at the ranch work for your father and put on a show."

Lud scoffed. "Always the optimist, aren't you?"

Nin continued, ignoring Lud's comment. "Hypocrites. All of them." With that, he walked ahead towards the guard booth.

Shem felt a pang of guilt at Nim's words, realizing that he used to be one of them until recently.

Noticing Shem's troubled expression, Bartel offered words of comfort. "You are right, though, this world is only going to get darker as we travel further from home."

Shem nodded solemnly at Bartel's words, his eyes scanning the bustling activity around the eastern gate. The weight of their journey ahead seemed to settle on his shoulders.

As they approached the gate, Shem felt a mix of excitement and apprehension. The intricate wooden arch loomed before them, marking the boundary between the familiar world of his family and the unknown lands beyond.

"Well, this is it," Elam said, his voice tinged with nervousness. "Once we pass through, there's no turning back."

Shem, sensing that Elam was still conflicted about his decision to follow him, said, "I don't know what I'd do without you, Elam."

Lady Aryana stepped forward, her black attire now clad with unadorned brown leather armor, which was a stark contrast to the vivid white and blue that they were familiar with. "I've arranged for supplies to be waiting for us just beyond the gate. Enough food for at least a week's journey."

Shem, wishing he could hug his grandfathers one last time, took a deep breath to steel himself for what lay ahead. "Alright, let's do this."

As they approached the gate, Nin stepped forward with a gruff looking guard in tow. "This is Edward. He will lead a contingent of city guards to travel with us east." He was a man of sturdy build and an even sterner expression.

Shem nodded respectfully to the man, while Bartel and Halvin introduced themselves and exchanged handshakes with him and the rest of his soldiers--six of them in total. It was clear that these men were well-trained and experienced in guarding caravans through dangerous territories.

They moved through the gate, which stood tall and imposing, its iron bars intricately designed with patterns of vines and leaves. As they passed through, Shem couldn't help but feel a sense of foreboding and uncertainty about what lay ahead.

Further down the path, their trusted gallimimus awaited them. The majestic creatures stood tall with their colorful feather-like fibers ruffling in the gentle breeze. Their saddles were already in place, ready for the companions to mount.

Behind them, Audrey's galli was also outfitted with extra packs and supplies, securing all of their belongings for the journey.

The guards, however, rode on traditional horses--sturdy and reliable animals trained for long journeys. With their weapons at their sides and their steeds' hooves pounding against the ground, they were prepared for any danger that may come their way on this adventure.

As they mounted their gallis, Shem felt a surge of anticipation. The creatures chirped softly, sensing the excitement of their riders. Shem patted his galli's neck, feeling the smooth fibers beneath his hand.

Lud grinned, adjusting his position on his saddle. "Let's hope these dinos are up for a long journey. I'd hate to have to walk all the way home."

Eloise rolled her eyes at Lud's comment but couldn't hide her small smile. "Keep telling stupid jokes and you'll be walking anyway."

With a final glance back at the gate of Center Grove, Shem urged his galli forward. The creature responded immediately, its powerful legs propelling them down the path. The rest of the group followed suit, their mounts falling into formation behind Shem.

As they rode, the enormous trees of Center Grove began to fade away, replaced by smaller groves of trees and terrain crisscrossed with streams. The air grew warmer as they ventured deeper into the wilderness, small stone bridges connecting the road east over hills that the streams meandered around.

"Keep your eyes peeled," Edward called out from his position near the rear of the group. "We're entering the Pishon Marsh, and it's less patrolled territory with many places to hide."

For hours, the companions journeyed through untamed countryside, crossing numerous rivers and valleys on a road that seemed to have existed for centuries. The landscape was alive with an abundance of wildlife - towering brontosaurus and tiny turtles coexisted peacefully in the warm, humid valleys. As they continued on, Edward shared his knowledge of the area - small settlements scattered throughout this part of Eden, but few and far between. A full day's ride would bring them to more open land and eventually to the breathtaking coast of the inner sea itself, a sight not to be missed. The air was thick with the rich scents of earth and flora, and the sounds of nature filled their ears as they forged ahead on their journey.

Their journey had been long and arduous. The road they followed was a winding path of worn cobblestones and pieced together planks. But as they reached a crossroad, their eyes were met with a sight that made Shem's blood run cold.

In the middle of the intersection lay the shattered remains of a wagon, its wooden frame splintered and broken. Surrounding it were the dead carcasses of two large horses, their once powerful bodies now lifeless and still.

Shem's hand instinctively reached for his dagger as he surveyed the area for any potential danger. To his left, the path continued on through endless hills and rivers like those that they had already traveled through. But to his right, the path led uphill towards a place that was spoken about only in hushed whispers - The Great Forest. And at its center lay a forbidden place, one that no mortal could ever enter - The Garden of Eden.

As Bartel dismounted from his horse and drew his sword, Shem could hear the rest of their group following suit. They all approached the wreckage cautiously, their weapons at the ready. The tension permeated the group as they examined the scene before them.

"What do you think happened?" asked Elam, coming up behind Shem.

Bartel knelt down to examine the debris and replied grimly, "I think...this was no accident."

The guards, still mounted on their steeds, formed a protective ring around their group, now on foot.

Nin crouched down along the side of the path that led into the Great Forest, pushing his hat back to peer into its dark depths. "From the looks of these footprints in the mud," he said slowly, "it seems there were multiple individuals involved in this attack."

"And it appears they headed into the forest," added Aryana, her sharp eyes scanning the area. "And it seems they took the travelers prisoner." She picked up a small pouch lying on the ground and opened it, revealing a large amber gem. "I've seen this before."

Shem's heart sank as he also recognized the gem, remembering the cute girl from the market. "That belonged to Sedee," he said with a heavy heart, recalling the horrifying events surrounding that gem.

Aram's face paled as he spoke up, his voice trembling. "The girl from the market? And...the boy that was...possessed?"

Chapter 16

The Dark and Foreboding

Shem's heart was pounding as he looked from the shattered wagon to the ominous forest path. The implications of what they'd discovered were stomach-turning.

"We have to go after them," Shem said, his stomach twisting in knots. "We can't leave Sedee and her uncle to the mercy of whoever attacked them."

Aram nodded in agreement, but Bartel held up a hand in caution. "Hold on, son. We have a pretty good idea of *who* attacked them. This could be a trap."

"They need our help," Aryana argued, her hand resting on the hilt of her sword.

Edward stepped forward, his face etched with concern. "With all due respect, our mission was to escort you east. Venturing into the Great Forest wasn't part of the plan."

"But we can't abandon them either," Shem argued, his hand tightening on his dagger. "We were led here for a reason. We have to help. Especially if it's the invaders, as Bartel suspects...and they are part of the plan."

"Eden's High Counsel did speculate about the invaders calling this forest their base of operations." said Aryana, nodding at Shem.

Edward, pressing his concern, said, "This is no place to enter lightly. Legends speak of ancient spirits and dark magic within its depths."

Nin snorted.

Shem looked between Edward and Nin, weighing their conflicting perspectives. The forest loomed before them, dark and foreboding, yet he couldn't shake the feeling that this was where they needed to go.

"I understand the risks," Shem said, meeting Edward's concerned gaze. "But, we need to discover if the invaders are using the forest as cover to attack Eden."

Halvin stepped forward, his face set with determination. "Shem's right. We didn't come all this way just to play it safe. If there's even a chance that this will lead us to save Eden, we have to try."

Lud nodded, a wry smile on his face. "Well, I didn't sign up for a boring journey anyway. Might as well add 'rescuing damsels from an evil forest' to our mission."

Bartel stroked his beard thoughtfully. "We should at least be cautious and watch for traps. Let's move slowly."

Nin, already moving towards the forest's edge, said, "The trail's fresh. Shouldn't be too hard to follow."

Shem nodded, feeling a mix of determination and apprehension as he gazed into the shadowy forest. "Alright, we'll be vigilant. Nin, take the lead. You're the best tracker among us."

Nin grunted in acknowledgment and began carefully examining the ground at the forest's edge. The group began to make their way into the forest, leading their mounts, with Nin taking point to follow the trail.

As they moved deeper into the forest, the air grew thick and heavy. The canopy above blocked out most of the sunlight, casting everything in an eerie green glow. Strange bird calls and the rustling of unseen creatures filled the air.

"Stay alert," Edward whispered, his hand on his sword hilt.

"There's no telling what we might encounter in here."

"Does anyone else feel...off?" Eloise whispered, her eyes darting nervously from tree to tree.

Lud nodded, moving closer to Eloise, his hand resting on the hilt of his sword. "There's something unnatural about this place. It makes me feel...uneasy."

Shem felt it too - an unsettling heaviness in the air that seemed to press in on them from all sides. The forest itself felt alive, watching their every move with unseen eyes.

"Stay close," Bartel murmured to his companions. "And keep your voices down."

They continued on for hours, following Nin's expert tracking. The trail led them deeper into the forest, winding between massive tree trunks and over gnarled roots. Strange, luminescent fungi dotted the forest floor, casting an otherworldly glow.

Suddenly, Nin held up a hand, signaling the group to stop.

He crouched low, examining something on the ground.

"What is it?" Shem whispered, moving closer.

Nin pointed to a small scrap of fabric caught on a thorny bush. "Looks like it came from someone's clothing."

Shem's heart was in his throat as he examined the torn fabric. It was a deep burgundy color, similar to the cloak Sedee had been wearing when he last saw her in the market.

"It's hers," he whispered mostly to himself, his voice tight with worry. "We're on the right track."

Elam pointed at the ground, his brow furrowed. "But look at these markings," he said, pointing to a series of strange indentations in the soft earth. "These don't look like human footprints."

Aram nodded grimly. "Whatever took them, it's not just men we're dealing with. Or there's something worse out here with us."

Shem's heart pounded as he studied the bizarre tracks. They could be a dinosaur's tracks. But they could be something else entirely - large, three-toed prints with long, curved claw marks at the tips.

"We should turn back," Edward urged, his voice cracking in near panic.

Nin shook his head, his usually stoic face showing frustration at Edward. "Your superstition is taking over your mind. This wood does not see much human traffic, so wouldn't it make more sense, that it's simply a beast of some kind?"

Shem considered Nin's words, feeling torn between caution and the urgent need to press on. "Nin's right," he said finally. "We can't let fear cloud our judgment. Beast or not, Sedee and the others need our help."

Aryana nodded in agreement. "Besides, if it is some kind of creature, we need to know what we're up against."

With renewed determination, the group pressed deeper into the forest. The air grew thicker, almost soupy, and strange mists began to curl around their ankles. The eerie silence was broken only by the occasional snap of a twig or rustle of leaves.

Suddenly, a high-pitched roaring shriek pierced the air, causing everyone to freeze in their tracks.

"What was that?" Eloise whispered

Shem's hand instinctively went to his sword as he scanned the shadowy forest around them. The roar had been unlike anything he'd ever heard before - not any animal that he was familiar with.

"Tight formation," Edward commanded to his men in a hushed tone, his eyes darting from tree to tree.

Another roar rang out, closer this time, followed by the sound of something large crashing through the underbrush. The group huddled together, weapons drawn, as they tried to pinpoint the source of the noise.

"There!" Lud hissed, pointing to a dense thicket of ferns.

The lush foliage parted. A monstrous creature emerged. Shem's blood run cold. Towering over them like a building, it had an oversized head with forward-facing, hungry red eyes that seemed to bore into their very souls. Its massive jaws were filled with robust, serrated teeth that dripped with saliva, and as it let out a deafening roar, the ground trembled beneath their feet. The creature's front claws and arms were surprisingly small in comparison to its overall size - almost comical if not for the sheer terror of its presence. But there was nothing funny about the way it charged towards them with unbridled aggression, smashing through the undergrowth with its powerful hind legs and lashing tail.

Shem's heart pounded as he stared up at the monstrous creature bearing down on them. His mind raced, trying to recall anything from his training that could help them face such a beast.

"Scatter!" Bartel roared, snapping everyone into action.

The group split apart, diving for cover as the creature's massive jaws snapped shut where they had been standing moments before. Shem rolled behind a fallen log, his breath coming in quick gasps.

"Is that a tyrannosaurus?" Eloise cried out, her voice shrill with fear.

"It looks like one," Nin shouted back. "But I've never seen one attack a human before!"

The creature let out another ear-splitting roar, its head swiveling as it tried to decide which prey to pursue first. Its eyes locked onto Elam, who had stumbled in his retreat and was now scrambling backwards on the forest floor.

Shem's heart leapt into his throat as he saw the monster zero in on his friend.

"Elam!" Shem shouted, leaping to his feet. Without thinking, he grabbed a fallen branch and hurled it at the beast's head. The makeshift projectile struck true, causing the tyrannosaurus to flinch and turn its attention away from Elam.

"Over here, you overgrown lizard!" Shem yelled, waving his arms. His heart thundered in his chest as the massive creature fixed its gaze on him, but he stood his ground.

Aryana seized the moment, darting forward with her dual swords drawn. She slashed at the creature's leg, barely breaking its scaly skin. The tyrannosaurus roared with fury, whipping around to snap at her. Aryana barely managed to dive out of the way of its massive jaws.

"We need to work together!" Bartel shouted, taking command. "Surround it!"

The group sprang into action, spreading out to encircle the enraged tyrannosaurus. Bartel and Halvin moved to flank its left side, while Lud, Aram and Nin took the right. Aryana, Raphael and Eloise positioned themselves behind the beast, leaving Shem and Elam to face it head-on. Edward and the guards hung back, unsure if they wanted to engage or not.

The tyrannosaurus' head swiveled back and forth, its red eyes blazing as it tried to keep track of all its potential prey. It let out another deafening roar, causing the trees around them to shudder.

"Now!" Shem bellowed, unleashing a fierce battle cry that echoed throughout the entire forest. His yell reverberated through the forest as he charged forward, his sword Davar held high, emanating a blinding light that illuminated every dark corner. With each step of Shem's powerful strides, his determination grew, fueled by the pulsing energy of his glowing sword.

As one, the group attacked. Bartel and Halvin hacked at the creature's left flank, while Lud, Aram and Nin assaulted its right side. Aryana, Raphael and Eloise darted in to slash at its legs and tail. Edward and the guards joined the melee, slashing at the creature when it came near. The tyrannosaurus roared in pain and confusion, spinning in circles as it tried to fend off the attacks coming from all sides.

Shem and Elam faced the beast head-on, dodging its snapping jaws as they looked for an opening. The tyrannosaurus' small arms flailed uselessly as it tried to defend itself.

"Aim for its throat!" Elam shouted, ducking under a swipe of the creature's tail.

Shem nodded, gripping Davar tightly. The sword's light pulsed even brighter, as if sensing the gravity of the moment. With a yell, Shem charged forward, Davar humming with energy. The tyrannosaurus lunged at him, jaws gaping wide. At the last moment, Shem dropped and slid beneath the creature's massive head. With all his strength, he thrust Davar upward, driving the glowing blade deep into the soft flesh of the beast's throat.

The tyrannosaurus let out a gurgling roar, stumbling backward. Dark blood gushed from the wound as the creature thrashed wildly. Its tail whipped around, catching Lud and sending him flying into a tree trunk with a sickening thud.

"Lud!" Eloise cried out, rushing to his side.

The rest of the group continued their assault, hacking and slashing at the wounded beast. With a final earth-shaking bellow, the tyrannosaurus crashed to the ground. The forest floor trembled under the impact, sending leaves and debris raining down from the canopy above. For a moment, the forest fell eerily silent.

Shem stood, panting heavily, his arms trembling from the exertion. Davar's light dimmed, but a faint glow still emanated from the blade. He looked around at his companions, relief washing over him as he saw they were all still standing – albeit battered and shaken.

"Is everyone alright?" Bartel called out, wiping blood from a gash on his forehead.

"Lud!" Eloise's panicked cry snapped everyone back to attention. They rushed over to where she knelt beside Lud, cradling his head gently.

Shem and Elam rushed over to check on their friend. Lud groaned, his eyes fluttering open.

"Did we win?" Lud mumbled, wincing as he tried to sit up.

"Easy there," Eloise said softly, gently easing him back down. "You took quite a hit."

Shem knelt beside his friend, relief flooding through him.

"We won, thanks in no small part to you. How are you feeling?"

Lud managed a weak grin."Like I picked a fight with a mountain and lost. But I'll live."

Bartel approached, his face etched with concern. "We need to get him patched up and set up camp. Night will be falling soon, and who knows what other creatures might be acting out of character."

Edward was frantic. "You actually want to stay here? Since when can you remember any animal attacking a human...it's against the natural order of things." He kept looking around, his eyes wide. "This place is possessed! We are all going to die!"

Nin's quiet voice rang out, cutting through the tense silence like a sharp blade. "All men die," he said, slamming his hat back onto his head with a resounding thud. "But if you don't find your courage now, it won't just be death you face tonight." His eyes scanned the dark jungle around them, searching for any sign of danger. "If that beast *was* possessed, then only the gods know what else is lurking out there waiting to prey on us." With a determined look, he straightened a fallen log and declared, "I'll take first watch. We can't afford to let our guard down for even a moment."

The camp was hastily thrown together, a few tents scattered around the clearing, their fabric worn from use. The fire pit in the center was surrounded by logs and rocks for makeshift seating. The crackling of the fire, the rustling of leaves, and the occasional call of nocturnal animals created a symphony of sounds that seemed to surround the weary travelers. The dimming light of the setting sun cast an eerie glow on the whole scene.

The evening air was thick with the smell of sweat and fear, and the darkness beyond the campfire's reach held unknown dangers that threatened to close in. But within the circle of light, there was a sense of camaraderie and determination as the companions prepared to face whatever horrors the night may bring.

The group huddled around the campfire, their faces etched with worry and exhaustion. Lud lay on a makeshift bed of leaves, his chest rising and falling steadily as Eloise tended to his wounds. The others sat in tense silence, their eyes darting to the shadows beyond the firelight.

"What do you think possessed that tyrannosaurus? A demon?" Aryana asked, breaking the uneasy quiet. "I've never seen an animal act like that before."

Elam shook his head, his brow furrowed in thought. "It's not natural. Something dark is definitely at work here."

"We should have never entered this accursed forest," Edward muttered, his hands shaking as he gripped his sword.

Shem began to understand Nin's perspective. This man's timidity was taking control. He was supposed to be a guard, someone reliable and unyielding. But instead, he crumbled at the first sign of danger.

Shem sighed, understanding Edward's fear but knowing they couldn't give in to it. "We're here now, and we have a mission to complete. Sedee and her uncle are still out there, and we can't abandon them."

Nin nodded approvingly at Shem's words. "The boy's right. Odds are good that the invaders are there too."

One of Edward's men spoke up. He seemed to be no older than Halvin. "There are old stories about this forest-tales of dark magic and ancient spirits. I always thought they were just legends, but after that beast..."

An older guard, sitting close to the one who spoke, added, "Legends often have a kernel of truth," he said, his eyes reflecting the flickering firelight. "My father used to speak of creatures called the Feeorin-small, pixie-like beings that were said to steal men's souls."

Bartel stroked his beard thoughtfully. "We should take turns keeping watch through the night. Two at a time, in shifts."

As the others discussed the watch schedule, Shem found his gaze drawn to the dark forest beyond their camp. The trees seemed to loom closer, their branches reaching out like grasping fingers. Strange sounds echoed in the distance - chirps, growls, and other noises he couldn't identify.

Shem's heart skipped a beat as Halvin materialized from the dense woods, his face beaming with a wide smile. "All the galli's are picketed and fed for the night," he announced, his voice warm and jovial.

"What happened to the rest of the men that were with you?" Bartel inquired, referring to the three guards who had been helping Halvin.

Halvin pointed back towards the picket line. “They're just beyond the galli's…chopping up the tyrannosaurus.” He shrugged, a look of confusion crossing his features as to why they would bother.

Edward answered their unspoken question. “Back in Center Grove, travelers pay good money for their hides. For boots, and even some clothing.”

“Seems like a waste of time out here,” Bartel remarked. “It's just more weight we'll have to carry out.”

Edward simply shrugged. “We don't get paid much for this gig. So, it's an opportunity to supplement our pay.”

“That actually sounds like a great idea,” Lud chimed in, starting to rise from his makeshift mat on the ground.

But before he could get far, Eloise gently pushed him back down. “Oh no you don't. You're in no shape to cut up a carcass or add to your load. You can barely carry your own weight right now.”

“Yeah, that head alone must weigh a ton!” Elam exclaimed.

He slumped back down with a mock pout on his face, eliciting laughter from his friends. Shem caught a conspiratorial wink from Elam as their eyes met.

Despite the heaviness in his heart from the loss of Adi, Shem found joy and contentment in the company of his friends and new companion, Eloise. It felt like it had been so long since they all gathered together like this, and Shem couldn't help but feel a sense of togetherness and comfort. He knew that Adi could never be replaced, but he also felt that she would approve of Eloise.

As he sat there, surrounded by familiar faces and laughter, Shem finally felt a weight lifted off his chest—all thoughts of revenge a distant memory. For the first time in a while, he could breathe without the pain of sorrow consuming him. And he knew that this newfound peace came from Yahweh, the only one who could bring true healing to his wounded soul.

As the fire burned low, Shem found himself on the first watch of the night with Nin. The prospect of spending time alone with him after their last conversation filled Shem with a mix of emotions. He couldn't shake off the tension that had been building between them since that night, and he dreaded the thought of being left alone with those unresolved feelings.

Shem felt Nin's presence next to him before he saw him. Nin broke the silence first. "Wanna talk?"

Shem hesitated, not sure if he was ready for another difficult conversation. But he couldn't refuse Nin's request. "Sure," he said quietly.

"I feel I was too hard on you," Nin began. "We have too much history to let this come between us."

Shem didn't know what to say. He loved and respected this man like a second father, and it pained him to see their relationship strained by recent events.

"I was defensive," said Nin remorsefully. "I don't like to be challenged."

Shem nodded, grateful for his attempt at an apology but still struggling to process everything that had happened between them. "It felt deeper than that though," he said softly. "Are you upset that I placed my faith in Yahweh? After everything that has happened..."

Nin pushed his hat back on his head and looked directly at Shem. "I was frustrated by that too," he admitted. "For years I helped raise you as my own, teaching you to be self-sufficient and courageous. Then overnight, I watched you suffer and I couldn't do anything to protect you." His voice got quieter as he continued, "When you turned to your god for help, I was disappointed...but each of us has our own path to walk. You chose yours and I have no right to take that away from you." He rested a hand on Shem's shoulder. "And for that, I am truly sorry."

Shem felt a surge of compassion for this man who had been like a father to him. "You said you raised me as your own. Did you have any children of your own?"

Nin's expression softened as he reminisced about his past. "I did, once upon a time. I was the ruler of a kingdom, with a princess and children just like in the stories you tell at camp." Shem's eyes widened in surprise. He had always thought of Nin as a simple farmer, not someone with such a grand past.

"What happened?" he asked softly.

"The same thing that always happens on Adamah," Nin said bitterly. "War...violence...hatred. My own family was of royal descent and I married the most beautiful princess, giving up my own claim to the throne. We ruled together for centuries and had children together." Nin's voice broke as he continued, "But then we got caught up in someone else's war and I lost everything. My wife and children were murdered, leaving me with only this scar to remember them by." He removed his hat and traced the long, jagged scar on his face. Tears welled up in his eyes as he gazed at Shem. "I may have lost my family, but I gained another in you. You are like a son to me."

Shem reached out and embraced Nin, feeling the weight of their shared pain but also the strength of their bond. They sat in silence for a while longer, each lost in their own thoughts before returning to their duties as watchmen for the night. But now, there was a new understanding and forgiveness between them that Shem knew would carry them through whatever challenges lay ahead.

With his time at watch finally completed, Shem allowed himself to drift into a peaceful slumber. The warm glow of the dying embers from their campfire cast a comforting light over him as he slept, the faint crackling sounds adding to the serene atmosphere. The night air was cool and crisp, carrying with it the distant songs of nocturnal creatures. Despite the dangers that lurked in the darkness, Shem felt safe and at ease in this tranquil moment, surrounded by nature's lullaby.

Shem's peaceful slumber was abruptly shattered by a high pitched, otherworldly shriek. His eyes snapped open, heart racing as he bolted upright.

The camp was in chaos. His companions were stumbling from their bedrolls, wrestling with unknown creatures.

"What was that?" Eloise gasped, holding on to her belongings in fear.

Before anyone could answer, Shem felt his pack violently pulled away from him. Rolling over on his side to face his assailant, he looked right into the eyes of a humanoid figure no taller than his forearm.

"Feeorin," the older guard yelled, his voice trembling. "By Yahweh, the legends are true."

CHAPTER 17

Ancient Spirits

The small creature appeared to be a female, her emerald green dress blending in seamlessly with the surrounding foliage. Her vibrant red hair was tied back in a wild tangle, and her pointed ears twitched as she darted through the shadows.

Shem's hand shot out instinctively to grab his pack before she could escape with it. In response, she hissed at him, revealing a row of razor-sharp teeth. Taken aback by her sudden aggression, Shem stumbled backwards as she darted off into the darkness with his belongings in tow.

Everyone else was also engaged in a chaotic game of chase with these elusive creatures all around their campsite.

Without hesitation, Shem sprang into action and chased after the thief and his stolen bag. The forest seemed to blur past him as he dodged trees and leapt over roots and fallen logs in pursuit of his possessions. The little creature was fast and agile, easily evading Shem's attempts to catch her.

But Shem persisted, driven by the need to reclaim what was rightfully his. He couldn't let this mischievous thief get away with his pack. Surrounded by the sounds of laughter and rustling leaves, he pushed himself harder, determined to catch up to the elusive creature and retrieve his things.

As Shem chased the nimble Feeorin through the dense forest, his heart pounded in his chest. The creature's emerald dress flashed between the trees, always just out of reach. Sweat trickled down his brow as he pushed himself to run faster.

"Come back here!" he shouted, his voice echoing through the woods.

The creature glanced back, her eyes glinting with mischief. She darted left suddenly, forcing Shem to skid and change direction. As he regained his footing, he became concerned. The forest looked unfamiliar now, the trees looming ominously overhead. *How far have I run?*

His stomach tightened as he remembered the tyrannosaurus they'd encountered earlier. *What else is in these woods?*

Shem slowed his pace, glancing around warily. The Feeorin had vanished from sight, leaving him alone in this dangerous forest. His chest heaved as he caught his breath, straining his ears for any sign of pursuit or danger.

Great...now I'm lost. What do I do now? Shem took a deep breath, trying to calm his racing heart.

He closed his eyes, focusing on the sounds around him:the rustling leaves, the distant call of unfamiliar birds, the babbling of a nearby stream. When he opened his eyes again, he spotted a faint path through the underbrush. *Is that the way?*

Making his way down the path, he heard a twig snap as though someone, or something, stepped on it. Shem froze, listening intently. Voices drifted through the trees, too low to make out the words. Feeling exposed, he dropped silently to a crouch, concealing himself in a thick patch of ferns.

Shem's chest pounded as he peered through the ferns, straining to make out the source of the voices. As the voices drew near, he recognized one of them - it was Nin! *Who is he talking with?*

Shem shifted slightly, careful not to rustle the leaves, and caught sight of a small figure walking beside Nin. It was a male Feeorin, his copper-colored hair glinting in the dappled sunlight.

"You've done well," Nin was saying, his voice low and conspiratorial. "Here's the payment we agreed upon."

Shem watched in disbelief as Nin reached into his pocket and pulled out a small pouch, handing it to the small creature. Its eyes gleamed as he weighed the pouch in his hand.

"The first part of the plan is complete," Nin continued, his voice barely above a whisper. "Although your beast failed."

The little man put his hands up in protest. "Those sharp tooth's are barely controllable anymore...and that sword is powerful."

"Yes it is," said Nin. "Nevertheless, Eden's armies have been alerted to move east, just as I'd hoped."

The Feeorin nodded, a sly grin spreading across his face. "And what will you do with these...travelers?"

"I'll worry about them. Just get word to the others. Everything will still proceed as planned. Oh...and, Oisin? Make sure the boy gets where I need him..."

Shem's mind reeled. *Nin's a traitor!*

He leaned forward, desperate to hear more, but his foot slipped on the damp forest floor. A twig snapped loudly beneath his weight.

Nin's head whipped around, his eyes scanning the underbrush. "Who's there?" he called out sharply.

Panic surged through Shem's veins. Without thinking, he bolted from his hiding place.

His heart pounded in his ears as he tore through the forest, branches whipping at his face and arms. Behind him, he could hear Nin's voice calling his name, growing fainter as he put distance between them.

But Shem didn't slow down. His mind was reeling from what he'd just witnessed. Nin, his friend and mentor, was a traitor. The very thought made his stomach churn.

As he ran, the forest seemed to close in around him. Shadows deepened, and unfamiliar sounds echoed through the trees. A howl in the distance made him stumble, his foot catching on a root. He sprawled forward, landing hard on the damp forest floor.

For a moment, Shem lay there, gasping for breath. Tears pricked at his eyes as the full weight of the situation sank in. *Did I make the wrong choice?*

Shem pushed himself up, brushing dirt and leaves from his clothes. His hands trembled as he ran them through his tangled hair. The forest loomed around him, vast and unfamiliar. Every rustle and snap made him flinch.

"Yahweh," he whispered, his voice cracking. "Are you even there? Are you protecting me at all?"

No answer came, just the eerie silence of the forest. Shem hugged his arms around himself, feeling utterly alone and betrayed.

Nin had been like a second father to him, guiding him, teaching him. And it had all been a lie. *Who can I trust now?*

A twig snapped nearby, and Shem's head whipped around. His heart raced as he scanned the shadows, expecting to see Nin or one of the Feeorin emerging from the darkness. Instead, a small rabbit hopped into view, its nose twitching as it regarded him.

Shem let out a shaky breath, relief flooding through him at the sight of the harmless creature. He watched as the rabbit nibbled on some nearby leaves, seemingly unconcerned by his presence. Its peaceful demeanor helped calm Shem's frayed nerves.

"At least you're not trying to betray me," he murmured to the rabbit with a weak smile.

Taking a deep breath, Shem tried to gather his thoughts. He needed a plan. He couldn't stay here in the middle of the forest, but he couldn't go back to camp either. Not with Nin there. But what of his friends? *Think Shem.*

Seeing the little rabbit hop off, he pushed himself to his feet, his legs shaky but determined to follow. He had to warn the others about Nin's betrayal but was unsure how. As he pondered his next move, he continued to force his legs to move, the ground beneath his feet began sloping upward. The trees thinned out, revealing glimpses of a starry sky above.

Driven by a mix of fear and curiosity Shem pressed on, his breath coming in short gasps as he climbed. Suddenly, the forest ended abruptly, and Shem found himself teetering on the edge of a steep cliff. He windmilled his arms, heart leaping into his throat as he nearly tumbled headfirst over the precipice.

Regaining his balance, Shem stepped back and took in the breathtaking view before him. Moonlight bathed the landscape, revealing a vast expanse of churning water far below. Across the distance, towering cliffs rose on the far side of the raging waters. Countless waterfalls cascaded down their faces, shrouded in mist and surrounded by lush greenery that seemed to glow in the moonlight. The sight was both beautiful and terrifying.

Shem's breath caught in his throat as realization dawned. "It can't be," he whispered, his voice barely audible over the distant roar of water. "Is this... the Garden of Eden?"

The stories flashed through his mind - tales of paradise, the place where humanity began and from which they were forever banished. A place no one could enter since Adam and Eve's exile.

As the realization washed over him, a wave of fear unlike anything he had ever experienced crashed through his body. His knees went weak, and he stumbled back from the cliff. Shem's legs gave out beneath him, and he collapsed onto the rocky ground, his eyes still fixed on the impossible sight before him. The Garden of Eden. The forbidden paradise. It was real, and he was looking right at it.

A cold sweat broke out across his skin as it hit him. This wasn't just about some invaders or even Nin's betrayal. This was something far bigger, far more terrifying.

Shem felt so small at this moment. *What've I gotten myself into?*

The beauty of the scene before him now seemed tinged with danger. The mist curling around the distant cliffs looked like grasping fingers. The roar of the waterfalls sounded like a warning. Even the moonlight felt ominous, as if it were exposing him to unseen watchers.

Shem's thoughts were a jumbled mess, trying to make sense of the scattered pieces of information he had gathered. *Why are Eden's armies being lured to the East? Did Nin manipulate me to go on this journey? Did I ever make my own choice?*

Part of him wanted to somehow rescue his friends, run away and return home, while another part felt drawn to capture Nin and force him to tell his plan. In all the ways he thought this journey could go, this wasn't one of them. None of his life experience prepared him for this, and he felt lost. *Lord, I need your guidance and help.*

He continued to walk for a ways, keeping the Garden to his left, lost in thought. The sun began to rise over the garden, bathing everything in a warm golden light and the thick fog that had blanketed the area began to dissipate, revealing a lush landscape. Far in the distance, two towering trees emerged from the lingering fog, their branches stretching towards the sky like tall fingers reaching for the sun. These weren't just any ordinary trees - they were massive, dwarfing even the largest ones he had seen in Center Grove. Their trunks looked as wide as houses and their leaves shimmered with an otherworldly green hue. He couldn't help but feel a sense of awe and wonder at the sight before him. These could only be the 'Tree of the Knowledge of Good and Evil' and the 'Tree of Life.'

In the midst of the quiet forest, a sharp snap echoed through the trees causing Shem to freeze. He swiftly drew his sword, Davar, its bright light casting long shadows around him.

Scanning the area, his eyes landed on a familiar, small feeorin standing before him, holding his pack in her tiny hands. Her green eyes met his with an unflinching stare, delicate features framed by messy locks of bright red hair. The only sound was the gentle rustling of leaves and the soft breaths of the two figures facing each other in the dawn's light.

Shem's grip tightened on Davar as he stared at her, his heart racing. She looked back at him calmly, seemingly unfazed by the glowing sword in his hand.

"You," Shem said, his voice hoarse. "You're the one who stole my bag."

The Feeorin nodded, her bright eyes never leaving his face. "I am," she said, her voice high and musical. "And now I'm returning it."

She held out the bag, and Shem hesitated before slowly reaching out to take it. As his fingers closed around the familiar leather, he felt a wave of relief wash over him.

"Why?" he asked, lowering Davar but not sheathing it. "Why take it only to give it back?"

The Feeorin's lips quirked in a small smile. "To lead you here, of course," she said, gesturing to the breathtaking view behind them. "You needed to see."

Shem frowned, confusion and wariness warring within him. *I followed the rabbit.*

"See what? The Garden? Why?"

The little creature's expression grew serious. "Because you're in grave danger. You, and your friends."

Shem's mind reeled. "Danger? You're one of the...ones helping Nin...whatever you are. Why should I trust you?"

"I am one of...them. The Nephilim. Or the ones you call Feeorin." she said, giggling. "I don't always agree with my brothers. Does your family all agree? "

Shem's eyes widened in shock. "You're...a Nephilim? But I thought..."

The feeorin-no, the Nephilim-smiled sadly. "You thought we were all ugly, evil giants?" She shook her head. "Adamah isn't that simple...it's filled with variety, no?"

Shem lowered Davar completely, his curiosity overcoming his fear. "So why help me? What's really going on? And my name is Shem..."

"I'm Binne," she said with a smile. Then she glanced around warily before speaking again in a hushed tone. "There's an abandoned city to the south...on the other side of the Gihon River. You'll find help there, people who know more." She paused, her green eyes meeting his. "But you should know-one of the mal'akh has been watching over you."

"The what?" said Shem, looking around in panic. He knew that the Gihon River was the natural border of Eden that ran all the way to Cush, but the revelation that something was watching him in secret caused him alarm.

Binne smiled at Shem's confusion. "The mal'akh - it's what we call the heavenly messengers of Yahweh. Your people might know them as angels."

Shem's eyes widened. "An angel has been watching me? But why haven't I seen him?"

"They don't always reveal themselves," Binne explained. "But they're there, sometimes as a human, or an animal, or even a breeze, protecting those in their charge."

Shem's mind was reeling. Angels, demons, Nephilim, betrayal - it was all too much. He took a deep breath, trying to focus.

"This abandoned city you mentioned... what will I find there?"

Binne's expression grew serious. "Soldiers and weapons mostly. But they can help you."

Reading Shem's confusion, Binne spoke quicker. "No time to explain. Come on, I'll take you." She grabbed Shem's hand and led him in the direction he was originally heading.

Shem hesitated for a moment, his mind racing with doubts. But something in Binne's urgent tone and the sincerity in her eyes made him decide to trust her. He nodded and allowed her to lead him forward.

They moved swiftly through the forest for what felt like hours, Binne's small form weaving effortlessly between the trees while Shem struggled to keep up. The terrain gradually changed, becoming rockier and the trees sparser. In the distance, Shem could hear the rush of water.

"The Gihon River," Binne said, as they crested a hill. "We'll need to cross it to reach the city."

As they approached the riverbank, Shem gasped. The Gihon was no gentle stream - it was a raging torrent, its waters dark and frothing.

"How are we supposed to cross that?" he asked, his voice filled with uncertainty.

Binne grinned, her sharp teeth glinting in the morning light. "We walk, of course."

Shem looked where she was pointing through the trees and his eyes widened in amazement. "Is that...a bridge?"

Binne nodded. "An ancient human construction. It was built to connect the old city to the rest of Eden. Follow me closely, an old road still exists in the undergrowth up ahead."

Shem stared in awe at the bridge before them. It was unlike anything he had ever seen in Eden. Massive stone pillars rose from churning waters, supporting an arched structure that spanned the width of the raging Gihon. Vines and moss clung to the weathered stone, a testament to its age.

"It's incredible," Shem breathed. "How old is it?"

Binne shrugged. "Older than me, and I'm pretty old," she said with a mischievous grin. "Come on..."

As they stepped onto the ancient roadway, Shem could feel the smooth stones, each the size of a man, worn by countless travelers from ages past. It was old, but it still stood strong against the river's fury.

"How did they build it?" He said in awe.

"Nephilim," she said, with a telling smile. "The big ugly ones!"

Shem laughed at her joke. The roar of the water below made his heart quicken, but he pressed on, following Binne's nimble emerald dressed form.

"Slow down," Shem said, out of breath from moving so fast for so long. He adjusted his pack and sword on his back and continued to follow her.

As Shem reached the peak of the ancient bridge, his eyes were drawn to a cluster of structures rising above the dense canopy of trees and overgrowth on the opposite side of the river. A broken wall encircled what seemed to be a forgotten metropolis. The towering buildings were constructed with colossal stones, now covered in vines and foliage, their roofs long ago crumbled away.

Descending the bridge, Shem could distinguish remnants of grandiose fountains adorned with massive statues, some as tall as buildings, paying tribute to ancient deities. The area was scattered with fragments of stone archways and massive blocks intricately carved by skilled hands.

He called out for Binne to stop, but she trotted ahead into the walled city as if heading to a celebration. A cheerful tune hummed from her mouth as she vanished through an opening in the wall.

Slipping silently to the side of the opening, careful to stay hidden among the tangle of vines, Shem pressed his body against the cold stone wall. His ears strained for any indication of danger within, but all he could hear was the soft rustling of leaves and the distant chirping of birds.

As he scanned the area for any other signs of life, his eyes fell upon a small plaque next to the entrance. It read in bold, weathered letters:

Eridu: Capital of the Eridushu Empire

Shem's heart raced with excitement and disbelief as he realized he was standing before the legendary Ruins of Eridu.

He wanted to shout out in excitement, but instead, he clapped a hand over his mouth, not wanting to alert anyone or anything to his presence. *I can't believe I'm actually here!*

Shem held his breath as he cautiously peeked around the corner, his eyes scanning the desolate streets of the once-thriving city. The crumbling buildings loomed overhead like menacing giants, their broken windows and jagged edges adding to the eerie atmosphere.

With weak knees, Shem mustered up every ounce of courage to take a step forward, feeling the weight of the abandoned city bearing down on him like a heavy cloak.

He couldn't believe his eyes as he took in the sight before him. The ancient city of Eridu sprawled out in a maze of crumbling stone structures and overgrown pathways. Massive trees had burst through cobblestone streets, their roots twisting around fallen columns and statues. Vines draped over everything, nature slowly reclaiming what was once a thriving metropolis.

Cautiously stepping through the entrance, Shem's foot caught on something. He looked down to see a rusted sword, its blade dulled by time but still recognizable. A chill ran down his spine as he realized this city hadn't just been lost to time - it had been abandoned in haste.

"Binne?" he called out softly, his voice echoing off the stone walls. "Where are you?"

There was no response. Shem's hand instinctively went to Davar on his back.

Shem crept further into the ruins, his eyes darting from shadow to shadow. The eerie silence was occasionally broken by the skittering of small animals or the rustle of leaves in the breeze. He tried to focus on finding Binne, but his mind kept wandering to the incredible history surrounding him.

As he rounded a corner, he froze. There, in a small clearing stood a group of soldiers. Their armor gleamed in the dappled sunlight, unlike anything Shem had seen before. It was made of a strange, black metal that reflected everything around it as they moved.

At the center of the group stood Binne, gesturing animatedly as she spoke to them with her hands waving around, obviously telling them a great story. One of the soldiers, a tall woman with close-cropped hair, noticed him first. She raised her hand, and the group fell silent. Looking in his direction, she said, "Shem...you're safe now."

The tall woman knew his name. *The little thief sold me out.*

Chapter 18

Suspicious Intensions

Shem's heart sank as he realized what had happened. Binne, his little guide, had led him into a trap. He felt a mix of anger and disappointment wash over him as he stared at the group of soldiers, their strange armor glinting in the fading sunlight.

"I... I don't understand," Shem said, his eyes darting between Binne and the tall woman. "What's going on here?"

The woman with the close-cropped hair stepped forward, her mechanical armor whirring softly with each movement. "We've been expecting you, Shem. Your little friend here has been quite helpful in filling us in on the details of your journey."

Binne avoided Shem's gaze, shuffling her feet nervously. Shem felt a pang of hurt at her betrayal, but he pushed it aside, focusing on the more pressing matter at hand.

Shem took a deep breath, trying to steady his nerves. "So this whole time... you were just waiting for me?" he asked, his voice tinged with disbelief.

The tall woman nodded, a hint of a smile playing at her lips. "We had to be sure you were who we thought you were. Can't be too careful these days."

One of the other soldiers, a burly man with a thick beard, chuckled. "Especially when dealing with Edeners. No offense, kid."

Shem bristled at the comment but held his tongue. He turned his attention back to the woman who seemed to be in charge.

"And who exactly do you think I am?"

"The son of Noah," she replied simply. "A boy on a mission to save Eden from invaders. Or so we've been told."

Shem's eyes widened. He glanced at Binne, who still refused to meet his gaze. "How much did you tell them?" he asked, his voice barely above a whisper.

The tall woman interjected before Binne could answer. "Enough. But we'd like to hear it from you, Shem. Why don't you join us by the fire and tell us your story?"

Shem hesitated, eyeing the strange group warily. Their mechanical armor and odd weapons made him uneasy, but he realized he had little choice. With a resigned sigh, he nodded and followed them to the fire.

As they settled around the flickering flames, Shem couldn't help but marvel at the intricate designs on their armor. Up close, he could see the faint glow of crystals embedded in the chest pieces, pulsing with an otherworldly light.

"Welcome, Shem, I'm Captain Damrina," the tall woman began, her voice surprisingly gentle. "This tall ugly one with the beard...who thinks he's funny, is Lieutenant Goriel." She smacked the big man's knee, with a hollow-sounding thud. "Tell us about Eden. And these invaders you're tracking."

As Shem recounted the events that led him here, the soldiers listened intently, their eyes reflecting the dancing firelight. He told them about the sudden attack on Eden, the chaos that ensued, and about Anu: The Destroyer, leaving out the part of Adi and his deepest pain.

"It all happened so fast," Shem said, his voice catching slightly. "One moment, everything was normal. The next, there were fires everywhere, people screaming..." He trailed off, lost in the memory.

Captain Damrina leaned forward, her armor creaking softly. "And that's when you decided to track the invaders?"

Shem nodded, leaving out Nin's betrayal. He was grateful for the soldiers letting him tell his story. *Maybe they can actually help me.*

Shem marveled at their equipment and unfamiliar technology. It was unlike anything he had ever seen in Eden. "Why are you camped all the way out here in an abandoned city? Couldn't you be somewhere more... comfortable?"

Captain Damrina's expression turned serious. "We're here on a mission, Shem. We're a scout group tasked with protecting the border of Assyria. This abandoned city provides an excellent vantage point."

The Assyrians? Shem coughed, masking his shock and realization that these soldiers are Eden's age old enemies.

Lieutenant Goriel, nodded, adding, "Plus, it's not as abandoned as you might think. There are still people living in the outskirts, trying to rebuild. We keep an eye on them too."

Shem's head reeling at this information, kept fishing for information. "Why haven't I seen it before? We trade with other cities and nations, but I've never encountered anything like this."

Captain Damrina's expression grew serious. "That's because we keep most of it secret, Shem. Assyria guards its technological advancements closely. But, the higher-ups...the rulers of Eden...they know what we want them to know. It's what we call a...deterrent."

Shem's brows furrowed as he tried to make sense of the information presented to him. He couldn't help but feel a creeping suspicion towards their true intentions. The wound of Nin's betrayal still stung deep within him. "What is this deterrent for? Why are you revealing all of this to me?"

Captain Damrina's expression softened slightly as she regarded Shem. "You're a sharp one, aren't you? The truth is, Shem, we're here because we believe you might be able to help us."

Shem's eyebrows shot up in surprise. "Help you? How could I possibly help soldiers with such things?" He gestured to the strange tube-shaped device in the Lieutenant's lap.

Lieutenant Goriel leaned forward, his armor creaking softly. "It's not about the technology, kid. It's about what you know and where you come from."

Captain Damrina nodded in agreement. "Eden has always been...different from the rest of Adamah. Your people have knowledge and skills that we don't fully understand. And it seems that we are both in a position to help each other."

How could I possibly have anything to offer these people? The warning bells in his mind were getting louder, and his mouth felt parched. "If you know who my father is...then you also know, my family is not very respected right now." Shem felt very uneasy with this conversation. "And, I'm just a farmer."

Captain Damrina's eyes softened as she regarded Shem. "You're more than just a farmer, Shem. You're the son of Noah, a man known for his wisdom and foresight. And you've shown great courage in pursuing these invaders into your enemies' land."

"Enemies?" Shem asked. *They haven't forgotten our history.*

The Captain just gave him a knowing look.

Shem shifted uncomfortably, overcome by a nagging sense that something wasn't quite right. "But what exactly do you want from me?" he asked cautiously.

Lieutenant Goriel leaned forward, his armor creaking softly. "Information, kid. We need to know more about what's happening in Eden, like with these invaders. More importan tly....what are your knights doing about it? Are they prepared properly?"

"And you think I have this information?" Shem asked, his voice tinged with disbelief.

Captain Damrina nodded. "You've seen things first-hand that we've only heard rumors about. Your perspective could be invaluable."

I thought they were going to help me. He glanced around at the soldiers, their strange armor glinting in the firelight. Part of him wanted to help, to be useful to these impressive warriors. But another part, the part that had been raised on tales of Assyria's treachery, screamed caution.

"I don't know anything." said Shem, folding his arms. "This doesn't feel right."

"Shem," Lieutenant Damrina said, her voice gentle but firm, "we're not your enemies. We want to help Eden, just as you do. But we need to understand what we're dealing with."

Lieutenant Goriel exchanged a look with Captain Damrina before turning back to Shem. "What about Eden itself? Its defenses, its resources... anything that might help us understand why it was targeted."

Shem's inner turmoil reached a boiling point, and he shot up from his seat in frustration, almost tripping over the large piece of debris he was sitting on. "I thought you could help me save my friends," he seethed, hands balled into fists at his sides. "I told you...I'm not involved in Eden's defenses...or resources. I would love to help, but..." His pacing became frantic, as he tried to escape from his own thoughts. "I would do anything to help them," he cried out, voice cracking with desperation. "I'm just...helpless." His words echoed around him like a cruel joke, taunting him with his own powerlessness.

Captain Damrina stood up slowly, her armor whirring softly. She approached Shem cautiously, hands held out in a calming gesture. "Easy there, Shem. We understand this is difficult for you."

Shem's heart pounded as his emotions raged out of control. He felt tears prickling at the corners of his eyes and blinked them back furiously. "You don't understand," he said, his voice barely above a whisper. "I left them. I left them all behind."

Lieutenant Goriel exchanged a concerned glance with Captain Damrina before speaking. "Left who behind, kid?"

Shem's shoulders slumped as the fight drained out of him. "My family. Everyone in Eden. I ran away to chase after the invaders, and now..." He felt so tired and lowered his voice to barely a whisper. "I left my friends with...him. I just...I feel so lost. I thought I knew what I was doing, but now..." He trailed off, unable to finish the thought.

Captain Damrina stepped closer, her voice softening, a hint of confusion on her face. "Shem, listen to me. You haven't abandoned anyone. You're out here trying to help your people. That takes courage."

Shem looked at her, blinking away his tears in embarrassment. "But what if I made the wrong choice? What if they needed me back there? If the invaders returned?"

Lieutenant Goriel stood up, his armor creaking. "Kid, sometimes the bravest thing you can do is leave. You're out here gathering information, seeking help. That's not running away--that's fighting smart."

Shem stopped pacing, his chest heaving as he tried to calm himself. He looked at the soldiers, their strange armor now seeming more alien and intimidating than ever. The weight of everything--the attack on Eden, Adi's death, slaying the giant, his journey, Nin's betrayal, and now this bizarre encounter--came crashing down on him.

Desperately trying to distract himself, he turned away from the huddle of soldiers gathered around the crackling fire and gazed up at a colossal statue perched atop a nearby abandoned fountain. The once-grand city square they now called home lay in ruins with crumbling buildings and rubble scattered about, but the statue still stood tall and proud, a symbol of a forgotten era. Its intricately carved features and outstretched arms seemed to reach out, as if calling those in its presence to bow and worship. The flickering flames, with the afternoon sun at its back, cast eerie shadows on its weathered face, giving it an almost lifelike appearance. As he studied the massive figure, he couldn't help but wonder what stories it could tell of the city's past glory. *Does it look like Nin?*

Shem's attention was drawn across the abandoned square to a group of heavily armored soldiers gathered around a large, box shaped carriage that seemed to have no beast in sight. Their shiny helmets gleamed in the sun, giving them an even more ominous and intimidating appearance than the ones around the fire. The sight of these fully armored warriors sent a shiver down Shem's spine, he imagined that their insect-like visages would evoke fear and dread in all who caught sight of them. Despite the lively atmosphere of the soldiers around the fire, these soldiers told a different tale.

Shem's gaze lingered on the armored soldiers by the strange transportation. Something about their rigid postures and the way they hovered around the vehicle unsettled him. He squinted, trying to make out more details in the shadows of the surrounding buildings.

"What's in that...carriage?" Shem asked, gesturing towards the group and still unsure what he was seeing.

Lieutenant Goriel followed his gaze, his expression hardening slightly. "The char? Oh, it's nothing you need to worry about, Shem. Just some supplies we're transporting."

Shem's eyes narrowed as he took a closer look. He thought he'd seen one of the soldiers, handing food to someone - or something - inside the back of the vehicle. "Are you sure? I thought I saw-"

"Okay...Okay. I guess there's no fooling you" Captain Damrina interrupted, sharing a glance with the Lieutenant. "It's just some vagabonds we picked up along the way. Petty thieves, mostly."

Lieutenant Goriel nodded, a bit too slowly. "Yeah, we're just holding them until we can transport them back to base for processing."

Shem frowned, unconvinced. The tension in the air was palpable, and he couldn't shake the feeling that something wasn't right. He looked back and forth between Captain Damrina and Lieutenant Goriel, noting their tense postures and the way they avoided meeting his eyes directly.

"Vagabonds?" Shem repeated skeptically. "Why would you need so many armed guards for petty thieves?"

Captain Damrina's smile tightened. "It's standard procedure, Shem. We can't be too careful out here on the borders." Shem took a step closer to the char, straining to see inside. The soldiers guarding it shifted uneasily, their hands tightening on their weapons.

"I don't think-" Shem began, but he was cut off by Captain Damrina.

She stepped forward, placing a firm hand on Shem's shoulder. "Shem, I know you're struggling with trusting us right now but believe me when I say it's better if you don't concern yourself with this. This is Assyrian business." Seeing that Shem wasn't convinced, she continued. "Look, Shem, you came to us for help, right? This has nothing to do with you. Remember the other...people...that I said occupy these ruins? Well, that's who we have detained. Okay?" Looking at the Lieutenant, she said, "Now, let's discuss how we can get you back to your friends, and maybe help Eden in the process."

Shem hesitated, torn between his curiosity about the mysterious char and his desire for help. He glanced back at the heavily guarded vehicle one last time before reluctantly turning away. "Could those be the ones I'm tracking?"

Captain Damrina's posture relaxed slightly as she guided Shem back towards the fire. "I'm not sure how they could be. They're just a group of religious zealots. They are what remains of the cult of Semyaza."

"How do you know it's not them?" Shem said.

"They are more concerned with meditation and rebuilding their idols," she said, gesturing up at the megalithic statue.

"That's him, the statue you were just admiring."

Laughing, Lieutenant Goriel, chimed in. "Besides," he said, tapping the sword on his hip. "They have no weapons to speak of. We don't allow it."

Shem's memory was stirred as he looked up at the statue. "Semyaza? That name sounds familiar."

Captain Damrina nodded, her expression grave. "They're not well-known outside of this region. They worship an ancient god they believe fell from the sky centuries ago ."

"Fell from the sky?" Shem repeated, his curiosity piqued despite his lingering unease. "Like... a star?"

Lieutenant Goriel chuckled. "Something like that, kid. They claim Semyaza was a god who was once part of the pantheon of The Serpent. Like Azazel. They believe that he was chief among all the gods."

Shem's eyes widened, as it dawned on him where he heard the name before. From his great-grandfather, Methuselah. *Semyaza was one of Satan's top two chieftains!*

Chapter 19

Children of the Gods

He thought it best to keep this information to himself. He wasn't sure how they would like their gods being referred to as fallen angels.

"I...I don't understand," Shem said, sensing they were still lying. "If they're just peaceful religious zealots, why are they being detained?"

Captain Damrina sighed, her armor creaking as she shifted her weight, "It's complicated, Shem. These people...they have beliefs that don't align with Assyrian interests. We can't risk them spreading their ideas. Plus, they are poor, and desperate people do desperate things."

Shem was alarmed by Captain Damrina's words, so he was glad he kept his thoughts about the fallen angel to himself, especially with the casual way she spoke of detaining people for their beliefs.

This unsettled him deeply. "In Eden, we're taught that all people have the right to their own beliefs, as long as they don't harm others." *Assyria hasn't changed at all!*

Lieutenant Goriel let out a bark of laughter. "And look where that's gotten Eden, kid. Attacked and vulnerable."

Captain Damrina shot the lieutenant a warning glance before turning back to Shem with a softer expression. "Shem, I know this must seem harsh to you. But the world outside Eden is a dangerous place. Sometimes we have to make difficult decisions to keep people safe."

Or force them? Shem shifted uncomfortably. "I appreciate you explaining things to me," Shem said carefully, "but I'm not sure I understand how detaining these people helps Assyria, Eden or anyone."

Captain Damrina's expression hardened slightly. "Sometimes, Shem, maintaining order requires difficult decisions. These cultists may seem harmless now, but left unchecked, their beliefs could destabilize the entire region."

Lieutenant Goriel nodded in agreement. "Better to nip it in the bud, kid. You'll understand when you're older."

Shem bristled at being dismissed as just a child but thought it best to hold his tongue.

Shem absentmindedly snacked on a handful of nuts and berries provided by the soldiers, while watching them discuss his situation. He figured it was best to let the 'adults' decide how to save his friends for now, so he kept his focus on the food in his hand.

Binne sat off to the side, her body tense and small as she tried to blend into the background. Shem decided to go join her, his steps slow and deliberate.

Binne glanced up at Shem as he approached, her eyes darting nervously between him and the soldiers. She hesitated for a moment before accepting a few berries from his outstretched hand.

"Thanks," she mumbled, popping a berry into her mouth.

Shem settled down beside her, close enough to talk quietly but not so close as to make her uncomfortable. He could sense her unease.

"You okay?" he asked gently. "You seem... worried."

Binne chewed slowly, her gaze fixed on the ground. "It's nothing," she said, but her tense posture betrayed her words.

Shem waited patiently, knowing from experience with his younger brother that sometimes silence was the best way to encourage someone to open up.

After a few moments, Binne sighed. "It's just... these humans. These...soldiers," she said, fidgeting with the hem of her bright green dress. "They're dangerous. And not to be trusted."

Shem leaned in closer, his voice barely above a whisper. "Why? I mean...you brought me right to them."

Binne's eyes darted around nervously before settling back on Shem. "Never-you-mind. I've... I've said too much. I never should've brought you here."

Shem's doubts returned. He glanced over at the soldiers, their armor glinting in the fading sunlight. "But they're helping me find my friends," he said, though his voice lacked conviction. "Right?"

Binne shook her head, her red curls bouncing. "That's what they want you to think..." She trailed off, her eyes distant and haunted.

Thoughts raced through Shem's mind as he thought about the attitude of the soldiers. *Is this all just a trap?*

He didn't want to push Binne for answers, thinking it best to tread carefully, so he changed the subject hoping she would reveal more on her own.

"Tell me about your family, Binne," Shem said, trying his best to show empathy.

A cool breeze rustled through the trees and the scent of pine filled the air around them, cooling the humid air, yet not doing much to shake off the unease that lingered in his gut, like a weight dragging him down into uncertainty.

Binne hesitated, her eyes darting around nervously, like she was suspicious of the breeze itself, before settling back on Shem. She took a deep breath, as if steeling herself to speak.

"My family... it's complicated," she began softly. "We're not like you humans. We're... different."

Shem leaned in closer to listen more intently. Yet, at this distance he almost snickered at her pointy teeth. *No kidding.*

Binne's voice dropped to barely above a whisper. "As you know, we're Nephilim. Children of the gods and human women."

Shem knew this much, and he had heard stories of the Nephilim's deeds, but had never thought to sit and speak with one.

Binne continued, her words tumbling out faster now. "There are many kinds of us that walk Adamah. The Emim enslave humans. The Repha'im cause fear just by their presence. The Gibborim are great heroes. The Zamzummim are the smart ones, helping build giant structures, like this city. The Awwim, like me, we're... sneaky... so say the humans. Not giants, but dangerous in our own way." She paused, her eyes distant. "And then there's the Anakim. The dumbest, but largest and most destructive. They wear the bones of those they've killed."

Shem shuddered at the thought. "Like Anu: The Destroyer, who attacked Ararat."

"That you killed by yourself," she smiled for the first time. "Quite the hero. Maybe you're Gibborim?"

"And... your family?"

Binne's voice grew softer. "Yes...my family. My father was a lesser-known god, Bezaliel. He came to Adamah, giving up his power so he could marry my mother. It was centuries ago, right here in this land before Eridu was built...before Assyria."

She plucked a blade of grass, twirling it between her fingers. "But when we were born - just a handful of tiny, red-headed pups - he..." Binne's voice cracked as she continued, "He was so enraged that his offspring weren't powerful giants. In his anger, he...he killed my mother. Then he just ran off, never to be seen again."

Shem's heart ached for her. He reached out and gently squeezed her hand. "I'm so sorry, Binne. That's terrible."

She withdrew her hand with a snarl. "It was her fault. She was weak!"

Shem just stared at her in shock.

She gave him a sad smile, her mood changing again. "My brothers and I have lived in the forest ever since. We keep to ourselves mostly. Humans tell stories about us stealing souls, but..." She let out a hollow laugh. "I've never taken one yet."

Shem felt a mix of fascination and sympathy, still not getting what he wanted. After a moment he tried a different strategy. "I miss my family."

Binne perked up, seeming excited for the change. “You mean the great Noah, and his giant slaying son?” She giggled at Shem’s expense.

Shem chuckled, shaking his head. “I’m not really a giant slayer. That was just luck… and desperation.” He paused, realizing he actually did miss them. “My family…we’re pretty simple, really. My mother, Emzara, she’s the kindest person you’ll ever meet. Always taking care of everyone, even when times are tough.”

He rubbed his chin in thought. *I need to shave.* “Then there’s my brothers, Japheth and Ham. Japheth’s the oldest, always trying to be responsible. And Ham…well, he’s the troublemaker.” Shem grinned thinking of a better time. *I wonder what they’re doing.*

Binne listened intently, her green eyes wide with curiosity.

“And your father? The famous Noah?”

Shem’s smile faded slightly. “Dad’s… complicated…He can be intense. You know about his prophecy. Everyone does.”

He paused, picking at a loose thread on his tunic. “The other people in Eden, they don’t really understand. They think he’s crazy. But he speaks the truth…I know that now.”

Binne tilted her head, intrigued. “Truth?”

“Yeah…the prophecy about Yahweh destroying Adamah. I thought you knew.”

Her mouth hung open in surprise.

“Because of the corruption of mankind,” Shem explained, feeling sad that the Nephilim are part of that reason. “Father says God told him to tell people to repent before it’s too late, that the end will be 85 years from now.”

“Why would the Creator destroy his own creation?” Binne looked skeptical, glancing around at the ruins around them. "I was told He was a cruel god that punished the wrong son of Adam. Now He's going to finish the job?"

Shem began to respond, but before he could say anything, a commotion near the city gate caught their attention. A woman adorned with a sword and leather armor came running up to Captain Damrina, and whispered urgently to her between labored breaths.

Binne, apparently hearing what was said, tensed beside Shem, her eyes darting around nervously. Without a word, she sprang to her feet and took off running, disappearing around a corner into the ruined city.

"Binne, wait!" Shem called after her, but she was already gone.

He was puzzled by her sudden departure. Something felt off, but he couldn't quite put his finger on what it was. *I don't like this.*

Suddenly, a familiar sound reached his ears - the distant barking of gallimimus. Shem's head snapped up, his heart racing in excitement. The soldiers around him had clearly heard it too, jumping to attention. Some ran off towards the city gate, weapons ready.

Through the gate, a figure appeared, hands raised in a gesture of peace. Shem squinted, then felt a surge of relief as he recognized Bartel, a familiar scowl on his face. The Captain and Lieutenant approached him cautiously.

Behind Bartel mounted on gallis came the rest of Shem's companions. Joy flooded through him at the sight of their familiar faces. They all looked unharmed, much to his surprise and relief. Maybe he had been wrong to worry so much. Maybe everything really was okay.

But as Nin came into view, Shem felt his blood boil with anger and fear. Their eyes met across the square, and

Shem clenched his fists, fighting the urge to draw Davar from its scabbard on his back.

Shem's his friends leapt from their mounts and rushed towards him, enveloping him in a group hug that made him feel like everything would be ok. Their relief was palpable as they squeezed him tight, having feared the worst.

"We thought you were dead!" Elam said, his voice muffled against Shem's shoulder.

"What happened to you?" Aram asked, pulling him at arm's length to examine him for injuries.

Shem opened his mouth to explain, but Lud cut him off. "You won't believe it, Shem! The feeorin were actually friendly. They were just playing with us the whole time!"

"What?" Shem's brow furrowed in confusion. "But I saw them attack you..."

"Turns out they're quite friendly," Eloise chimed in. "They actually led us here."

Shem's mind reeled, trying to process this information. It didn't make sense. He knew what he had seen - the feeorin attacking his friends, stealing their belongings. *Friendly*?

But, then again Binne was kind to him, leading him here. To the Assyrians.

"But... but where's Raphael?" Shem asked, his voice tight with concern, looking past his friends at the group of Center Grove guards that were still with the companions.

Eloise's face fell. "We haven't seen him since he went off searching for you. We had hoped he'd found you."

A knot formed in Shem's stomach. *Did Nin do something to him?*

As his friends continued to chatter excitedly around him, even Lady Aryana seemed genuinely happy, Shem's gaze drifted back to Nin. The man was speaking with Captain Damrina, Lieutenant Goriel, and Bartel, his posture relaxed like always. But there was something in his eyes that made Shem's skin crawl.

Nin caught Shem staring without a change in expression. He excused himself from the conversation with the officers and sauntered over to where Shem stood with his friends.

"Ah, Shem," Nin said, his voice smooth as silk. "I'm so glad to see you're safe. We were all terribly worried."

He actually sounds sincere. Shem clenched his jaw, fighting to keep his voice steady. "Were you?"

A hush fell over the group. Nin's smile faltered for just a moment before widening. "Of course I was worried. Why would you think differently? I thought we moved past this."

Shem's anger boiled over. "You know why!" he shouted, jabbing a finger at Nin's chest. "I heard you clear as day - you betrayed us! I heard you talking to that Feeorin!"

The sudden outburst drew everyone's attention. Captain Damrina and Lieutenant Goriel hurried over, hands on their weapon hilts.

"What's going on here?" Damrina demanded.

Nin raised his hands placatingly. "Just a misunderstanding, Captain. Young Shem here is understandably shaken from his ordeal-"

"Don't do that!" Shem snapped. He turned to his friends. "You have to believe me. Nin betrayed us!"

Uncertainty flickered across their faces. Elam stepped forward, brow furrowed. "Shem, are you sure? We're all okay."

"Hey, kid, your friends all seem to be ok," said Lieutenant Goriel, trying to keep the peace. "Is it possible you heard it wrong? Aren't these the friends you wanted us to find?"

Shem was speechless. He never told the soldiers about Nin, and now it was too late. *They'll never understand.*

Seeing Shem's distress, Bartel stepped forward, his face creased with concern. "Now hold on a minute. I've known Shem's family for years. They aren't liars. If Shem says he heard something, I believe him."

The lieutenant backed away from Bartel, one hand up in protest, the other on the strange tube-like weapon strapped to his shoulder.

Nin's eyes flashed dangerously. "Careful Bartel, sounds like you're insinuating something."

"Oh, I'm not insinuating," Bartel growled, squaring his shoulders. "I never trusted you, Nin. There's always been something off about you."

Shem's friends shifted uncomfortably, unsure what to do, as Bartel and Nin faced off in a battle of wills. Captain Damrina's hand tightened on her sword hilt.

"Always the storyteller," Nin said, his voice low and menacing.

Shem couldn't watch any longer. "Bartel isn't lying!" He was shaking in anger, feeling the sting of betrayal all over again. "I trusted you...only to find out that you planned all of this! Even the tyrannosaur wasn't a coincidence...you tried to kill us all!"

Shem could hear his friends gasp in surprise.

Nin simply folded his arms, his hat pulled down low.

"You're responsible for all of it...even...even, Adi's death." Shem's heart was pounding. He couldn't continue.

Captain Damrina broke her silence, addressing Shem. "Adi ? What is this?"

Bartel took the lead and answered for him. "She was his betrothed, and my daughter. Her...my other daughter, and my wife, all perished when Anu attacked Ararat." He put his hands on his hips to catch his breath at the painful memory.

"It's because of you, Nin, they all died. It's because of you that we left home..." Shem's voice was barely a whisper.

"Then, it's also because of you," said Eloise. "That my mother died."

Nin's face contorted with rage. "You dare accuse me?" he hissed, stepping towards Shem.

In a flash, Bartel's hand connected with Nin's chest, sending him staggering backward. The surrounding soldiers drew their weapons, the metallic ring of steel filling the air.

"Stand down!" Captain Damrina barked, but her order was lost in the chaos.

Shem's companions instinctively drew their own weapons, forming a protective circle around him. The air was heavy with tension as the two groups faced off, blades glinting in the fading sunlight.

Bartel, his face red with fury, shouted over the commotion. "Everyone, back down! This doesn't have to end in bloodshed!" He turned to Captain Damrina, his voice thick with urgency. "Captain, surely you can see that Nin is a traitor!"

Nin, rubbing his chest, locked eyes with Shem. A chilling smile spread across his face. "You're wrong about one thing," he said quietly, in response to Bartel. "It was always going to end in bloodshed."

In a blur of motion, Nin drew his sword and plunged it through Bartel's back. The blade erupted from Bartel's chest in a spray of crimson.

Shem watched in horror as Bartel's eyes went wide with shock and pain. His friend's mouth opened, but no sound came out. He slumped forward, sliding off Nin's blade and crumpling to the ground.

"No!" Shem screamed, lunging forward. Elam and Lud grabbed him, holding him back as he thrashed against their grip. "You monster!"

Chaos erupted as Bartel's body hit the ground, Shem's anguished cry piercing the air. His friends desperately struggled to hold him back. The Assyrian soldiers closed ranks around Nin, weapons drawn and pointed at Shem's group.

"Stand down!" Captain Damrina shouted, her voice cutting through the pandemonium. "Everyone, weapons down now!"

But her orders fell on deaf ears. Shem's companions were now joined by Edward and the town guard, swords and bows at the ready. Tension filled the clearing as both sides faced off, waiting for the slightest provocation to attack.

Nin wiped his bloody blade on Bartel's cloak, his face a mask of cold indifference. "Now, now," he said, his voice eerily calm. "Let's not do anything foolish."

"Foolish?" Shem broke free from his friends' grasp, drawing Davar from its sheath. The sword hummed with energy, responding to his rage and grief. He charged at Nin, who stood over Bartel's body with a cruel smile. "I'll show you foolish!" Shem roared, bringing Davar down in a powerful arc.

Nin sidestepped the blow with a superhuman speed, his eyes glittering with malice. "You have no chance, boy," he hissed.

Around them, the square had devolved into a war zone. Nin's blade clashed against Davar, the impact sending shockwaves up Shem's arms. The man's strength was inhuman, far beyond what Shem had expected. "You don't know who you're dealing with, boy," Nin snarled, his face inches from Shem's. His eyes flashed with an other-worldly light.

Shem gritted his teeth, pushing back with all his might. "I know exactly who I'm dealing with," he spat. "A traitor and a murderer!"

Around them, chaos reigned. The sound of clashing steel filled the air as Shem's companions fought against the Assyrian soldiers.

"You don't even know how that blade works," said Nin, swinging his sword at Shem's head.

Shem barely had time to react as Nin's blade whistled through the air, towards his neck. He stumbled backward, Davar rising just in time to deflect the blow. The impact sent shockwaves up his arms, nearly causing him to drop his sword. He was losing ground quickly and knew he couldn't win this fight.

"You're out of your depth," Nin taunted, pressing his attack. His movements were impossibly fast, each strike coming with inhuman strength.

Shem frantically parried, giving ground with each exchange. His arms burned with the effort of holding off Nin's onslaught. Around them, the battle raged - the clash of steel and cries of pain filling the air.

The ground trembled beneath Shem's feet as he stumbled back from Nin's ferocious assault. His heart racing, he frantically scanned the chaotic scene of battle, his eyes locking onto a herd of large dinosaurs stampeding down the road between the crumbling buildings that encircled the square.

"Everyone scatter!" Shem shouted, narrowly avoiding another strike from Nin's blade. "Run!"

He leapt out of harm's way as a herd of Pachycephalosaurus charged into the midst of the battle. Their thick skulls plowed through the technologically advanced soldiers, who were caught off guard by the sudden appearance of these stampeding beasts.

As Elam helped him to his feet, Shem caught a glimpse of Binne perched on top of one of the charging dinosaurs, her laughter ringing out in pure joy and excitement amidst the chaos of battle.

CHAPTER 20

Incredible Force

"Binne!" Shem yelled, his voice barely audible over the thunderous footsteps of the dinosaurs.

Binne's wild laughter faded into the distance as the Pachycephalosaurus herd barreled through the square, leaving a wake of bewildered soldiers in their path.

Shem shook his head in disbelief. "She's going to get herself killed."

"Or save us all," Elam quipped, scanning the chaotic scene around them.

The stampede had bought them precious moments, but Shem knew it wouldn't last long. "We need to do something, now!"

Shem tried to think quickly, as he surveyed the chaotic scene. Edward and his town guard were pressing their advantage, ruthlessly attacking the disoriented soldiers.

But on the edge of the chaos stood Nin, radiating malevolence, his wide-brimmed hat pulled low over his eyes. His dark smile made Shem feel weak as he locked his gaze on him, a chilling promise of impending defeat.

Shem's breath caught in his throat as Nin launched himself into the fray, moving with inhuman speed. Before anyone could react, the dark figure had cut down two of Edward's men, their bodies crumpling to the ground like discarded puppets.

"No!" Shem cried out, his voice echoing off of the surrounding buildings.

Elam gripped Shem's arm, his face pale with shock. "By the Creator...I've never seen him move like that!"

They watched in horror as Nin effortlessly dispatched the remaining guards, his blade a blur of deadly precision. Edward, realizing the futility of the fight, dropped his weapon and raised his hands in surrender.

"Please," Edward's voice carried across the square, "we yield!"

Nin showed no mercy. With a cruel smile directed at Shem and his friends, he drove his blade through Edward's chest.

"We have to get out of here," Aram said, tugging at Shem's sleeve.

Shem nodded grimly, his heart pounding. "You're right. We're outmatched here."

As if on cue, Nin's voice rang out across the square, "Captain! I want those children! Alive!"

Captain Damrina and Lieutenant Goriel began advancing with their troops, weapons at the ready.

Shem and his friends backed away, desperately searching for an escape route.

"There!" Aryana pointed to a massive stone structure looming behind them. "That building might offer some cover."

Shem squinted, noticing movement near the entrance at the top of a multi-tiered staircase. *Is that Raphael?*

Before he could confirm, the soldiers closed in. Acting on instinct, Shem raised Davar and slashed through the air. The sword struck one of the soldier's tube-weapons like a bolt of lightning, cleaving it in two. The weapon exploded in a shower of sparks, causing the nearby soldiers to recoil and shield their eyes.

Shem seized the moment of confusion. "Now!" he shouted to his friends. "Up the stairs!"

They bolted towards the monolithic structure, their feet pounding against the ancient stone steps. Shem's lungs burned as he pushed himself harder, hearing the angry shouts of the soldiers behind them.

"Stop right there, or I'll show you how the serpent works!" Lieutenant Goriel's voice boomed from below. His warning was followed by a high-pitched whine as his weapon came to life.

Shem glanced back just in time to see Goriel point the serpent at them. "Duck!" he yelled, throwing himself to the side.

A concussive blast struck the nearby column, sending chunks of stone raining down on them. Eloise yelped as a piece grazed her arm, but Lud pulled her along.

"Keep moving!" Halvin urged, his voice strained with exertion. "We're almost there!"

They stumbled through the entrance, coughing as dust billowed around them. Shem was shocked as he took in the vast interior. Smooth stone walls stretched upward, their polished surfaces barely touched by time. Fallen wooden doors and overturned tables, now nothing more than rotted remnants, littered the floor.

"This way!" Aryana called, gesturing toward a corridor, dimly lit by a few openings.

As they ran, Shem's mind raced. "Did anyone else see Raphael? I could've sworn—"

"Less talking, more running!" Elam interrupted, pushing Shem forward as the sound of boots on marble echoed behind them.

Shem's head was pounded, as they made their way deeper into the building, trying to process everything that had just happened. The treacherous soldiers, Nin killing Bartel, Edward and the town guard were dead, and now they were running for their lives from a person they believed to be their friend - it was almost too much to bear.

"Quick, in here!" Aram called out, gesturing to a partially open doorway.

They ducked inside what appeared to be a large chamber, its high ceilings lost in shadow. Halvin and Lud quickly pushed a heavy stone table against the door, barricading it.

"That should hold them for a bit," Lud panted, wiping sweat from his brow. "Unless they have another giant."

Shem leaned against a wall, catching his breath. "Okay, we need a plan. Any ideas?"

Eloise spoke up, her voice trembling slightly. "We need to find a way out of this building. There has to be another exit."

"Agreed," Shem nodded, pushing himself off the wall. "But we also need to figure out what's going on. What is Nin's plan?"

Elam ran a hand through his hair, his face etched with concern. "I hate to say it, but I think he's in charge of those...soldiers. We were so wrong about him."

"It doesn't make sense," Aram muttered, pacing nervously. "Did you see how he moved? It wasn't natural."

Lady Aryana's eyes were wide with fear, her voice trembling. "Who are they, Shem? They are unlike anything I've ever encountered. Those weapons…that armor…"

Her near panic was causing Shem's own nerves to fray. *What hope do we have if she's falling apart?*

"They're Assyrians," Shem couldn't blame her for being scared. "They've been developing their weapons for years."

"Well I for one, don't want to see what they can do to us," said Lud, looking around the room. "Can we go now?"

Halvin's fists clenched tightly as he growled, "Yeah, I agree. We need to find a way out."

A loud bang against the barricaded door made them all jump.

Shem nodded, his eyes scanning the dimly lit chamber for another exit. "Alright, spread out and search for any hidden passages or doors. This place looks ancient—there might be a hidden way."

As they fanned out across the room, another crash echoed from the barricaded entrance. The stone table shuddered, and a fine shower of dust rained down from the ceiling.

"They're using something to break through," Eloise whispered, her voice tight with fear.

Shem's hand tightened on Davar's hilt as he turned to face the trembling door. He could feel the floor shake under his feet, as another crash struck the barricade.

"Hey, I don't think it's going to hold—" started Lud from the other side of the room.

His words were cut off by a deafening boom. The stone table flew across the room, shattering against the far wall and showering them with debris.

Through the dust and chaos, Shem glimpsed the menacing silhouette of Lieutenant Goriel, his serpent weapon glowing ominously.

"There's nowhere left to run, boy," Goriel sneered, stepping into the chamber. Behind him, a squad of Assyrian soldiers filed in, their insect-like helmets gleaming in the dim light.

Shem's mind raced. They were cornered, outnumbered, and outmatched, but he refused to make it easy for them.

"Sorry," he whispered dejectedly, "I've run out of ideas." He raised his sword in resignation. *This is it.*

Goriel's lips curled into a cruel smile as he raised his serpent weapon. "Surrender now, and we'll end this."

Shem's grip tightened on Davar, his palms slick with sweat. He glanced at his friends, seeing the fear and determination in their eyes. They were cornered, but they weren't going down without a fight. *Lord, give me strength.*

Shem raised Davar high, its radiance shining even brighter and fiercer than before, as though it were answering his silent plea.

Goriel's laughter boomed through the room, as he faced the small group standing before him. "You really think you stand a chance against the might of the Assyrian army?" He sneered, dismissing them with a wave of his hand.

Shem couldn't respond, as the soldiers had already opened fire on his friends with more of their strange tube-like weapons. He watched helplessly as, one by one they fell to the ground, their bodies limp and lifeless as if a switch had been flipped and their lights extinguished.

Enraged, Shem lunged towards Lieutenant Goriel, determined to take him down at any cost. But just as he was about to reach him, the serpent weapon fired and Davar took the brunt of the blast, shielding Shem from its deadly force. The impact sent Shem hurtling backwards through what looked like a solid stone wall, but upon impact it shattered like brittle wood, splintering into pieces.

Shem crashed through the wall into another chamber, his body aching and battered but still fueled by anger and adrenaline. He could taste the blood on his lips as he rose to his feet, ready to take on the whole Assyian army by himself.

As he turned, Elam's voice cut through the chaos, bringing him back to reality. He saw his friend struggling to stand, blood streaming down his face from a deep wound. Shem reached out to help him up.

"What happened?" Elam asked, wincing in pain as he touched his head wound.

"We were thrown through a wall by one of their weapons," Shem replied, his ears still ringing from the blast. "My head is still spinning."

With Davar clutched tightly in front of him, its light shining bright, Shem shifted into a fighting stance. "They'll be on us any second. Can you fight?"

Elam started to reply, but before he could finish, the floor beneath them gave way and they found themselves tumbling into the unknown.

Shem and Elam plummeted through the darkness, their startled cries echoing off unseen walls. The fall seemed to last an eternity before they crashed onto a hard surface with a bone jarring thud.

"Oof!" Elam groaned, the impact knocking the wind out of him. "What in the name of—"

"Shh!" Shem hissed, his hand fumbling for Davar. The sword's faint glow illuminated their surroundings - a cramped, musty chamber filled with broken pottery and the pungent smell of long-spoiled wine.

"Where are we?" Elam whispered, wincing as he tried to move.

Shem carefully got to his feet, his body aching from the fall.

"Some kind of old storage room, I think. Are you alright?"

Elam attempted to stand but immediately fell back with a sharp cry of pain. "My ankle," he gasped, clutching his leg. "I think it's sprained... or worse."

Shem's heart sank. He knelt beside his friend, Davar's soft light revealing Elam's grimace of pain. "Let me take a look," he said, gently probing the swollen ankle. Elam sucked air through clenched teeth.

"Can you move it at all?" Shem asked.

Elam tried wiggling his foot, his face contorting. "A little, but it hurts like blazes."

Shem nodded grimly. "I'm no healer, but it just seems like a bad sprain. You won't be running anytime soon." He glanced around the dim chamber, searching for an exit. "We need to find a way out of here before those soldiers find us."

Elam gritted his teeth and tried to stand again, leaning heavily on Shem for support. "What about the others? Do you think they're...?"

Shem's stomach churned as he remembered the sight of his friends falling to the Assyrian weapons. "I... I don't know," he admitted, trying to keep his voice to a whisper. "It all happened so fast. But we can't help them if we're caught too. We need to focus."

As Shem helped Elam limp across the room, he noticed a faint breeze coming from one corner. "There," he whispered, "I think there might be a passage."

Shem helped Elam hobble towards the source of the breeze. As they got closer, Shem could make out a narrow opening in the wall, partially obscured by fallen debris. "Look," he whispered, "a passageway. It might lead us out of here."

Elam nodded, his face pale with pain. "Let's hope it doesn't lead us right back to those soldiers."

As Shem began clearing away the debris, Elam spoke up. "Shem, those soldiers... who or what are we dealing with here?"

Shem paused, thinking about what he actually knew. "They're Assyrians," he said, in a low voice. "They claimed to be monitoring the border of their empire, and that they were friends...but clearly, that was a lie. It looked like they were taking orders from Nin."

Elam's eyes widened. "But how? And why?"

Shem shook his head, resuming his work on clearing the debris. "What makes it worse, is I think the Eden council is aware of their power." He grunted as he pushed aside a large piece of broken pottery. "And I don't believe they realize the danger. It looks like the Assyrians are preparing for war...and somehow Nin seems to be completely involved."

"I can't believe it," Elam whispered, his face paling further. "Against Eden? And, what does Nin gain in all this?"

"I don't know," Shem admitted. "But he's been hiding it for a long time. We need to warn Eden, warn everyone."

Shem strained as he pushed aside the last piece of debris, revealing a narrow passageway. "There, that should do it," he said, wiping sweat from his brow. "Hopefully we can escape and find some help." *Lord, please send help.*

He helped Elam to his feet, supporting his weight as they squeezed into the passageway. The air was stale and musty, but Shem could feel a faint breeze on his face, giving him hope that it led somewhere.

As they shuffled along in the dim light of Davar, Elam spoke up again. "Just curious...where do you think we'll find help out here?"

Shem nodded, keeping his voice low. "I'm not entirely sure, but the soldiers mentioned having problems with a group of people that live on the outskirts."

Shem paused, listening for any sounds of pursuit before continuing. "They said they are part of a cult that doesn't believe what they believe. A few of them are being held captive. The enemy of our enemy, right?"

Elam winced as he put weight on his injured ankle. "Or...we could be walking right into another trap."

"True," Shem admitted, "but right now, do we have another option?"

They continued down the narrow passageway, the soft glow of Davar casting eerie shadows on the ancient walls. The air grew fresher as they progressed, giving Shem hope that they were nearing an exit.

Rounding a bend in the passage, he could see a faint glimmer of light ahead. Shem's heart began to race. He could hear muffled voices, but couldn't make out what they were saying. He slowed, pressing a finger to his lips, reminding Elam to be quiet.

They crept forward, the passageway opening into a small courtyard between the buildings. Shem peered around the corner, his breath catching at the sight before him.

Four of the Assyrian soldiers were gathered together in the courtyard, their armor shining in all of its intimidating glory. They spoke in hushed, yet unnatural tones, their insect-like helmets masking their true voices.

"I bet they're looking for us," Elam whispered, his voice barely audible.

Shem nodded, his mind racing. These soldiers would act without hesitation if they saw them, but with Elam injured they couldn't outrun them. *I need a distraction.*

"I have an idea," Shem whispered, carefully lowering Elam to the ground. "Stay here and keep quiet."

Elam's eyes widened. "Shem, no! It's too dangerous."

Shem shrugged nonchalantly and sheathed Davar. "It's just like when we used to sneak into old Katla's Bakery for sweet cakes back home," he declared confidently.

Elam rolled his eyes and muttered, "But you always got caught..."

Shem simply grinned and slipped out of the tunnel, behind a row of bushes that lined the courtyard, leaving Elam to sit in frustration.

He crept along the edge of the courtyard, his heart pounding in his chest. The bushes provided some cover, but Shem knew one wrong move could give him away. He glanced back at Elam, who watched with wide, worried eyes from the passageway.

Taking a deep breath, Shem picked up a small rock. He weighed it in his hand for a moment, then hurled it across the courtyard. It clattered against a far wall, the sound echoing in the stillness.

The effect was immediate. The Assyrian soldiers snapped to attention, their insect-like helmets swiveling towards the noise.

"Over there!" one of them barked, his voice distorted by the technology in his helmet. "Spread out and search!"

As the soldiers moved towards the far side of the courtyard, Shem moved from his hiding spot.

Shem darted from behind the bushes, keeping low as he moved towards a crumbling stone archway on the opposite side of the courtyard. His heart pounded in his ears as he tried to stay out of sight of the searching soldiers.

Shem darted for the archway, his mind filled with the hope of escape. But suddenly, a soldier lunged from the shadows with a violent force, his arm outstretched like a deadly branch. The breath was knocked from Shem's body as he was launched into the air, his feet flailing helplessly before crashing to the ground with a deafening thud, his body crumpling like a sack of potatoes. Pain shot through every limb as he struggled to regain his bearings.

With a grunt, he rolled onto his side and winced as his eyes adjusted to the afternoon sunlight. In the center of the courtyard, Elam was being dragged by the other soldiers, their curses filling the air as they pulled him unceremoniously from his hiding spot.

Shem's head pounded as he felt himself being yanked up from the ground by his attacker, his body protesting against the rough treatment. He was forced to join Elam in the center, surrounded by the others who yelled at them with varying levels of disdain and anger. Each breath burned in Shem's chest as he braced himself for what was to come next.

The soldier's boot ground into Shem's back, pinning him to the ground with incredible force. "They were right where he told us to look," he barked, his laughter laced with sadistic glee as he reveled in Shem's helplessness.

"Yeah, it's weird how the general knows the ins and outs of this place," said one of the others. "How old is he anyway?"

The soldier pinning Shem answered. "It doesn't matter. Let's just get back to the clearing and secure them with the others."

"Others?" Elam's voice trembled with fear and panic. He tried to get up, but his body betrayed him, only making it to his hands and knees. Suddenly, the soldier closest to him lashed out with the force of a large horse, delivering a brutal kick that sent Elam flying through the air. With a sickening thud, he hit the ground hard on his stomach, the wind knocked out of him. He lay there moaning in agony, helpless and at the mercy of his attackers.

"Leave him alone," yelled Shem, his anger getting the best of him. "Or I'll..."

The soldier lifted him off the ground by his throat; Shem held onto his arm for dear life. "You'll do what little Edener?"

Shem struggled for breath, his fingers clawing desperately at the soldier's iron grip. Black spots danced at the edges of his vision as he felt consciousness slipping away.

Suddenly, a blur of motion caught his fading sight. The soldier holding him jerked violently, loosening his grip as he stumbled backward. Shem dropped to the ground, gasping and coughing.

Through watering eyes, he saw a white clad figure moving with inhuman speed among the soldiers. There was a flash of steel, a spray of blood, and one by one the Assyrians fell.

As Shem's vision cleared, he saw Raphael standing over the fallen soldiers, his blade dripping red. The familiar man's eyes burned with an intensity Shem had never seen before. *Thank Yahweh, he found us.*

Covered in dust and struggling to get to his knees, Elam looked at Shem, his grin stretching from ear to ear. "I knew it!"

"Knew what?"

"That you always get caught," quipped Elam.

Shem could only roll his eyes.

CHAPTER 21

Dreadful Incantations

Shem, Elam and Raphael slinked through the abandoned city streets, careful to avoid any sign of movement or life. Their progress was slow, as Elam couldn't put much weight on his ankle. They weaved their way through decaying buildings, their footsteps muffled by layers of dust and debris. The late afternoon sun cast long shadows on them, making every step feel like a race against time.

As they neared the outskirts of the city, Shem could feel a sense of relief wash over him. Either they were almost free and out of danger, or they would run into the city's other residents and find possible help. But they didn't let their guard down, knowing that at any moment they could be captured and taken back to the soldier's camp in the town square.

As they rounded a corner, Shem held up a hand, signaling the others to stop. He peered cautiously around a crumbling stone wall, holding his breath. The street ahead appeared empty, but something felt off.

"What is it?" Elam whispered, his voice tight with pain and exhaustion.

Shem shook his head, squinting into the shadows. "I'm not sure. Just... stay alert."

They crept forward, the eerie silence broken only by the crunch of gravel beneath their feet and Elam's labored breathing. Raphael supported Elam's weight, both of them moving slowly behind Shem.

Suddenly, a flicker of movement caught Shem's eye. He froze, raising his hand again to halt the others.

"There," he breathed, pointing to a small alleyway that led to what appeared to be a clearing. "Someone is down there. Maybe they'll help."

Raphael shook his head, his expression turning grave as he lifted a warning finger. It was clear that he did not agree with the proposed plan.

Shem let out an exasperated sigh, throwing his hands up in frustration at Raphael's lack of vocal response. For as long as Shem had known him, he had never said a word, and yet he couldn't help but feel annoyed by his silence at this moment.

In response, Raphael's arm shot out in the opposite direction, his fingers pointing fiercely in the air.

Elam raised an eyebrow at the intensity of Raphael's gesture.

"I guess he really feels strongly about it."

Shem, on the other hand, shook his head slowly, uncertainty clouding his mind as he weighed his options. The wind tousled his hair, and a faint scent of pine lingered in the air around them. He furrowed his brow, deep in thought as he tried to determine the best course of action.

Elam's tone of concern broke through Shem's thoughts. "What do you wanna do?" he said, his brow furrowed in thought.

Shem's mind drifted back to the words of his father when they first left on this journey. "*I can assure you, that he is a gift, even if you cannot see it now,*" he had said, and that was part of what made this decision so difficult.

Shem didn't normally spend much time pondering his decisions, but for some reason he couldn't shake off the doubt that lingered in his mind. And he couldn't remember Raphael ever being so adamant about anything before.

After a moment of hesitation, Shem spoke up again. "Okay, Raphael," he said with a sigh. "I hope you know where you're going." His uncertainty still gnawed at him, making it hard to fully commit to this new plan. "But, we'll go your way."

His words were resigned, but underneath there was a glimmer of hope that this unexpected turn would lead them to safety.

Shem carefully took over supporting Elam from Raphael and they moved slowly down the road, following Raphael's directions. They cautiously navigated each crossroad, with Shem's eyes scanning for any signs of movement down the alternate routes. After what seemed like an eternity, they finally reached their destination-an open space that appeared to be an old marketplace, teeming with life and energy. Vendors called out their wares, children ran between stalls, and the scent of spices and freshly baked bread wafted through the air. Shem couldn't help but pause in awe at the bustling scene before them.

The clearing was vast, enclosed by the crumbling buildings of the old city on all sides except for the far end where a looming stone wall stood in all its megalithic majesty. The cobblestone path descended down steps into a large landing, lined with elegant benches and ornate planters filled with meticulously tended bushes and trees. Each leaf seemed to glisten in the warm sunlight, evidence that they were being carefully groomed by loving hands.

The bustling market area was a maze of tents and stalls, each selling their own unique wares. It was a city within a city, the central heart of these people. The buildings encircling the market showed signs of recent construction and repair, as they continued to rebuild and revive their once-great city from this central point outwards. The sound of hammers and saws echoed through the air, a symphony of progress throughout the ruins.

Amidst the bustling town, people rushed past each other in a whirlwind of activity. Some were tending to repairs, hammers and saws in hand, while others were chopping wood with sharp axes.

Each person seemed to be a puzzle piece fitting perfectly into the picture of a peaceful community that would've been right at home in Eden. Their clothes varied in style and quality, as if they had been carefully selected and imported from all corners of Adamah. Vibrant colors adorned their garments, giving the impression of a lively and diverse society thriving in their own corner of the world.

Shem spoke to Raphael over his shoulder.

"Well, it seems like you were right," he commented, turning to see Raphael's reaction. But to his surprise, Raphael was nowhere in sight.

"That's strange," Elam remarked, scanning the area. "He was here a second ago. Perhaps he's just scouting ahead?"

"Maybe," replied Shem, feeling a sense of unease creeping up on him.

Still processing the situation, Shem spied a group of people making their way towards him and Elam.

Two men and a woman, all armed with short swords at their hips, approached the boys. Their clothing was simple without any signs of armor, but Shem couldn't shake off his wariness. He scanned their surroundings, searching for potential escape routes in case things took a turn for the worst.

Shem tensed as the group drew closer, instinctively tightening his grip on Elam. The woman, her dark hair streaked with gray, stepped forward with a welcoming smile that didn't quite reach her eyes.

"Welcome, strangers," she said, her voice carrying a hint of wariness beneath its warmth. "I am Estrid, one of the elders here. What brings you to New Eridu?"

"We're... travelers," Shem said carefully. "My friend is injured, and we're seeking refuge and aid."

One of the men, a tall lanky, clean shaven man, narrowed his eyes. "Travelers, eh? From where?"

Elam spoke up, his voice strained but steady. "We come from the north," Elam said, his eyes meeting the tall man's gaze. "Our village was raided by bandits. We managed to escape."

Shem felt a flicker of admiration for Elam's quick thinking, even as his stomach twisted with guilt for his friend, whom he never heard lie before.

Estrid's eyebrows raised. "I'm sorry to hear that. We've had some dealings with...bandits." She glanced at Elam's injured ankle. "Come, let's get you to a healer."

As they followed Estrid through the bustling marketplace, Shem felt his unease increase with the amount of people surrounding him. He scanned the crowd, searching for any sign of Raphael, but their silent companion was nowhere to be seen.

They led Shem and Elam through the winding tent city of New Eridu, the sounds of the marketplace all around them. Shem's eyes darted from face to face, searching for any sign of hostility or recognition. But the people they passed seemed genuinely curious, if a bit wary, of the newcomers.

They arrived at a small, circular tent with a red roof. Smoke curled lazily from a hole in the center, carrying with it the pungent scent of herbs.

"This is our healing house," Estrid explained, ushering them inside. "Mara will tend to your friend's injury."

An elderly woman with kind eyes and gnarled hands emerged from the shadows. She gestured for Elam to sit on a low wooden bench.

As Mara began examining Elam's ankle, Shem turned to Estrid, his curiosity getting the better of him. "This place New Eridu - how long has it been here?" he asked, trying to keep his tone casual.

Estrid's eyes narrowed slightly, but her smile remained in place. "We've been rebuilding for years now," she said. "After the... wars." Her smile disappeared. "You should've seen it before. It was majestic."

Shem nodded, not wanting to press further and risk upsetting her or arousing suspicion. He glanced at Elam, who was wincing as Mara prodded his swollen ankle.

"It's a bad sprain," Mara announced, reaching for a jar of pungent-smelling salve. "But with rest and this ointment, you should be back on your feet in a few days."

As she worked, Estrid cleared her throat. "We have a gathering tonight, to honor our god and seek his guidance. You're our guests. Please, join us."

Shem felt a prickle of unease at the mention of "their god," but he forced a smile. "That's very kind of you. We'd be honored."

Elam shot him a questioning look, but Shem gave a subtle shake of his head. They needed to play along, at least for now.

"Excellent," Estrid said, clapping her hands together. "I'll have someone show you to the gathering spot, when you are done here. The ceremony begins at sundown in a few hours."

Later, as they followed a young boy through the winding tents towards the meeting spot, Shem leaned close to Elam. "Keep your eyes open," he whispered. "Something feels off about this place."

Elam nodded subtly, his eyes scanning their surroundings as they walked. "So...I guess we don't trust they'll help us?"

"Trust is in short supply right now. Like, where's Raphael?"

"I see your point," said Elam, clenching his jaw in concern.

The sun was sinking low on the horizon, casting long shadows across the bustling marketplace. And near the edge of the tent city, a large bonfire was being prepared in a cleared area.

"There," the young guide said, pointing to the gathering crowd. "The ceremony will start soon."

Shem and Elam exchanged a wary glance before following the boy to the edge of the crowd. People were settling onto logs around the pit that was blazing with an impressive bonfire. The air buzzed with anticipation.

Taking their seats, Shem leaned close to Elam. "Any sign of him?" he murmured.

Elam shook his head. "Nothing. It's like he vanished."

A hush fell over the crowd, pausing any further conversation, leaving only the sounds of boots hitting the ground in unison. The firelight flickered ominously as a procession emerged from the shadows.

Shem's breath caught in his throat as he saw the elaborate face tattoos adorning each member of the group come into view. Each was adorned in black leather armor, as though prepared for war. It was the invaders they'd been searching for.

At the center of the procession was a woman, her face a canvas of swirling patterns radiating out from an eye tattooed on her forehead. She moved with an otherworldly grace, her eyes distant and unfocused. The crowd began to murmur in anticipation.

Shem tensed, ready to spring up, but a firm hand gripped his shoulder from behind. He had similar facial markings, his expression stern. "Stay seated," the man growled softly.

The tattooed woman, whom Shem presumed to be a priestess, lifted her arms, instantly silencing the crowd.

"Brothers and sisters," the priestess' voice rang out, eerily melodic. "Tonight, we gather to honor our great leader, General Ouza, and present him with a gift of glory."

Shem felt his heart racing in his chest as the priestess' gaze swept over the crowd, finally landing on Shem and Elam. A cold smile spread across her face. "Behold, the offering our master has long awaited."

Shem's muscles tensed as he attempted to flee, but the grip on his shoulder tightened painfully.

The color had drained from Elam's face.

"And now," the woman continued, her voice rising, "I present to you, our glorious leader, General Ouza!"

A cheer erupted as a tall figure, dressed in black, emerged from a nearby tent.

Shem's blood ran cold as he recognized the familiar face. *Nin!*

The man who had betrayed them, who had sent the giant Anu to destroy his home, now stood before them as the revered leader of these cultists. And his name was General Ouza, a name that he and his friends had heard many times around the fire, a name from legends of old.

Nin - or General Ouza as he was known here - strode forward, his eyes gleaming with triumph as he surveyed the bowing crowd. When his gaze fell on Shem and Elam, a cruel smile twisted his lips.

"My faithful followers," Ouza's voice boomed across the gathering. "Our patience has been rewarded. The boys who thought they could challenge us have been delivered into our hands."

Fury and desperation surged through Shem. Slipping from the tattooed man's grip, he drew Davar, the sword springing to life in his hands. Brilliant light erupted from the blade, momentarily blinding those nearby.

"Traitor!" Shem shouted, his voice cracking with emotion. He lunged forward, intent on striking down Ouza where he stood.

But rough hands grabbed him from behind before he could strike. Shem struggled against his captors, the sword's light flickering wildly. He heard Elam cry out in pain beside him.

"Drop the sword, boy," Ouza's voice was calm, almost bored. "Or your friend dies."

Shem froze, his heart pounding. He turned to see one of the tattooed cultists pressing a wicked-looking knife against Elam's throat. His friend's eyes were wide with fear, silently pleading for help.

Time seemed to stand still as Shem's mind raced. The sword in his hand pulsed with power, urging him to strike. But the sight of the blade against Elam's skin made his stomach churn.

He couldn't risk his friend's life, not even to stop Ouza. Feeling the sting of hopelessness, Shem lowered Davar. The brilliant light faded, plunging the gathering back into the flickering shadows of the bonfire.

"Let him go," Shem said, his voice hoarse. "I'll do what you want."

"I have no doubt." Ouza, sounding cruel and mocking, stepped closer, his eyes gleaming with malice in the firelight. "Drop the sword, Shem. Now!"

Shem's fingers tightened around Davar's hilt, every instinct screaming at him to fight. But as the cultist pressed the knife harder against Elam's throat, drawing a thin line of blood, he knew he had no choice. With a shaky exhale, he let the sword fall from his grip. It clattered to the ground, its wooden blade sounding like a useless branch in the tense silence.

"Bind them," Ouza said, to the tattooed soldiers, who seized Shem and Elam, forcing their arms behind their backs.

As iron shackles bit into his wrists, Shem locked eyes with his old mentor. "Why?" he demanded, his voice raw with anger and betrayal. "Why did you turn against us? Against Eden?"

"Why...indeed," said Ouza, looking strangely amused. "That...Is a tale for another day. We have business to attend to."

Turning to the priestess, Ouza gave a terse command. "Begin the ceremony."

The woman bowed deeply, then raised her arms to the darkening sky. Chanting in an ancient, guttural incantation, the priestess' voice rose above the crackle of the fire, her words weaving spells into the air. She held aloft a chalice, pouring the offering of its contents in the fire, which erupted in a burst of green and purple flames.

With a deep breath, she began the final incantation, her voice steady despite the weight of what she was about to do. "I summon thee, Samyaza. Enter this vessel, become one with me, for the greater good."

A familiar sense of dread filled Shem as he watched the priestess begin to convulse, her eyes rolling back in her head. The crowd around them fell to their knees, pressing their foreheads to the ground in reverence.

The air grew thick, charged with an otherworldly energy. The flames of the bonfire twisted into forms of faces, snarling and laughing, as if the very essence of the fire was alive with the presence of this otherworldly being.

Suddenly, the priestess's body went rigid, and when she spoke again, it was with a voice that was not her own. Deep and guttural, it seemed to come from everywhere and nowhere at once.

"Who dares to summon me?" the voice growled.

Shem's blood ran cold as he somehow knew the demonic voice. It wasn't Samyaza at all - it was Azazel. The same fallen angel who had taunted them in Eden, now speaking through the possessed priestess. These cultists had no idea of the true nature of the being they worshipped.

Ouza stepped forward and bowed low. "Great Samyaza," he intoned, "I, your faithful servant Ouza, have brought you the prize you seek."

Azazel's laughter boomed through the priestess's mouth, making the flames dance wildly. "Ah General, yes, you have done well."

The demon's eyes, glowing an unnatural amber through the priestess's sockets, fell upon Shem and Elam. A wicked grin spread across the woman's face, twisting her features into something inhuman.

"Shem, son of Noah," Azazel's voice rumbled. "How delightful to see you again, boy. I'm sure...by now... you realize there is no place I can't find you."

Shem gritted his teeth, fighting against the urge to lunge at the possessed woman. "You won't win, Azazel," he spat. "Yahweh will—"

"Yahweh?" Azazel interrupted with a mocking laugh. "Your precious Yahweh has abandoned you, child. Just as He abandoned this world to us long ago."

The demon's gaze swept over the bowing cultists. "They worship me in complete devotion, and soon, so will all of Adamah."

Azazel's eyes locked onto Shem once more. "You and your pathetic lineage have lost. The line of Seth will be stamped out, and with it, any hope for your Yahweh's precious Redeemer."

Shem felt his heart pounding, a mixture of fear and rage coursing through him. He wanted to shout, to deny Azazel's words, but the demon's confidence shook him to his core.

Laughing, the demon turned its attention to Ouza. "My faithful general. You have done well in delivering these boys to me. But our work is not yet finished."

Bowing low, Ouza said, "What would you have me do, lord?"

Azazel's eyes gleamed with malice. "Take them and the others to Asshur for the celebration. And since you've succeeded in luring Eden's knights east, you may have your revenge. Go command my armies and strike the capital of Eden itself, in the west."

Shem railed against his captors, trying without success to break free. *I've gotta get home!*

At Ouza's command, the tattooed cultists roughly hauled Shem and Elam to their feet. As they spun around, Shem felt his knees go weak. There, at the edge of the clearing, stood the Assyrian soldiers awaiting their new prisoners.

The box-like char was with them and it now hovered above the ground, emanating an eerie blue light. Shem's heart skipped a beat as he saw it, knowing all too well what that ominous vehicle was used for - transporting prisoners. He hoped that his friends were in the transport and in one piece.

Ouza barked orders to Captain Damrina, who marched forward with military precision. "Place them with the others," he commanded, a cruel smile playing on his lips. "Our revenge is at hand."

As the soldiers roughly grabbed Shem and Elam, dragging them towards the char, Shem desperately scanned the crowd. *Where is Raphael?* Had their silent companion abandoned them, or had he too been captured? Or worse-did he betray them, too?

Approaching the transport-char, Shem caught a faint murmur of voices and saw shadows moving inside. A surge of hope filled his heart as he spotted familiar faces pressed against the bars of the back window. His friends were all there. *Thank you, Lord!*

"Shem! Elam!" Lud called out, his voice muffled. "You're alive!"

"Not for long," Captain Damrina sneered, roughly pushing Shem forward.

The rear door of the char swung open with an ominous creak. Inside, Shem could see the rest of his friends huddled together in the cramped space. They appeared haggard and defeated, but their eyes lit up at the sight of Shem and Elam.

As they were shoved inside, Shem stumbled, nearly falling on top of Sedee. She was huddled next to an older, bald man that he recognized from her vender stall back in Center Grove.

"Steady there, lad," the older man said, steadying Shem with a weathered hand. His kind eyes crinkled with concern. "You alright?"

Shem nodded gratefully, trying to regain his balance in the cramped space. "Not really."

"Come...sit," the man replied with a tired smile.

"Sedee, here is my niece, and they call me Bog."

Before Shem could respond, Elam was roughly shoved in behind him, the door slamming shut with a resounding clang. The char hummed to life, an eerie blue light cast strange shadows across their faces.

"What happened?" Lud whispered urgently, his face pressed close to Shem's. "How did they catch you?"

Shem shook his head, his voice low and bitter. "It was Raphael. He led us right to them."

A collective gasp rippled through the cramped space of the char. Shem felt the weight of disbelief and betrayal settle over the group.

"Raphael?" Eloise whispered, her voice trembling. "But... he seemed so...trustworthy."

Elam shook his head, wincing as he shifted his injured ankle. "We don't know for sure. He disappeared right before we were captured. Maybe he was taken too, or..."

"Or he was working with them all along," Lud finished grimly.

"I...I...just don't know any more," said Elam, dejectedly.

Shem leaned his head against the cool metal wall of the char, closing his eyes briefly. The events of the past few hours swirled in his mind - the revelation of Nin as General Ouza, Azazel wanting to destroy Eden, and now the uncertainty surrounding Raphael's true allegiance.

As the char drove off to places unknown, Shem could hear Ouza's voice outside, addressing the gathered cultists. "My faithful followers, our time of revenge draws near! Soon, we will strike at the very heart of Eden itself!"

A chorus of cheers erupted, fading as the char picked up speed.

Inside, the prisoners exchanged worried glances.

"Eden?" Halvin whispered, his eyes wide. "Haven't they already been attacking Eden?"

Shem nodded grimly. "That was just a ruse to lure the Eden Knights East. He and Nin...General Ouza, are working together and plan to attack the capital out west with the Assyrian army."

"Did you just say, General Ouza?" asked Lud, with a look of complete shock on his face. "As in...THE General Ouza? The same one from the Assyrian War?"

"The same," said Shem, still in disbelief himself.

"Didn't the stories say that Anatu killed him during the war?"

"Let's ask his sister," said Aram, joining the conversation.

Realizing that they were all waiting for a response, Aryana put her hands up in protest. “I wasn’t even born when that happened. I was told the same stories as everyone else.”

“Leave her be,” said Halvin, coming to her rescue. “It doesn’t matter. Ouza’s alive now, and Eden is in trouble! That’s all that matters right at this moment.”

“We have to warn them somehow,” said Aryana, her voice tight with desperation. “We must get a message to the high council.” She looked lost, as tears filled her eyes. “If only I had Alouette. Hopefully she recovers soon and finds me.

PART FOUR
Empire

"The Nephilim were on Adamah in those days, and also afterward, when the sons of Yahweh came into the daughters of men and they bore children to them.

Those were the mighty men who were of old, men of renown."

–The First Book of Moses:
Genesis: Chapter 6, Verse 4

CHAPTER 22

A Heavy Weight

"Have you completely lost your mind?" Halvin yelled, his face flushed with rage. His argument with Lud had been ongoing for hours now. "Do you honestly believe that we would have been safe if we stayed home?"

They had been going back and forth since their capture, which felt like an eternity ago. The Assyrians' convoy had left the forest behind and was now travelling through unfamiliar lands, with their prisoner transport in tow. Aryana sat by the back window, trying to keep an eye on their surroundings, but she had no idea where they were or where they were headed.

The rest of the companions were mostly silent, too scared or too tired to speak up or discuss their situation. Eloise sat between her two arguing friends , looking like she would rather be anywhere else. Of course, everyone wished for that.

Shem could see it in their weary faces. *This is a nightmare.*

Ouza had confirmed his fears - Shem was the prize that his master sought. The attack on Ararat wasn't *just* a ploy to lure the knights out. Which meant that Adi's death wasn't an accident. And since then, with every decision he made, and every time Nin agreed with Shem's plans, more people ended up getting hurt or killed. He was pulled along like a branch stuck in a strong river current. *Lord, how many more need to suffer for my destiny?*

"Just face it," Lud said bitterly, his usual cheerful demeanor nowhere to be found. "We have no hope against this evil."

Eloise reached for Lud's hand, attempting to calm him down, looking to Aram for help. But he just sat there in silence, examining the light on the roof of their mobile prison.

Shem noticed that Elam seemed like he wanted to say something several times, but he always stopped himself. He probably agreed with Lud but didn't want to take sides. So he remained silent too.

Sedee and Bog kept to themselves during the whole exchange, sharing quiet conversation. They were new to the group, and Shem figured they were just attempting to catch up with the whole ordeal. *It wouldn't surprise me if they were part of Nin's plan, too.*

Taking advantage of a break in the heated conversation, Bog spoke up. "Something occurred to me just now. I know you've all been through a lot, but hear me out. Maybe your man, Raphael, didn't actually betray you."

Shem perked up, intrigued. "Why do you say that?"

Bog leaned forward, making sure he had everyone's attention before continuing. "Sometimes when we think we know what's best, Yahweh knows another way." He turned to Sedee. "Tell them what you overheard, dear."

Sedee nodded and spoke up. "When the soldiers were looking for Shem, I heard them talking. They were hoping Shem would come their way so they could catch him and...

tear him apart. That was their words." She gave a pointed look at Shem. "Like you did to some of their friends?"

Shem grimaced, recalling the incident, and added, "Before we were captured, Raphael showed up and took care of some of the soldiers who were probably going to kill us."

Sedee smiled sadly. "Looks like they didn't get their revenge after all."

"Was that luck, or divine intervention?" Bog asked, earning silent stares from the group.

Lud shook his head in disbelief, grumbling to himself.

Shem leaned back against the rough wooden wall of the cart, his mind racing. Could Raphael really still be on their side? The thought gave him a glimmer of hope, but he couldn't shake the feeling of guilt that had settled in his chest.

"Even if Raphael is still trying to help us," Shem said quietly, "it doesn't change the fact that we're in this mess because of me. Either because of who I am, or who they think I am."

Elam, who had been holding his opinions, finally spoke up. "You can't blame yourself for the actions of evil men, Shem. We all chose to follow you--to fight for what's right."

Shem sighed heavily, his shoulders slumping. "But at what cost?" he repeated softly. "How many more lives will be lost because of me?"

Halvin, who had kept to himself, suddenly spoke up. "Listen, Shem," he said, his voice firm but not unkind. "You're not responsible for the choices of others. We all knew the risks when we left Ararat, and then again in Centergrove. And if you think for one second that any of us regret following you, you're dead wrong." He looked pointedly at Lud, who in turn, looked at his feet.

Shem looked up, meeting Halvin's steady gaze. His eyes were filled with a fierce determination that Shem hadn't seen before.

"He's right," Aryana chimed in, her voice gentle but resolute. "Plus, second guessing won't change our situation."

Even though Shem wasn't completely convinced, he looked around at his companions and could read the support in their eyes, knowing that most of them were. Only Lud refused to make eye contact, keeping his head down.

"I…I got nothing," Shem stammered, overwhelmed by their acceptance-or even loyalty.

Aram, always the one to choose his words carefully, finally spoke up. "Then don't say anything, Shem. We're with you, no matter what."

With a gleaming smile, Bog said, "And this is what it means to be united in friendship and faith. In our unity, our Lord is with us."

Elam's face was filled with amazement as he looked at Bog.

"What? You didn't think the Edeners were the only ones who knew about Yahweh?" Bog playfully teased, his innocent eyes sparkling. "There are Sethites outside of Eden who follow Him, too."

Elam stuttered, unable to believe what he was hearing. But Bog just patted his leg and chuckled.

"It's okay, son. Our numbers are few, but that only makes us stronger." He then shared the story of how he and Sedee met an old man named Lamech who introduced them to Yahweh, His promise of redemption, and the coming judgment.

Shem was excited by this connection. "He's actually my grandfather."

"He's quite a character," Bog said with a grin. "But more importantly, he opened our hearts to faith in Yahweh and the promised Redeemer."

Elam couldn't believe the coincidence and remarked that it's a small world after all.

But Bog's expression turned somber as he spoke about their struggles to stay in the village because they were different. "But we will never stop spreading the truth and hope of our Lord, Yahweh," he declared with determination.

"Alright, so let me get this straight," Sedee said, pointing her finger dramatically at Shem, Elam, and Aryana. "I met you guys at my cart when you returned my stolen gem from that pesky kid. But how in the world did you all end up here?"

Lud chuckled, seemingly back to his normal self. "You can't tell? We're here to rescue you!"

Sedee rolled her eyes at Lud's quip, but a small smile tugged at her lips. "Oh, is that so? Well, great job."

The cart jolted suddenly, causing everyone to grab onto something for balance. The cart no longer moved smoothly, making it obvious that their route had changed.

"I think we're slowing down," Aryana said, peering out the small window. "We turned off the main road."

Shem felt his heart rate quicken. "Everyone, be ready for anything," he whispered urgently.

Coming to a stop, they could hear muffled voices and footsteps approaching the char. Suddenly, the door swung open, flooding the dim interior with harsh sunlight. Shem squinted, trying to make out the figures silhouetted against the bright sky.

"Out! All of you!" Lieutenant Goriel's gruff voice commanded.

Shem exchanged glances with his companions before slowly rising to his feet. As they filed out of the cart one by one, he took in their new surroundings. They had stopped at a small outpost surrounded by small buildings. The air was warmer here, and a light mist hung in the air, giving everything an otherworldly feel.

Several Assyrian soldiers stood guard, their weapons at the ready, armor gleaming in the evening sunlight. Shem's eyes darted around, searching for any sign of Ouza or a chance to escape, but found neither.

"Line up," barked the lieutenant, looking more surly than usual with his calculating eyes.

Shem and his companions reluctantly formed a line, exchanging nervous glances. The lieutenant paced in front of them, boots crunching on the gravel, his menacing armor reflecting the companions' wary faces back at them.

"Listen up," he growled. "We'll be stopping here for the night. You'll be given food and water, but don't get any stupid ideas."

As if to emphasize his point, more soldiers appeared from the nearby buildings, their weapons glinting in the fading daylight.

"What's going to happen to us?" Elam asked, his voice barely above a whisper.

The lieutenant's eyes narrowed. "That's not for you to worry about. Just be grateful you're still alive."

Shem felt a surge of anger at the man's callous words. He opened his mouth to retort, but Sedee subtly shook her head, warning him that this wasn't the time.

Shem clenched his jaw but remained silent, surprised that he was so willing to follow her advice.

The lieutenant continued his intimidating pacing, eyeing each of them suspiciously. "You'll be split into groups and taken to separate holding areas," he announced. "Any attempt to communicate between groups or escape will be met with severe punishment."

Shem's mind raced, trying to figure out a way to keep everyone together, knowing it was futile. As the soldiers separated them, he caught Elam's eye and gave a subtle nod. *Just play along, for now.*

The soldiers marched the three of them to a small, windowless building on the outskirts of the outpost. The door creaked open, revealing a sparse interior with nothing but a few thin blankets on the dirt floor.

"Don't try anything stupid," one of the soldiers grunted, shoving them inside.

The door slammed shut behind them, followed by the ominous sound of a heavy lock sliding into place.

Immediately, Shem began inspecting their new prison, running his hands along the rough wooden walls, searching for any weak spots or hidden openings. Aryana and Sedee watched him silently for a moment before joining in the search.

"It's solid," said Aryana, after a few minutes, frustration evident in her voice. "No windows, no gaps in the walls or roof. They've chosen our prison well."

Slumping down onto a blanket, Sedee's spirits were dampened. "Now what?"

Shem sat down beside her, running through it in his head. "We wait," he said finally. "Nothing else to do," Then he added, trying to offer her some comfort. "I'm sure your uncle's ok."

She nodded in response.

Aryana nodded grimly, settling down on another blanket. "Shem's right. We need to be patient and observe. We don't want to put the others in danger."

The three of them sat in silence for a while, each lost in their own thoughts. The only sounds were the muffled voices of guards outside and the occasional scurrying of what Shem hoped were just mice in the corners.

As the light fading through the cracks in the walls grew dimmer, Sedee spoke up. "You know, I've been thinking about what Uncle Bog said earlier. About Yahweh knowing another way."

Shem looked up, intrigued. "What do you mean?"

Sedee's eyes had a faraway look as she continued. "Maybe... maybe all of this is part of a bigger plan. Something we can't see yet."

Aryana scoffed, but there was no real bite to it. "Does He have a plan?"

Sedee shrugged, a small smile playing on her lips. "I know it sounds crazy, but think about it. What are the odds that we'd all end up here together? That you'd meet my uncle and me, other Sethites, at Centergrove, then find us in the middle of nowhere?"

Shem nodded slowly, considering her words. "I guess I never thought of it that way. "

"Well," Sedee said, her voice growing more animated. "Maybe this is the Lord's way of bringing us all together for a reason. Maybe we each have a part to play in something bigger."

Shem considered Sedee's words, her positive outlook. Part of him wanted to dismiss the idea outright--after all, how could their current predicament and all this death be part of some divine plan? But another part of him, the part that gave his heart to Yahweh, the part that still clung to hope despite everything, wondered if she might be right.

Aryana still looked skeptical, but her expression had softened. "I suppose stranger things have happened. But what do you propose? Just sit here and wait for Yahweh's plan to unfold?"

Sedee shook her head. "Look...I know you are used to relying on your skill and swords, but maybe...just maybe they aren't the only answer. We should find comfort in knowing that the Lord has a greater purpose for all of this and hasn't forsaken us."

As if on cue, they heard the sound of footsteps approaching their prison. The three of them tensed, exchanging worried glances. The lock clicked, and the door swung open to reveal a young Assyrian soldier carrying a tray of food and water.

"Here," he said gruffly, setting the tray down just inside the door.

As he turned to leave, Shem noticed something odd about the young soldier's demeanor. There was a hesitation in his movements, and his eyes darted around nervously, as if he was afraid of being caught.

"Wait," Shem called out softly, causing the soldier to freeze. "Can you tell us anything?"

The soldier turned back slowly, his face a mask of conflict. He glanced over his shoulder before stepping closer and lowering his voice. "I... I'm not supposed to talk to you.

But I overheard some of the officers talking. They're planning to move you again at dawn, to the capital of Assyria-Asshur."

Aryana stood up, her eyes narrowing. "Why are you telling us this?"

The soldier swallowed hard. "Because I don't think this is right. What they're doing to you, to all the prisoners. It goes against everything I thought I was fighting for."

The young soldier's words hung in the air, heavy with implication. Shem exchanged a quick glance with Aryana and Sedee before turning back to the conflicted Assyrian.

"What's your name?" Shem asked gently.

The soldier hesitated, then whispered, "Eshkar."

"Eshkar," Shem repeated, "thank you for telling us this. It must be difficult for you."

Eshkar nodded, his eyes darting nervously to the door. "I... I should go. If they catch me talking to you..."

"Wait," Sedee interjected softly. "What are they planning that has you so upset?"

Eshkar's eyes widened in fear. "I-I can't. They'd kill me." His eyes darted nervously between the three prisoners, clearly torn between his duty and his conscience. Finally, taking a deep breath he spoke in a hushed tone. "They plan to use you as leverage against your people," he whispered. "Especially you." He nodded at Shem. "They say you're some kind of chosen one, that your capture will force your people to surrender."

Shem felt his stomach drop. Once again he was reminded that his destiny was the reason they were all in this mess.

Aryana stepped forward, her eyes blazing. "And what about the rest of us? What do they plan to do with our friends?"

Eshkar shook his head. "I don't know the specifics, but it's not good. There's talk of dark rituals. Sacrifices..." He trailed off, unable to meet their eyes.

Shem exchanged alarmed glances with Aryana and Sedee.

Eschkar paused before leaving. "Be careful. I've always trusted science...what I can see with my own eyes. But if you pray...I would do so."

With that, he was gone, the door closing behind him, latch clicking back in place.

Shem, Aryana, and Sedee huddled together in the dim light, discussing what they learned.

"Dark rituals? Sacrifices?" Aryana whispered, her voice tight with fear. "We have to get out of here, Shem. We have to warn the others."

Shem nodded grimly. "I know. But how? We're locked in here, and even if we could escape, we don't know where the others are being held."

Aryana's eyes suddenly lit up. "Wait a minute. That soldier, Eshkar - he seemed conflicted about what's happening. Maybe we could use him."

"It's risky," Shem said, running a hand through his hair. "If we're wrong about him, we could make things even worse."

"But what choice do we have?" Aryana argued.

"There's always a choice," said Sedee, twirling her hair in concentration. "We could get him in trouble. Or worse."

Shem's heart twisted in guilt as he struggled with his doubts about trusting the young boy. His past actions weighed heavily on him, making it hard to trust himself. "I'm not sure what the right move is," he said, his voice strained.

Aryana's eyes flashed with anger at his words. "I don't know who you are right now, Shem," she snapped. "Where is the fearless man who bravely fought against a giant? We can't save Eden from a locked room!"

Shem felt a pang of hurt, not wanting to let down his friends but also afraid of leading them into danger. "That man...he's just a scared and lost boy," he admitted, meeting her gaze with desperation. "Everything we do has consequences, and I can't bear the thought of someone else dying because of a quick decision. I just don't know, Aryana."

Aryana looked away, her body tense with frustration. "It's Lady Aryana," she corrected coldly before turning her back to Shem and Sedee, seeking solace in the comfort of her blankets.

Shem felt a wave of shame wash over him at Aryana's cold words. He opened his mouth to apologize, but Sedee placed a gentle hand on his arm, shaking her head slightly.

"Give her some time," Sedee whispered. "We're all on edge."

Shem was grateful for her gentle touch. "Thanks, Sedee. I just...I don't know what to do anymore. Every choice I make seems to lead to more suffering." *Lord help me.*

Sedee's eyes softened with understanding. "Sometimes the hardest thing is to just keep going. But that's when you leave it to Him. Whatever is going on...this battle is not yours, it's Yahweh's."

Shem nodded, swallowing the lump in his throat, while contemplating her wisdom. *She knows exactly what to say.*

He retreated to his own corner of the small room, wrapping himself in one of the thin blankets. As he sat there in the growing darkness, he couldn't help but replay the events that had led them to this point. Every decision, every misstep weighed on him, tying his stomach in knots.

Finally, in his despair, he cried out to Yahweh in a silent prayer. *Lord, hear my cry for help. Please come to my rescue and my friends; I know you are faithful and righteous. Please, don't let my friends suffer judgement for my decisions, even though we all deserve it. Lord, the enemy has captured me and desires to destroy me and my family. My heart and spirit are so heavy and I'm weak. I don't even have your sword, Davar, to protect us. I remember the promise you made to my family, and remember all the works your hands have done. Now I spread out my empty hands to you and beg like a man who has no water. Lord, for your name, preserve my life and my friend's lives. In your righteousness, help us. In your love, silence and destroy my enemies. I will trust your will, and am your servant, my Lord-Yahweh.*

He drifted off to sleep and the night wore on, filled with uneasy silence broken only by the occasional sound of guards passing by outside.

Shem jolted awake, his heart pounding. The nightmares had been vivid - images of his friends suffering, of dark rituals and sacrifices. He blinked in the dim light, trying to orient himself. As his eyes adjusted, he realized dawn was approaching. Faint light filtered through the cracks in the walls, illuminating Aryana and Sedee's sleeping forms.

Hearing footsteps approaching, his body tensed, remembering Eshkar's warning about them being moved at dawn. The lock clicked, and the door swung open.

One of the soldiers, the same one who had brought them to this room, stood in the doorway with a group of his comrades.

CHAPTER 23

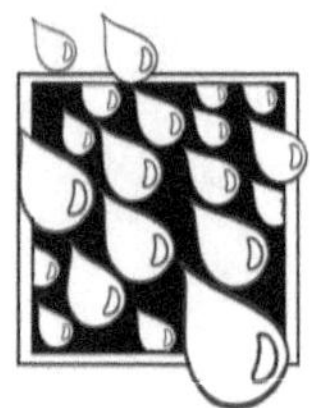

Great Value

The armored soldiers held iron restraints in their hands and were sharing a boisterous laugh at some unknown joke. “Come on,” one soldier barked, motioning for them to follow. “Don’t give us any trouble.”

With their wrists bound, Shem and his companions were led out of the small house and towards the waiting char. As they walked, he could see his other friends emerging from the other buildings, their faces showing signs of relief and exhaustion.

About halfway to the transport, Shem’s attention was drawn to a group of soldiers gathered around Captain Damrina. Their gazes were fixed on something on the ground - another soldier’s lifeless body. Some of them were laughing as they surveyed the scene before them.

Shem’s heart started racing as he approached the body on the ground, fearing it could be one of his friends that was responsible. Around them, the soldiers laughed and continued on, pushing them towards the back of the char.

Lieutenant Goriel stood waiting, a sickening smile on his bearded face. “So, did we all sleep well?”

Shem, ignoring his taunt, asked, “What happened?”

The lieutenant’s laughter turned cruel. “You actually surprised us, little Edener. We thought for sure you would take the bait.”

A sinking feeling settled in Shem’s gut. “What are you talking about?”

Goriel’s smile vanished, replaced by a dangerous glint in his eyes. “You better watch your tone, boy.” He leaned in close. “Private Eshkar was becoming increasingly opposed to our ways, so we figured he would try to help you escape. We watched him all night.” The sound of their laughter was like daggers in Shem’s ears.

Pushing through the feeling of dread that was creeping up, Shem asked, “You watched him for what reason?”

“We placed bets on how long it would take for him to free you,” Goriel said with a dark chuckle, his attention divided between the prisoners and two of his men flipping through a book of some kind. “Especially since he defied my orders and spoke to you,” he said, leaning in towards Shem. “I lost.”

Shem felt panic as he realized they had monitored every moment. “And then...you killed him anyway?” *That could’ve been us.*

The lieutenant stepped dangerously close, his voice low and menacing. “Consider this a warning, boy. Our orders are to bring you to Assher, that much is true. But any attempt at escape will have dire consequences.”

“Evil,” Aryana whispered, shaking her head.

“Call it what you want,” Goriel sneered. “Just remember, if we are willing to do this to our own traitors, imagine what we would do to you.” With that, he turned his back on the shocked group, snatching the book from his men. "Put them in the box. Playtime is over."

Shem's mind reeled as he took his place back in the cramped prisoner transport. The stench of fear and sweat filled his nostrils as the door clanged shut, plunging them into darkness. He felt Sedee trembling beside him and wished he could offer some comfort, but his bound hands made it impossible.

The char lurched into motion, whirring as it picked up speed. Through the thin sides of their mobile jail, Shem could hear the soldiers' raucous laughter fading into the distance. His stomach churned with a mixture of anger and dread.

"I can't believe they killed him," Sedee whispered, her voice barely audible over the rumbling of the char. "He was just trying to help us."

"They're monsters," Aryana spat. "All of them."

Shem leaned his head back against the cold metal wall, trying to steady his breathing. "We can't lose hope," he said, almost a whisper, trying his best to convince himself.

The char jolted suddenly, nearly toppling them over. Shem could feel the vehicle beginning to climb, the angle of ascent growing steeper. The transport strained louder, vibrating through the metal box.

"What now?" Elam asked, his voice tense.

"Oh, you know, just another bad situation," said Lud, looking at the roof. "Probably a dragon swooping down to eat us!"

Elam just shook his head, trying to suppress a smile.

A heavy silence fell over the group, broken only by the humming of the char and their own ragged breathing.

The cruel laughter of the soldiers still echoed in Shem's ears, mingling with the haunting image of Private Eshkar's lifeless body. Shem clenched his jaw, fighting back a wave of nausea that threatened to overtake him.

The char continued its ascent, the angle growing ever steeper. Shem's stomach lurched as they crested what felt like the peak of a hill, then plummeted down the other side. The metal box rattled and creaked ominously.

"I think I'm going to be sick," Aryana groaned.

Looking like he was losing the battle to hold his breath, Aram said, "THAT's actually funny."

Aryana appeared wounded. "When I fly, it's not usually in a metal box!"

Looking at the floor, Aram laughed.

After traveling for most of the morning, a muffled shout from outside caught their attention. The char jerked to an abrupt halt, nearly sending them sprawling.

Before anyone could recover, the door to their prison was yanked open and harsh sunlight flooded in, momentarily blinding them.

Adjusting to the bright light, Shem saw Lieutenant Goriel standing there, flanked by two armed soldiers.

His face twisted into a sneer. "Out," he barked. "Now."

Shem stumbled as he was roughly pulled from the box, his legs stiff from hours of confinement. The others followed, blinking and squinting in the sunlight. As Shem's vision cleared, he gasped at the sight before him.

They stood on a vast, grassy plain that stretched as far as the eye could see. The wind whipped across the open expanse, causing the tall grass to ripple like waves on a green sea, carrying with it the scent of unfamiliar wildflowers. In front of them Shem could see they were at an outpost of some kind, by the cluster of small buildings that filled the area. But it wasn't the landscape or buildings that had caught Shem's attention.

Looming before them was an enormous oval structure, unlike anything Shem had ever seen. His heart skipped a beat as he took in the massive sight before them, breath catching as he realized it was suspended in midair. The oval shape was covered in a patchwork of metal plates and fabric, with thick cables and pipes running along its surface. Surrounding it was an intricate web of scaffolding that reached high into the sky, giving the entire thing an otherworldly appearance.

"What in the world is that thing?" Halvin whispered, his voice filled with awe and a hint of fear.

Lieutenant Goriel chuckled darkly. "That...is an air-char. The pinnacle of our technology and the ticket to your final destination."

Shem's mind reeled as he tried to process what he was seeing. *An air-char? A machine that could fly through the sky like a bird?* It seemed impossible, yet there it was before his very eyes.

As they were marched closer to the enormous transport, Shem couldn't tear his eyes away from the incredible sight. The structure seemed to dwarf everything around it, casting a long shadow across the grassy plain. The wind picked up, carrying the scent of oil and metal.

"How does it even stay up there?" Aram muttered, his grounded, mechanical mind expressing a tone of wonder.

"Quiet!" one of the soldiers snapped, shoving Aram forward.

Massive fans were attached to frames jutting out from the main structure, their blades gleaming in the sunlight. Below the oval body, a smaller compartment hung suspended - what looked like some sort of command center. Men in crisp uniforms bustled about, calling out orders and checking instruments.

Lieutenant Goriel led them to a long staircase that wound its way up through the scaffolding. Shem's legs burned as they climbed higher and higher, the ground falling away beneath them. The wind whipped at their clothes, growing stronger with each step.

Finally, they reached a hatch in the underbelly of the massive air-char. Goriel yanked it open with a loud creak. "Move," he barked, shoving Shem forward.

Shem stumbled inside, his companions close behind. They found themselves in a narrow metal corridor lit by glowing crystal lamps. The air was stuffy and carried a sharp tang of oil and sweat.

They were led through a maze of corridors and up another set of stairs. Shem tried to keep track of their route, but it was hopeless. The interior of the air-char was a confusing labyrinth of metal passageways and cramped rooms. Eventually, they were shoved into a small chamber barely large enough for the group to stand. "Welcome to your new accommodations," Goriel sneered. "Enjoy the ride. It'll be your last."

The door slammed shut with a resounding clang, leaving them in near darkness save for a single dim lamp. Shem could feel the others pressed close around him in the tight space.

"Well, this is cozy," Lud muttered sarcastically.

A deep rumbling vibration began to course through the floor and walls. The noise grew louder, accompanied by a high-pitched whine that made Shem's teeth ache.

"What's happening?" Eloise asked, her voice trembling.

"Are we moving?" Lud asked, in answer to her question.

The vibrations intensified, and Shem felt his stomach lurch as the floor seemed to tilt beneath them. A collective gasp went up as they all realized what was happening - the massive air-char was lifting into the sky.

Shem's heart raced, a mix of terror and exhilaration coursing through him. He had dreamed of flying as a child, imagining what it would be like to soar above the clouds like a bird. But this was nothing like those childhood fantasies. The reality was far more terrifying.

"We're going to die," Lud moaned, his usual bravado completely gone. "This thing is going to fall out of the sky and we're all going to die."

In response, Sedee pressed closer to Shem. He wanted to offer her some sort of comfort, but the restraints made that impossible. The air-char continued to climb, the motion making Shem nauseated.

"We should be fine," Bog said firmly, trying to project confidence that no one else felt. "This...air-char thing has clearly flown before. I doubt they would transport their own people if it wasn't safe."

"Safe?" Lud scoffed."Nothing about this is safe!We're prisoners being taken who knows where in a giant metal death trap!"

"Lud, you're not helping," Aram hissed. "Just...try to breathe, okay?"

His voice rose as Lud began to talk faster. "Sure I'll breathe. I'll breathe as we fall to our doom. Hey...maybe we'll get lucky and it'll bounce!"

"Lud, please..." said Eloise, in clear distress.

"No, no, hold on," he said to her before continuing his tirade. "In your expertise, Aram, do you think we'd survive the drop? And, if so, will we just roll to whatever pit they plan on tossing us into-or bounce? This was the biggest mistake of our lives. I said from the start we should return home...but, nooooo, you..." The air-char lurched again, stopping Lud's rant, mid-sentence.

Shem attempted to focus on steadying his own breathing. The vibrations coursing through the metal floor seemed to penetrate his very bones.

"Sorry to drag you against your will," Aram murmured with an edge to his voice which was barely audible over the droning of the engines.

Shem swallowed hard, wishing he could calm his friends' mood, but he didn't know how. *Maybe I made the wrong choice.*

"I'm going to kill them all," Aram growled, his voice strained. "They've taken enough from us!"

Shem, initially shocked at his friend's outburst, suddenly came to the realization of what happened. "They have your book."

That book was Aram's most important possession-beside his father's watch. Shem grew up watching his friend sketch everything and everyone that mattered to him in that leather bound volume. Always a talented artist, he had drawn diagrams and even journal entries going back for years on the blank pages within. There were others, of course, with various doodles and studies, but this was the important one; the one he would never leave home without.

"Oh no..." said Lud, his voice tight, clearly upset for his brother. "I forgot it was in your pack."

Feeling horrible, Shem offered an explanation. "I saw it back at the last stop, with the Lieutenant, he..."

"Forget it," said Aram, cutting him off, obviously uncomfortable with the exchange.

The air-char continued to vibrate around them as it climbed higher into the sky, causing the pressure to change in Shem's ears, making them pop uncomfortably.

The group fell into an uneasy silence, each lost in their own thoughts as the air-char continued its ascent. Shem tried to focus on the steady rhythm of his breathing, pushing away the images of plummeting to the ground that kept flashing through his mind.

After what felt like hours the vibrations began to change. The upward motion seemed to level off, and the engine noise settled into a more constant drone.

"I think we've reached our flying height," Aryana observed, her voice tight but controlled.

Shem nodded, figuring that she was the only one who could understand the motion associated with flight.

The sourness that had been building in his stomach began to ease slightly as they maintained a steadier course.

Just as they were adjusting to their new reality of flight, the sound of heavy footsteps echoed down the corridor outside their cramped chamber. The door swung open with a metallic screech, revealing a stern-faced guard.

"You," he barked, pointing at Shem. "Come with me." Shem's companions tensed, exchanging worried glances.

"Where are you taking him?" Sedee demanded, her voice wavering slightly despite her attempt at bravery.

Elam jumped in. "What's going on? Why are we prisoners?"

The guard's hand moved to the weapon at his hip. "That's none of your concern. Now move, boy, unless you want trouble."

Shem swallowed hard, trying to quell the fear rising in his chest. He met Elam's eyes, seeing his own anxiety mirrored there. "It's okay," he said, forcing a calm he didn't feel into his voice, for his friends' benefit.

Shem stepped forward, his legs shaky from the combination of fear and the unfamiliar sensation of being airborne. The guard roughly grabbed his arm and pulled him out of the cramped chamber.

"It'll be okay," Shem called over his shoulder, trying to reassure his friends. The last thing he saw before the door slammed shut was Sedee's worried face.

The guard marched Shem down a series of narrow corridors, the metal floors clanging beneath their feet. The air was thick with the familiar scent of oil and machinery. Shem's mind raced, wondering what fate awaited him.

After several twists and turns, they emerged into a large, open space that took Shem's breath away. It was a vast room filled with tables and chairs, reminiscent of the main hall of an inn back home. But what truly captured Shem's attention was the far wall, lined entirely with glass-paned windows that offered an unobstructed view of the sky. Shem's breath caught in his throat as he took in the endless expanse of blue, dotted with wispy clouds that seemed close enough to touch.

"Welcome to the lounge," a familiar voice said.

Shem turned to see General Ouza approaching with a smile that didn't quite reach his eyes. The man had undergone a dramatic transformation since their last encounter. Gone were the simple clothes of a rancher. Now he was dressed in the full regalia of a high-ranking military official.

His lightweight black armor gleamed in the sunlight that streamed through the windows. Unlike the other soldiers, his chest plate lacked the glowing crystals, and his arms were bare of that protection. Beneath the armor, Shem could see a well-tailored black uniform.

The general's high collar was adorned with intricate filigree, and his polished, black, knee-high boots gleamed. His dark hair was pulled back into a tight ponytail, and his clean-shaven face bore an expression of cool authority. Yet, he still managed to look completely relaxed.

"Remove his restraints," General Ouza ordered the guard, who quickly complied.

As the restraints were removed, Shem rubbed his wrists, relishing the feeling of freedom even as his mind was filled with questions and fears.

"Come, sit with me," the general said, gesturing to a pair of comfortable-looking chairs facing the windows. As Shem hesitated, Ouza's voice hardened slightly. "That wasn't a request, Shem."

Shem followed, acutely aware of the guard retreating to stand by the far doorway. As they sat, he perceived that the chairs were positioned on a slightly lower level, allowing an unobstructed view of the landscape below. His breath caught as he took in the sight.

The world stretched out beneath them like a living map. Vast prairies rolled by, dotted with herds of hadrosaurus with their duck-like bills or stegosaurus with long rows of plates lining their backs, all looking like mere specks from this height. Rivers snaked through the landscape, glinting in the sunlight. Farms and roads created a patchwork pattern reminiscent of his mother's quilts. It was breathtakingly beautiful and utterly terrifying all at once.

"Quite a view, isn't it?" General Ouza remarked, his tone almost conversational. "It never ceases to amaze me what man is capable of...no matter how many times I see it."

Shem nodded, unable to tear his eyes away from the landscape. "It's...incredible," he admitted.

"Indeed it is," the general agreed. "Adamah is beautiful."

Something about his previous statement struck Shem as odd. "No matter how many times you see it?" he asked, becoming more confused as he mulled it over. "You lived in Ararat for my whole life, and probably for hundreds of years before that. And they just recently built this wonder...as far as I can tell. How could you have seen Adamah from this view before now?"

General Ouza's eyes narrowed slightly, a fleeting expression of annoyance crossing his face before his practiced smile returned. "Perceptive, aren't you?" he asked, his tone carrying a hint of warning. "Let's just say I've had... opportunities to see Adamah from above before. But that's not why I brought you here."

He leaned forward, fixing Shem with an intense gaze. "I think it's time we had a frank discussion about your situation and what I expect from you."

Shem felt a chill run down his spine despite the warmth of the sunlight streaming through the windows. He straightened in his chair, trying to project a confidence he didn't feel. "Do you actually think I'll do anything for you, General?" he asked, proud that his voice remained steady.

The general's smile widened, but it didn't reach his eyes. "You're a smart boy, Shem. I'm sure you've figured out by now that you're quite important to...my master's...plans." adding the last part, like it made him ill. "You're in a rather precarious position."

Shem swallowed hard, but met the general's gaze. "You mean flying around in a giant metal egg?"

A low chuckle escaped Ouza's lips. "You deflect. Your spirit is admirable...if misplaced. But let me be clear--you are here because you have great value to me. You could change the course of history."

"You're referring to the promised Redeemer and the prophecy of the coming cataclysm." Shem whispered, his heart heavy.

"Precisely," Ouza nodded. "Azazel once believed that holding you would give him leverage to stop Noah from bringing the destruction of Adamah. Or that he could persuade you to join us against him."

Shem was amused at how Ouza paid less attention to his father's sermons than he did. "You know that my father has nothing to do with it. He's just the messenger. A prophet." The thought of his encounter with Azazel made him feel nauseated. "I had a taste of your master's persuasion. You see how that worked out."

"I'm aware," said Ouza, looking out the window in thought.

Ouza turned back to Shem, his expression grave. "I've met Yahweh, you know? And I know how he works. If He says he will do something, then He will. So, we know that in order to fulfill his promise to Eve, he has to preserve a remnant after he destroys Adamah."

"You met...Yahweh?" Shem's brow furrowed in confusion. "What are you talking about?" *How could he meet Him and not be a follower?*

The general leaned forward, his voice low and intense. "If Azazel can't have you, then neither can Yahweh. That is what he believes. He believes that if he can wipe out your family line, then he can stop Yahweh's plan to destroy Adamah."

Even though Shem was warned by his grandfather that this could be Azazel's plan, it didn't feel any better to hear it from the enemy. "You believe this too?"

"Oh, it would probably only delay it," said Ouza. "I believe that Yahweh could call whoever he wants, and that He would find a way to keep that promise." He sat back in his chair and returned his gaze to the expansive landscape. "My way would be to kill Azazel."

"What?" He couldn't believe what he was hearing. "You can't kill a demon...can you?"

CHAPTER 24

A Dizzying Destination

Ouza chuckled darkly, his eyes still fixed on the horizon. "Oh, but you can kill a demon, young Shem. You most certainly can."

Shem's heart raced, his mind reeling at the implications. He leaned forward, unable to contain his curiosity. "How? I mean, they're not mortal like us, are they?"

The general turned back to face him, a glint in his eye. "Not mortal, no. But not invincible either. There are... ways. Ancient weapons, forged for this very purpose."

Shem's eyes widened. "Weapons that can kill demons? I've never heard of such things."

"Few have," Ouza replied. "It's not the kind of knowledge that's shared freely. But I've seen it done. I've witnessed a 'demon,' as you call them, fall."

The air seemed to thicken around them as Ouza's words hung heavy in the silence. Shem felt a chill run down his spine despite the warm evening breeze.

"You've... seen it?" Shem asked, his voice barely above a whisper. "How is that possible?"

Ouza's lips curved into a grim smile."There's much you don't know about the world, boy. These 'demons' as humans call them - they're actually known as 'The Sons of Yahweh.' Heavenly beings created to serve Him. Messengers actually."

Shem nodded slowly, recalling fragments of stories his father had told him. "I've heard something like that before. The Shining One... Satan?"

Ouza's eyes darkened as he continued, "The Son of the Morning believed he should rule creation himself. He desired Yahweh's throne. He and those countless 'sons' who followed him in that belief were cast out of the heavenly realm for their treachery."

Shem nodded slowly, pieces falling into place. "My father Noah told me some of this. And my grandfathers too. But what does that have to do with you and Azazel? And how do you know they can be killed?"

A wry smile twisted Ouza's lips. "Ah, now we get to the heart of it. You see, Samyaza and Azazel were Satan's top generals. They devised a plan to empower humanity and be lost to Yahweh for eternity."

"How?" Shem asked, leaning forward.

"By teaching forbidden knowledge. Metallurgy, forging weapons, and more," he explained. "They got His attention." Ouza paused, his eyes distant as if lost in memory. "But Yahweh gave the line of Seth the means to fight back. To stop the spread of those creations."

Shem's brow furrowed. "You mean--the ancient weapons?"

"Relics," Ouza said, his voice low. "Powerful weapons that can kill a 'demon,' 'god,' or whatever you choose to call a son of Yahweh." His eyes locked onto Shem's. "The relics I speak of are swords, and one of those is Davar - The Sword of the Spirit."

Shem's mind reeled in surprise. He shook his head, struggling to process this flood of information. "How do you know all this? And why are you telling me?"

Ouza's lips curved into a bitter smile. "The Eden Knights were created for this very purpose. Their swords, forged from a tree, from The Garden of Eden by Noah himself."

Shem remembered his father sharing about the sword when they left home. "My father mentioned something about 'singing' Davar from a Gopher tree, or something like that, when he gave it to me." He wasn't about to remind him that there was a singular forest of these trees hidden somewhere.

Ouza nodded. "Indeed. When Assyria sought to assimilate the rest of Adamah into their empire, it was the Eden Knights who stood in their way. With those very swords, they defeated the might of an empire that included demons, giants, and technology far beyond what they were capable of."

The general's gaze grew distant, his voice tinged with a mix of awe and resentment. "All with swords made from trees. It sounds impossible, doesn't it?"

Shem shook his head in disbelief, still unsure how this all fit together. "Where are you going with all of this?"

Ouza's face darkened, his fingers unconsciously tracing the long scar that ran down his face. "I was there. I fought in that war... for Assyria." His eyes narrowed as he fixed Shem with an intense stare. "And this scar? A courtesy of your hero, Anatu -Lady Aryana's brother."

Shem's jaw dropped, his mind reeling from this revelation. He stared at Ouza, seeing his former mentor in an entirely new light. The pieces were falling into place, but they formed a picture he wasn't sure he wanted to see.

"What do you want from me?" Shem sputtered, gesturing helplessly. "You have my sword, and I'm your prisoner. How can I possibly—"

Ouza cut him off with a sharp wave of his hand. "At the right time, I'll give you the opportunity and your sword. But make no mistake, boy - if you try to escape before then, I'll kill you without hesitation." His eyes narrowed. "And your friends too."

Shem felt trapped. He had no doubt Ouza meant every word. The man he had once looked up to as a mentor now seemed like a stranger - dangerous and unpredictable.

"I won't serve you," Shem said carefully, his mind racing. He suspected Ouza might try to kill them all anyway, regardless of his cooperation. All trust between them had evaporated like morning dew.

"Oh, you will when the time comes. You'll have no choice."

A suffocating stillness descended upon them, heavy as a leaden blanket. The man Shem had once respected as Nin was gone, replaced by a malevolent general devoid of any shred of empathy or care. With a heavy heart, Shem observed his former mentor turn away, no longer acknowledging him, and gaze out into the vast expanse of Adamah below, a reminder of all that had been lost and destroyed.

Shem's mind was still whirling with the weight of Ouza's revelations, when something high in the clouds caught his eye. He squinted, hardly daring to believe what he saw. It looked like... a pterosaur? Could it be Alouette, somehow healed from her wounds? His heart leapt with hope, but he quickly schooled his features, not wanting to draw Ouza's attention. The general seemed oblivious, his gaze fixed on the horizon.

Suddenly, the air-char began to pivot, and Shem's breath caught in his throat. Before him sprawled the most wondrous man-made sight he had ever beheld, a testament of their ingenuity. A vast city rose from the banks of a wide river, its walls embracing the water's edge. Giant statues, reaching to the heavens, guarded the entrance to a bustling harbor teeming with boats and skiffs. The city itself was a marvel, with soaring towers and bridges crisscrossing between multiple layers, each built atop the last as it spread outward from the harbor.

Monolithic structures of colossal stone blocks surrounded the harbor, adorned with steps and columns. Smaller rivers branched out from the main waterway, with countless bridges and walkways connecting the maze of roads and paths. Rising from the harbor to another level, a giant amphitheater dominated the center, along with more megalithic buildings with multiple multi-spires reaching for the heavens, ringed by roads that tied the sprawling metropolis together. The opposite side of the city, facing the expanse of wilderness, was surrounded with walls, terminating in a multiple tiered castle with ramparts and towers.

Beyond the castle walls stood three massive pyramids, beyond which nestled buildings and farmsteads into the distant foothills. Shem's eyes widened in awe at the sheer scale and grandeur before him.

"Behold Asshur," Ouza declared, a hint of pride in his voice.

Shem was speechless as he took in the incredible sight. The city of Asshur was unlike anything he had ever imagined. As his eyes roamed over the sprawling metropolis, he noticed movement among the buildings and streets. His breath caught in his throat as he realized what he was seeing.

"Are those... giants?" he whispered, hardly believing his eyes.

Ouza nodded, a smirk playing on his lips. "Indeed. The Nephilim walk freely here."

Shem watched in amazement as the massive figures moved through the city, towering over the thousands of regular-sized citizens going about their business. But the wonders didn't stop there. His shock grew as he spotted brontosaurus, elephants and other large beasts adorned in beautiful fabrics and jewels as they lumbered through the streets with people perched atop them.

Shem's eyes were drawn to movement on the far side of the city, beyond the castle. His heart sank as he realized what he was seeing. "Is that... an army?"

Ouza's smile grew cold. "Very observant, boy. Yes, that is the might of Assyria - larger than anything Eden could ever hope to muster."

Shem swallowed hard, trying to comprehend the sheer scale of the force arrayed before him. Thousands upon thousands of soldiers stood in perfect formation, their technologically advanced weapons glinting in the sun. The sight filled him with a mix of awe and dread.

As the air-char continued its descent, Ouza pointed to a high point near the edge of the city. "There. That's our destination."

Shem squinted, making out a structure that looked similar to the scaffolding they had used to board the air-char. His stomach churned as he realized their journey was coming to an end.

Ouza's voice cut through Shem's thoughts, cold and threatening. "Remember our deal, boy. It's pointless to resist."

Shem nodded stiffly, his jaw clenched. He had no illusions about the precariousness of their situation. As the air-char began its final approach, Shem's mind raced, trying to find some way out of this impossible situation.

The craft stopped its progress while Ouza barked orders toward the guard at the doorway. He approached Shem, his face impassive.

"Take him back to the others," Ouza commanded. "Make sure they're ready to depart."

As the guard roughly grabbed Shem's arms, he caught one last glimpse of the sprawling city of Asshur before being led away. His mind reeled, trying to process everything he had seen and learned. As the guard shoved him down a narrow corridor, Shem's thoughts turned to his companions. He had to find a way to warn them, it was time to come up with a plan.

The guard's heavy footsteps echoed down the metal corridor as he approached the door to the room where Shem's friends were being held. Another guard, his face etched with weariness and disinterest, stood just outside.

Shem's escort, a young man with fidgety hands, struggled with the latch on the door. His awkward movements and unsure grasp hinted that he was unfamiliar with the mechanism or perhaps clumsy. The other guard couldn't help but smirk at the sight, clearly amused by his companion's ineptitude. After several failed attempts, the latch finally clicked open, causing the first guard to let out a victorious grin before pulling the door open with a creak.

The door exploded open with a deafening crash, nearly tearing off its hinges as Aram and Lud burst out of the room like raging beasts. With a force that could rival a small giant, they collided with their target, sending him hurtling across the hall and crashing into the opposite wall with bone-breaking impact. Before the guard could even process what was happening, Lud was on top of him, unleashing a relentless barrage of fists that pounded his face with fury and vengeance. At the same time, Aram seized the second man and dragged him into the room, where Shem could hear his fate being sealed by the sound of grunts and shattering bones as the others in the room carried out their plans.

"What are you doing?" Shem yelled, feeling the panic well up within him. "You've alerted the guards!"

Aryana emerged from the room, her eyes blazing with determination. "We're escaping, that's what and we have no time to debate. Now move!"

She grabbed Shem's arm and yanked him down the corridor, away from the sounds of guards that were alerted by all the noise. Sedee was already ahead, working frantically to remove her mechanical restraints with a key she must have taken from the guard they incapacitated in the room.

"We need to talk about this," Shem protested as they ran. "I'm not sure if this is the right move!"

"Shem, we're not doing this again," Aryana snapped. "We. Are. Leaving!"

Behind them, Elam, Halvin, Eloise, and Bog spilled out into the hallway, following close on their heels.

Shem was racing against his own fear. The sound of approaching footsteps echoed behind them, growing louder with each passing second.

"This way!" Aryana hissed, pulling Shem around a sharp corner. Sedee was just ahead, her fingers fumbling with the lock on her restraints as she ran.

"You go," Shem gasped, trying to catch his breath. "I saw Alouette! She might be able to get you to safety!"

Aryana's eyes widened for a moment, and she gave Shem a sly smile. "Even better. Keep moving!"

Suddenly, a crossbow bolt whistled past Shem's ear, embedding itself in the wooden wall beside him. He turned to see Lieutenant Goriel at the end of the hallway, reloading his weapon with practiced efficiency.

"You leaving, boy?" Goriel laughed, as the rest of his men flooded the hall. "You have nowhere to go!"

"Watch out!" Elam yelled, but it was too late. Another bolt flew through the air, this time finding its mark. Aram cried out in pain as the projectile struck his shoulder, sending him stumbling into the wall.

"Aram!" Lud shouted, stopping to help his fallen brother.

"Go!" Aram gritted through clenched teeth. "Get Shem out of here!"

"I'm not leaving you," said Lud. "We'll face them together!"

The delay was costly. In the chaos, the companions found themselves cut off from Shem as more guards flooded the hallway behind them. His heart sank as he watched his friends disappear from view, surrounded by armed soldiers.

"We have to help them!" Shem cried, trying to turn back.

"No!" Aryana grabbed him forcefully, pushing Shem forward. "We can't help them now!"

Shem struggled against her grip. "But our friends—"

"Will be killed if we don't warn Eden!" Aryana shouted, her eyes flashing with intensity. "An attack is coming, Shem. This was our plan all along - to get you out. You're the one they really want."

The words hit Shem like a physical blow. He stumbled forward, his mind reeling. Behind them, he could hear the sounds of fighting - cries of pain, the clash of metal, orders being shouted. His friends were putting up a fight, buying them time to escape.

"There!" Sedee called out, pointing to a door at the end of the corridor. "That might lead outside!" Her face flushed with anxiety.

They sprinted towards the door, hearts pounding. Shem reached it first, yanking it open to reveal a narrow metal ladder leading upwards through the center of the air-char's hollow center.

"Up! Quickly!" he shouted, gesturing for the Sedee and Aryana to go ahead of him.

Sedee scrambled up first, her nimble fingers finding purchase on the rungs despite her shaking hands. Aryana followed close behind, pausing only to grab Shem's sleeve and haul him onto the ladder after her.

"Move it, farm boy!" she said, her voice tight with urgency.

Shem moved quickly, hearing shouts and pounding footsteps growing closer. As he climbed, the wide open space was unnerving, giving him the feeling that he was suspended in a giant cavern. The air was surprisingly still for being such an open area.

Shem's arms burned as he climbed the ladder, trying to control his breathing. The open space of the air-char's envelope yawned around them, a dizzying void that threatened to swallow them whole. Above, he could see Sedee and Aryana scrambling towards a hatch that presumably led to the exterior.

"Almost there!" Sedee called down, her voice echoing strangely in the cavernous space.

Just as Shem thought they might make it, a shout from below froze his blood.

"Stop right there!" Lieutenant Goriel's voice boomed up from the bottom of the ladder. "One more move and I'll shoot!"

Shem glanced down to see Goriel aiming his crossbow upwards, a cruel smile twisting his features. Time seemed to slow as Shem's mind raced, desperately seeking a solution. *Lord, please help my friends.*

Shem's heart pounded as he clung to the ladder, torn between the urge to climb, the fear of Goriel's threat, and concern for his friends. He looked up to see Aryana and Sedee had reached the hatch at the top.

"Hurry!" Aryana yelled down to him. She turned her face to the sky and let out a piercing whistle, calling for Alouette.

The sound galvanized Shem into action. With a surge of desperate energy, he began climbing again, his muscles screaming in protest. Below, he heard Goriel curse and the twang of a crossbow being fired.

Bolts whizzed past Shem's head as he climbed, missing him by inches. He pushed himself to the brink of exhaustion, feeling as if the ladder stretched endlessly upward.

Shem hauled himself out of the hatch into the bright afternoon sunlight, gasping for breath. The wind whipped around him as he took in the dizzying height. Aryana was already astride Alouette, pulling Sedee up behind her onto the saddle.

"There's more of them!" Aryana yelled, her eyes wide with urgency. Shem stumbled forward on his hands and knees, his legs shaky after the frantic climb. He was vaguely aware of shouts coming from another hatch further down the air-char's exterior-more guards emerging to give chase.

He scrambled to his feet, attempting to shut the hatch behind him, but before he could take a step, a crossbow bolt ricocheted off his leather armor with a dull thud. The impact, though glancing, threw him off balance. His foot slipped on the curved surface of the air-char, and suddenly he was sliding, tumbling towards the edge.

Chapter 25

Dangerous Territory

Shem fought with all that was within him to find a firm grip on the smooth material. His fingers found nothing as he picked up speed, the world blurring around him. The wind whipped his hair into his eyes, and he could barely make out the dizzying drop below.

"Aryana!" he yelled, his voice torn away by the rushing air.

He caught a glimpse of her, still astride Alouette, diving towards him. But they were too far away, too slow. The edge of the air-char loomed, and then he was falling, tumbling end over end into the open sky.

Shem's stomach lurched as he plummeted. The ground rushed up to meet him, a patchwork of fields and the dark smudge of the Assyrian army. He flailed his arms, as if he could somehow fly, but succeeded only in spinning himself faster. The world became a dizzying blur of sky and earth.

Just as he was certain he'd become a messy splatter on the ground, he felt a sharp pain in his shoulders. His descent jerked to a halt so abruptly that he thought his arms might pop out of their sockets.

"Gotcha!" Aryana's triumphant voice came from above.

Shem looked up to see Alouette's talons gripping his leather armor, the pterosaur's wings beating furiously as she struggled to keep them aloft. He could feel her laboring under their combined weight.

"We're too heavy!" she shouted over the wind. "She can't hold all of us!" Aryana's face was a mask of determination. "Hold on!"

They were losing altitude fast, the castle walls looming closer.

Shem silently prayed as they skimmed over the castle walls, Alouette's wingtips nearly grazing the stone. He could see the shocked faces of the guards, their mouths agape as the unlikely trio sailed over their heads.

"We're not gonna make it!" Shem yelled, his eyes widening as he saw the courtyard rushing up to meet them.

Aryana gritted her teeth. "Oh yes, we are!" She leaned forward, whispering encouragement to Alouette. The pterosaur let out a shrill cry and gave one last powerful beat of her wings.

They barely cleared the inner wall, Shem's boots scraping against the top as they plummeted towards the courtyard.

Alouette gave one final burst of strength, her wings straining to lift them over the smaller city-side wall. With a sharp descent, they hurtled towards the cobblestone streets below, the ground rushing up at an alarming speed.

Just narrowly avoiding a collision with a bridge, Alouette released her grip on Shem, sending him tumbling and rolling until he finally came to rest on his back. Gasping for air, he lay there looking up at the towering buildings surrounding him. *Thank you, Lord.*

Shem lay on the cobblestones, his chest heaving as he tried to catch his breath. Every part of his body ached from the rough landing, but he was alive. He heard the soft thud of Alouette touching down nearby, followed by Aryana's and Sedee's boots hitting the ground.

"Shem! Are you alright?" Sedee's voice was tinged with worry as she rushed to his side.

He groaned and slowly sat up, wincing at the pain in his ribs. "I think so. Nothing seems broken, at least."

Aryana knelt beside him, her eyes scanning him for injuries. "That was too close. I thought we'd lost you back there."

Shem managed a weak smile. "For a moment, so did I. That was close."

A commotion from the street drew their attention. People were emerging from buildings, pointing and murmuring at the sight of the pterosaur and the disheveled trio. Some looked frightened, others curious. A group of city guards pushed through the growing crowd, their hands on their sword hilts.

"We need to move," Aryana said urgently, helping Shem to his feet. "Can you walk?"

He nodded, grimacing as he tested his weight. "I'll manage. But where to? We're strangers here, and that landing wasn't exactly subtle."

Sedee glanced around, her eyes landing on a narrow alley between two tall buildings. "This way," she whispered, gesturing for them to follow. "We need to get off the main street."

As they hurried towards the alley, Alouette let out a low, distressed cry. Aryana turned back, her face torn. "Go ahead, girl," she said, "go get some rest and something to eat. I'll be fine."

With that, Alouette took a few steps, and gracefully soared into the sky, smoothly clearing the buildings and disappearing from sight.

They ducked into the alley just as the guards reached the spot where they had landed. They pressed themselves against the warm walls, listening to the shouts and confusion behind them.

"Where exactly are we going?" Shem whispered, glancing nervously over his shoulder.

Sedee's voice was low and urgent. "To find an old... acquaintance. Trust me."

Do I have a choice? Although, in spite of the betrayals and attacks he'd endured recently, he found himself willing to follow her into the unknown.

They descended through the levels of the city, the buildings growing more cramped and run-down with each turn. The air became thick with the smell of spices, sweat, and something Shem couldn't quite place.

"We're nearing the old market," Sedee explained. "It's where the common folk trade. We might be able to blend in there."

As they emerged onto a wider street, Shem's senses were immediately overwhelmed. The old market was a cacophony of sights, sounds, and smells. Colorful awnings stretched overhead, providing patchy shade from the harsh sun. Merchants shouted their wares from wooden stalls, their voices competing with the bleating of goats and the squawking of chickens in wicker cages.

"Stay close," Sedee warned, weaving through the dense crowd. "It's easy to get lost here. And...be careful."

Shem tried to take it all in as they moved. He saw fruits he'd never encountered before, their vibrant colors enticing even from a distance. Spice merchants stood behind mounds of fragrant powders, the air around them thick with exotic aromas. A group of children darted past, laughing as they chased a stray dog through the throng.

"Are those...Zamzummim?" Shem whispered to Sedee, nodding towards one of the giants carefully picking his way through the crowd. *Is he shopping?*

Sedee nodded, looking impressed that he knew that. "He might be. Or possibly a Gibborim. Who can tell? These in the city are more...civilized, if you can say that about any Nephilim."

Shem couldn't stop staring as they walked down the bustling avenue. Everywhere he looked, there were people dressed in revealing, scandalous outfits - a far cry from the conservative standards of his home in Eden. Even Aryana couldn't help but blush and tug at her hair as they passed by men with their bare muscles on full display and women showing way more skin than any of them were used to seeing.

Sedee chuckled and nudged them, "Stop gawking, you two! You're sticking out like sore thumbs."

"We already stand out just by wearing clothes," said Aryana, cheeks a bright red.

Shem could only mutter in embarrassment and wish for invisibility to get out of this awkward situation. So, thinking it better to just focus on something else, he decided to fixate on the unique architecture that surrounded them.

The buildings lining the avenue were a mix of old and new, with intricate designs and vibrant colors adorning their facades. Some stood tall at two or three stories, while others seemed to lean in towards the street, beckoning to passersby. From balconies, revelers threw beads and trinkets to those below, their voices carrying in the lively atmosphere. But Shem figured out quickly not to look up for too long, as some women were using this as an opportunity to flaunt their bodies in exchange for the colorful souvenirs.

In the far distance, a magnificent sight was on full display. The avenue gradually sloped downward, leading travelers and merchants to a breathtaking view of the multi-spired structure he saw from the air-char upon their arrival. The central tower soared towards the heavens, its glimmering domed peak visible for miles like a beckoning jewel. Surrounding it were smaller towers adorned with similar grandeur and parapets of varying sizes and dimensions. Even from this distance, one could sense the palace's immense size and opulence, clearly belonging to a person of tremendous power and influence

Shem couldn't believe how big it was. "What is that place?" he asked, his voice barely above a whisper.

Sedee followed his gaze and nodded grimly. "That's the capital palace. Home of Lilith, the first mother of the Nephilim. She's the sister-wife of Tubal-Cain and daughter of Lamech the Cainite. Although all of Assyria believes she is the first mother...of ALL humans."

Aryana's eyes widened. "Lilith? I've heard stories about her. Is she not ancient then?"

"Oh, she is that," Sedee confirmed. "But not THAT ancient."

As they continued through the market, Shem considered their situation. "So, this person you know," he said, trying to keep his voice low, "how exactly can they help us?"

Sedee's eyes darted around, checking for eavesdroppers before responding. "He's...well-connected. Has his fingers in all sorts of pies, if you know what I mean. If anyone can get us information, it's him."

"And weapons?" Aryana asked, her hand instinctively moving to where her dual swords would have been on her back.

Sedee nodded. "They won't be cheap though."

Shem frowned. "We don't have any money. How are we supposed to—" He thought about it for a second before he asked, "What do they even use for money?"

"We do have this," Aryana interrupted, pulling out the gem she had recovered from Sedee's ambushed wagon wreckage. It looked like a small amber egg that glinted in the sunlight, its smooth, rounded sides casting tiny rainbows on the nearby market stalls.

Sedee's eyes widened at the sight of the gem, tears filling her eyes. "I thought it was gone forever."

Shem recognized the jewel. "What is it?"

"It's a rare gem that has been passed down through my family," Sedee explained in a hushed tone. "I'm not sure where it's from originally, but it's very valuable." Her voice strained, she added. "It should be enough to get us what we need."

"We'll figure out another option," said Shem, feeling sad that she was willing to give up something so important.

"What option?" asked Aryana, with a tone that dripped with sarcasm.

Shem didn't feel that it was theirs to barter. "I don't know right now. But we will."

With a huff, Aryana let the topic go.

Continuing through the market, Shem noticed a change in the atmosphere. The crowds were thinning, and the stalls became sparser. The buildings around them looked more rundown with narrow alleys branching off into shadowy depths.

"We're getting close," Sedee murmured. "Stay alert. This isn't the safest part of the city."

They turned down a narrow side street, the sounds of the market fading behind them. Shem felt closed in as the buildings seemed to shut them in, blocking out much of the sunlight. The air grew thick with the smell of rotting garbage and something more sinister that he couldn't quite place.

"Are we close?" Shem whispered to Sedee. He didn't like the feeling that they could be jumped at any moment and never see it coming .

Sedee's face was grim as she replied, "Almost there. Just... let me do the talking."

They came to a stop in front of a dilapidated building with boarded-up windows. A faded sign hung crookedly above the door, its words long since worn away.

Sedee took a deep breath and knocked three times in quick succession, then twice more-slowly.

For a long moment, nothing happened. Then a series of clicks and scrapes echoed from behind the door. Shem held his breath as it creaked open, revealing a sliver of darkness beyond.

A gravelly voice emerged from the shadows. "Well, well, well. If it isn't little Sedeqetelebab. Thought I'd never see *you* again."

"Who?" Shem mouthed under his breath, in confusion.

Sedee straightened her shoulders. "Hello, Rakham. We need your help." Then turning to Shem with a smirk, she whispered, "Shut up...it's my name."

Eyes wide, Aryana snorted as she unsuccessfully tried to suppress a laugh, evoking a cross look from Sedee.

The door opened wider, and Shem got his first look at Rakham. The man was short and wiry with a face like crumpled parchment and eyes that gleamed with cunning. He wore a patchwork coat that seemed to be made entirely of pockets.

Rakham's calculating gaze swept over Aryana and Shem, his lips twisting into a grin. "New friends? I wonder where that clever uncle of yours is hiding."

Sedee glanced nervously behind her before pleading, "Come on, Rakham. Let us in. *Please.*"

Shem's instincts screamed at him to leave, but he forced a smile and asked, "Are you sure this is a good idea, Sedee?"

Sedee laughed, fidgeting with the buttons that ran down the front of her one piece jumper, eventually thrusting her hands into her oversized pockets. "Trust me, my uncle and I have history with Rakham. He'll help us."

Shaking his head in reply, he couldn't help but notice a few stray curls had escaped from her hastily swept back dark hair, framing her face. Even though she did her best to hide her nervousness, the attempt made her that much cuter to Shem, who suddenly wanted to do everything in his power to ensure that she would always smile.

Finally gaining entrance to the small building, Shem followed Sedee inside. "I'm still not so sure about giving Rakham your family heirloom." His mind raced, searching for any other options, but there seemed to be no escape from this dangerous situation.

"Calm down, Shem," said Aryana. "We need his help. Let this play out."

The interior of Rakham's home was nothing like its run-down exterior. The room was cozy and well-kept, filled with an eclectic array of furniture and decorations that spoke of a lifetime of collecting. Ornate rugs covered the floor, and shelves lined the walls, each one packed with curios and trinkets Shem couldn't begin to identify.

Rakham shuffled further into the room, gesturing for them to follow. "Make yourselves comfortable," he said, indicating a plush couch. "I'll be back in a moment."

As the old man disappeared into what Shem assumed was the kitchen, he turned to Sedee. "Who is this guy?" he whispered. "You actually know him?"

Sedee's expression was amused. "My uncle and him go way back, and he has no love for the Assyrian Empire. So, it's all we have right now."

Aryana, meanwhile, had begun wandering around the cluttered room, picking up various objects that caught her eye. "Some of these look...interesting," she murmured, turning a small pair of spectacles with multiple lenses and gears over in her hands.

"Be careful," Sedee said. "He's very particular about his things."

Shem lowered his voice further. "This guys a friend?"

Sedee shrugged, her eyes scanning the room as she spoke. "As I was saying, they go way back. Before my parents were...killed, and he became my guardian. They've had all sorts of adventures together - or so they claim. Usually when I see them, they're just sitting around playing that game." She pointed to a round table tucked between two overstuffed chairs. On its surface was an intricate game board with winding paths and colorful pieces.

"The Game of the Serpent," Sedee explained. "They can spend hours hunched over that board, arguing about rules and old stories."

Aryana rejoined them, her eyes still roving over the cluttered shelves. "How long's it been?"

Sedee's brow furrowed in thought. "About a year ago, I think. He was living here with his roommate, Lahar, when I last saw him." A small smile played at the corners of her mouth. "Though I suspect their relationship was... more than just roommates."

Before Shem could ask what she meant, the sound of shuffling footsteps announced Rakham's return. The old man carried a tray with steaming cups of what smelled like spiced tea and a plate of dried fruits and nuts.

"Thought you might be hungry," Rakham said, setting the tray down on a cluttered side table. "So...what sort of trouble have you gotten yourself into this time, Sedee?" His eyes twinkled with amusement.

Sedee sat back on the couch with resignation written all over her face. "You already know. Don't you?"

A small laugh escaped Rakham. "Word travels fast in this city, you know. A flying dinosaur and three strangers causing quite a stir? Tsk tsk."

Shem felt his face grow hot. "We didn't mean to-"

Rakham waved a hand dismissively. "No need to explain. I'm sure you had your reasons." He settled into one of the overstuffed chairs next to the board game, eyeing them each in turn. “Now, what brings you to my humble abode? I doubt it’s just for a friendly game of Snakes.” He gestured towards the round game with a telling smile.

Sedee leaned forward, her voice low and urgent. “We need information, Rakham. About the Assyrian army’s plans. And weapons, if you can spare them. And where would they make a sacrifice to Azazel?”

Rakham’s bushy eyebrows shot up. “My, my. You don’t ask for small favors, do you?” He stroked his chin thoughtfully. “That’s dangerous territory, even for me. And Azazel? That’s a big ask, isn't it?”

Sedee produced the gem from her pocket. It glinted in the dim light of the room, casting tiny rainbows across Rakham’s weathered face. “We can pay,” she said, shaking the shiny treasure between her two fingers.

Rakham’s eyes widened at the sight of the gem, a hungry look crossing his face. He leaned forward in his chair, fingers twitching as if to snatch it away. “Well now, you are desperate, aren’t you?” He chuckled, a dry, rasping sound. “Wasn’t that your father’s?”

Sedee looked down at the gem, sadness etching her features.

Rakham sat back, stroking his chin thoughtfully. “The Assyrians don’t look kindly at those snooping around their business.” He shook his head. “And, they have spies everywhere.”

A loud creak echoed through the house, causing Shem and Aryana to jump to their feet in alarm. The sound of a door opening from the other room filled the air, making them tense and ready for any danger that may come bursting into their sanctuary.

"Stay calm, son," Rakham said calmly, gesturing with his hands for Shem to sit back down. "It's just Lahar." He pleaded with his eyes for Aryana to follow suit.

Though he wanted to trust the old man's words, Shem couldn't shake the feeling of impending danger. He exchanged a wary look with Aryana before reluctantly settling back down.

"Rak, have you noticed all the extra guards patrolling today?" Lahar asked as he entered the room, assuming he was speaking only to Rakham. "They're on high alert for a boy and two girls who arrived on...a pterosaur," he finished slowly, realizing he wasn't alone in the room.

Rakham stood to his feet and took Lahar by the hand. "Lahar, I'd like to introduce you to Shem and Aryana." Then gesturing towards Sedee, "And of course, Sedee, you already know."

Lahar's pleasant demeanor changed quickly, as he pulled his hand away. "You need to leave. Like...right now!" He said, as he walked to the front door and slid the trap door aside, to look out front, panic filling his voice. "Those guards are everywhere."

Shem's heart raced as he watched Lahar peer anxiously out the front door. *We're putting them in danger now, too.*

"Calm down, Lahar," Rakham said, his gravelly voice surprisingly soothing. "No one saw them come in. We're safe for the moment."

Lahar's body tensed as he spun around, his eyes wide with panic. "Safe? With half the city guard hot on their trail? Rakham, this is pure madness. It appears they are part of a larger group, and they're planning to unleash chaos at the festival tonight!"

Sedee jumped to her feet, her face hardened into a determined mask. “Festival? What kind of festival?”

Shem couldn’t believe what he was hearing. *The whole city will be looking for us now!*

Lahar’s expression turned grim as he looked at Rakham. “You know exactly what festival...the one dedicated to Azazel.” He turned to Shem, his voice filled with warning. “Whatever trouble you kids have gotten yourselves into...we want no part of it. Leave now through the back door before anyone sees you.” His desperate eyes pleaded with Rakham as he added, “or I’ll have no choice but to turn you in.”

Shem could feel his face turning red, directing his vitriol towards Rakham. “Did you know our friends would be at this *festival* the whole time?”

Rakham slowly turned to Sedee, a heavy weight of grief evident in his expression. “The festival is always held inside the colosseum. Just head towards the palace when you leave from the backdoor...you’ll see it.”

“Oh Rakham...” started Sedee, sadly.

He gently grasped her hand, holding the gem tightly. “I wish I could do more for you. But this...this is beyond our abilities. If you’re truly facing Azazel, you’ll need divine intervention. I’m sorry.”

Placing the gem back into her pocket, Sedee leaned towards Rakham, kissing him gently on the cheek. “I understand, Rakham. And yes...Yahweh is with us..” She turned to Shem. “Let’s go,” and she left through the doorway to the kitchen.

Shem, taking her cue, followed her with a nod towards the two men, Aryana close on his heels.

CHAPTER 26

Anticipated Darkness

Shem and Sedee found themselves alone in a dark alley some distance away from Rakham's house and the main thoroughfare. The sun had set, replaced by evening in the large city, lit by lighting lining the main streets. Aryana suggested that she go and scout ahead and told them to wait while she slipped away into the darkness of the alley.

Shem leaned against the cool stone wall, frustrated that they could get no assistance from Rakham. The alley was quiet except for the distant sounds of the city beyond. He glanced at Sedee, her face half-hidden in shadow.

"Sorry, he was no help," said Sedee, reading his frustration.

"It's not your fault. I guess it's hard to trust strangers."

Sedee looked into Shem's eyes; searching. "It's just that I was really hoping for some help. I'm so worried about Bog. He's the only family I have left."

"What were they like? I mean...if you don't mind me asking." *That was awkward.*

Sedee's eyes met his, a flicker of sadness passing through them. "They were good people. Honest. Kind." She paused, taking a deep breath. "Brave."

Shem felt a pang of regret for bringing up what was clearly a painful topic. "I'm sorry, I didn't mean to—"

"No, it's okay," Sedee interrupted, offering a small smile. "It happened a while ago. A Nephilim attack on our town in Blaine Falls, in the Valley. It was...horrible. I was told that the giants just appeared out of nowhere, tearing through buildings like they were made of paper." Sedee's voice grew quiet, her eyes distant. "My parents... they did their best to help others escape, but were unable to save themselves. I was with my uncle at the time and couldn't help them. I blamed myself for not being there."

Shem felt a lump form in his throat. He reached out, hesitantly placing a hand on Sedee's shoulder. "I'm so sorry. That must have been terrible." He didn't add that he was thankful that she wasn't there. *She may have been killed with them.*

She nodded, blinking back tears. "I'm so thankful that the Lord found me. I was broken, and Yahweh was the only one that could give me peace."

Shem swallowed hard, thinking of his own losses. "I understand."

"Someone close?"

"Her name was Adi. We were to be married."

Sedee's eyes softened. "Tell me about her?"

"I don't talk about it much," Shem began, his voice rough to his ears, like gravel underfoot. "Not because I don't want to, but because every time I do, it's like I'm back there. Smelling the smoke. Hearing the screams."

Sedee tilted her head slightly, saying nothing, just letting the space between them breathe. It was enough to nudge him on.

"She was... incredible. Smart, brave, and she had this laugh that could light up a room." He smiled at the memory. "We grew up together in Ararat."

Sedee nodded, encouraging him to continue.

"The invaders that captured you, had invaded our town first. They hit fast. Killing many people I knew. It's why we started on this journey--my misguided ideas of revenge. You see...she was killed by a giant, as well." Shem's gaze drifted from her face to the ground, flexing his fingers to try and shake off the memory.

Sedee placed her warm hand on Shem's arm without saying a word.

"When she died, I thought my world had ended," Shem's voice cracked, and he swallowed hard. "But now...I can finally remember her without feeling like I'm drowning in grief. I know I'll see her again someday, when I leave this world."

The silence that followed was heavy, thick with the weight of what he'd laid bare. Sedee shifted her weight, the sound pulling his eyes up to meet hers. There was no pity in her expression, no empty platitudes--just a quiet understanding that pierced through the haze of their mutual grief.

"Can I ask what changed your perspective? Sedee asked softly.

"I had a run-in with Azazel that scared me to death. After that...with Bartel's leading, I saw that Yahweh was the answer all along. The next time I faced him, I could feel the Lord in Davar, my sword. Yet, after all of that, I still pursued those invaders, and Bartel died. I just don't know anymore. Bartel was Adi's father and I'll never be able to tell him how thankful I am."

"I'm sure he knew. And don't ever discount yourself or have doubt just because bad things have happened. He will give you what you need. These trials shape us--make us who we are."

Shem's chest tightened, but not from the memories this time. It was her-Sedee-standing there with her own scars laid open, mirroring his. He studied her face in the street-light: the soft line of her jaw, eyes that reflected compassion, the way her lips pressed together like she was holding back more. She wasn't just listening. She got it. And that realization hit him harder than he expected. "You sound like my father," he said with a small chuckle. "He said that I had to be forged in fire, or something like that."

Sedee smiled. "I hope that was a compliment. Your father sounds like a wise man."

He nodded slowly, the knot in his throat loosening just a bit. For the first time since he left home, he didn't feel alone in it. And as the light danced across her features, he noticed something else--a pull, a warmth that wasn't just from the setting sun. She was strong, steady, beautiful in a way that didn't shout but whispered, tugging at something deep inside him. He hadn't expected that. Hadn't wanted it, maybe. But there it was, stirring in the space between them, fragile and real.

"You're easy to talk to," he said, the words clumsy but honest, feeling a faint flush creeping up his neck.

She smiled, small and unguarded, and it lit something he thought had burned out forever. "Good," she said. "Because I'm not going anywhere.

He was about to respond when a flicker of movement caught his eye.

Aryana emerged from the shadows, her face grim.

"What did you see?" Shem asked, straightening up.

Aryana's eyes darted between them, suspiciously. "Thousands of people are heading towards the center of Asshur, to the colosseum."

"Thousands?" asked Shem, shocked. "What could be drawing such a crowd?"

Aryana shook her head, her expression troubled. "I'm sure it's this festival of Azazel, and I'm sure it can't be good. Whatever they have planned, it's big."

Sedee frowned, her brow furrowed in thought. "We need to get closer, find out where Bog and your friends are being held."

"Agreed," said Aryana, "but we have no weapons. How can we mount a rescue like this?"

Shem felt a surge of determination, like a tugging from within his core. "You'll have no choice," he said, almost to himself, recalling Ouza's words on the air-char.

"What was that?" asked Aryana.

Shem shook his head. "Just learning how the Lord works."

Sedee nodded, a glimmer of hope in her eyes. "What's the plan, then?"

Shem took a deep breath, firm in his resolve. "We blend in with the crowd," he said decisively. "It's our best chance to get close without drawing attention."

Aryana nodded in agreement. "Good idea. The streets are packed; no one will notice three more faces going the same direction. Even if we are the only ones properly clothed."

As they prepared to leave the alley, Shem felt a strange certainty settle over him. *He'lll be expecting me. I just know it.*

Sedee looked at Shem with concern. "Are you...okay?"

Shem took a deep breath and squared his shoulders. "I am. I finally know what I need to do."

They emerged from the network of back alleys, and were immediately engulfed by the surging crowd. The air was thick with excitement and the pungent smell of sweat mixed with the floral scents of mingling perfumes. Bodies pressed against them from all sides as they were swept along with the flow of people.

"Stay close!" Shem called out to Sedee and Aryana, reaching back to grasp Sedee's hand. He felt her fingers intertwine with his, anchoring them together in the sea of humanity.

The noise was deafening. Shouts, laughter, and the thunderous sound of thousands of feet pounding the cobblestones filled Shem's ears. He could barely hear himself think over the din.

Moving closer to the center of the city, Shem caught glimpses of the massive colosseum looming ahead. Its stone walls seemed to touch the sky, lights from banks of crystals illuminating the approaching crowds.

"Look there!" Aryana's sharp voice cut through the noise. Shem followed her gaze, his heart quickening as he saw what had caught her attention. High above the colosseum, the giant egg-shaped air-char hovered above the thousands of people gathered below.

"That means they're here!" Sedee gasped, squeezing Shem's hand. "They must've brought them right to the top of the colosseum."

"We need to get inside," Shem said, his hand tugging on Sedee and Aryana's arms as they pushed through the crowded streets. Their movements were disguised among the throngs of people, using the press of bodies as cover.

Despite the grumbles and curses thrown their way, they persisted forward towards the entrance of the stadium.

Once inside, Shem caught sight of the main arena. And it was so large that it could fit a small village within its boundaries.

In the center stood a grand stage, flanked by soldiers standing at attention. And there, chained together in the middle, were their friends: prisoners of war.

The backdrop behind the stage was an imposing skeleton of a giant Nephilim, sitting on a throne made of monolithic stone, with two more of these fearsome creatures, alive, and standing guard on either side of the long platform. Behind the prisoners, two large human sized thrones sat empty, surrounded by smaller cushioned chairs.

As they were pulled along with the crowd, Shem felt his heart racing. The sheer number of people was overwhelming, bodies pressing in from all sides as they moved deeper into the colosseum. The air was thick with the smell of sweat and incense, and the noise was a deafening mix of excited chatter, shouting vendors, and the occasional blast of horns.

Shem kept a tight grip on Sedee's hand, afraid to lose her in the crowd. He could just make out Aryana's golden hair bobbing ahead of them as she navigated the throng of people.

"This way!" Aryana called back over her shoulder, gesturing towards a set of wide stone steps leading down to the arena floor.

As they descended, the full scale of the colosseum became apparent. Tens of thousands of people filled the tiered seating, a sea of faces all focused on the arena below. Shem's eyes were drawn to the massive fire pit in front of the stage, flames leaping high into the air. The heat from it was palpable even from this distance.

Reaching the bottom of the stairs, Shem overheard snippets of conversation from those around them.

"Did you see last year's sacrifice? This one's supposed to feature something special," a woman whispered excitedly to her companion.

"I heard Lilith might make an appearance," another man said, his voice tinged with awe. "They say she is so beautiful that she is favored by the gods."

"Tubal-Cain will be there too," someone else chimed in.

"What a sight that will be!"

Shem felt cold despite the oppressive heat. He exchanged a worried glance with Sedee, whose face had gone pale. The mention of sacrifices and powerful figures like Lilith and Tubal-Cain only heightened their sense of urgency.

As they pushed forward through the crowd, a man next to Shem leaned in close, his breath hot on Shem's ear. "All this superstition and ritual," he muttered, "it's outdated. We should be focusing on science and progress, not appeasing imaginary gods."

Before Shem could respond, the man's wife grabbed his arm, her eyes darting nervously. "Hush!" she hissed. "Someone might hear you!"

Shem felt a flicker of hope at overhearing the man's whispered dissent. Perhaps not everyone in Asshur was completely under Azazel's sway. He filed the information away, focusing on the more pressing matter at hand.

As they neared the arena floor, the crowd began to thin slightly. Shem could now see the stage more clearly. His heart clenched at the sight of his friends chained there, looking battered but defiant. He itched to rush forward and free them but knew it would be suicide with the Nephilim guards looming nearby.

"We need to get closer," Shem murmured to Sedee and Aryana. "Maybe if we—"

His words were cut off by a sudden hush falling over the crowd. A horn blasted, the sound echoing off the stone walls. Shem's skin prickled with unease as the crowd fell silent. All eyes turned towards the grand entrance at the opposite end of the arena.

The crowd erupted with a renewed vigor as a procession emerged, led by a tall, imposing figure clad in gleaming armor. General Ouza. His black eyes swept the arena, and for a moment, Shem could have sworn their gazes locked. At his side he held Davar, Shem's sword.

Behind Ouza came a stunningly beautiful woman that could only be called obscene, her fire-red hair cascading down her back, adorned with jewels that glittered in the firelight. She had huge antlers rising from her headdress and a sheer red gown draped over her shoulders that moved in the wake of her deliberate grace, exposing her lack of modesty. Her feet were painted black to her knees, as were her arms to her elbows. Her presence seemed to captivate the entire crowd, her presence a slow burn of intensity that unsettled as much as it drew them in, eliciting a collective sigh from the masses as they worshipped this woman who radiated evil personified.

"That's Lilith," whispered Sedee, with a tone of disgust. "At least the name she took, after giving birth to the first Nephilim."

Shem had to look away from this boldly provocative figure who commanded attention with an almost magnetic pull. She was both enchanting and unnerving, forcing him to clench his teeth in embarrassment.

Next came a towering mass of muscle, every sinew and tendon rippling under his bronzed skin, glistening slightly with sweat. His beard, thick and wild, cascaded down his chest, a stark contrast to his otherwise bare torso. It was white, streaked with black, giving him an air of seasoned wisdom or perhaps untamed fury. His only garment was a simple loincloth, secured around his waist with a thick, leather belt. Tubal-Cain. In his hands, he wielded an enormous hammer, its head larger than a man's torso, forged from dark, gleaming metal that seemed to absorb light. His eyes scanned the colosseum, daring anyone to challenge him.

"That's..."

"Tubal-Cain?" whispered Shem, anticipating Sedee's commentary.

"Obvious, huh?" she said, under her breath.

A colorful parade of attendants and devotees trailed behind them, each dressed in their own unique style and fashion, or lack thereof. The vibrant hues of their outfits blended together in a kaleidoscope of colors, ranging from deep blues to bold reds and everything in between. Each person's attire was a reflection of their individual tastes and personalities or status, making the procession a visual feast for the eyes. Some wore intricate patterns and detailed designs, while others opted for simple yet elegant ensembles. With them were mixed in a contingent of Assyrian soldiers in their glimmering black armor. The air was filled with anticipation, the crowd's chatter and laughter rising like a wave as they made their way down the path.

Shem's heart pounded as he watched the procession make its way to the stage. The crowd was caught up in the shared thrill; a chaotic yet joyful celebration as the parade mounted the platform. He felt Sedee's hand tighten in his, her palm slick with nervous sweat.

As Ouza, Lilith, and Tubal-Cain took their places on the thrones, one of the attendants took the center stage. He wore long red robes, and a three-tiered headdress adorned with gold, silver and jewels. He was pale, with gaunt features and black eyes. Eyes that were painted in shadow and outlined in blacks and purples, extending outward, creating a menacing, predatory look. As he raised his hands out to speak, the red color painted on his lips gave the impression of dried blood, making him appear even more ghastly. The crowd went silent.

The man's voice boomed across the arena, unnaturally loud and echoing. "People of Asshur! Faithful citizens of Assyria! Tonight, we gather to celebrate The Festival of Azazel!" Shem felt his stomach churn as the crowd roared in response. He glanced at Sedee and Aryana, their faces mirroring his own concern.

"For too long," the master of ceremonies continued. "The followers of Yahweh and armies of Eden have sought to undermine our great society. But no more! Tonight, we will show them the true power of Azazel!"

Another deafening cheer erupted from the crowd. Shem gritted his teeth, fighting the urge to shout out in defiance.

He calmed the crowd with a gesture. "Bring forth the chosen!" the master of ceremonies commanded.

A large group of parade participants was brought up onto the stage, their emotions ranging from tears streaming down their faces to joyous clapping. They were lined up along the front edge of the stage, just a few feet away from the blazing fire pit. The crowd erupted once again.

Shem couldn't help but worry that they might catch on fire if they weren't careful. He could feel the sweat dripping down his own face.

The master of ceremonies spoke a few words to the group, his voice carrying over the cheering crowd. Shem strained to make out what was being said, but he couldn't make it out, over the deafening noise; the crowd's cheering and excitement was palpable and contagious.

Shem noticed that many in the crowd were covering their mouths in anticipation of what was to come, overhearing someone close say, "...such an honor." His own imagination ran wild awaiting the next part of the ceremony with dread.

The master of ceremonies presented to the crowd once again. "Behold, the willing sacrifices who will usher in a new era of power for Azazel our lord!"

Shem's blood ran cold. Sacrifices? He exchanged horrified glances with Sedee and Aryana.

"No," Sedee whispered, her face pale. "I can't watch this."

Shem put his arm around Sedee as the master of ceremonies raised his arms dramatically. "Let the ceremony begin!"

A low, haunting chant began to rise from the crowd. The fire in the pit before the stage flared higher, casting eerie shadows across the arena. Shem watched in horror as Lilith rose from her throne, her movements fluid and hypnotic. She approached the line of participants, a cruel smile playing on her lips.

"Children of Azazel," she purred, her smokey, seductive voice carrying unnaturally across the arena, "your sacrifice will not be in vain. Through your devotion, our lord will rise to his rightful place, and Assyria will gain the power to crush our enemies and rule all of Adamah!"

The chanting grew louder, more frenzied. Shem felt dizzy, the heat and noise overwhelming his senses. He saw Lilith raise her arms, her fingers splayed wide. The fire in the pit surged impossibly high, licking at the night sky.

"Now!" Lilith cried. "Step forward and embrace your destiny!"

To Shem's horror, the first person in line - a young man barely older than himself - stepped towards the edge of the stage. His eyes were glazed, a blissful smile on his face, as he leapt into the roaring flames.

"No!" Shem cried out, unable to contain himself any longer. But his voice was lost in the roar of the crowd.

Letting go of Sedee, he lurched forward instinctively, but Aryana's iron grip on his arm stopped him cold.

"Shem, no!" she hissed. "You'll get us all killed!"

He knew she was right, but the sight of the young man's body consumed by flames made him feel physically ill. One by one, the other sacrifices stepped forward, faces rapturous as they plunged into the inferno. The stench of burning flesh filled the air, mixing sickeningly with the crowd's ecstatic shouts.

Lilith's laughter rang out, cruel and triumphant. "Feel the power, my children! With each sacrifice, Azazel grows stronger!"

Shem felt bile rise in his throat as he watched the horrific scene unfold. The acrid smell of burning flesh mingled with the crowd's frenzied cheers, creating a nightmarish mix of senses. He wanted nothing more than to look away, to run from this madness, but he forced himself to watch. He had to bear witness to this evil, to remember why they were fighting.

Beside him, Sedee had buried her face in his shoulder, her body shaking with silent sobs. Aryana stood rigid, her face a mask of barely contained fury.

As the last sacrifice stepped into the flames, the fire pit erupted in a column of sickly green light. The crowd's chanting reached a fever pitch, and Shem felt a wave of malevolent energy wash over him. He staggered, nearly falling to his knees.

Then, as if conjured from the depths of a dark, smoldering shadow on the stage, a figure appeared. He stood tall and commanding in the vibrant glow of the emerald flames. His presence was enigmatic and mysterious, like a forgotten legend come to life.

Shem's blood ran cold as he laid eyes on the newcomer, his heart pounding in fear and recognition. Azazel. He stood out from the crowd in his pristine white attire, his skin almost translucent and giving off an otherworldly glow. But it was his dark, soulless eyes that sent shivers through Shem's body.

Without a word, Azazel raised his hands towards the crowd and immediately Tubal-Cain, Lilith, General Ouza, and all those in attendance fell to their knees in worship. The sound of their collective bowing echoed throughout the colosseum, drowning out the gasps and cries of the thousands of citizens who had also been compelled to submit to their god.

But Shem, Aryana, and Sedee remained standing, their defiance palpable in the air. Azazel's smile widened as he locked eyes with Shem, an unspoken challenge passing between them. Time seemed to stand still as they faced off, good and evil at odds with each other.

Shem felt a surge of determination course through him. Without a word to Aryana or Sedee, he began pushing his way through the kneeling crowd towards the stage. Gasps and cries of shock rippled through the arena as people noticed his defiance.

"Shem, no!" Sedee cried, reaching for him. But he was already out of her grasp, moving with purpose towards his destiny. Her and Aryana had to move quickly to keep up with him.

Approaching the left side of the stage, the Nephilim guard moved to intercept them, but Azazel's voice rang out, clear and cold. "Let them pass."

The giant hesitated, then stepped aside, towering above the potential threat, while Shem climbed the steps, undeterred by the knot twisting in his stomach. At the top, Lieutenant Goriel stood waiting, a smirk playing on his lips.

Shem met his gaze steadily, refusing to be intimidated, noticing a particular book jutting out of his belt. *Aram's journal.*

Behind him, he could sense Aryana and Sedee's presence, lending him strength. The acrid smell of smoke and burnt flesh still hung heavy in the air, a grim reminder of the horror they had just witnessed.

Azazel's voice cut through the tense silence. "Rise," he commanded, his words meant only for those on stage.

Tubal-Cain and Lilith took their seats on their thrones, their expressions a mix of amusement and boredom. General Ouza, however, strode purposefully towards Shem, his hand still holding Davar - Shem's own sword.

"Now, Shem," Ouza said, his voice quiet, evoking memories of Nin back on the farm, "it's time."

Shem felt a strange calm wash over him as he faced General Ouza. The man who had once been like a father to him now stood as his enemy, wielding Shem's own sword against him. The blade was dark; just a beautiful piece of wood. *Nin can't use its power!*

"I guess it is," said Shem, his voice steadier than he felt.

Ouza's smile died on his lips from Shem's response. "You're not clever, boy. I set you on this path, and we will finish it together. This is my will."

Behind him, Shem heard Sedee's sharp intake of breath. He didn't dare turn to look at her or Aryana, knowing their faces would be etched with worry and fear.

"You're wrong," Shem said, his voice growing stronger with each word. "My destiny was set by Yahweh, before I was born. You cannot escape his will."

Ouza turned to face the crowd, with a parting word for Shem. "We shall see." He raised his hands to the masses who erupted in a deafening roar.

"My fellow Assyrians," he proclaimed, his voice echoing through the square. "I, General Ouza, have returned to you after centuries of absence, having fought valiantly in the treacherous land of Eden." The crowd seethed with animosity towards their despised neighbors, but he silenced them with a commanding gesture. "You were assured of an extraordinary offering at this year's celebration, and I am here to fulfill that pledge. As a devout tribute to our revered god Azazel, I present to you Shem, son of Noah himself!" The sea of people erupted once more in a deafening cacophony of cheers and applause, their voices rising and falling in a rhythmic chant of "Ouza, Ouza!"

CHAPTER 27

Heir of the Promise

The energy in the colosseum was electric, pulsing through the air with an almost tangible force. Each clap was like a drumbeat, keeping time with the chant as it echoed across the packed arena.

Shem's eyes darted between Aryana and Sedee, knowing that his next move could put everyone in danger; especially his captive friends. "Be ready," he whispered urgently to Aryana, who nodded with steely determination. His heart beat rapidly as he turned to Sedee, gripping her arm tightly. "Protect our friends," he said, his voice trembling slightly with fear and resolve. He held her gaze for a moment longer, hoping it wouldn't be their last knowing that chaos would soon erupt around them.

Ouza, casting a brief glance at Shem before resuming his oration, declared with fervor, "Noah, the esteemed high priest of Seth's lineage in Eden, has foretold the impending judgment of Yahweh!" The crowd erupted in a clamor of dissent towards Noah's proclamation.

"Listen to me, people! This message is nothing but a deceitful lie!" Ouza's voice echoed through the crowd as he stood on the podium, his eyes blazing with conviction. "Yahweh cannot destroy Adamah because He promised a supposed Redeemer. How can He break His promise and still be considered just?"

The murmurs in the crowd grew louder as the deception of Ouza's words sunk in, sowing confusion in the crowd.

"What about Noah's son?" someone shouted out, their voice filled with desperation.

Ouza scoffed, his laughter tinged with malice. "Ah, yes. Shem. The only way Yahweh could fulfill His promise is if He preserves the family line. But we will put an end to that here and now." A sinister grin spread across his face as he raised Davar above his head.

The crowd erupted into cheers and jeers, fueled by blind devotion to Azazel and hatred for the one true God. "With this sacrifice," Ouza shouted over the noise, "with Shem's death, Yahweh's plan will fail, and Assyria shall reign supreme!"

The final part of his statement was drowned out by the deafening roar of the crowd, their applause and cries drowning out all reason and sense. The atmosphere was charged with frenzy and anticipation as they prepared to offer up a human life in defiance of Yahweh.

Shem knew it was almost time as he watched Ouza raise Davar high, the sword's blade dark, even in the torchlight. The crowd's frenzy reached a fever pitch, their chants for his blood echoing off the stone walls. They were completely enthralled with the provocative speech that Ouza gave, having no idea that Shem had brothers or that Yahweh could use whoever he chose.

In that moment, time seemed to slow. Shem locked eyes with Aryana, her face a mask of determination. He gave her a slight nod, and she tensed, ready to spring into action.

Suddenly, Ouza spun towards Shem, his eyes wild. "Now!" he bellowed, hurling Davar through the air.

Shem's breath caught in his throat as the sword arched towards him. Instinctively, he reached out, his fingers closing around the hilt just as it was about to strike his chest. The crowd fell silent, shock rippling through the masses.

The weight of Davar felt familiar in Shem's hands, its power thrumming through his body. The sword glowed with an otherworldly light, illuminating the stunned faces around him. Azazel's laughter died in his throat, his eyes widening in surprise.

Without hesitation, Shem swung the sword in a graceful arc, slicing through the chains binding his friends. The metal links shattered like glass, falling away with a musical tinkling.

At the same time, in a blur of motion, Aryana launched herself at Lieutenant Goriel, catching him off guard. Her piercing whistle cut through the air, calling Alouette to her rescue.

Shem's eyes locked on Azazel. The fallen angel's face contorted with rage as Shem closed the distance between them, Davar's light blazing ever brighter.

"You fool!" Azazel snarled, his voice like grinding stone. "You think you can defeat me?"

Shem didn't waste breath on a reply. He could hear the chaos erupting behind him - shouts of confusion, the clash of metal, Alouette's piercing cry. But he kept his focus on Azazel, trusting his friends to handle the rest.

Nearing his target, Shem caught glimpses of movement in his peripheral vision--Tubal-Cain rising from his throne, face twisted in shock and fury and Ouza across the stage, closing in on Azazel from another angle.

Davar's glow intensified with each step. Shem's heart pounded in his ears as he closed in on Azazel, the fallen angel's eyes blazing with hellfire.

Azazel stood his ground, his face contorting into an evil smile.

But Shem didn't falter. He remembered Ouza's words that demons could be killed. He had to believe it was true.

With a cry that tore from deep in his chest, Shem lunged forward, Davar aimed straight at Azazel's black heart. The demon's hand shot out with inhuman speed and grasped Shem's wrist before the sword could find purchase.

Shem's arm trembled as he pushed against Azazel's iron grip, Davar's tip mere inches from the demon's chest. Azazel's eyes blazed with hellfire, his lips curled in a sneer.

"Did you really think it would be that easy, boy?" Azazel hissed, his fetid breath washing over Shem's face.

But Shem wasn't alone. A blur of motion caught his eye as Ouza appeared behind Azazel, his face set in grim determination. In one fluid motion, Ouza grabbed Azazel's shoulder and yanked him backwards, throwing the demon off balance.

"Now, Shem!" Ouza roared.

But it was already too late. Azazel's arms swung out with a ferocity that sent both assailants flying back, their bodies hitting the ground with a painful thud. Davar clattering to the stage, dark once again.

Shem stumbled to his feet, near panic as he searched for Davar amidst the chaos. But before he could even process what was happening, Azazel had already reached the fallen sword and was lifting it from the platform with a smirk forming on his face.

Thinking he had more time, Ouza lunged towards the demon, hoping to catch him off guard. But Azazel was too quick and swung the dark blade at him with deadly accuracy, slicing across his face in a spray of blood. With a cry of pain, Ouza tumbled off the edge of the stage and out of sight, leaving Shem frozen in shock at the turn of events before him.

Shem stood facing Azazel, helpless, as his friends struggled against overwhelming odds. He could see Tubal-Cain approaching on his left, his face twisted with rage. A massive Nephilim was climbing onto the stage from where Ouza had fallen, its inhuman eyes fixed on Shem. The piercing screech of Alouette filled the air as she dove at the Assyrian soldiers, talons extended.

The colosseum erupted into utter chaos. Screams and the clash of weapons echoed off the stone walls as the pitched battle raged on the stage and pockets of fighting broke out in the crowd.

Azazel's laughter boomed over the cacophony as he held Davar high above his head. "Foolish mortals," he sneered, his eyes gleaming with malice. "Did you truly believe you could kill a son of Yahweh?" With a sickening crack, he brought the sword down over his knee. The blade snapped in two.

A blinding flash of energy exploded from the broken sword, sending a shockwave across the stage. Shem's feet left the ground as his body was hurled backwards off the stage and crashed onto the arena floor next to the giant Nephilim skeleton. The impact knocked the wind from his lungs, leaving him gasping.

As the spots cleared from his vision, Shem pushed himself up on shaky arms. The scene before him was one of devastation. His friends lay scattered and motionless across the stage. Even the towering Nephilim had been brought to its knees. The Assyrian soldiers were sprawled in heaps, groaning in pain.

Despair washed over Shem as he slumped back on his knees. He had failed. Davar was destroyed, his allies incapacitated. Even Ouza, for all his cunning, had been cast aside like a ragdoll.

Shem felt the full weight of defeat as he knelt on the arena floor. The failure pressed down on him, threatening to crush his spirit. With trembling hands, he reached down and grasped a handful of sand letting it sift through his fingers.

"Yahweh," he whispered, his voice barely audible over the groans of the fallen, "I don't know what to do. Please... help us."

As the last grains of sand slipped from his grasp, a shadow fell over him. Shem's breath caught in his throat as he raised his eyes, expecting to see Azazel looming over him ready to deliver the final blow.

"Why do you despair, son of man?" Shem had never heard the voice before, but he knew immediately who it belonged to: Raphael. "Who was it that called to you on the breeze? Who saved you from certain death when the abomination first came? Who broke the spell of the fallen? Who gave you the strength to defeat the giant? Who gave you the wisdom to save your friends? Who directed your path leading you to this very moment? Where does your faith reside, son of Noah-chosen of Yahweh?"

Shem could feel his body tremble in fear before this being. He kept his eyes firmly on Raphael's plain sandaled feet.

Could it be? "I am unworthy, my Lord..."

"I am NOT him. I am but a faithful servant, a messenger sent to give you help," said Raphael, guiding Shem to his feet with a tug of his sleeve. "A gift," he said, with a warm, gentle expression on his face.

Shem was embarrassed and looked to the ground. "The sword my father gave me broke. I lost it."

"Was it a sword made of gopher wood that delivered you? Or was it The Sword of the Spirit...The Word of Yahweh Himself?" Raphael continued to smile at Shem with a tenderness that spoke of true love for him. There was no accusation in the question.

Shem stood in silence-confused. His father had explained that it was a powerful symbol of the Word of Yahweh. *I don't understand.*

Suddenly it washed over him, like a bucket of cold water while he was sleeping. It wasn't the sword that had the power--that was just a tool in a believer's hands. It was actually the Lord that held all the power, working through him.

As this revelation hit him, he realized that the Lord didn't need a physical weapon to fight evil - only a servant of Yahweh. "How much faith is required?" he asked.

Raphael simply held up his thumb and index finger, barely a space apart, indicating that even the smallest amount of faith was enough. "You were born of the line of Seth, but it is by faith that you are an heir of the promise."

This epiphany filled Shem with a newfound understanding and strength. And, as if a curtain was lifted, his eyes were opened to the spiritual realm merging with the physical all around him. Raphael appeared before him, transformed into a glorious being of radiant light and towering wings. And he was not alone - countless angels fought around him, their flaming swords clashing against dark and sinister beings. Shem witnessed a grand battle between the faithful sons of Yahweh and those who rebelled against Him.

On the stage of this celestial war, Shem watched in awe as angels and demons were locked in a fierce struggle. The forces of light seemed to be losing ground against a horde of malevolent creatures, led by the largest and most fearsome of them all: Azazel. With bat-like wings and fiery eyes, he exuded terror and malice.

"Go forth, son of man," commanded Raphael with a voice that echoed like a hundred men. "This day, the LORD will deliver them into your hands." And with that, he soared towards Azazel, ready to face off in a showdown of epic proportions.

Renewed with a new sense of understanding and purpose, Shem looked around frantically for a weapon. His eyes fell on the giant Nephilim skeleton sitting on the throne. Grabbing the closest thing he could use, he took hold of the lower leg bone that was nearly as tall as himself and, to his amazement, he ripped it free with surprising ease.

Gripping the massive bone, Shem launched himself back onto the stage. Tubal-Cain stood waiting, hammer raised high. As Shem's feet hit the platform, he swung the bone with all his might, impacting Tubal-Cain's head with a sickening crunch. The blow sent the man flying backwards into the fire pit without so much as a cry.

Panting heavily, Shem took a moment to survey the chaos around him. His friends, now free from their bonds, were fighting back against the guards and attendants with fierce determination. Aryana soared overhead on Alouette, diving at the eyes of the Nephilim on the far side. *Where's the other one?*

He whirled just in time to dodge a crushing blow from its massive spear.

The weapon's haft was as thick as Shem's leg, but leaping forward, he gripped the spear and wrenched it from the Nephilim's grasp. In one fluid motion, Shem hurled the bone at the giant's head, striking with pinpoint accuracy between the eyes sending the behemoth staggering backward. The Nephilim crashed to the ground with an earth-shaking thud, seemingly incapacitated.

With the Nephilim defeated, Shem turned to face the true threat - Azazel. The fallen angel was locked in fierce combat with Raphael, their forms shifting between human and angelic as they battled. It was a dizzying sight, like two images superimposed and fighting for dominance.

Taking a chance to help Raphael, Shem lunged forward and grabbed Azazel from behind, wrapping his arms around the demon's neck. He pulled backwards with all his might, lifting Azazel's human form off the ground. The effect was immediate and terrifying. Azazel let out an unholy scream that set Shem's teeth on edge - it was the sound of a thousand tormented souls crying out at once.

Azazel's sword flickered and went dark as he thrashed against Shem's iron grip. But Shem held fast, his arms trembling with the effort of restraining Azazel, Yahweh's strength flowing through him.

Raphael lowered his sword, his celestial form blazing with holy light as he addressed the writhing demon. "Azazel,"

Raphael's voice boomed, "your defiance has come to an end. The Lord's power flowing through him has you trapped in your human form, unable to flee, like the Watchers who took mortal wives. Your judgment is at hand."

Azazel's struggles intensified, his screams growing more frantic.Raphael continued, his words heavy with divine authority: "You shall be chained in a prison of darkness, in the place called Dudael, until the day of the great judgment. Then you will be cast into the lake of fire for eternity."

As Raphael spoke, glowing silver chains erupted from the floor beneath Azazel's feet. They snaked upwards, wrapping around the demon's thrashing form. Shem felt the chains brush against his arms as they encircled Azazel, and he released his grip, stumbling backwards.

Azazel's screams reached a fever pitch as the chains cocooned his entire body in pulsing silver light. The demon's eyes blazed with terror and fury as he was slowly dragged downwards. The floor beneath him seemed to liquefy, swallowing him up inch by agonizing inch.

"No!" Azazel howled, his voice distorting into an inhuman shriek. "This cannot be! I am eternal! I cannot be bound!"

But his protests were in vain. With a final, gut-wrenching scream, Azazel disappeared beneath the shimmering surface, leaving only eerie silence in his wake. The effect was immediate and profound. Demons scattered in panic, fleeing at the sight of their leader's defeat. The oppressive darkness that had hung over the colosseum began to lift.

Shem turned to Raphael, his heart pounding. The angel's radiant form was already beginning to fade, but he offered Shem a warm smile and a respectful salute before vanishing entirely.

As the veil between worlds closed, everything seemed dim in comparison. Shem blinked, his eyes adjusting to the mundane reality around him. Even the sounds of battle diminished, but what remained were muted now.

A low rumble drew Shem's attention skyward. The massive air-char was now descending rapidly, its shadow falling over the stage. Crossbow bolts began thudding into the stage around him. He ducked instinctively, his eyes darting to the other end of the platform where his friends were fighting their own battle.

Lieutenant Goriel's headless body lay crumpled on the ground, with Eloise, Lud, and Bog standing over it, their faces grim but determined. Shem couldn't tell which of them had dealt the fatal blow, yet Lud was holding his brother's journal in one hand and a sword in the other.

Nearby, Sedee was comforting Elam as he knelt beside Halvin's still body, who was sprawled face-down with a dagger protruding from his back. Blood pooled beneath him, and Shem's heart clenched with the loss of yet another friend.

The master of ceremonies lay dead not far away, his elaborate robes stained crimson. There was no sign of the second Nephilim, but Alouette circled the arena keeping watch for more foes.

Shem's heart raced as he surveyed the chaotic scene. The air-char loomed ever closer, its massive presence engulfing the stage. More crossbow bolts rained down, splintering the wood around them.

Aram rushed to Shem's side, his eyes wide with urgency. "We need to take that thing down," he shouted over the din. "It's their key to launching an assault deep into Eden. We'll be skewered if we don't act fast!"

"How?" Shem asked, ducking as another bolt whizzed past his ear.

"Fire," Aram replied grimly. "I overheard from the soldiers that whatever keeps it aloft is vulnerable to flame."

Without hesitation, Shem sprinted to where the fallen Nephilim's spear lay. He snatched it up, quickly wrapping a strip of cloth around its tip. "Aryana!" he called out, catching her eye as she swooped low on Alouette. "When I strike the air-char, grab one of the hanging ropes!"

"When you what?" asked Aryana, shock written all over her face. "Forget I asked," she added, seeing the giant spear in Shem's hand. Urging Alouette higher, she began circling just out of crossbow range.

Shem ran to the fire pit, plunging the cloth-wrapped spear tip into the flames. It ignited instantly. Taking a deep breath, he hefted the massive weapon, its weight straining his muscles.

With a mighty heave, Shem launched the flaming spear towards the descending air-char. It arced through the air, trailing smoke and sparks. For a heart-stopping moment, Shem feared it would fall short. But the spear found its mark, piercing the air-char's midsection with a dull thud.

At first, nothing happened. Then, with a whoosh, flames erupted from the impact point, spreading rapidly across the craft's surface. Panicked shouts echoed from within as the fire ignited.

Alouette swooped down, her talons grasping one of the dangling ropes. She dropped the end near Shem, who seized it; making the line taught. Gritting his teeth, he began to pull with all his might, dragging the flaming behemoth towards the stage.

His friends could only watch in disbelief as Shem singlehandedly tugged the massive craft downward. The air-char lurched and shuddered, its occupants scrambling in vain to regain control.

"Get out of here!" Shem shouted to his companions, his voice strained with effort. "Get clear!"

As his friends began to retreat, Eloise's voice cut through the chaos. "Lilith!" she shouted, pointing towards the back of the stage. "I saw her escape through a trapdoor!"

Shem's companions began making their way towards the hidden exit, but Sedee and Elam hesitated, looking back at Shem with concern.

"Hurry up!" Sedee called out, her voice trembling. "I won't lose you!"

Shem's arms burned with exertion as he continued to pull the flaming air-char downward. He could feel the heat intensifying as it drew closer, the wood of the stage creaking ominously beneath his feet.

With a final burst of strength, Shem yanked hard on the rope, ensuring the air-char's trajectory was set. It was now descending rapidly, completely out of control. Satisfied it would crash into the stage, Shem released the rope and sprinted towards his friends.

"Go!" he shouted, waving his arms frantically. "Get down the trapdoor!"

Sedee and Elam didn't need to be told twice. They disappeared through the opening, with Shem close behind. As he dropped down into the tunnel, he heard the deafening crash of the air-char smashing into the stage above.

The narrow passageway was dimly lit by gems along the walls. Shem's companions were already running full-tilt down the corridor, their footsteps echoing off the stone. He pushed himself to catch up, his lungs burning with each breath.

Suddenly, a massive explosion rocked the tunnel.

Chapter 28

Divine Judgement

The concussive force of the explosion sent debris hurtling through the air, knocking everyone off their feet. Shem tumbled forward, skidding across the rough stone floor. His ears rang from the blast as he struggled to regain his bearings.

Coughing and sputtering, Shem pushed himself up onto his hands and knees. Dust filled the air, making it difficult to see or breathe. He could hear the pained groans of his companions around him.

They were bruised, bleeding, and shaken, but miraculously, and thankfully, all were alive. *Thank you Lord.*

As the dust settled, Shem struggled to his feet, wincing at the various aches and cuts covering his body. Squinting through the hazy air, he attempted to take stock of his companions.

"Everyone okay?" he asked, his voice rough from the dust.

One by one, his friends responded:

"I'm here," Aram coughed, emerging from a cloud of dust. He was rubbing a gash on his shoulder.

"Present," Elam groaned, helping Sedee to her feet.

"Just peachy," Lud muttered, rubbing a nasty bump on his head. He was supporting Eloise who gave Shem a half smile in acknowledgement.

Bog gave a weak thumbs up as he extricated himself from a pile of debris.

Shem's heart sank at the realization of Halvin's absence. He met Elam's level stare, and he shook his head slightly.

The loss of their friend hung heavy in the air.

"We need to keep moving," Aram said quietly, breaking the somber silence. "There's no telling if that explosion sealed off our exit or if it will bring down the rest of the tunnel."

Nodding grimly, Shem helped Bog to his feet. "Aram's right. We're not safe yet. Let's go."

The group stumbled forward, supporting each other as they made their way down the dim corridor. The gems lining the walls flickered eerily, casting long shadows as they passed.

"Where do you think this tunnel leads?" Eloise whispered, her voice echoing slightly.

"Hopefully beyond the stadium walls," Lud muttered.

As they approached a turn in the tunnel, the companions slowed down hearing crying from up ahead. Shem held up a hand, signaling the others to stop. Cautiously, he peered around the corner.

In the dim light, he could make out a figure huddled against the wall. It was a woman wrapped in a blanket, her body shaking with sobs. Next to her lay the still form of another woman, covered in blood.

Shem's eyes widened in recognition at the disheveled figure. "Lilith," he whispered.

Her elaborate headdress was gone, her red hair a tangled mess. The paint on her face was smeared, tears cutting tracks through the powder and eye make-up. She looked nothing like the regal, intimidating, sensuous figure they had seen earlier.

As Shem and his companions cautiously approached, Lilith's head snapped up.

Her eyes were wild with fear and grief. "Stay back!" she shrieked, brandishing a blood-stained dagger. "Haven't you done enough?"

Shem held up his hands in a placating gesture towards this young, scared woman. "We're not here to hurt you," he said softly.

Lilith let out a bitter laugh. "Not here to hurt me? You've destroyed everything! If you had just accepted your fate, none of this would have happened!"

Aryana stepped forward, her brow furrowed in confusion. "Wait...you're not Naamah, are you? Tubal-Cain's sister? How old are you? Why are you called Lilith?"

Lilith's face crumpled, fresh tears spilling down her cheeks. "No," she whispered. "I...I'm barely 100...Naamah died years ago during the great expansion and Tubal-Cain died some time after that. Some battle with one of the lands. I don't know which. I used my true name once, during a public appearance, and they wrote it into the narrative."

She wiped her nose with the back of her hand, smearing black paint on her face, looking suddenly very young and vulnerable. "The Conclave - they're the ones who really run everything. They decided it was best to keep up the myth that we are demigods and use us as stand-ins to play the parts."

Her voice broke as she glanced at the still form beside her. "I'm only allowed out for public engagements. Dalula...she was my only real friend."

Shem felt a pang of sympathy, despite everything. He took a cautious step forward. "I'm so sorry about your friend," he said softly. "But why is she...?" He trailed off, gesturing to the blood-covered body.

Lilith's face crumpled, fresh tears spilling down her cheeks. "It's your fault!" she wailed, brandishing the bloody dagger. "I had to do it! I had to sacrifice her to Azazel, to save her from you Sethites!"

A collective gasp went up from Shem's companions. Sedee's hand flew to her mouth in horror.

"You... you killed your only friend?" Elam asked, his voice thick with disbelief.

Lilith nodded miserably, her shoulders shaking with sobs. "I thought... I thought it would protect her."

Shem felt sick from Lilith's confession. The young woman before them was clearly broken, manipulated by forces beyond her control into committing an unthinkable act.

"Lilith," he said gently, taking another careful step forward. "You've been lied to. Azazel is defeated. He has no power anymore."

Lilith's eyes widened in disbelief. "No... that's impossible. He's a god!"

"He was a fallen angel," Eloise explained softly. "And now he's been bound. I used to believe as you do, but the Conclave, Azazel - they've all been using you."

Lilith's grip on the dagger loosened as the truth of their words sank in. "Then... Dalula died for nothing?" Her voice was barely a whisper.

"Not for nothing," said a voice from further up the corridor.

"Sacrifice is true worship. Wouldn't you agree, son of Noah?"

Shem recognized Ouza's voice, even though it was muffled and began backing up. "I thought you were dead."

"Many have thought that over the centuries. Much to their regret." General Ouza came completely into view, revealing that the lower part of his face was wrapped in black cloth, hiding the injury he received from Azazel. Despite the covering, Shem could see the cruel glint in his eyes.

"Lilith, my dear," Ouza said, his voice dripping with honey. "You've done well. Come, let me help you."

He extended a hand towards the distraught young woman. Lilith hesitated for a moment, then dropped the dagger and allowed Ouza to guide her to her feet. She leaned against him, seeking comfort in his open arms.

Ouza wrapped an arm around Lilith's shoulders, then turned to address Shem and his companions. His eyes blazed with triumph as he spoke.

"You see, Shem, the defeat of Azazel was always part of my plan. You've served me well."

Shem bristled at Ouza's words, anger rising in his chest. "You're delusional," he spat. "I serve only Yahweh. You're no different than Tubal-Cain or Azazel - just another evil man who will fade away."

Ouza's eyes narrowed dangerously. "You think I'm like them? Oh, Shem. You have no idea who I truly am."

"Then enlighten us," Shem challenged. "Why do you think you're so special?"

A cruel smile spread across Ouza's face. "I've gone by many names over the centuries. Ouza is my personal favorite, but I've also been called Nin, Aza, Semihazah, Sahjaza,

Samiarush, Shemhazai, Shemyazaz..." He paused for dramatic effect. Ouza's eyes glinted with malice as he delivered the final revelation: "But my original name, the one I held as a 'son of Yahweh', was Samyaza."

A collective gasp went up from Shem and his companions. Even though Shem had suspected the truth, hearing it confirmed still shocked him to his core. His mind reeled as he tried to process this information.

"But... how?" Lud sputtered. "We've known you most of our lives. You were Nin, Noah's foreman!"

"Why would you deceive us like this?" Elam demanded, his voice trembling with a mix of anger and betrayal.

Samyaza laughed, the sound echoing ominously through the tunnel. "Oh, it's quite simple, really. Love."

Samyaza's grip on Lilith tightened as he continued. "I gave up my place in heaven, my spiritual kingdom on Adamah, all for love. To marry Naamah, the first mother of the Nephilim."

Lilith gasped, her eyes wide with shock. The rest of the companions stood in stunned silence.

"That skeleton on the throne," Samyaza said, his voice tinged with pride and sorrow, "was my child. He was the first of the Nephilim, named Assur. It was in his honor that Tubal-Cain named the city Asshur, recognizing my service to the empire."

He paused, his eyes growing distant. "Our home was Eridu of Eden in those days. We fought for Assyrian expansion, but the Eden Knights...they destroyed everything. My wife, my son were both killed.

Samyaza's eyes grew dark with anger as he continued his tale. "The Conclave of the Serpent - the true power behind all the cults - they thought I was killed as well. They decided to keep Naamah's death a secret, replacing her with a...stand-in. It's been their way ever since, allowing them to maintain their grip on power."

Shem felt a mix of emotions wash over him - pity for Samyaza's loss, but also revulsion at the choices he had made. "I understand your grief," Shem said carefully, "but it was your choice to turn away from the Creator and serve the will of Satan."

A flicker of something - regret perhaps - passed over Samyaza's face before his expression hardened once more. "Perhaps," he conceded. "But it changes nothing. I don't need...or want your pity. I will rule Adamah, and Eden will pay for what they've done. The Conclave will answer for their insolence. No more pretenders will be tolerated."

As he spoke those last words, Samyaza's hands moved to cup Lilith's face in what seemed like a tender gesture. But before anyone could react, there was a sickening crack as he violently twisted her head. Lilith's body crumpled to the ground beside her friend's.

Screams of horror and protest erupted from Shem and his companions. Eloise covered her mouth in shock, while Aram lunged forward, only to be held back by Lud.

Samyaza stepped over Lilith's lifeless form, his eyes burning with cold fury. "You will all bow to me," he declared, "Or die."

Shem stepped forward, his heart pounding but his voice steady. He remembered Raphael's words: "This day, the LORD will deliver them into your hands." Drawing strength from his faith, Shem faced Samyaza.

"We don't fear you," Shem declared. "Yahweh is our Lord, not you."

Samyaza's face contorted with rage. He lunged at Shem, one hand reaching to grab him while the other drew his sword. But Shem, empowered by Yahweh's strength, moved with lightning speed.

In one fluid motion, Shem grabbed Samyaza's throat with one hand and seized his sword arm with the other. To everyone's shock, including Samyaza, Shem lifted the fallen angel off the ground.

Samyaza thrashed and struggled, but couldn't break free from Shem's iron grip. His eyes bulged with shock and fury as he realized his superhuman strength was no match for Shem's divinely empowered might.

"Impossible!" Samyaza choked out, clawing at Shem's hand around his throat.

Shem's friends watched in awe, hardly believing what they were seeing. The once-mighty fallen angel, now reduced to a desperate, flailing mortal in Shem's grasp.

"Your power is broken," Shem declared, his voice resonating with authority. "Yahweh has judged you, Samyaza. Your reign of terror ends here."

For a moment, fear flashed in Samyaza's eyes - true fear, perhaps for the first time in millennia. But Shem, not wishing to murder the now-mortal fallen angel, released his grip and threw Samyaza forcefully against the tunnel wall.

"It's over," Shem said firmly. "We're leaving." He turned to his friends. "Let's go. There's a staircase over there - that must be how he got down here."

They all moved towards the stairs, with Elam lingering behind, his eyes fixed warily on Samyaza's crumpled form.

They had barely reached the base of the staircase when a blood curdling cry echoed through the tunnel. Samyaza charged at them, his face contorted with rage and madness.

As Samyaza came rushing at them with a bloodthirsty cry, Shem braced himself for another confrontation. But suddenly, the fallen angel stopped short, his eyes wide with shock.

Shem looked down to see Lilith's blood stained dagger protruding from Samyaza's stomach. There stood Elam, hand on the dagger, his face grim but resolute.

Samyaza stumbled backwards, his hands grasping weakly at the blade embedded in his flesh. He looked up at Elam, then at Shem, disbelief etched across his features.

"How...?" he gasped, the sound of blood bubbling behind his face covering. "I was...second only to The Son of the Dawn, himself..."

As Samyaza slumped to the ground, Shem approached him. Despite everything, he felt a pang of sorrow for his old mentor, and this fallen being who had once been so mighty.

"I loved you once," Shem said softly, kneeling beside Samyaza. "Nin...you were like family to me. I'm sorry it had to end this way."

Samyaza's eyes once blazing with hellfire now were lined with pain as his life ebbed away. He attempted to speak, but only a rattling breath escaped. Then, with a final shudder, he slumped over. Still.

Shem stood, his heart heavy. He turned to his companions, who watched him with a mixture of awe and concern.

"It's over," he said quietly.

Emerging from the secret tunnel, they were plunged into a pandemonium of terror. The world outside was a maelstrom of chaos, filled with the terrified screams of people fleeing the fiery destruction. Flames licked at the sky, their sinister dance fueled by the wreckage of the exploded air-char. The once grand colosseum now had a huge section in ruins, smoke billowing from its broken skeleton like ghostly specters.

In this chaos, Shem and his friends managed to steal an abandoned char. Aram's technical abilities proved invaluable as he quickly deciphered how it started, while Elam took over driving duties, bravely navigating through the chaotic scene with a determination that belied his lack of experience.

They weaved their way through groups of panicked citizens and even darted between a towering, colorfully adorned, brachiosaurus' legs, their hearts pounding in sync with each thunderous step of the giant creature as they barely dodged its long swiping tail.

The group of royal looking passengers, high on the dinosaur's sloping back, hurled down curses and fruit in protest of being jostled by the beast's sudden change in stride.

In their frantic race for survival a sudden gasp broke the silence, a sharp intake of breath that echoed in the quiet night. It was Eloise. Her eyes were wide and wild, reflecting the flickering flames that devoured Asshur's once grand arena.

"We must go back! We can't just leave Halvin there!" She cried out, her voice trembling with fear and grief.

Bog moved closer to her, his deep-set eyes filled with understanding and compassion. He reached out and gently took hold of her shaking hands.

"Eloise," he began softly, "Halvin is not there anymore."

"But his body..." she choked on her words, tears glistening in her eyes.

"Our bodies are but vessels," Bog explained gently. "His spirit has already joined our ancestors with Yahweh. That's where he truly belongs now."

They continued to weave through the maze-like streets of the city, skillfully dodging humanity, beasts, and patrols.

Shem was overcome with relief as they passed through the gates of the towering walls of Assur to the countryside beyond. With Alouette soaring overhead, her wings cutting through the sky in graceful arcs, he was grateful to see Aryana was alive and well upon her back. *Thank you, Lord.*

They reached the outskirts where expansive fields stretched out before them. As they put distance between themselves and Asshur, they were overcome with a mix of relief and trepidation.

Their victory was bittersweet - a hard-won battle against formidable foes but at a cost that weighed heavily on them all. Looking back at the burning silhouette of Asshur beyond the gigantic pyramids, they knew one thing for certain - this chapter may have concluded, but their story was far from over.

As the companions huddled close around a small fire in the tranquil countryside just outside of Asshur, the three majestic pyramids stood tall and proud in the distance. Their smooth, angular sides glimmered in the light of the moon, and artificial lighting from within, making them seem almost otherworldly. The group had miraculously escaped from the chaos and turmoil of the city, much to Aryana's surprise and overwhelming relief. Now, exhausted but still alive, they gathered to discuss their next course of action under the shadows of the awe-inspiring structures. The stars glittered above them like scattered jewels in a dark velvet sky, providing a sense of peace and tranquility amidst the uncertainty of their situation.

Aram cleared his throat. "I've decided to stay in Asshur," he announced. "I want to join the School of Engineering, maybe even the Engineering Guild someday. I'd love to learn how those power plants work," he said, gesturing to the well-lit pyramids in the distance. "I think I could be of help to Eden from the inside."

Shem frowned. "Are you sure that's wise? It could be dangerous."

Aram nodded, looking down at his watch. "I know the risks. But it's always been my dream to complete what my father started. This feels right."

"You sure it's not about something else?" asked Lud, standing up to face his brother.

Aram stood up, turning his back on Lud and said, "Can you blame me?"

Lud put his arm on Aram's shoulder. "Maybe he doesn't want to be found. Did you ever think that?"

"Maybe," said Aram, turning to look his brother in the eyes. "But I need to know for sure. Besides, you have someone else to keep you in line now."

Lud turned to look at Eloise, who in turn, looked at the ground, her face red. With a smile, He faced his brother.

"Yeah, she's pretty special. Be careful, Aram." Then, pulling Aram's journal from his belt, he passed it to his brother. "You may need this."

Aram, with tears in his eyes, said, "Thank you. And take care of mom...give her my love."

Nodding to his brother, he addressed the rest of them. "Well, I guess you should all know," said Lud, fidgeting with his shirt. "We've decided to return to Ararat together."

Shem and the others exchanged knowing glances - they all started laughing.

"We thought maybe I could help out with my knowledge of the forge," said Eloise, smiling softly at Lud.

"Wow! Not even a joke," said Elam with a huge grin on his face.

Everyone else just looked down, hiding their own laughter.

Lud mumbled his response. "I didn't think it was funny."

Lady Aryana, still smiling, cleared her throat. "I'll be returning to Stone Crest," she said firmly, her expression becoming serious. "The council needs to know everything that's happened here. We need to prepare for the future."

Her eyes scanned the group, her expression grim. "We may have cut off the head of Assyria's snake, but this Conclave will find replacements. They'll pick up where they left off eventually. And other nations like Havilah and Nod may feel emboldened if they had spies here and find out what went on."

Elam nodded thoughtfully. "I agree. The world is so much more dangerous than we initially thought, and it's time to see if my dad needs another deputy in Ararat. I'll go see if we can make things a little more secure back home. " He glanced at Shem. "What about you, Shem? What are your plans?"

Shem took a deep breath, his eyes reflecting the flickering firelight. "I'll stop home first to let my father know all that's happened. Maybe learn more about Yahweh from him. But after that..." He paused, looking towards the distant mountains. "I think I'll travel to Stonecrest. Maybe see about lending my knowledge and experience to the Eden Knights." A small smile played at the corners of his mouth. "It was my dream, after all."

Aryana gave him a solid punch to the shoulder in prideful agreement.

A moment of silence fell over the group as they absorbed Shem's words. Then, almost as one, they turned to look at Sedee and Bog. "What about you two?" Elam asked. "You're welcome to come with us to Ararat, if you'd like."

"Oh, I'll leave those big choices up to my niece," said Bog, smiling at Sedee.

Sedee looked up, her eyes meeting Shem's briefly before darting away. She fidgeted with the hem of her tunic, clearly uncomfortable being the center of attention.

"I... I'm not sure, I..." she said softly, before walking away from the comfort of the fire.

Shem felt a pang of guilt, remembering the moment of shared grief they shared in the city. He got up and followed her.

The night pressed heavily around Shem, the silence split only by the fading crunch of Sedee's boots on the gravel and his friend's laughter around the fire. He stood rooted near the flickering light, watching her shadow stretch and dissolve into the blackness beyond. His chest tightened-she was the deciding factor in whether or not she and her uncle would return to their old life. *Did I push her away? Was all of this too much?*

His mind kept tossing around the fleeting moment, the shared ache that had tethered them together. Her presence had been warm, steady, and a comfort against the raw edge of grief. *But now? Does she even want to be near me, now that our journey is over, or am I just a reflection of her own pain? A reminder?*

He shifted his weight, boots scuffing the dirt. She stopped at the edge of the light, her figure small against the vast dark, and his gut twisted. *Was she thinking of home?*

She turned then, stepping fully into the shadows, and something snapped in him. *I can't let her go-not without knowing.*

"Sedee!" The word tore out of him, rough and louder than he'd meant, shattering the quiet. He moved before he could second-guess it, jogging after her.

She stopped, half-turning, her face catching just enough light to show her eyes; wide, searching. His pulse hammered as he closed the distance, slowing to a stop a few feet away. *What is she thinking? Am I a burden to her? A friend?*

"I..." His throat closed up, and he swallowed hard, forcing the words out. "You don't have to go back to the Pishon Valley. You and your uncle...there's room at the ranch. For both of you." His eyes dropped to the ground, then flicked back to hers, softer now, unguarded. He couldn't stop this pull. *Too soon?* "And maybe...maybe we could figure this out. Whatever *this* is." The words hung there, shaky with a hope he barely dared to name.

THANK YOU

Thank you for reading The Sword of the Spirit, Book One of the Heir of the Promise series. Whether you came for the adventure, the message of faith, or simply curiosity—I'm so glad you joined Shem's journey.

This story was written to reflect a deeper truth: that we are all part of a greater story, authored by a faithful God. If you're a believer, I hope this book encouraged your walk. And if you're not, thank you for taking a chance on something outside your usual path. I invite you to keep exploring—sometimes questions lead to the most powerful discoveries.

If the story moved you, please consider leaving a review on Amazon, Goodreads, or sharing it on social media. Your voice can help others to find this journey too.

With heartfelt thanks,

Chad

Acknowledgements

Every story begins with a spark—but it takes the faith and kindness of others to bring that spark to life.

To Tom and Bobbi Cervini—thank you for investing in this dream when it was little more than an idea. Your generosity and belief made this book possible.

To Anna Muessig—thank you for your keen eye and endless patience with my runaway commas. Your work brought clarity and polish to every page.

With a full and grateful heart,

Chad

"Now to him who is able to do immeasurably more than all we ask or imagine, according to his power that is at work within us..."

—Ephesians 3:20

About the author

A graduate of Word of Life Bible Institute, Chad Muessig serves as a Chaplain and Worship Leader, which enriches the spiritual fabric of his writing, offering readers an insightful journey through themes of faith, redemption and hope. Drawing on a career in law enforcement, he weaves a narrative rich with insights into justice and order.

Residing in South Jersey with his loving wife and five children, Chad enjoys drawing or driving his gecko green Jeep Gladiator, fondly named "Preacher."

www.ingramcontent.com/pod-product-compliance
Lightning Source LLC
Chambersburg PA
CBHW020008120726
47903CB00004B/1196

9798998999406